The Agathas

KATHLEEN GLASGOW & LIZ LAWSON

ROCK THE BOAT

A Rock the Boat Book

First published in Great Britain and Ireland
by Rock the Boat, an imprint of Oneworld Publications, 2022
Reprinted, 2022

Published by arrangement with Random House Children's Books,
a division of Penguin Random House LLC

ISBN 978-0-86154-477-6
ISBN 978-0-86154-478-3 (ebook)

Interior design by Ken Crossland
Printed and bound in Great Britain by Clays Ltd, Elcograf S.p.A.

Oneworld Publications
10 Bloomsbury Street
London WC1B 3SR
England

Stay up to date with the latest books,
special offers, and exclusive content from
Rock the Boat with our newsletter

Sign up on our website
oneworld-publications.com/rtb

To best friends/teen detectives everywhere!

Agatha Christie

AKA Dame Agatha Mary Clarissa Christie, Lady
Mallowan, DBE (née Miller; 15 September 1890–
12 January 1976)

An English writer known for her 66 detective
novels and 14 short story collections.

Also known as the bestselling author of all time.

Also, one bad bitch.

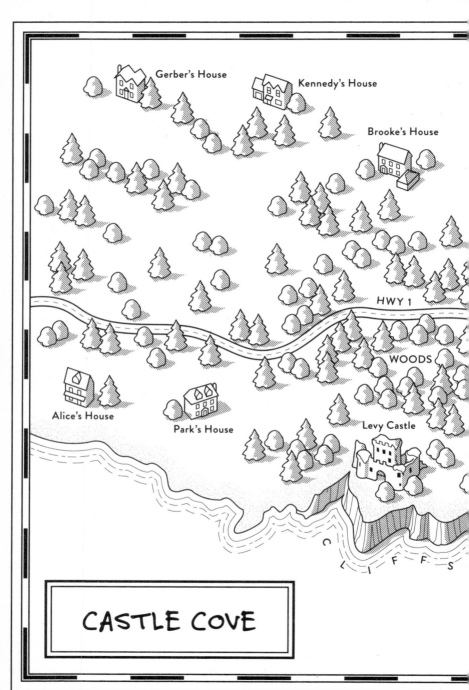

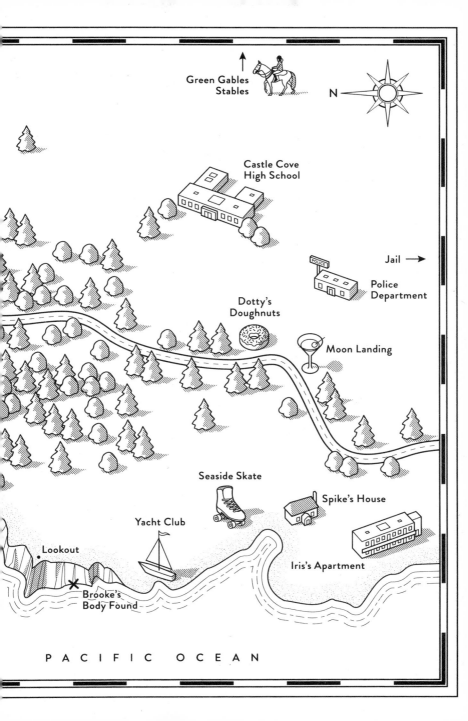

Green Gables
Stables

N

Castle Cove
High School

Jail →

Police
Department

Dotty's
Doughnuts

Moon Landing

Seaside Skate

Spike's House

Yacht Club

Iris's Apartment

Lookout

Brooke's
Body Found

PACIFIC OCEAN

CHAPTER ONE

ALICE OGILVIE
OCTOBER 31
7:50 A.M.

"These blondes, sir, they're
responsible for a lot of trouble."
—AGATHA CHRISTIE,
THE LABOURS OF HERCULES

ALICE OGILVIE IS CRAZY.

The words are huge, written across my locker in thick black marker, impossible to miss. I see them from down the hall as I approach, the words like a pin to the eye. My first day back from house arrest, and this is what greets me. I can't say I'm surprised.

Rebecca Kennedy snickers from across the hall, where she stands watching with Helen Park and Brooke Donovan. My former friends. My former *best* friends.

I wonder if one of them wrote this. Not Brooke; she would never do something like this, but I wouldn't put it past Kennedy. This is *exactly* something she'd do. A small ache starts in my center, but I think to myself: What would Agatha Christie do right now? Would she let them get to her? Run out of the school? Is that what she did when her first husband cheated on

1

her? Hell no. She squared her shoulders and became a multi-national bestselling author.

I whirl around and level a glare at the three of them. Kennedy's smirk sags.

"Can I *help* you?" I say in my most bored voice. The last thing I want is for them to know I care.

Park, of course, sinks back against the lockers, pretending she's not involved, letting her straight, shiny black hair curtain her face. She's terrible at confrontation. Kennedy rolls her eyes. And Brooke . . . well, her red-painted lips tremble like *I'm* the one who did something wrong.

"Alice," Brooke says softly, like she's about to get into things—things that I would much prefer *never* to get into, thank you very much. I force myself to meet her eyes, and it's only then that I notice what she's wearing. I glance around at the other kids in the hall and confirm that, yup—*everyone* is wearing them. Except for me.

Costumes. Because today is Halloween. Great. My re-entrance to social life at Castle Cove High School is already crashing and burning.

Brooke and Kennedy and Park are dressed as bloody cheerleaders. How *original*. The three of them are decked out in short blue-and-white pleated skirts, hair curled to perfection, blood all over their clothing but none on their faces. Wouldn't want to actually commit to the costume *too* much and mess up their makeup.

I, on the other hand, look foolish. I am the only person in this hallway—perhaps the entire school—who is not dressed to the nines in a costume.

As if I needed yet another reminder about how I no longer

fit in, the universe apparently decided to make that fact *explicit*. I clear my face of emotion, toss my hair over my shoulder, and unlock my locker door. I know everyone is watching. Waiting to see what I'll do. If I'll react.

But I won't.

Because *I don't care*.

I'm struggling to stay awake in third-period math when the door to the classroom swings open and some freshman child pops his head in, face flushing as every head swivels in his direction simultaneously.

"Uh," he says, voice cracking. "Uh, sorry. I have a note?" He hurries over to Ms. Hollister and holds it out to her, but before she can take it, the paper slips from between his fingers and floats to the ground. The kid flushes an even brighter shade of red as he scrambles to grab it before it hits the linoleum floor. "Sorry, sorry. Here," he mutters, and thrusts it into Hollister's hand, then darts out of the room. What a production. At least it stopped Hollister's droning about pre-calc.

Hollister opens the note and reads it, and then her gaze falls squarely on me.

"Alice," she says in her nasally voice, fingering the oddly expensive-looking necklace she's wearing. My back stiffens. Three hours back at school, and I'm already in *trouble*? Good lord, I've barely had time to pee. "You're wanted in Ms. West-macott's office."

My stomach sinks. I'm not in trouble. It's much, much worse than that.

I'm being called to the guidance counselor's office.

—

I knock softly on the door, hoping against hope that maybe Ms. Westmacott won't be there. But almost immediately I hear an overeager "Yes?"

I've never had the displeasure of being inside Westmacott's office before, but I've heard rumors. When I push the door open, I see all of them are true. She truly does have her name spelled out in gigantic gold sparkly letters on the wall behind her desk. There really is a bulletin board on the wall called the *Feelings Board*. And that corner that everyone talks about? The one set up with the beanbags so she can have "jam sessions" with students?

That's a real thing, too.

No wonder Brooke didn't want her dad to marry this lady.

"Hello!" she cries. "Come in!" She waves me in, and I comply, mostly because I don't have a choice. "Shall we sit over there?" She motions to the beanbags.

Um, no. "My . . . knees are bad," I lie. There is no way I am sitting on a beanbag. "The chair is fine." I take a seat before she can protest.

After a moment's hesitation, she slides into her chair, folds her hands on the desk, and leans forward.

"We're glad to have you back, Alice." She's wearing a tunic with a bunch of weird shapes glued around the neckline and has her brown hair pushed back with a headband. Not a cool headband, mind you, but one of those thick ones that I've seen in pictures of people from the 1990s. "We know things have been . . . rough over the past few months." She makes a sympathetic face, and my stomach turns. I know what's coming. "We

4

all thought it would be best if you and I had some time to chat." She raises her eyebrows like it's a question, but I know it's not a question. I know I don't have a choice.

"We can just jam, talk about how things are going. How school's treating you. Stuff like that!" She smiles.

"Uh-huh" is the best I can manage in reply.

She ignores my lack of enthusiasm and continues, "To get started: Let's talk about Brooke and Steve. They're dating. How are you dealing with it? Clearly, it hasn't been easy on you. . . ."

Jesus, she's really going there? She's the first person to directly mention the two of them to me since everything happened. Brooke was my best friend since birth, so I always knew she wasn't the perfect angel she would have you believe (two words: Cole Fielding). I used to appreciate it; you need a little spice to keep things interesting. But I never expected her to steal my *boyfriend* right out from under my *nose.*

Steve and I started dating my sophomore year, his junior, when he became the breakout star on the varsity basketball team. He'd always been in the background before that, spending a lot of his time at training camps that his mom worked two jobs to afford, but I guess they paid off, because one day I heard these girls talking about him in the bathroom, about how random it was that some kid no one had ever heard of was carrying the team, and I knew I had to have him. We started dating a few weeks later. I gave him popularity. A social life. Access to my *world*. And what did he give me in return? He *dumped me.*

So, back in June, after he told me he wanted to break up because I was too bossy (rude), I went to Egypt with my mom to visit the set of some movie she was working on. My dad was out of town working, like he is 99 percent of the time, and Brenda's first grandchild was due and she went down to San Diego for that, so it was either go with my mom or mope around the house, alone. I thought it would be a good distraction, maybe make Steve miss me, and that while I was gone, I could figure out how to patch things up with him. Also, if I'm going to be totally honest, which I am usually not about *feelings,* I thought maybe my mom and I could have, you know, fun together.

Well, to no one's great surprise, it ended up being yet another trip where she worked twenty-four hours a day and I sat in a hotel room alone. Thank god for room service and the Agatha Christie novels I found in the lounge.

Let's just say that my mom and I didn't bond, but Brooke and Steve certainly did.

I shiver at the memory of Brooke showing up at my house to tearfully inform me that she never meant for it to happen— she never meant to *fall in love with Steve.* When Steve and I were dating, he and Brooke always got along—something that I was stupid enough to think was a *good* thing—but clearly wasn't.

"Can we not?" My voice shakes. I clamp my lips together. Get yourself under *control,* Ogilvie.

Westmacott's eyes soften. "Of course. Why don't we start with homeschooling? Tell me how you've been over these past few months, homeschooling when you were on . . . er . . ."

"House arrest?" I finish for her.

"Um, yes."

"It was fine." I cross my arms tight against my chest.

"I imagine it might have been a little lonely."

"It was *fine*," I say. God, why is she so intent on pressing this? "My parents got me a horse," I add, for no reason other than to keep her quiet for a few more seconds. "For my birthday, a few months ago. Right before . . ." I trail off.

Her eyes light up. "A horse! That's fantastic! What breed?"

It's really *not* fantastic. It's more exactly what my parents do: buy me something—something I cannot stand—because it's expensive. I shrug. "Um, brown?"

"Are you boarding her at the Green Gables Stables?"

I nod. A perfectly silly name for a place with perfectly monstrous beings. Although apparently my parents don't know this, I've hated horses ever since the summer after fourth grade, when my mom decided that having a daughter who rides would be good for her image and signed me up for horseback riding camp. I went along with it, because at least she had temporarily remembered I existed. It wasn't too terrible . . . until it was.

The last day of camp, we were showing our horses when Marinda Kelly fell off hers and tumbled to the ground, breaking her hip and both her legs. Talk about traumatizing. The ambulance had to come. After that mess, I vowed never to go within thirty feet of a horse again. A vow my parents clearly did not remember.

"I love that place! I board my Oliver there!" Westmacott says this as if we're about to bond over a shared love of horses.

Of course she's a horse lady. Of course she is.

"Cool." What kind of horse name is Oliver? I keep my thoughts to myself, though. The last thing I need is to get suspended from school the first day I'm back. I plaster on a smile.

She chats on about her favorite horses, her riding schedule, but at least she's stopped asking me questions about myself.

The bell finally rings, marking the end of the period and my chance to escape. I rise to stand, but she stops me. "Wait, wait," she says, smacking her hand against her forehead. "I forgot to tell you one of the reasons I called you here in the first place! Since you missed the first few months of school, we've set you up with a tutor." She pauses. "Well, your *parents* set it up. I'm the go-between."

A *tutor*? "I'm good," I protest. "I don't need——"

"Alice." She raises an eyebrow under her thick-rimmed glasses. "Your at-home efforts were . . . let's just say we found them wanting. The only subject you've kept up in is French. Consider this not so much a suggestion as a requirement." Her smile drops away and her too-cheery voice grows hard. Something pricks along my back. "Okay?"

I blink and nod.

"Great!" She claps her hands, voice returning to its overly enthusiastic pitch, like she wasn't just growling at me. "We've assigned you to Iris Adams."

"Who?"

"Iris Adams. You don't know her?"

I shrug. A lot of kids go here. How am I supposed to know all of their names?

Westmacott raises her eyebrows. "You've gone to school together since kindergarten," as if that's supposed to jog my memory.

I shake my head.

She looks down at the slip of paper in her hand. "Well, here's all the info. She's going to come to your house after school today. We all agreed to set it up that way because——"

"Great." I cut her off. I grab the piece of paper from her hand. "Thanks."

I see a flash of irritation in her face before her smile reappears. "Okay. Perfect. Oh, and Alice?"

"Yeah?"

"Life gives you lemons, but you can make lemonade!"

I give her a thumbs-up.

I can hardly wait.

CHAPTER TWO

IRIS ADAMS
OCTOBER 31
11:45 A.M.

THERE ARE MANY PERKS to being invisible.

I don't mean the *actual* kind of invisible, like the whole vaporous thing in the movies. I mean being the type of person that people simply don't really see, because the type of person you are (the type of person they *think* you are) is not one that interests them. Because people don't see you, you have free rein to listen in on conversations, observe behavior, and learn patterns. All of these things are essential to surviving life, particularly high school.

For instance, I was able to divert Kennedy—first name: Rebecca, but all the Main Kids at Castle Cove High refer to each other by their last names, which I think is a curious and loathsome habit and makes them sound like male stockbrokers on an ill-advised bourbon bender—from some routine mean-girl behavior in AP Biology today by dropping some information I'd gleaned while dressing for PE.

Kennedy isn't happy to be my lab partner, even though I'm carrying her to an A in this class. Every lab day, she looks at me and sighs, rolling her neck like I've sliced her carotid, and then says, "Flannel, *again*?" If I wanted my clothes critiqued, I'd sit with the Stitch Bitches during lunch. They make their own clothes, which is admirable, but makes for tedious conversation. And please, of all people, Kennedy should not be critiquing my clothes when today she's dressed like some sort of dead cheerleader. It's Halloween, but still.

Usually, I let it ride. I can tune people out pretty well, but today was not the day, because all day I'd been confronted with the painful return of Alice Ogilvie, and what that was going to mean for me.

I'm sorry, *Ogilvie,* as her clan calls her.

Kennedy was starting in on my hair when I decided to cut her off while slicing open the abdomen of our frog, which made her grow very pale.

"Rebecca," I said. "I'm so sorry to hear about Cole. What a blow that must be."

She fanned her face. "It's *Kennedy.* And *what* are you talking about?"

I fixed my face into a perfect, sympathetic shape: lips slightly pursed, chin tucked, head tilted. "Oh wow, no, sorry, I thought you *knew.*"

"What the f," she said. "What the f are you talking about, Eileen?"

"Iris," I reminded her firmly. I carefully spread the skin of the frog so she could get a good look at its gleaming, spongy insides. The insides of things are so much different than the outsides. Most people don't care to find that out.

"He's going with Madison—I mean, *Fletcher,* to the regatta ball. Wasn't that supposed to be you?"

It's like dealing with little kids, really. You have to distract them from whatever it is you don't want them to be doing. Offer a chocolate, a brightly colored game on your phone, and there you are: crisis averted. I knew mentioning this would sit poorly with Kennedy; all the Mains adore the annual regatta ball at the Yacht Club. It's their time to buy obscenely expensive gowns and pretend they're some kind of local royalty while chugging back bottles of booze that cost so much they could pay for an entire year of college tuition.

I handed Kennedy the scalpel and sat back.

It really was quite a joy to watch Kennedy annihilate that poor frog. Good thing it was already dead.

At lunch I take my usual spot in the back of the cafeteria with Spike and the rest of the Zoners. That's our allotted spot. The social layout of the Castle Cove cafeteria is strictly adhered to. Zoners at the back, in the last tables. Punks to the right, by the exit doors, in case one of the more athletic Mains decides to mess with them; they need a quick exit. To the left of us are the Stitch Bitches, nestled in a clump of hemp clothing and messy buns pulled together with vintage pins. The front of the cafeteria is taken over by the APs, iPads out and glasses smudged. Dance team is next to them, almost to the center, gleaming and perky.

The athletic Mains, all gusto and swears and decked-out team tees, scatter the left tables, two trays of food each. And in the center, the very center, because the rest of us revolve around their brilliance, are the main Mains. Glossy and full of health and money, they ooze easy life. The center is the best place for them; that way, whatever they do, they have us, a willing (or not) audience.

The Zoners are the friends I have at Castle Cove, and we've been thrown together mostly out of necessity our whole lives. Because, and get ready for it: we are *poor.*

My mother works in a bar. It would be different if she owned the bar, and especially if it was a nice one, but she doesn't. She's the one at the Moon Landing who slops the drinks and dries your tears and holds your damp, crumpled bills up to the fan to dry them off, because we need that money. In Castle Cove, you are either the served or the server. Spike's dad is one of the janitors at Castle Cove High. You want your palatial seaside home polished and sparkling? That's how five of the Zoners' parents pay their rent.

I mean, to me, some of us scrape by and some of us are fine, but compared to everyone else in this cozy coastal town and school, we're at the bottom.

Spike and the other Zoners are deeply involved in a conversation about who's going to be the next Dungeon Master. I pull out my sandwich. Down at the end of the table, Cole Fielding is napping, his tousled blond head nestled on his arms. Even sleeping, he's distractingly attractive.

Zora catches me looking and giggles.

"You like guys in leather, Iris?" she asks.

Cole Fielding belongs to no group. Except if you count some of the girl Mains. They pass him around like candy. He's widely known to have special *talents.*

"Ha," I say. "But no, thank you."

Not that I don't *think* about it. Especially when I'm at Seaside Skate and he's handing my wheels to me over the counter and says, "Hey, Iris," in that lazy voice of his, smiling. It's the way he says Iris. *Eeeyyyee-rissss.* Like it's a word that feels good in his mouth.

I shake my head. I have a strict keep-to-myself-policy, because I've learned that romance = tragedy. But there's nothing wrong with a little fantasy, though it would be easier to ignore Cole if he was a jerk.

There's a stir as heads turn to the front of the cafeteria.

You know how in the movies those scenes happen where everyone and everything suddenly goes dead quiet?

That's what happens.

Even the Zoners look up.

The most famous Main of all has appeared.

Alice Ogilvie, Castle Cove's very own disappearing girl.

I mean, I get it. You can't just . . . disappear. I mean, you *can,* and plenty of girls *do,* but usually in dark and horrible ways mainly perpetrated by disturbed men.

Not many just . . . poof.

And then . . . come back.

I don't know the whole story, only bits and pieces, parts of which I think have to do with a broken heart and petty jealousy, but I do know the town of Castle Cove spent an awful lot of time and money trying to find Alice and that her last-named friends even held a candlelight vigil for her when they could have been TikToking or whatever it is they do with their time. And now they are *pissed.*

Alice Ogilvie is frozen at the front of the cafeteria.

Normally, she'd swan right over and sit with Henderson, Kennedy, Park, and Donovan, but they've closed themselves into a kind of turtle shell and won't look at her.

You might think Alice would hold her head high and sit anywhere, but she doesn't. She just stands there.

Her mouth quivers.

"Man," Spike murmurs. "This is kind of sad."

For a moment, I feel sorry for Alice Ogilvie.

That pain of knowing no one wants you.

There's a rustle at the Main Girls table. Brooke Donovan, basically the human equivalent of cotton candy, stands up and waves at Alice. Kennedy tugs her back down.

But Alice Ogilvie, whose mouth was quivering just a moment before, stares Donovan right in the face and slowly draws up her middle finger, then turns around and stalks out of the cafeteria.

Suddenly I feel a brief, startling admiration for Alice Ogilvie.

She basically just told kindness to fuck off.

After school, it's time for my appointment with Westmacott. Her office is reviled by many, but not me.

I don't mind her sparkly decor, her beanbags, and the inspirational posters pinned to her walls. I mean, what do you want out of a guidance counselor? Thanos? Come *on.*

Plus, she has snacks. Granola bars, fruit gummies, Cheetos, kale crisps, you name it. She told me once this is because a lot of girls don't want to be seen eating at Castle Cove High (that's another issue we don't need to get into), and she knows when they come see her, they're starving. If she closes the door, they'll eat.

When I walk in, she tosses me a pack of strawberry gummies, which I immediately tear open, because I'm not an idiot (free food), and plus, I have a long bike ride to Alice Ogilvie's house.

Ms. Westmacott pushes the file folder across her desk. "Here it is. Lucky you."

I stare at the blue folder greedily. This is no ordinary blue folder. It's a blue folder worth three thousand dollars. Three thousand dollars that will get me closer to getting my mother and me out of Castle Cove, and away from the Thing, for good.

I steel myself. I'm not going to think about the Thing right now. Right now, I'm on a mission.

"I don't think she had a very good first day back," I say, sliding the folder into my backpack. "Cold shoulder from the clique."

Ms. Westmacott nods. "Alice dug her own hole. Now she has to stew in it for a while. Actions have consequences."

Her eyes drift to a box in the corner of the office. Slopping out the top are overly large sneakers, some *Lost* DVDs, and a disturbingly massive collection of Michael Jordan memorabilia.

She turns her eyes back to me, then looks down at her desk. Uh-oh. I think my guidance counselor is about to cry. We all know she was with Coach Donovan for all last year. How could we not? She was always a little too close to his side during assemblies and absolutely the loudest person in the stands during home games.

Not to be callous, but I don't want to counsel my counselor. Hurriedly, I zip my backpack and hoist it over my shoulders.

Westmacott pulls a tissue from a box on her desk and finally glances up at me. "My allergies are really acting up, excuse *me.*"

"Well, I should go," I say tentatively.

Her misty eyes lock onto mine.

"How are things at home?" she asks pointedly.

I tighten my hands around the straps of my backpack. She's poking for a soft spot, looking for that opening. Westmacott can be kind, but at times, a little pushy. Pressing too hard for information. You always have to be on your toes.

In August, there was . . . an incident. I should have been safe from anyone knowing, since school wasn't back yet, but I ran into Westmacott at the pharmacy while my mom was getting my pain meds filled. I could tell she absolutely did not buy the excuse I gave her about falling at Seaside Skate.

Ms. Westmacott wanted to draw funny faces on my cast, but I wouldn't let her.

I change the subject. "So, I only have to do this until the end of this quarter, right? And even if she doesn't get As, I get paid? Even if she fails, I get paid?"

"Correct. Her parents agreed. She's brighter than you think. I have a feeling the key to Alice is that she simply needs someone to believe in her."

"Ms. Westmacott," I say. "I don't mean to be rude, but I cannot be the Alice Whisperer. I'm tutoring, and that's it."

"Maybe she'll take you horseback riding, Iris. Maybe you'll become friends. The world is full of unlikely things." Ms. Westmacott smiles. "It wouldn't be the worst thing in the world. To have a friend."

"Oh," I say, turning to go. "It would be if that friend was Alice Ogilvie."

—

By the time I get to the end of Alice Ogilvie's massive brick driveway, my stomach is rumbling. I'm regretting not taking more snacks from Westmacott.

Her house looms above me. I'm not surprised it's mammoth; that's the norm for Castle Cove, where people have indoor swimming pools and home theaters and their own bowling alleys. The boats at Castle Cove Yacht Club alone are like floating mansions. If it's not big and outrageous, it's not Castle Cove. The Yacht Club's been undergoing renovations for the past year; the reopening will be during the annual regatta this year. It's a huge deal for the town. If Alice hadn't been dumped by Steve, she'd probably be having her gown fitted for the regatta ball by now.

I'm locking my bike outside the double front doors when they open and a kind-faced woman in a brown sweater and gray pants peers out.

"You must be Iris," she says, smiling. "Come in. Alice is upstairs."

I don't mean to, but the moment I step inside, I kind of stop breathing. I've never been in a house like this before, only seen them from the outside. The place is the size of an airplane hangar. The ceilings are at least fifteen feet high, and one entire wall is just huge windows, looking out to the beautiful, placid sea.

I mean, I live by the ocean, too, but on the dumpy side of downtown, in a two-bedroom apartment with my mom. The beach is there, mostly rocky, and the beautiful waves, but we don't have a wall of windows devoted to it. There's one window you can look out of, and a long set of rotting wooden steps that you can take to the beach.

For a minute, I allow myself to feel a pang of want, which I usually don't do, because it hurts. I love my mother and our life, but sometimes . . . I'd like to have a beautiful window on the sea. I'd like to walk right outside my door and be able to feel the sand in my toes, instead of always having to wear shoes on the sharp rocks that make up our portion of the beach. Sometimes I feel like my whole life is navigating sharp rocks, and I would just like soft sand once in a while.

"It's lovely, isn't it?" the woman says.

"Yes," I say, snapping back to attention. "Absolutely. Are you Alice's mom?"

I hope she can't hear my stomach growling.

The woman laughs. "Oh no, no. I'm Brenda. I take care of Alice."

"Alice is seventeen," I say.

She smiles. "Even Alice, at seventeen, needs some care."

She pulls out her phone, taps the screen, and holds it to her ear. I hear a phone ringing far off in the house.

"Your friend is here," Brenda says into the phone.

From somewhere deep on the second floor, Alice Ogilvie screams, "TUTOR."

Brenda points to a twisting white staircase. "Fifth door on the right."

I don't often feel small, but right now, in Alice's house, I feel about as small as that frog in biology earlier today.

You know how you go to someone's house and they have cute kid photos on the walls? Birthday cake smushed on cheeks, playing in sand with plastic buckets and shovels, gap-toothed school photographs?

The expensively framed and exquisite photographs of Alice

that line the walls of the staircase are not those. Even small Alice, maybe three or four, is handsomely attired in satin dresses with perfect hair, settled on velvety pillows. And there are no photographs of Alice with her parents. Just Alice, alone.

In fact, the whole house is kind of eerie and lonely-feeling and I'm kind of regretting we have to meet here, but it's better than being at my place. I don't need Alice Ogilvie *there*.

I count the doors on the second floor. Seven in all. I knock on the fifth one.

"Just come in, already!" Alice shouts.

I open the door. Alice is splayed across an enormous bed.

"Jerks," she murmurs, throwing the phone beside her on the bed. She rolls over, eyeing me. I can tell she has no idea who I am, even though we've shared at least two classes a year since Castle Cove Elementary.

She's taken off the weird outfit she had on at school today—some short-skirted monstrosity more suited to a movie premiere than math—and is dressed in yoga pants and a T-shirt.

"Welcome to my hell," she says bitterly. "How much are my parents paying you?"

"Ask them yourself," I say. "I get paid whether you pass or not, just so you know."

"Well, then what an easy gig for you," she sighs. "Just sit anywhere so we can get started. I'm quite busy."

Alice lies on her bed, perfectly still. She does not, in fact, look like she has anything to do, at all, now or ever.

I walk over to the couch by her bed, kicking a slew of paperbacks out of the way. I sit down, unzipping my backpack. She sighs again.

"Go ahead already, ask me."

"I'm sorry?"

"Just ask me. You know you want to. Everybody wants to."

"Ask you what?" I decide to play dumb. Of *course* I want to know all about where she was. But I'm also getting the feeling Alice is rather like a cat: When you want to play, they don't. They prefer play on their own terms, especially when it involves disrupting you.

"About what happened. About where I was. What I did. You know you want to, Irene."

Alice has very pretty ice-blue eyes and a lot of soft-looking, exquisitely lovely blond hair. The kind of hair that means weekly trips to a stylist, the kind of place that gives you lemons in water and a hot cloth on your face and all that jazz.

"Iris," I say. "My name is Iris."

"Whatever."

"Actually, it's not whatever, that's my name. Would you like me to call you Abigail?"

She smirks. "Touché. Ask me."

"It's not really any of my business," I tell her.

I mean, but I *am* dying to know. Obviously, I have watched enough true-crime shows to know she wasn't harmed in any way; she'd have been trucked off to the hospital if she had. It would have been in the *Cove Gazette* and on KWB. But those things didn't happen. In fact, *nothing* happened. No new reports in the paper. Everything about Alice Ogilvie just . . . stopped. She was taken into her house and there she stayed, until today. My sneaking suspicion is that she wasn't alone, wherever she went.

Alice is staring at me in a way that's a little unnerving. I look down, pull out the blue homework folder, and catch sight of one of the paperbacks. I pick it up.

Death on the Nile. Agatha Christie.

The paperback is well thumbed, with sentences underlined, dog-eared on several pages.

"I like mysteries," Alice says. "How you never know what really happened until the very end. You have to put everything together as you go along."

She blinks at me and then flips over.

"Funny," I say. "That you like reading this stuff, and somehow you ended up at the center of one of Castle Cove's biggest mysteries. Currently unsolved."

She shrugs one shoulder. I sigh. I'm getting tired, and we have work to do. "Where do you want to start, Alice? Lit or history?"

"It's not what people think, anyway," she says, her voice muffled.

"I don't know what people think," I say slowly. "Maybe you ran away. Maybe you were abducted by some creepy cult leader, and you managed to escape before you drank the Kool-Aid. Maybe you had transient amnesia. Who knows? Personally, I'm betting you took off to teach somebody a lesson."

She flips back over and sits up.

"And why," she says coolly, "would you think that?"

I tick off my fingers. "One, you'd just had a bad breakup, right? And your bestie is now with your ex? That's gotta hurt. Two, the news said a vase was shattered in your house? But they didn't find any fingerprints but yours, your parents', and your housekeeper's. Maybe you broke it yourself? To throw people off?"

"Nanny," Alice interjects. "The housekeeper is Bibi."

"Whatever," I say. "My point is, and I have no judgment

here, if you disappeared on your own? Good for you. If things are crappy for you where you are, leave."

"Is that what you'd do?" Her voice is still cool, but her eyes are very bright, like she's . . . interested.

"Everybody has the right to abandon ship," I say mildly, pulling the Greek mythology handout from our lit class out of the homework folder. "If anything, Alice, maybe you flew too close to the sun, like Icarus."

She tilts her head. "Like who and the what now?"

"Your homework. The reading on Icarus. He and his dad built wings so they could escape, but the wings were made of feathers and wax, and his dad told him not to fly too close to the sun, because it would melt and burn his wings, but Icarus didn't listen, because he was headstrong and prideful, and that's exactly what happened, and he drowned. You had your chance, Alice, but it came crashing down."

Alice considers me. "Huh. Look at you, a little detective. But I don't think you really know much at all."

Is she going to cry? Because I didn't sign up for that. Like I told Westmacott, I'm not going to be the Alice Whisperer.

She doesn't cry, though. She sniffles briefly and then asks, "Okay, so what else do I need to know about the winged guy?"

On my way out of the house, Brenda hands me a Tupperware filled with pasta. "For you. It's dark out now. You'll be hungry when you get home."

Suddenly I want to cry, taking the plastic container from this nice woman who so obviously heard my stomach growling in this lonely, too-big house.

Sometimes I forget that people can be kind. That you don't have to ask them. They just are.

"Thank you," I say.

"Oh," Brenda says. "Let's exchange numbers. Just in case? I have all of Alice's friends' numbers. I'd like yours, too."

I blink. "I'm just tutoring her. We aren't going to, like, hang out or anything."

She waves her phone at me. "I just like to keep an eye on her. I think you can guess why."

I drop my backpack on the floor and unzip it, sliding the Tupperware inside. I pull my phone from my pocket and tell Brenda my number. She texts me right away.

Hello, new friend of Alice's!

The Tupperware thunks against my back as I ride home, the sharp sea wind cutting against my face. My hands are cold. The trick-or-treaters are out, pillowcases and buckets and masks. My mom always used to make sure to get a couple hours off from work to take me out. I miss that, her hand in mine. When it was just us.

I feel a brief flare of pain in my wrist as I angle the bike handles. Even though the cast is off, and I do my daily wrist exercises, it still hurts every once in a while, a constant reminder of the Thing.

My stomach coils into knots.

Whatever Alice did, winged or not, wherever she went and why, she made one fatal mistake, in my opinion.

She came *back*.

Rebecca Kennedy: Don't kill me. My dad texted me a second ago and said DJ Porcini can't play the party tonight . . .

Helen Park: OMG WHAT

RK: I know; I'm sorry. I guess he got pulled away to some last min gig in Ibiza, and . . . ugh. I'm sorry. It sux

RK: But, do you know who IS coming?

RK: Any guesses?

HP: Steve?

RK: What?

HP: Steve is coming?

RK: . . . um, clearly. Right BD?

Brooke Donovan: Yes. We will be there

RK: OK I'll tell you. COLE

HP: Kennedy! Awkward

RK: What? It's not like Donovan owns him

Ashley Henderson: Unsubscribe

BD: Henderson are you coming?

AH: No duh I'm going to be in LA. My dad has a premiere

RK: okkkkk thx for the update

BD: Kennedy

AH: It's fine I know shes just jeal

RK: Hardly

HP: Is there anyone else who can DJ? Is Feral Bunny around? Ask your dad, Kennedy

RK: He claims no

RK: Brookie, so sorry bout Cole. Figured it would be OK since you're with Steve now.

BD: I don't care

RK: Good. you can't claim ALL the guys in school, lol

RK: You have to let us have at least a few of them

HP: Maybe DJ UnderCeej? Your mom knew him a little when he was dating Trevor Pennington, right Brookie?

BD: What's that supposed to mean, Kennedy?

RK: LOL nothing. Just saying, you don't need to get upset bc you have steve now. Not everyone can be yours brookie lol

BD: I KNOW that kennedy

HP: Are we going to have to just listen to music on someone's Bluetooth speaker? This is a disaster.

RK: OMG PARK. Get over it. My dad said he'll make sure Frank Sea is there for the regatta ball, k?

AH: Frank Sea is playing the premiere!

HP: WHAT!

RK: At least your chef made those signature cocktails, right?

HP: I guess

RK: Just suck a couple down and you won't even be able to tell the diff

HP: Ugh, fine

CHAPTER THREE

ALICE

OCTOBER 31

8:50 P.M.

*"Why shouldn't I hate her? She did the worst thing
to me that anyone can do to anyone else."*
—AGATHA CHRISTIE, *THE MIRROR CRACK'D
FROM SIDE TO SIDE*

WHEN IRIS SHOWED UP in my room, I recognized her immediately, and, I hate to admit, I felt kind of bad that I had never
bothered to learn her name. I mean, *sure,* if I spent my time
learning the names of all the people at school, I wouldn't have
time to do much of anything else, but . . . I guess I could have
made a little more of an effort.

She wasn't as bad as I was expecting. Her hair was kind of
cool—she had that messy bedhead thing going on that most
people can't pull off, but she makes work. And weirdly, her outfit wasn't actually out of style—she had the right parts—the
flannel, the Chucks, but like was missing that extra thing to
tie it all together. I could help her, maybe. I appreciated that
she didn't rub her smartness in my face, unlike so many of the
other smart kids at Castle Cove. I know I'm not stupid; it's just
that school has never interested me much.

Now, with her gone, it's quiet in my room. Too quiet. All I can think about is the fact that it's Halloween night, and all my old friends are at the annual party at Levy Castle while I'm sitting here alone.

I'm sure Brooke is there, glammed out and wandering the halls of the Castle with Steve, reminding him that her family used to own it and her grandmother used to live there back in the day. Their heads bent together, laughing, holding hands, like they don't have a care in the world. Like the only reason that they even know each other isn't because of me. Like I don't even exist.

That image plays in my head, over and over. I grab my iPad and turn on something mindless on Netflix, but even that doesn't help shut my brain up. All I can think about is that party and Steve and Brooke and what happened this summer and how unfair it all is. . . .

I can't take it anymore. They're all there, having fun, while I sit here alone. I deserve to be there as much as any of them. Brooke stole *my* boyfriend, and somehow *I'm* the bad guy?

I jump out of bed, throw my closet door open, and pull on clothes.

Once dressed, I sneak downstairs. Brenda's in her room, so I manage to get outside and to my car—another guilt gift from my parents—without fielding any questions. In the distance, the surf slams into the cliffs below our house, the fall wind rolling the waves angrily. I'd say that there's something in the air tonight, something creepy, but I'm not the type of person to believe in that sort of thing.

I turn up my music as high as it'll go, drowning out any

more racing thoughts, and take off down the driveway out to Highway 1.

The road is busy tonight. It wraps along the cliffs, between the ocean and the hills, and there are only a few houses to the west of the highway. Downtown Castle Cove is on the east side of things, cut into the bottom of the hills.

I pass Park's driveway; her house is on the cliff side of the street like mine but surrounded by high gates. Her dad is an international businessman, whatever that means, and is super paranoid about everything. Kennedy and Donovan live a few minutes in the other direction from where I'm heading; their houses are up in the neighborhoods in the hills on the east side of the highway. If I kept driving, I'd hit the town center, where the high school is and all the restaurants where *Top Chef* losers come to set up shop. The winners open their places down the coast in LA, obviously.

But, before I hit downtown, I reach my destination—the Castle. It's on the west side of the road, set on ten acres, the biggest parcel of land on the cliff side of the highway. It was built by Brooke's great-grandfather about eighty years ago as a residence for their family.

It sits on the ocean side of Highway 1, with a veranda that has a gigantic outdoor pool and sweeping views of the Pacific Ocean. The public is only allowed in certain rooms of the Castle, but because of the various parties over the years I've seen it all—and it's literally insane. Like, tall, stained-glass windows, an ornate indoor pool with mermaid fountains that spit water, and more bedrooms than I can count.

Back in the day, Brooke's great-grandfather used to hold

court there, throwing these elaborate weekend-long parties and inviting all the entertainment industry people up from LA. Tons of movie stars used to hang out there, and at least one of them died under mysterious circumstances.

It's been here since before Castle Cove was even really a town, and all the property on the cliff side of the road used to belong to it—according to what I've heard from Kennedy, at one point it had like one hundred acres, all to itself. Legend has it that Brooke's great-grandmother used to have a zoo on the property, with llamas and tigers and everything.

Developers bought up most of that land over the years and built huge houses like mine and Park's. I guess it brought in a bunch of money to the town—made Castle Cove more of a livable place rather than just a tourist destination. More recently, they've turned their attention to revamping the Yacht Club. Kennedy's dad has something to do with it, I think, which I only know because a few months ago she spent, like, a solid week moaning about how her dad had canceled their summer vacation to Barcelona because he had to stay in town to help with the deal.

I pull off the highway into the lot for the Castle and stop beside Park's car, a green Porsche Cayenne that her parents bought her for no reason other than she exists and they *love* her.

As I slip out of my car, I hear them: loud voices in the distance, a scream of laughter. Brooke's laughter. It scrapes through my skin, down into my heart, and for a moment I actually consider getting back into the car and driving away. Maybe driving away like I did three months ago.

That night, last summer, after I'd just gotten back from Egypt and Brooke came over and said what she said to me about her and Steve . . . it was like my heart stopped beating. Like my brain short-circuited. All I could think about was Agatha Christie, what she did after she figured out her husband was cheating on her. How she straight up disappeared for eleven days, and half the population of England was convinced he'd murdered her. Like, how badass is that? It's not that I *wanted* Steve to, you know, get arrested or anything, but at the same time, I didn't mind the thought of people searching for me. Wondering about me. *Thinking* about me.

So, I got into my car and started to drive. I left my phone at home along with this vase I'd accidentally knocked over in the foyer on my way out . . . which sort of made everyone think I'd been kidnapped, and Steve had to go into the station for questions, and the town organized this whole search party to look for me. . . .

Anyway, when I got back five days later, everyone was pretty freaking mad. Mad enough that my parents had to negotiate with the city, and everyone agreed that house arrest was the appropriate punishment for what I'd done.

Another peal of laughter punctures the night air. We started having this party at the Castle three years ago, when we were freshmen, courtesy of Brooke's connections. The first year it was mostly just people from our school, but word got out and now kids from neighboring towns drive in for it, too. Kennedy's dad, who's a music agent down in LA, gets one of his clients to play. Everyone ships in the most elaborate costumes possible. It's become a whole thing.

As I round the corner to the front of the Castle where we always set up, I hear music but don't see a DJ. Which means Kennedy's dad didn't come through with one of his clients. Park must have had a *fit*.

There have to be at least two hundred people here, spread out everywhere, laughing, talking, crying. Everyone having a grand old time without me.

Across the lawn a bit, on a wide stone terrace behind the back entrance to the Castle, a bar is set up, manned by a bartender wearing a penguin costume. I catch sight of Cole Fielding hanging in front of it, talking to Kennedy, who's still dressed as a bloody cheerleader. Her blond hair is tied up on her head in a messy top knot that I'm sure took her over an hour to perfect, and she has one manicured hand placed on Cole's arm.

Even *Cole* is here? That had to be Kennedy's doing. She's wanted to get with him for years. I wonder if Brooke was okay with it.

On the lawn overlooking the sea, someone—probably Kennedy's house manager—has set up a big bonfire and surrounded it with floor pillows and faux fur blankets and other glamping paraphernalia. I spot Park and Donovan and Steve right away. They're sprawled across a giant pillow. Brooke is basically lying on top of Steve, and Park is, as usual, sitting awkwardly close to the two of them. She has no sense of personal boundaries. Both of them are still wearing their bloody cheerleader outfits, too, and Steve just has a green mask perched on top of his thick, brown hair. He's never really been into dressing up, which annoyed me to no end when we were dating.

My heart starts thumping in my chest as I take it all in. And of course Kennedy chooses this moment to spot me.

"Oh my god. *Ew,*" she says loudly. The music basically screeches to a stop, and every single person turns in my direction and stares. Merde. This is not the entrance I anticipated. In my mind, it went something like this: I walk in, Brooke sees me and collapses into a ball of tearful guilt, and every single one of these people apologizes to me for how rude they've been. Even though I saw them at school earlier and that didn't happen, I somehow thought that it might now. I swear to god, sometimes I don't know what I'm thinking.

Instead, a little voice in my head is screaming *run run run run run* over and over again. I can't leave now, though. How pathetic would that be? I ball my hands into fists and remind myself that I have just as much right to be here as the rest of them.

I keep walking across the lawn toward the fire.

Steve starts to stand when he sees me approaching, and Brooke topples off his lap onto the blanket, which gives me a little kick of satisfaction. She glares at him and then drags herself up off the ground, brushing her short pleated skirt off and turning to face me with an angry glare.

It's Steve who speaks first, though. "What are you doing here, Alice?" he asks quietly.

I stop in front of them. "I just . . ." I trail off, heart pounding.

Brooke starts to move between us, and he puts out a hand to stop her. "I'll take care of this," he says, then to me, "C'mon." Then he grabs my elbow and starts to lead me through the large crowd that's gathered. I put my head down, trying not to make eye contact with anyone.

We're almost back to the side of the Castle when we're stopped by a voice behind us. Brooke.

"Where are you *going*?" She sounds upset.

Steve and I both turn back, and Steve says, "Brookie, give me a minute, okay?"

Her expression falls. "You're going to go off into the dark? With *her*?" she whines, barking a bitter laugh.

For a moment, a foreign emotion runs through me—something that might be close to guilt, but then Kennedy appears behind Brooke. "Are you sure that's a good idea, Steve?" she says. "You know what she did last summer."

"Kennedy. *God,*" Brooke snaps, and turns back to me and Steve, a frown tugging the corners of her mouth down. "What are you even *doing* here, Alice? Haven't you done enough damage? Why can't you just leave us alone!"

She has got to be kidding. She's playing it off like *she's* the victim? "Haven't *I* done enough damage? You're the one who stole my boyfriend—"

"I didn't *steal* him," she interrupts. "Jesus, Alice. You are so dramatic. You were in *Egypt.* You guys were broken *up.* And then you disappeared—why did you *do* that? That was so scary—"

"Enough!" Steve yells, cutting us both off. Now his voice isn't so quiet. Or nice. He sounds mad.

Brooke's face flushes. She must be thinking what I'm thinking—I've *never* heard Steve speak like that before, not to anyone. Last summer, after I reappeared with no explanation, everyone was so pissed off, but Steve just ignored me—in fact, this is the longest conversation the two of us have had since the day he dumped me. He's just not an angry guy.

He sucks in a breath and then turns to Brooke. "I am going to walk Alice back to her car. It's dark and it's Halloween. Who knows what kind of pervs are out there. I have to do this, Brooke."

She folds her arms across her chest. "Fine. Come back soon, okay?" Her voice is tight, but she manages a smile. Something squeezes in my stomach. God, the two of them—two peas in the same annoyingly kind pod. A whisper of regret floats into my brain, but I squash it before it can grow.

"I will." He smiles at her and walks over to where she's standing. He bends down to kiss her cheek, and suddenly, I'm invisible.

By the time we get to the parking lot, Steve is practically dragging me by the arm. Every time I tried to stop and say something to him, he gave me this *look* and kept right on going. Now, under the streetlamps, I can see his face clearly for the first time, and he does not look happy.

We stop a few feet away from my car, and he drops my arm. "Why did you come here, Alice?" he asks again.

"I . . ." What *am* I doing here? My fantasies about everyone begging for my forgiveness seem ridiculous now. The anger drains out of my body. I'm tired. Tired of holding myself up straight. Tired of all of this. "I'll go." Clearly, I'm not going to get whatever I was looking for from this place.

Steve's face softens, because of course it does, because he's Steve and he's too nice, even to me. "Alice, are you okay?" He puts his hand on my arm, gently this time. His face is close to mine and his eyes are kind.

The words pierce a hole in my midsection, and the warmth of his hand on my arm is almost too much. I miss him, but more than that, I miss my *life*. I miss friends. I miss . . . Brooke. It makes me want to cry, even though I do not cry, as a rule. I suck in a shaky breath.

"Steve."

A voice hisses out of the dark. Brooke Donovan's voice, to be precise. Who apparently followed us, along with Kennedy and Park. Kennedy has her phone out, recording everything, Park hopping around behind the two of them excitedly.

Steve's hand drops off my arm. My mouth clamps shut.

"Alice, it's time for you to go," Brooke says.

I open my mouth to respond, but I have nothing left to say. Instead, I muster up all the strength I have and, without so much as a glance back, get into my car and drive away.

CHAPTER FOUR

IRIS

OCTOBER 31

9:20 P.M.

THE PASTA THAT ALICE'S—nanny? maid? caretaker?—gave me was something warm and cheesy with sun-dried tomatoes and broccoli and tangy nuts. I rinse the empty Tupperware in the sink and set it to dry on the dish rack.

Alice's house smelled like good things. Fresh flowers, food cooking somewhere I couldn't see, the aroma wafting through the enormous front room.

Our apartment smells like trash that needs to be taken out. Laundry we haven't yet hauled down to the dreary basement, where we'll have to lift out someone else's clothes, musty and already half-dry from being left in the washer too long.

The ceiling bulb goes dark, then pops back to life. The landlord always says he's going to fix it.

I open the window above the sink so the ocean air pours in, cool and salty. Maybe it'll freeze the tears brimming in my eyes.

When you're little, people tell you how great your life will be one day. Tell you that you can be anything or anyone you want as long as you work hard and are kind and never give up.

But I do all of those things, and I'm still a girl alone in a crappy seaside apartment with wonky wiring.

I turn back to the kitchen table, boot up my iPad. I have two assignments due tomorrow and a calc quiz to study for. Right? Because isn't that supposed to be my ticket to getting out? Using my brain for a college scholarship? I'm a junior. This is all I'm supposed to care about.

I can hear footsteps outside the door. I know it's just somebody who lives in the building, because *he* can't come back. He's not allowed to.

Still.

I start to shake. Don't think about him. Don't.

But it's too late. I can feel his hands on my chest, pushing me. I'd wedged myself between them after he lunged at her. The snap in my wrist as I hit the linoleum.

Old Man from C11 pounding on the front door. *What's happening in there?*

The Thing staring down at me, face red, then him staggering to the door, pushing past the old man.

Of course he called days later, sorry, crying, like he always does. My mother changed her number. Again.

The apartment, the blinking lightbulb. The air around me closes in, making me smaller, smaller, nothing, everything inside me disappearing.

I grab my peacoat, my phone and keys and headphones, and run from my own home.

—

I take deep breaths as I walk down Highway 1, wiping my face dry in the cold air, my heart a loud drum in my chest.

Breathe in, breathe out, breathe in, breathe out.

At the lookout spot, I stop. I like to stand here and gaze down at the waves and listen to the sound of the water crashing against the bottom of the cliff. There's something mesmerizing about the way the water rolls up into curls of white and then rolls back out again.

I'm not thinking about anything dire. It's just peaceful, that's all.

I step back, noticing I'm too close to the edge. You have to be careful. Every year, there's always a referendum or something like that to put in a guardrail, but it gets shot down. Instead, there are signs posted with figures midtumble, surrounded by a spray of pebbles, and *Watch Your Step,* and a broken fence.

I will miss the sea when I finally get me and my mom out of here. I don't know where I'll take us, but it has to be far from this place. Somewhere he can't bother us ever again.

I slip my headphones back on, turn around, check carefully before crossing the highway. The road's super curvy around here, and who knows who might be driving too fast on Halloween night. I need to stay by the woodside to be safe.

A horn blares and I jump back, my heart racing.

A silvery car whizzes past, southbound. Is that Alice Ogilvie driving like a bat out of hell? I could only make out waves of blond hair, but it looked like her car.

What would Alice be doing out? Her friends hate her. And

she should be, you know, reading about Icarus. Oh well. It's not my fault if she doesn't study, I tell myself. I'm glad I'm getting paid, no matter what happens with her grades.

About fifteen minutes down the road, I hear the sounds of thumping bass from way up the hill. A seething mass of brightly colored figures staggering around a bonfire flickering on the lawn of the Castle.

Right. Levy Castle. The Halloween party the Mains throw every year. Even kids from neighboring towns come, swanked out and itching to get their drunk on.

I keep walking, angling my direction so they can't see me, when two figures spill out of the clearing ahead of me. They're pulling at each other, which is just great. Now I have to walk by a fight. I keep my headphones on, ducking against a tree to wait it out when I realize who it is—Steve Anderson, a green mask pulled on top of his head, and Brooke Donovan in a short skirt. She must be freezing out here.

They've stopped tugging at each other. Steve looks . . . well, not like Steve usually does, kind of happy-go-lucky and nice. He's probably the nicest of the Mains, to tell you the truth.

But he's not smiling now. Instead, he looks kind of pissed. And a little . . . messed up? He's kind of weaving every which way. I didn't think Steve was a drinker. He's pretty straight-edge because of basketball.

Brooke's crying and her hair is in her face. Brooke has always been pretty cool, and she doesn't even have to be. She's literally the most famous, richest girl in town. I mean, entire books have been written about her family history, which apparently involves some mysterious deaths at sea, a fortune made, lost, and remade, and an infamous custody battle involving her grandmother that made headlines around the world. All this means Brooke could be the biggest bitch in town, but she isn't.

The silver car from earlier flashes in my memory then, and it hits me. That *had* to be Alice. But why would she come here after everything? From Spike and Zora, I knew all about Steve stepping out on Alice over the summer with Brooke. Then, when Alice disappeared, Zora was pretty convinced for, like, a day that Steve had done something to her, and I guess the police thought so, too, because he was questioned and the whole shebang. They had a search party, Amber Alert, all the bells and whistles and then . . . Alice reappeared in her parents' driveway, miraculously fine, with nary a scratch on her.

Steve grabs Brooke by the shoulders, startling me. I tense up, slide my headphones off.

I sink farther into the tree as Brooke twists away violently.

"I knew it," she screams. "I knew you'd go back to her. Everyone is always leaving me."

"I'm not leaving you, just calm down," Steve yells back, and grabs her arm.

I take a step forward and stop. Where are her friends?

"Let go of me. Get away from me, *now*!" Brooke screams.

"I'm not going to let you run away from me," Steve says.

Suddenly, an army of Mains clutching red Solo cups descends from the long steps leading down from the Castle into the lot. They all have their phones up, filming Brooke and Steve, but no one's stepping in to stop what's happening.

Brooke shoves Steve, and he stumbles backward.

And then Steve shoves her back.

"Hey, man, come on, now." It's Cole Fielding. He moves like he's going to stop Steve, but Nelson and Gerber, Steve's basketball buddies, hold him back.

"Brookie." Kennedy rushes over, helping her up.

"What the hell is your problem," Park yells at Steve, slugging him in the arm.

Brooke straightens her skirt. Then she turns and runs.

Toward me.

Steve starts to go after her, but Park blocks him, her hands pressing against his chest.

"Brooke," he shouts. "You can't do this to me, Brooke!"

I step back farther in the trees so her friends can't see me. I know it would not be good if they knew I was here.

Brooke runs past me, tears streaming down her face, phone clutched in one hand, face wild. She looks like my mom used to after a fight with the Thing when I was little. Desperate and in her own world.

Instinctively, I go still. It's scary to see Brooke look like my mom did.

It's only after she's passed me that I come out of the trees. Her friends are still standing in the lot. Kennedy hesitantly calls out, "Brookie! Come on, come back."

But then Kennedy shrugs and turns her back. Park is guiding Steve away, her arm in his. I guess Brooke is just a drunk nuisance to them, which doesn't seem very friend-like to me.

If her friends aren't going to help her, I will. I take off after her. A girl shouldn't be allowed to run away into the dark on her own.

By the time I reach the first bend of road, though, there's no one there, just the sound of the sea washing up against the cliffs below. I walk along Highway 1 and call her name, but I don't get an answer.

Brooke Donovan is gone.

CHAPTER FIVE

ALICE

NOVEMBER 1

7:52 A.M.

"There is no such thing as a really calm sea.
Always, always, there is motion."
—AGATHA CHRISTIE, *EVIL UNDER THE SUN*

I'M EXHAUSTED THIS MORNING. After I left the party, I drove south for a while, trying to take my mind off of everything. When I got home, it took forever for me to fall asleep and when I finally did, I had all these weird dreams about cliffs and crashing waves and Brooke crying in that stupid Castle.

I'm almost to my locker when a hand adorned with multiple designer rings grabs my arm. I jerk away, surprised, and snap, "Get off."

Kennedy holds her hands up, that smirk of hers plastered on her face. "Sorry. Jesus, Ogilvie. Didn't know you were so jumpy."

I roll my eyes. "Whatever. What do you want, *Rebecca*?" I say her first name with a sneer. I know she hates it. And, sure enough, her face flushes red for a moment. *Good.*

"Well, *Alice*," she says, as if I hate my first name also, which

I do not, thank you very much. "Thanks to you, Brooke and Steve got into a massive fight after you left last night. I'm sure you heard about it. Nice work."

I glare at her. I am running on four hours of sleep, and dealing with Kennedy and her attitude is the last thing I can handle right now. "How was that my fault?"

She makes a face. "Um, how was it *not* your fault. Showing up like you did. Brooke was super upset, you know. After their fight, she took off. She didn't even sleep at my place like she was supposed to."

I clench my jaw and exhale slowly. What a joy it is to deal with Kennedy bright and early in the morning. "First of all," I say. "*I* don't control Steve and Brooke. Them fighting is their own issue. And second, why aren't you talking to *Brooke* if you're so concerned with her well-being?" I motion vaguely at the kids passing in the hall. "Where is she anyway? Why don't you go annoy her instead of me?"

Kennedy's face darkens. "I haven't seen her yet. I texted her a bunch of times this morning but haven't heard back. I assume she's still upset from having to deal with *you.*"

I roll my eyes. "Well, thanks so much for the update." I hike my bag back up onto my shoulder and prepare to exit this most charming of situations. "I'll see——" I start, but Kennedy interrupts me.

"Coach!" she yells, and I turn to see Coach Donovan heading our way. He waves to her and stops in front of us.

"Yes, Rebecca?" he says. He looks exhausted, dark bags sagging under his eyes, and his normal congenial smile is nowhere to be found. Apparently, no one slept well last night. "Aren't you ladies due in class soon?"

"Where's Brooke?" asks the ever-so-pleasant Kennedy abruptly.

"Brooke?" he asks, glancing between the two of us.

"Yes," she says. "Where is she? I've been looking for her all morning."

His brow furrows. "Isn't she with you? She slept over at your house."

"No." Irritation flickers across Kennedy's face, but she knows better than to be rude to a teacher—especially Coach. "She didn't sleep at my house. Didn't she sleep at home?"

Coach narrows his eyes. "No. She slept at your house."

Kennedy sighs. "*No.* She slept at——"

"Good lord," I interrupt. "Did she sleep at your house?" I direct the question to Kennedy first, who shakes her head. "At home?" I ask Coach.

"No," he replies. "She went to the Castle party and told me she was going to sleep over at Rebecca's."

The three of us lapse into a short silence, the two of them presumably stumped over how Brooke could not have slept at the other's house.

"Okay, then. Where is Brooke?" I ask, looking between them.

Coach pulls out his phone, taps it a few times, and presses it up against his ear. "I'm calling her." After a few moments, he hangs up. "No answer." He sighs. "I'd like to say this isn't like her, but . . ." He trails off for a moment, and a faraway look crosses his face. "I'm sure she'll show up soon. She's probably with Steve. I'm heading to class, but if you girls see or hear from her, please tell her to find me."

Kennedy and I watch as he departs, and then I turn back to her. "What the hell?"

Kennedy purses her lips. "Not that it's any business of yours,

Alice, but Coach and Brooke haven't exactly been getting along recently. She's been staying at my house and at Park's a bunch, or sometimes with Steve at the Insley Arms or whatever."

"They haven't been getting along?" Brooke and Coach have always been close, although since Brooke's mom died, I know it's been hard, and there *has* been tension. I always chalked that up to grief, though. "Why not?"

Kennedy shrugs. "Who knows. Money stuff, I think. Whatever. You know, I bet he's right, though. Brooke and Steve probably found each other after the party and made up." Her eyes cut to my face, waiting for me to react, but when I don't, her face falls. "Anyway, I gotta get to class." She marches about two feet away from me before stopping in her tracks.

"Steve," I hear her mutter.

"What?" I'm confused for a moment, and then I turn.

And there's Steve, standing in front of his locker. Alone.

He's a mess. His hair is everywhere, pants stained, a rip in one of the knees. He's only wearing one shoe, and there's dirt streaked across his face. He's hanging on to his locker door like it's holding him up. I look at Kennedy and she cuts her eyes to me. I know we're wondering the same thing.

What happened to him? I've never seen him like this—even after his basketball games, he puts himself back together. Never goes into public all sweaty and gross like some of his teammates.

Kennedy marches over to him and I follow. "Steve!" she yells, and he turns toward us, wincing. As I get closer, I realize he stinks like garbage and old shoes. Kennedy wrinkles her nose. She must smell it, too. What is he thinking, showing up at school like this?

"What?" he says. From his exhausted expression, it appears

it took a massive effort for him to get that one word out of his mouth. If I didn't know any better, I'd say he was hungover, or maybe even still drunk, but Steve doesn't usually drink much, especially not with basketball season coming up so soon.

"First of all"—she pinches her nose—"you smell like a dumpster. You need to go home."

He shakes his head. "Woke up in the woods. Got an exam. I'll clean up in the bathroom."

This is such typical, dutiful Steve. Showing up for an exam that he'll probably fail—he looks like he didn't sleep a wink last night.

Kennedy shakes her head. "Right. Anyway, more importantly—where's Brooke? Did you find her after you left the party?"

An odd expression crosses his face. "Brooke?"

"You know, your girlfriend?" she says. She glances at me and smirks. "Sorry, Alice." She just can't help herself.

"What do you mean . . . ?" He pauses. "Wait. She's not here?"

My heart drops.

Kennedy shakes her head. "No. She isn't with you? She was supposed to sleep at my house, but she never showed up, and Coach Donovan said she didn't sleep at home, either." For the first time this morning, she looks worried. "The last time I saw her was when she ran off after your fight last night."

"What?" he says. Any color that existed in Steve's face, which was not much, drains out. We have his attention now. "I haven't seen her since then, either. Where is she?"

"That's the thing," Kennedy says. "Nobody seems to know."

With that, Steve holds up a finger and says, "I gotta puke." Then he runs past us, straight into the boys' bathroom, leaving

Kennedy and me standing there, alone. We look at each other, eyes wide, and a trickle of fear starts down my spine.

Brooke still hasn't appeared by the time third period ends, but word about what happened last night is out. The hallway is buzzing with rumors about Brooke and Steve . . . and me.

I'm in the bathroom when I overhear two girls talking on the other side of the stall about how Steve showed up drunk this morning to school and got sent home, but instead went to Brooke's house and banged on her door until her neighbors called the cops on him. Apparently, the cops hauled him down to the station for disturbing the peace, and now he's at home. Hopefully sleeping off whatever happened to him. It's weird; it's not like Steve to drink so much, especially during the basketball preseason, when he's in training.

"I heard Mr. Carpenter ask Coach Donovan if Brooke was okay—he said that she's fine . . . probably just took off for the night," continues one of the girls. "I bet you anything that she's probably just pulling an Ogilvie."

Excuse me? What sort of inane gossip is this? Why is Coach telling people that Brooke is fine? Isn't he worried about her? And what do they mean by *pulling an Ogilvie*? Is that, like, a term people are using now? Ugh, this school.

I flush the toilet and then slam open my stall door. "Oh hi," I say sweetly. Sarah Keller's face goes white, and her friend's jaw drops.

"I'd appreciate it if you two would shut your mouths about all of this. You know nothing about Brooke, or Steve, or me." I smile with all my teeth. "And I don't care what Coach says. Brooke would never"—I make air quotes with my fingers—

"*pull an Ogilvie.* Understand? Please be on your way now. Spreading rumors is rude."

They both nod, eyes wide.

I turn on my heel and leave the bathroom with my head held high, but a very bad feeling has started to settle in my stomach. What parent doesn't immediately freak out when their child goes missing? Why isn't Coach doing anything? It doesn't make any sense.

Something feels very, very wrong about this.

By the time the final bell rings, I can barely concentrate. I leave my last class in a haze, and I'm so deep in my own head trying to puzzle this out that I almost walk into an open locker door.

I've heard the phrase *pulled an Ogilvie* more times than I can count today, and half the school, including Coach, seems like they've accepted that Brooke just took off for a couple days, like it's just what teenage girls do. Like it's normal.

I don't think she would have taken off like I did, but what this past summer showed me more than anything is that people are sometimes not what they seem. Kennedy did say Brooke was having issues with Coach. Maybe she *did* run away.

As I'm about to leave the building, though, I see Coach. He's standing in the hallway, chatting with another teacher, and he looks . . . normal. Like he doesn't have a care in the world, like his only daughter hasn't disappeared.

I walk over to him and stand there until his conversation peters to an end, and the other teacher awkwardly says her goodbye.

I don't waste my time on hellos. "Have you heard from her?" I ask Coach.

An annoyed expression skitters across his face. He tries to disguise it by plastering over it the fakest smile I've ever seen, but it's a weak try. "Hello, Alice." He pauses, like he's waiting for me to respond with some silly nicety, as though that matters right now.

And, suddenly, I'm mad. Like, rip-roaring, raging mad. I'm getting the feeling that no one is looking for Brooke because of me, and maybe part of my anger is actually shame, sure, but also, what in the actual *hell*. "Why aren't you worried about her?" I ask him. I don't care if I'm being rude. I just don't care.

He sucks in a breath like he's trying to stay calm. "I am concerned, Alice, but as I told you earlier, it isn't the first time Brooke has done this recently. Not to mention . . ." He narrows his eyes. "You should know better than anyone that sometimes people just need a break. To cool off or whatnot. I'll have her get in touch with you as soon as she gets home; I'm sure she'll appreciate your concern. Now, go home, and try not to worry. I'll see you tomorrow, alright?" He turns and pushes through the double doors out into the afternoon sunlight, leaving me behind to fume.

I cannot believe he's brushing this off. Brooke may have hurt me, but she used to be my best friend. And I've had just about enough with everyone's lack of concern for her safety.

And I know exactly what to do about it. I reach into my bag, pull out my cell, and go to my contacts. I scroll until I find who I want. Lilian Levy.

Brooke's grandmother.

You told me to text you if Brooke was ever in trouble, I type. *Have you heard from her? She never came home last night. Worried. SOS.*

A moment later, my phone rings.

CHAPTER SIX

ALICE

NOVEMBER 2

8:05 A.M.

"Why harrow oneself by looking on the worst
side? . . . Because it is sometimes necessary."
—AGATHA CHRISTIE, *SAD CYPRESS*

AGATHA CHRISTIE WOULD BE proud of me for trusting my
instincts. Because Brooke still hasn't appeared, but Lilian Levy
has swept into town from New York City, and things are finally
starting to happen.

Beginning with this morning's assembly, which is being
held in lieu of zero period, and everyone is required to attend.

I slip inside the auditorium, finding a seat toward the back.
Down in the front of the room, I catch sight of Coach, a grumpy
expression on his face, being lectured by an older, genteel
woman who's holding a cane. Lilian Levy.

I smile. Coach looks like a little kid being scolded by his
mom, or, in this case, his mother-in-law. Back when Brooke
and I were friends, I'd go with her every year to upstate New
York to visit her mom's family's vacation home in the Adiron-

dacks. Lilian is a force to be reckoned with, and I know she never liked Coach much.

As the room starts to fill with my classmates, I bury my head in my phone to try and avoid eye contact with anyone. The last thing I want is to hear more comments about what I did last summer. Everyone in this town really needs to learn to move on.

Good old Lilian Levy. I knew I could count on her.

A hush falls over the room, and I look up. Steve, Park, Kennedy, Henderson, and the others are all sitting in the front row on the other side of the aisle from me, worried expressions on their faces. Steve looks like he's been crying.

Lilian Levy makes her way up to the stage, followed by Principal Brown and Ms. Westmacott. They confer for a few moments, and then Brown walks over to the microphone.

"Hell——" The microphone gives a loud *screech,* and she pulls back. Some jerk down front yells, "Where's Brooke!" and a few people laugh. Brown glares at them before continuing. "Hello, everyone. We're here today because Brooke Donovan is missing. The last time she was seen was around ten p.m. Halloween night, leaving the Castle grounds, heading south on Highway One. I'm going to let her grandmother"—she motions back to Lilian Levy—"talk for a moment, but if anyone here—anyone at all—has information regarding the whereabouts of Brooke Donovan, we need to know." She retreats from the mic and stands next to Westmacott, and Lilian takes her place.

It's been a year since I've seen Lilian, and she's impeccable as always even with the addition of the cane she's leaning on, dressed in a tweed Chanel jacket and tailored pants, her makeup subtle and classy. And, as always, she's wearing her signature red-framed glasses, the ones Brooke and I always coveted.

"Good morning, everyone. As most of you have heard by now, my granddaughter, Brooke Donovan"—for a moment, her voice wobbles and she clears her throat before continuing—"has been missing since Halloween. That night, she attended a party at the Levy Castle, but never made it home. I'm told she was wearing a cheerleader outfit. A short skirt and crop top. It's possible she had been drinking. I understand my late daughter's husband"—Lilian's mouth puckers in distaste—"initially suspected Brooke had run away from home, but at this point, I think we all can agree that is simply not the case."

Lilian continues, "If anyone has any information on where she is, please let the authorities know. I am offering a *substantial* award to anyone who helps us locate her. The first seventy-two hours are the most critical in a missing persons case. This is a very serious matter." She glares menacingly in the direction of Coach for a moment before walking back to join Principal Brown as Westmacott steps forward.

Westmacott clears her throat into the microphone. Her face is pale. "Hi, everyone. Like Ms. Levy said, if anyone knows where Brooke might be, please come forward. And, if anyone needs to talk, my door is open. Thank you."

And with that, we're dismissed.

CHAPTER SEVEN

I'M IN THE CAFETERIA, trying to do my calc homework, when I notice a flurry of activity.

I look up and am surprised to see blue uniforms and stern looks as a group of police officers gaze around the sea of kids. The principal is with them.

I elbow Spike. "What's up with this?"

"You live under a rock, Iris? That rich girl, Brooke, I guess she's missing?" Spike frowns at me.

Zora crunches a carrot. "Didn't you go to assembly this morning, Iris?"

"No, I . . ." I watch the cops walking slowly. "I never go to that stuff." I had skipped it, instead secreting myself into the farthest corner of the library and reading on the floor. Mrs. Henley and I have an agreement: I can hide as long as I help reshelve. I'd heard little buzzes, though, that Brooke wasn't in school yesterday, but didn't pay attention. She's a Main. They skip all the time. I had other things on my mind, anyway, like how to go about changing your identity.

Prickles start to creep up my skin.

Spike chews his salt-and-vinegar chips thoughtfully. "That Castle party they have on Halloween. She never made it home."

Never made it home. My body runs cold, the scene on Halloween playing in my head. When I ran after her, she disappeared. It was really dark out, getting late, and I went home.

I bite my lip. "She never went home at all? Or anywhere else?" I mean, I guess I thought maybe her friends would find her after the party, or that she texted someone. I never thought . . .

What have I done?

Zora pulls a sheet of paper from her backpack and slides it across the table to me. "Here. Fifty flippin' K to whoever finds her. They passed these out at assembly. Brooke's grandmother showed up and gave a little speech."

I look at the flyer, but my vision is blurry from panic. The image of Brooke on the paper, sweet and pretty, swims before my eyes.

I saw her, I ran after her. She vanished. I went home. I got home around 10:15 p.m. It's lunchtime now, and cops are here in the cafeteria. How long has no one heard a word from Brooke? I saw Coach this morning on my way to class. He looked the way he always does: kind of grumpy, clutching his class folders and a clipboard.

If his kid is missing, why is he even *at* school?

The smell of Spike's chips suddenly makes me feel ill. I fold up the flyer and shove it into my backpack.

I watch as the cops amble down the aisles with the principal, who's pointing to kids. Slowly, each one gets up.

Kennedy, Park, Henderson. Steve Anderson, who looks like hell, by the way. Puffy face, slumped shoulders.

Park is starting to cry. I can tell by the way she's hunching her shoulders and letting her long hair fall across her face. The Mains usually look bored, but they look a little freaked out right now. Even Kennedy, who prides herself on remaining cool at all times, is nervously chewing a bright pink nail. Steve looks like a deer caught in headlights.

Brooke was running and then she was gone.

The cafeteria is dead silent as we watch the Mains grab their stuff and follow the cops out.

I watch them being led from the cafeteria.

"I'm voting for a good old-fashioned kidnapping and ransom deal," Zora murmurs, tucking a bright orange strand of hair behind her ear. "I mean, her family is loaded. That grandma was practically dripping money."

Brooke ran right by me.

I ran after her and called her name, but . . . nothing. And then I just . . . went home. I mean, why didn't her *friends* go find her?

I feel like I can't breathe.

"I bet it was one of them," Neil says, gesturing to the cafeteria exit, where the Mains have just filed out.

"Those girls? No way," Spike says. "They couldn't *murder* anyone. They wouldn't want to break a nail. There are plenty of perverts in Castle Cove. I mean, Remy Jackson? They never found who did *that.*"

"They've never figured out a lot of stuff. Mona Moody? The movie star who died at Levy Castle in the thirties?" Zora deepens her voice. "So many mysteries in our fair sea town."

I feel like I'm being swallowed by an enormous dark cloud.

Ten years ago Remy Jackson was found in a dumpster, wrapped in Hefty bags and duct tape. She was fourteen. They never solved it. Case closed.

That night keeps running through my head. Brooke, fighting with Steve, who seemed *not-Steve,* and then running right by me, and then the empty road when I turned the curve in the highway.

"Iris?" Spike says, poking me in the arm. "Hey, Adams, you alright?"

Shakily, I pull my phone from my back pocket and text my mom.

Mom something bad happened. I need you.

I stand up, shoving my iPad and lunch bag into my backpack.

"She's probably just imitating Ogilvie," Zora muses. "It's the new trend for the Mains. Disappearing!"

"Iris?" Spike says, softly. "Where are you going?"

"It was me," I tell him. "I think it was me. The last one who saw her."

I start walking away quickly. Spike calling after me, "Iris! Hey, Iris!" but I don't turn back.

What Zora said burns in my brain: Maybe, possibly, cotton candy–sweet Brooke left all on her own after a fight with her boyfriend, but what if she *didn't*? What if I was the last person to see her before she went missing?

The detective's name is Thompson and he seems irritated with me, which I think is a little unacceptable since a girl is missing. The room we're in looks exactly like it does in TV shows: long, crummy table, window on one wall that I can't see through. Who's on the other side, watching us? Maybe I shouldn't have come here. After all, what do I know? And this guy doesn't really even seem to *care*.

"So," he says gruffly. "You were out walking on Highway One, you saw a fight in the clearing? At the Castle party. Ms. Donovan and her boyfriend, correct?"

"Yes, like I told you on the phone. She pushed him and he pushed her back. And then she ran away."

"Would you characterize the fight as violent?"

"Well, there was pushing. And yelling?" I say.

He makes a note on his pad. "Why were you out so late, walking alone?"

"I don't . . . why is that important?" I ask. "I take walks. I was on a walk."

The video camera next to us whirs.

"You a friend of Ms. Donovan's?"

"No, not really," I answer.

"What time would you say she ran past you?"

"I don't know. Nine-thirty, nine-forty-five, maybe? I didn't look at my phone or anything."

"Had Ms. Donovan been upset at school prior to this? Anything you might have noticed?"

"I don't know. I mean, like I said, we weren't friends. Sometimes she seemed sad. I mean, her mom died, but that was a while ago."

I shift in my seat. We weren't friends, but I liked what I knew of her. I'm not sure if a fight with your boyfriend is enough to make you take off on more than a momentary basis, but add in some alcohol, shoving, and leftover grief, well, that might be a different story. But also . . .

"Why was her dad at school?" I ask. That fact is still poking at me. "I mean, wouldn't you be at home, or out looking, if your kid was missing? And what about her boyfriend? Have you questioned him? They did fight." I feel a little guilty about this, tossing Steve out, but I have seen enough shows where it's always the boyfriend, as nice as they might seem in the beginning.

Thompson looks up from his notes and gazes at me.

"I think that's something for us to worry about, not you, Ms. Adams. Don't worry, we've got everything under control."

I don't like the cool look in his eyes. It reminds me of when the police came, after the incident with the Thing. How they looked at me and my mom like we were somehow to blame. Like we were a nuisance. Like we were lying. Like they didn't want to be bothered.

"Yes, but do you? My mom and I took Highway One here and there's no one out there. That's where I saw her. Shouldn't you guys be out there? You know, *searching?*"

Detective Thompson sets his jaw. "You know, Ms. Adams, I was a teenager once, too, but you don't see me sitting here lecturing you on how to teenage. So maybe just because you've seen a couple of TV shows about cops, don't think you know how to do *my* job, okay? I'm getting enough of that from the girl's grandmother, to be perfectly honest."

Right. Lilian Levy. The assembly speech I missed. The reward money. I guess Thompson just doesn't like listening to women, period.

Thompson pops a piece of gum into his mouth. "Back to the matter at hand, Ms. Adams. So, Ms. Donovan had a fight with her boyfriend and she ran past you and you ran after her and then she was gone? Poof?"

Something about the way he says *poof* irks me. And the fact he didn't really answer me about searching. Like he's not taking this seriously.

"Do you always refer to girls going missing as *poof*?" I ask, an edge to my voice.

Thompson puts his pencil down. "I'll be straight with you, Ms. Adams. I'm glad you came in. We're talking to some of Brooke's friends right now. Looking around a bit. Interviewing party guests. But we also have to entertain the fact that Ms. Donovan may have simply left on her own. Teenager fights with her boyfriend, maybe a little drunk, decides to teach him a lesson. Get a little attention. We saw a bit of that this summer, didn't we? And it's my understanding that Ms. Donovan was friends with the girl who disappeared over the summer. We're thinking this is a copycat situation. You know how girls are."

I stare at him. "How girls *are*? We're so overly emotional we decide to disappear to make our boyfriends upset or something?"

He looks at my hands, coiled tightly on the table. My knuckles are white.

And then he *smiles*. Like it's funny, my anger.

"You okay, Ms. Adams? Anything going on with *you*? I looked you up. Had a little trouble at your apartment over the summer."

I speak slowly, trying to stay calm. "I don't think that has anything to do with this."

He shrugs. "Maybe trouble follows you around. You seem very upset for a girl who didn't know the girl who's missing."

"I'm very upset you don't seem to be taking this seriously. One girl isn't the same as another. I mean, what if she, you know, fell from the cliffs? It was a party. Maybe she was drunk. Are you even *looking*?"

"Like I said, we're talking to her friends, her family. We're checking the area. Back to you and that night. What did her friends do when she ran off?"

I think about Halloween night. "They didn't go after her," I tell him. "But they're also kind of awful, if you want to know the truth, so I'm not entirely surprised."

"But you went after her. So according to what we have so far, you were the last person to see her. What did *you* do after you realized she was gone?"

"I . . ." Why is my voice shaking? He's giving me such a hard look, it's making me nervous. "I went home. I finished my homework, turned it in on the portal, and went to bed."

Detective Thompson puts down his pencil and picks something out of his fingernail. "You didn't call us? Report a distraught girl on the road? Go back to the party, tell her friends you couldn't find her? You just . . . went home? Maybe you didn't think much of it, either, then."

My heart sinks. I never should have come here. This guy, he obviously doesn't *care.*

The video camera wheezes. Thompson knocks it, and it stops.

"Thanks for coming, Ms. Adams," he says finally. "We have

an approximate time now, and location, for the last-known sighting of Ms. Donovan. You were very helpful. If we need anything more, we'll be in touch."

He stands up.

"That's it?" I ask, surprised.

"That's it," he says. He holds out his hand, like we're supposed to shake or something, but I don't take it.

I grab my backpack and stand up, cross the room to the door.

At the door, I look back.

"It's true that a girl disappeared this summer, and it turned out to be something else," I say, "but this might not be like that. We're not all the same."

CHAPTER EIGHT

IRIS

NOVEMBER 2

3:15 P.M.

MY MOM STARTS THE car and waits, like we always do, for the weird chugging noise to even out, then pulls out of the Castle Cove Police Department parking lot.

"You did the right thing," she says. "That poor girl. Maybe she's just holing up with a friend. I hope it's nothing worse, or anything like that Ogilvie girl over the summer. Aren't you tutoring her?"

"Her name is Alice and yes, I'm tutoring her, but why does everyone think Brooke is just being a copycat? She's still not *home*. And if her friends are hiding her, they sure put on a show today at school, freaking out in the cafeteria when the cops showed up."

Holing up with a friend still means coming home after several hours, a day, tops. Once, Zora had a fight with her mom and stayed with Spike for almost two days. But *her* mom knew where she was. Alice Ogilvie was gone for five days, five long days in which no one heard from her and in which her car was found totaled in a completely different town. That wasn't "holing up." *That* was long enough to be scary.

Brooke's no troublemaker. I don't think, anyway. And Steve did seem angry. She looked scared as she was running. Is Steve really a threat? And again, why would Coach come to school if his daughter never came home?

As we're driving down Highway 1, we pass maybe three cars, and some blue uniforms poking around the woodside and by the Lookout. Shouldn't there be scores of cop cars around, cops from all over looking for Brooke? Shouldn't there be yellow caution tape, people in white suits with special gloves, the whole deal? And where are the boats? Maybe she fell over the Lookout cliff. People do. The fence is shoddy and it was dark and she was frantic and maybe wasted.

I shudder at the thought. I can feel my mom's eyes searching my face, but I keep my gaze locked on the ocean outside my window. The sky is shifting a bit over the water, dark clouds gathering.

My mom's voice falters. "I guess I just want to hope, Iris, that she is just hiding somewhere. Because the alternative is . . ."

The air between us is thick. I tense up.

Missing girls suddenly found. In riverbeds. On the sides of roads. Bound up in dumpsters, like Remy Jackson.

"Right," I say softly.

Rebecca Kennedy: What did they ask u

Helen Park: Who was at the party

HP: What happened between Brooke and Steve

HP: If I've heard from her

RK: Yeah, they asked me that too

HP: Have you?

RK: No have you?

HP: No

HP: They also asked about Alice. About last summer. How she left

RK: Same

RK: What'd you say?

HP: Just that I didn't think Brooke would do that

RK: Yeah but did you ever think Alice would have?

HP: Honestly, yea

RK: Ok fair

RK: I bet Brooke is copying her. You know they were always trying to one-up each other

HP: IDK maybe

RK: Did they ask you about me?

HP: What do you mean?

RK: Like where I was that night

RK: Where I went after

RK: That sort of thing

HP: A little I guess

RK: What did you tell them?

HP: I said you were at the party and then you went home

RK: That's all you told them?

HP: Yes. I obviously didn't tell them about the video if that's what you mean

RK: OK good

HP: What did you tell them

RK: About where I was?

HP: No about me

RK: What about you?

HP: IDK just where I was that night at the party and stuff

RK: I mean there isnt anything to tell is there? You were just hanging with brooke and steve like usual right?

HP: Yeah

RK: Why are you acting weird

HP: I'm not

RK: Uh ok Park whatev gtg

CHAPTER NINE

ALICE

NOVEMBER 2

3:20 P.M.

"I do not argue with obstinate men.
I act in spite of them."
—AGATHA CHRISTIE,
THE MYSTERY OF THE BLUE TRAIN

AFTER THE ASSEMBLY, I thought things would turn around and people would start taking things seriously, but apparently my classmates aren't as intimidated by Lilian Levy as the Castle Cove cops are. Even after the police showed up at lunch and took a bunch of my old friends out of school to talk to them, the phrase *pulled an Ogilvie* is floating around in the hallways like my dumb classmates still think all of this is a joke.

Principal Brown catches me as I'm heading out of the building to let me know that the cops request my presence down at the station. Considering what happened at lunch, I'm unsurprised by this turn of events.

One minute later, I pull into the parking lot of the station. It's only a few blocks from the high school, but the sky has turned a disturbing shade of dark gray and the wind is kicking up. Since we're right on the coast, the storms we get in Castle Cove come up fast and violent, and getting caught in them is decidedly unpleasant.

The station is in the center of town, adorned by tall palm trees that I'm pretty sure are not native to this area. All I know is, Kennedy's dad, who's head of the Castle Cove Planning Commission, keeps having them imported and replanted every time they die. Seems like a lot of work for some trees, if you ask me.

I slip out of my car, head held high like my heart isn't thumping in my chest at one hundred miles per hour. The last time I was here was right after the *incident* last summer, and those memories are threatening to surface.

When Detective Thompson comes out of the back and spots me, he grimaces. We aren't exactly the best of friends. He was one of my least favorite people to deal with after my return, which is really saying something. There were a lot of contenders on that list.

"Alice," he says, "always a pleasure to see you. It's interesting, how often you seem to end up in my station. Follow me."

I roll my eyes and he holds open the low door, allowing me behind the counter. I trail behind him to the back of the station into a small interview room straight out of *Law & Order: SVU.* It's the same as the last time I was here. Ugly.

In all of Agatha Christie's books, interviews with witnesses and suspects are conducted in a more elegant manner, in classy drawing rooms and aboard luxury steamers. The next time I'm involved in a mystery, I'd prefer it to be somewhere more interesting than Castle Cove.

Thompson starts in on me immediately. "Alice, I'm sure

you know why you're here. We were told that you were in attendance at the Castle party on Halloween, the night Brooke Donovan disappeared. Is that correct?"

"Yes," I respond.

Thompson writes something in his notebook. "We were told by several witnesses that you and Brooke had an altercation that night."

"*Altercation* seems like a strong word to use, but yeah, we got into an argument. I have to tell you, though——"

"What was it about?" he interrupts.

I pause. Heat creeps up my neck, but I force my voice to stay steady. "She wasn't pleased that I showed up."

Thompson cocks an eyebrow at me. "Oh? Why's that?"

"I wasn't exactly welcome there."

"Mmm . . ." He writes something else down in his notebook. "So, you show up, uninvited, at the party. You and Brooke argue. Was Steve Anderson there? If I recall from our conversation earlier this year, you two dated, correct? And now he's dating Ms. Donovan?"

"Yes, but——"

"Was Steve involved in this altercation?"

"A little. But——"

"Do you remember if he was angry when you left?"

I pause, trying to figure out the best way to respond.

"Please answer the question, Alice. I'm trying to determine Steve Anderson's state of mind when you left the party. I'll ask again—was he angry?"

"Yes, he was upset, but——"

"And when did you leave the party?" He cuts me off *again*. God, this man is frustrating. Hercule Poirot never treated his interviewees like this, and he was so pompous that Agatha Christie couldn't stand him. And she *created* him.

I purse my lips. "Around nine-forty-five p.m., I think? Everyone else was still there."

"Did you go straight home? Or did you linger?"

"Linger?"

He frowns, shrugging. "Sometimes people linger. You know, after arguments. They want to have the last word. Hash it out. Did you stay around there? Maybe talk to Brooke again? Argue some more, this time in private?"

My mouth drops open. "Excuse me? Why are you asking me that?" I know why he's asking me that—I'm not stupid—but I want it confirmed to my face. They think *I* am a suspect.

"Please just answer the question."

I'm tempted to snap back, but I pull in a breath to stay calm. After this past summer, I learned the hard way what happens when you talk back to a cop.

"No! I didn't stay there. I went home. To my *house.*"

Thompson pauses, considering my answer. "Did anyone see you? At home?"

Brenda was asleep when I got back, and clearly neither of my parents was there. I shake my head. "No."

"Interesting." He makes another note, then looks back at me. "It's strange, how you disappeared a few months ago and then showed back up like nothing even happened, and here we are with another disappearing girl on our hands. And, you and Brooke were friends. Did you ever tell her about what you did when you left? Give her some tips on how to run away?"

I bristle. Oh, *here* we go. *This* is why I'm here. "You're trying to say Brooke just ran away. Like I did?"

He shrugs. "You have to admit, it's quite the coincidence."

"Sometimes coincidences happen, don't they? I know you spoke to Steve and Kennedy and Park and *all* of them. Have they heard from her? Has *anyone* heard from her in the past two days?"

"No, Alice, but that doesn't mean——"

"She wouldn't do that. I'm telling you she wouldn't. Now, why won't you all——"

He cuts me off. "Alice, please. Who's conducting this interview? You or me?" He ignores my glare and pushes his chair back from the table with a screech, standing. "Thank you for your cooperation. That's all we need from you at the moment." He motions for me to get up.

I stay put. I am going to say what I came here to say if it's literally the last thing I do. Miss Marple wouldn't take this crap, and neither will I. Miss Marple is a badass older woman in Agatha Christie's books who isn't a detective or a cop or anything, and a lot of people dismiss her for those reasons. But she never lets that dissuade her from finding the truth; she's extremely intelligent and understands how human beings tick.

"Brooke wouldn't do that." I give him my best Alice Ogilvie stare. "She did not run away. Look, at first I thought maybe she was copying me, too. I mean, she clearly is into doing whatever I do these days. But, like you said, *no one has heard from her.* Doesn't that strike you as even a little weird?"

He has the audacity to roll his eyes. How absolutely rude. "I *greatly* appreciate your input, Alice, but we are handling it."

"You are not——"

He ignores that I'm trying to speak and just talks over me. "Not that I owe you an explanation, but we *are* conducting searches. Unfortunately, however, it's starting to storm, so we have to hold off on our big one until tomorrow morning. We are trying to make the best use of our *very* limited resources so what happened to us last summer doesn't happen again. As I'm sure you remember, that didn't turn out very well, now, did it? Lots of time and money were wasted. You know that better than anyone."

I shake my head vehemently. "You have got to listen to me. This is different. She's not me. There's something fishy about all of this. Brooke would have gotten in touch with someone by now, if she was okay. I'd suggest that you rethink how you're conducting this investigation."

"Oh, you would, Alice?" Thompson says sarcastically. "And how would *you* suggest we go about searching for a missing girl?"

"Well, first of all," I say, "I'd consider *character*. Brooke would never make people worry so much about her." I hold up a finger. "Even if she's mad at Coach, she still would have called one of her friends. The fact no one has heard from her means she's in trouble. And that means you need to start looking in Castle Cove, right now."

He snorts. Actually *snorts*, like he's my freaking horse or something. "Is that right, Alice? Last summer, did *you* bother to pick up the phone and let anyone know that you were okay? I've heard about enough, thank you. It's time for you to go. I know you're young, but one day, you'll learn that people can surprise you," he adds, like I didn't already know that. Like I'm not an *expert* on the topic.

"That might be, *Officer*," I say sweetly. "But anyone who knows *anything* about solving mysteries knows that understanding psychology and character are the keys to solving a crime."

CHAPTER TEN

IRIS
NOVEMBER 2
4:10 P.M.

"ALICE?" I PEER AROUND the room. It's dark in here. The curtains are closed. It has that air of sad desperation, like the person inside has suffered a great indignation and is holing up.

"What?"

A muffled voice from under a mound of pink and purple blankets on her massive bed.

"Uh, time to get tutored?" I make my way across the room to her couch, careful not to step on any of the clothes or books strewn across the floor. "Athena and Arachne wait for no one."

I pick up one of the books, a beat-up paperback called *Five Little Pigs.*

The mass of blankets shifts.

"Who and the what now?"

"Basically two bitchy ladies who get into an art war, and one ends up a spider."

"Interesting."

I try a gentler approach. "I know Brooke was your friend and all. You must be upset."

"She ceased being my friend the moment she hooked up with my boyfriend, but yes. I'm upset. About a lot of things. Having to go to the police department and be interrogated, having them seem to, you know, accuse *me* of having something to do with Brooke being missing. Yeah, all of *that*."

I thumb through the paperback. It's kind of interesting. Mostly I prefer thrillers, something with a little more edge. Agatha Christie always seems so cozy and old-ladyish, but maybe I'm wrong.

"I went in, too," I say tentatively. "To the station."

Alice emerges from the blankets, her face creased, her hair mussed.

"What the hell for? What do you have to do with any of this? You aren't even friends with her. You aren't even friends with anyone, are you?" She pats her hair delicately, smoothing out the rumpled bits.

I ignore her comment about friends, because I'll bet if I'd been Brooke Donovan, Spike or Zora or one of the Zoners would have run after me, or looked for me, or something. None of Brooke's friends did that for *her*. Apparently not even Steve or her dad, either.

I wish I hadn't said anything, but it's too late now. "Because I was there, that's why. Not at the party, but near it. I was taking a walk."

I decide not to mention she almost ran me over, since obviously she never even noticed, or doesn't care.

Alice is staring at me in a curious way, her eyes bright and intent on my face. It's making me nervous, so I start babbling.

"I saw the fight. Between Brooke and Steve. They were pushing each other. And then she took off running, and she passed by me. You know, the first twist in the road? I went after her, because none of the Mains did. But she was gone by the time I got to the bend. I can't figure out where she went, though. I mean, Alice, where *is* she?"

"The 'Mains'?" Alice says. "What is that, some kind of code?"

My face reddens. "It's, uh, what everyone calls you. I mean, you and your . . . people. The Main Kids. Because you're, well, I mean, you run the school."

"That's a little rude. I mean, we don't lump all of *you* together."

"Don't you? Do you think we named *ourselves* the Zoners?"

Alice ignores that and lifts her chin. "That was nice of you. To go after her. I can't believe no one else did." She pauses. "Well, maybe I *can.* I mean, even her own dad seems to think it's nothing. I had to be the one to call her grandmother." She twists the edge of her blanket in her fingers.

"*You* did that?" I ask.

"Yes! Because obviously Coach wasn't going to."

"Alice." I hesitate.

"What?" She sounds annoyed, picking at her cuticles.

I take a deep breath, because what I'm going to say is kind of scary, to be honest. And if I say it, it might make it more real.

"Alice, I mean, do you really think Brooke just ran away,

like you? Don't you think, maybe, it's something . . . some*one* else? That kind of thing?"

Alice tenses up. "I definitely think she didn't run away. She's not built for that, trust me. She likes comfort too much. But the other . . . it can't be that. It just can't."

Softly, I say, "It can. I mean, what about Steve? The boyfriend—"

"No," she says firmly, fixing me with a hard look.

"It is possible, too," I say slowly, "that she, you know, went over the cliffs. I saw some cops out there after my interview, but I didn't see any boats on the water. Are they not even searching the coastline?"

Alice doesn't look at me. She's very still.

"I don't want to think about that," she says finally. "All I know is, it seems like the police are blaming *me*, like she's copying what I did."

I pull my notebook out of my backpack and grab a pen. "Okay, let's just go through this, one by one."

"I'm sorry?" Alice says.

"Let's just write down what we know and what we think. Your friend is missing. You don't think she ran away. Maybe talking through possibilities will help you, or, like, trigger a memory. Where she might possibly have gone."

Alice closes her eyes and sighs. "I went to the party. Brooke was mad that I was there. We yelled at each other. Steve walked me to my car. Brooke followed us. I left. I drove home, I took a bath, I read my book. The next morning, I went to school and Kennedy told me about Steve and Brooke fighting, like that was *my* fault. Kennedy can be so—"

"Focus," I say gently.

"Ugh. Kennedy said Brooke was supposed to stay the night at her house, but she never showed. Kennedy thought she ended up going home, but Coach thought she was at Kennedy's."

I write that down. "You don't think Kennedy is covering for Brooke? Like maybe Brooke is at her house, chilling in the rec room or something?"

"Rec room? What is this, 1975?"

"Is it possible Kennedy would lie for Brooke?"

Alice considers this. "Yes and no. I mean, who doesn't lie for their friends every once in a while? But she seemed honestly worried when Coach didn't know where she was, and why would she be that way if it wasn't true?"

"People lie," I point out.

"Kennedy isn't a good liar. She's like a colander when you need a vault." Alice frowns. "Then we thought, oh, maybe Steve found her after the party. I thought for a second that maybe she went to a hotel—Brooke liked staying at the Insley Arms, by the way, she was always taking Cole there—"

"Wait, Brooke and Cole were hooking up?" I try to keep my voice neutral.

But my face betrays me.

"Iris Adams," Alice coos. "Do you have a thing for Cole Fielding? My, my."

"Shut up," I say. "Back to our original conversation."

"But then we saw Steve and he looked like crap. He was missing a sneaker, he was dirty, and he seemed genuinely surprised when we said Brooke was missing."

I look up from my scribbling, and Alice's face is creased in thought.

"What bothers me the most is, wouldn't you be worried if your daughter hadn't been seen since a party the night before? Wouldn't you call the police right away? Brenda did, for me. But Coach just went along to teach his first-period class. That's why I texted Lilian."

I look at my notes. *Coach—suspicious behavior? Steve—fights with Brooke, claims not to know where she is. Kennedy—claims Brooke never made it to her house.*

Alice continues, "I'm pretty sure it was Lilian who called the police."

I tap my finger on the notebook page. "If I saw Brooke around ten p.m., that's a solid eleven hours before anyone knows she's missing. Presumably."

"And?" Alice says impatiently.

"Well," I say slowly. "That's a lot of time for a lot of things to happen. One, she runs down Highway One, maybe hides in the woods for a bit? Or maybe walks to the Lookout and slips over."

Alice shudders.

"You can't ignore that possibility."

"Go on," Alice says.

"Two, someone came for her. My friend Zora thinks it's a ransom-kidnapping deal, but she tends to blow things out of proportion."

Alice takes my notebook from me. "I'm marking that down, because who knows. She's a freaking heiress."

"Three," I say. "Brooke texted somebody to pick her up and she is hiding somewhere. Or she called an Uber and is copying you and is in some other town, which makes me wonder—"

Alice snaps her fingers. "Where *is* her phone? Nobody's said anything about a phone. Can't they ping that or something?

She would never give up her phone without a fight. But I have to disagree on her leaving town. She's never used public transportation in her life, and she prefers comfort. I mean, I *know* that girl. She would *pack* before running away. Me? I just took off."

I take my notebook back gently.

"Four," I say, "is the bad one, but it's necessary. Harm came to her from human means."

"Well, that's certainly an ominous thing to say, Iris," Alice says. "Thanks a lot."

"You can't rule it out." I look at my notes again. "It's either running away, an accident, or the bad thing. There were a *ton* of people at that party; who knows who might have been driving along Highway One and seen her? And who knows when we'll find out, because not much seems to be happening in the *way* of finding out."

Alice huffs off her bed and begins pacing the room. "Can you believe the police aren't even going to search anymore today? That detective told me they called it off because of the storm. A little rain is too much for them to look for a missing girl?"

Thinking about the incompetency of the Castle Cove Police Department, plus all the homework we still need to do, is giving me a headache. I close the notebook and put it on the floor.

"I guess we should get to work," I say, pulling my iPad from my backpack. A bunch of loose papers tumble out with it and I go to collect them, only to see the "Missing" flyer that Zora passed to me in the cafeteria, staring up at me from Alice's carpet.

I look at the flyer. It's Brooke's sophomore-year photo, her long brown hair shining, her eyes clear and bright blue. She's tucked into the crevice of a tree, beautiful and perfect. *Have you seen me?* the flyer says. *Missing since October 31st, 10 p.m., on or near Highway 1, off the Castle exit, possibly by the Lookout. Brooke Donovan, 5'5", 105 pounds, brown hair, blue eyes.*

There's something so sad about seeing a girl you know, even just glancingly, reduced to a photo on a piece of paper and a plea for help.

At the bottom, the flyer says, *$50,000 reward for information leading to the whereabouts of Brooke Donovan.*

Alice motions to the flyer. "That's all Lilian, by the way. Coach is just a normal guy. When he married Victoria, he had to sign a prenup or something. There's an estate trustee, I guess, who takes care of Brooke's living expenses and the upkeep for the house. Coach gets a monthly stipend, but that ends when Brooke turns eighteen in December. She talked about it sometimes. After her mom died."

I put the flyer back into my backpack, careful not to crumple it. It must be nice, for Brooke and Alice and the other girls like them, to just . . . have money.

Fifty thousand dollars.

Certain thoughts, like about what that reward could mean for me, and how I could get it, start wiggling in my brain, but I also feel a little ashamed of them. A girl is gone. *That's* what I should care about, not those scribblings in my notebook about Steve, Coach, and Kennedy. But fifty thousand dollars would get me and my mom out of Castle Cove and away from the Thing.

Whatever.

I turn on my iPad. "Would you rather work on history? It's monarchy time in Devlin's class. She likes to throw easy bones like this. All you need to do is pick four of Henry the Eighth's wives, read the bios, and write a summary. That's it."

"Iris?" Alice's voice is suddenly steely, and I look up. "Why are we just sitting here?"

"Because we have homework?"

"My friend is missing. The cops are dragging their feet, and now they called off the search by the cliffs, which is the last place she was seen, because of a little rain? I care about Brooke. I mean. I don't like her, but I still love her, if that makes sense. And I'm worried. And I want to do something. I don't just want to sit here and read about some gross dude who chopped off his wives' heads."

"Well, he didn't chop *all* of them off—"

"Iris," Alice sighs, grabbing my hand and pulling me up. "I can't just do nothing. And I can tell you care, too, because you were taking notes. You are kind of *into* this."

"Into what?" I ask suspiciously, extracting my arm from her hand. "I'm into homework, that's for sure. And not fail—"

"Into finding Brooke. And I'm bored. So let's go." Her eyes gleam.

"Go *where*?"

"Let's go. To the cliffs. The Castle. Walk around the last place we think Brooke was. Investigate. If the cops aren't going to do something, why can't we? You think Miss Marple would sit around worrying about Henry's wives? I think not."

She's already sliding on shoes, hunting for a coat.

"But that would be disturbing evidence."

Alice looks at me with a glint in her eye. "Iris Adams, I thought you were the kind of girl who might like to disturb things. Or was I wrong about that?"

I look down at my iPad, think about our homework. Brooke

Donovan is missing, and no one seems to think it's any more than a silly teenage girl off somewhere on a lark.

Alice is right. We'll just take a look around. Probably nothing will happen. We won't find anything. It's better than reading about a horrible king who got what he wanted by killing his wives.

CHAPTER ELEVEN

ALICE
NOVEMBER 2
4:54 P.M.

"Intuition is like reading a word
without having to spell it out."
—AGATHA CHRISTIE,
THE MURDER AT THE VICARAGE

BY THE TIME WE pull into the empty Castle parking lot twenty minutes later, the sky has opened up, rain pounding down on the windshield of my car hard and fast. In any other circumstance, I'd suggest we go home and have a nice hot cup of tea rather than walking around out in this weather, but it's been two full days and no one has heard from Brooke. No one at all. And we need to do something about it, *now.*

If Lilian hadn't arrived in town when she did, would the cops even have started looking for her yet? Coach was so insistent that she just ran away that first day; why didn't he think it was odd that she wasn't in touch with anyone? What sort of parent doesn't immediately look for their missing child? I know my disappearance last summer left a bad taste in everyone's mouth, but I also know that I am not Brooke and *Brooke* is not *me.*

I park, then grab from the center console the big, heavy-duty flashlight I took from home. It's going to be getting dark in the next hour, and who knows how long this is going to take. We don't know how much ground Brooke covered that night.

Iris reaches into the back seat and grabs the umbrellas we got from the coatroom at my house. "Ready?" She holds out one of the umbrellas, and I take it from her.

I nod and exit the car into cold rain, trying to figure out what to do and where to go first. What would Agatha Christie do? I try to channel the queen. It's not like I investigate missing girls on the regular. Especially ones that I know.

"I saw her run that way." Iris breaks the silence from the other side of the car. She walks around the front of the car, holding her umbrella up as best she can against the rain, and points down the road. "She and Steve were arguing there"— she gestures to an area close to the main pathway into the Castle—"and then Brooke took off running. She went up that way toward the bend in the road. If I think about it, I'm guessing maybe she went into the woods? Who would just keep running down the highway, right? I'd want to get off the road, chill for a while—" The ringing of her phone cuts her off. "Hold on," she says, and grabs it out of her back pocket.

I'm starting to protest that whoever is on the other side cannot be more important than what we're doing, but she's already talking.

"What? No, Spike, I'm not—I'm *out*. With who? I—" She glances at me and lowers her voice. "Alice." She pauses. "Yes, *Ogilvie*. You know I'm tutoring her—she wanted to go to the Castle to look for—yes. In this rain. Right. Yes. What? No, Spike, do not . . . hello? *Hello?*" A moment later, she drops the phone from her ear.

"Friend of yours?" I say, raising an eyebrow.

"Oh, that was just Spike," she replies, like the name is supposed to mean something to me.

"Spike?" I repeat.

"Yes. My friend. Spike. He's with a couple of our other friends. They're all in the forensic science club, and they're really into this sort of thing, especially Neil. They're on their way here. To help us."

"*Help* us?" Sure, I don't really know what I'm doing, but I also don't need a bunch of random kids showing up here to mess everything up before we even begin.

Iris sighs. "Yeah. Once Spike gets his mind set on something, there's no stopping him. I do think, though, that they might be useful right now. I mean, I don't know what I'm doing . . . do you?"

I purse my lips and shrug. "I suppose not."

Iris hesitates. "Also, not that I think we will . . . but if we *do* find anything, like, major, I wouldn't mind having some other people here." She shivers, rubbing her arm with her free hand. "I was the last person to see her," she says, her words quiet under the blustery wind. "I should have done *more*. Run faster, stuck around. Called the cops right then and there." She bites her bottom lip, cheeks turning red. Is she going to cry? I am not good with criers. My mom informed me years ago that crying was an unattractive quality in a person, and after that I stopped doing it.

I pat her shoulder awkwardly. "There, there."

She glances at me, a tiny smile on her face. "Did you just say 'there, there' to me?"

Now it's my turn to redden.

"Sorry, I—" I start, but am cut off by a car squealing into the lot. It pulls up, hitting a giant puddle and sending a spray of water directly at Iris and me before coming to a halt. "What the hell?"

"We made it here in record time," says a guy climbing out of the driver's seat, pumping his fist. He's short and stocky and has one of those awkward, scraggly beards that teenage boys seem to think are attractive. He blows on his hands. It's chilly out here, the wind coming in off the ocean and the rain growing heavier by the second.

"Helped that we were already in the car, but okay, Neil," mutters a girl as she climbs out from the back of the two-door car, maneuvering herself around the driver's seat and finally breaking free. She has short orange hair cut in a bob, eyes rimmed with heavy black eyeliner. Holding one totally ineffective hand over her head, she hurries around to the back of the car and pops the trunk. "Good thing we had these with us." She pulls out a small black duffel bag and several umbrellas.

"What is that bag?" I direct the question to Iris, but the third of the trio answers as he exits the passenger side of the car. He's tall and gangly, with brown curly hair that falls to his shoulders, and is wearing an oversized green military jacket that sort of swallows him whole.

"It's our forensic kit from our club. Hey, Iris." The guy waves to her and smiles a shy little smile. I recognize that smile. It's the same one I saw on Steve's face whenever Brooke was around in the weeks before he broke up with me. I didn't really register it back then, but I certainly know what it means now. Someone has a crush. Interesting.

"Hey, Spike," Iris says back, walking around me to meet

her friends. I recognize them from the table at the back of the cafeteria where the weirdos sit; it's possible that Spike-the crusher was in my geometry class last year, but I'm not one hundred percent on that. Most of my attention at the time was eaten up by Steve and coordinating with him to be certain he would meet me after class and walk me to my next one.

"So," says the first guy, pushing a hand through his wet hair and hopping from foot to foot excitedly. "Where do we start? We're tracking Brooke's steps that night, correct? It's going to be a little hard because of this rain, but Iris, you said you saw her. Can you tell us the path she took? Even if a lot of her footsteps have been washed away, we still might be able to find—"

"Excuse me," I interrupt, pursing my lips. I know they are here to *help,* allegedly, but who even are they? "I am Alice." I tap my chest. "And you are?"

They stop scurrying around and stare at me. "We know who you are, Alice," says the boy-who-loves-Iris, a funny look on his face. "*Everyone* knows who you are."

In the past, someone telling me that would have given me a little thrill of pleasure, but the shiver that runs through my body right now is anything but. "Great. Right. But who are you?" I know technically Iris just said hello to him, but I'd appreciate a formal introduction, please and thank you.

"Spike," he says. The one who called Iris and insisted on coming here. Makes sense. "And that's Zora. And Neil." They wave.

"*Thank* you. Now we can proceed."

"Great." Neil doesn't even hesitate. He grabs the bag off Zora's shoulder, and she gives him a dirty look that he either doesn't notice or ignores. He throws it onto the closed trunk of his car and starts pulling random things out of it: ziplock bags, plastic gloves, a small black round thing.

"Is that a *compass*?" I ask.

"Yes," he says, serious. "We might get lost in the woods. Safety first." He puts the things back into the bag.

I open my mouth to argue that we can just use the compasses on our *phones* if that happens, but Iris gives me a look like *Let it go,* so I shut it back up. Whatever. Bring a compass; see if I care. I look at the time on my phone. "Can we please hurry this along? This rain is out of control and it's going to be getting dark soon." I shiver. "Iris said that she saw Brooke run from there"—I motion toward the entrance to the Castle grounds where the Halloween party is held—"that way." I point up Highway 1 away from us, toward the woods. "Is that right, Iris?"

"Yes." Now that her friends have arrived, Iris seems different somehow. More comfortable. Her eyes sparkle with excitement. "Okay, we should maybe split up?"

"Split *up*?" Neil repeats, like the idea personally offends him. "No, no. No. We stay together. It's getting dark outside, and this *weather*. Also, there are mountain lions. Safety in numbers, Iris. Not to mention, the murderer could be here. They like to do that. Show up at crime scenes and get a thrill."

At the word *murderer,* a sick dread creeps into my stomach. I know Iris and I talked about just that earlier. I know that's the other option, right? If she didn't run away or get kidnapped. But, still. Hearing it out loud is something different.

"She's not *dead,*" Iris tells him with a shaky voice. I'm not sure she believes her own words.

He shrugs. "Are you sure? It's been two days. Forty-eight hours, almost. And I read earlier today that in 88.5 percent of cases, kids who are kidnapped are dead within twenty-four hours. . . ." I bristle. Iris inches closer to me, putting a warm hand on my arm. *Sorry,* she mouths. I wave her off. I know better than anyone that you can't control your friends. He starts across the parking lot toward the spot where Iris saw Brooke disappear.

Once there, we trudge up the slippery bank off the highway, heading up the hill and into the redwoods. The trees are so tall in here it's hard to see the sky. Only a few feet in, the canopy blocks most of the rain, but the chill in the air grows. I shiver. Brooke must have been super upset to run in here. She knows that at night, there's almost no way to see.

Neil and Iris, who have been leading the pack, stop short in front of me, Neil slipping on a patch of ground and catching himself on the nearest tree trunk.

"I don't know where she went from here," Iris says, frustrated. "She could have gone anywhere, really."

Neil points up ahead of us, where the hill becomes steeper, rockier, sharper. "Unless she had on rock-climbing gear, I doubt she went far in that direction. My bet is that she stayed along the road, probably heading in the direction you saw her going. Staying close to the lights of passing cars, you know?"

Iris nods, and after a second, I do, too. Fine, he *is* good at this. Maybe having Iris's friends along isn't the worst idea ever.

There's grunting behind us as Zora and Spike, the stragglers, catch up. Zora puts her free hand on her knee and sucks in a breath. "I did not realize that tonight's activities would involve cardio."

Spike snorts. "Zora, we were going to go *roller skating. That's* cardio."

She sighs. "Oh please. You know I was mostly along for the

ride. And the eye candy." She winks at Iris, who blushes. Eye candy? Who are— I realize with a start that they must be talking about Cole Fielding. He's worked there forever. When he and Brooke were hanging out, Brooke forced me to go to the skating rink to see him.

Good god, is *everyone* in this town in love with that kid? Poor Spike.

Neil ignores them. I'm quickly coming to realize that he is not here for the small talk at *all*. He reaches into the duffel bag, which is slung cross-body over his shoulder, and pulls out the latex gloves and ziplock bags. "Here. Everyone take a set and put them on." He hands them to the four of us. "We don't want to contaminate the crime scene, any more than the rain already has." He turns to me. "Also, before we start. Alice, is there anything you can tell us about that night? I know you and Donovan had a knockdown fight at the Halloween party and you threatened Donovan—"

"Ex*cuse* me?" I arch a brow. "I did what?" Is that what the rumor mill is saying? Jesus, no wonder the cops dragged me in yesterday.

Neil has the decency to look ashamed. "Uh, sorry, that didn't come out right."

Spike steps between us. "I think what Neil"—he punches him in the arm—"is trying to say is that if you remember anything that Brooke said that night that could be useful, it might be good to let us know."

I shake my head. "No. She was mostly just mad. At me . . . and Steve."

Zora mutters behind me darkly, "You ask me, it's *always* someone close to the victim. Like a parent . . . or the boyfriend."

I turn on her. "And you know that how?" I challenge, arching a brow. "With your degree in psychology and forensics?" Who does this girl think she is?

She shrugs. "Whatever. Anyway, did you guys see the reward money her grandma is offering? Pretty decent chunk of change." I make a face. I am not a fan of that girl.

"Okay," Neil says, diverting my attention, "let's fan out and walk, say, a quarter mile or something. No one go too far, but Spike, you're wearing the best shoes for this weather, so you take the path farthest up into the trees, where it's most slippery—"

"Oh, thanks," mutters Spike.

"And Zora, you next, and then me, and then Iris." He nods at her. "And then you, Ogilvie."

I purse my lips at him using my last name but comply. As I slowly make my way down toward the road, I hear Zora ask how we're supposed to know how far a quarter mile is, which is a fair question. He tells her to just walk until he shouts for us all to stop. Neil is certainly not shy about taking charge.

It's weird, looking for something when you don't really know what *it* is. I'm trying to see it like Poirot would. How Miss Marple would. How the brilliant Agatha Christie herself would. Clearly, not everything is a clue. Like the silver gum wrapper I spot buried in a small pile of leaves. I pick it up and shove it into my pocket, just in case, but things like that won't help us at all, I don't think. They're probably more of a distraction than anything; we need to concentrate on the big things, the things that might actually lead us to her. Like, I don't know. Something like a weapon, or two sets of footprints? Or like tire tracks from a getaway car. Some sort of sign that someone took her.

As we walk, I keep glancing into the woods. I can just barely make out Iris above me, head down, searching. We've been walking for a few minutes when I spot a small piece of wet fabric, half tucked under the concrete foot of a bench. I bend down and grab it—a star shape made out of denim—and stuff it into my pocket next to the gum wrapper.

A few minutes later, Neil calls, "Okay, everyone stop. Head down the hill. Alice, stay where you are." I wait for them, pulling my light jacket tighter around my body. I definitely did not dress well for this rain. The daylight is disappearing beyond the cliffs, and it is getting cold as hell out here.

"Anyone find anything of interest?" Neil asks when we're all back together.

I think of the stuff I have in my pocket and am about to mention it when Iris speaks.

"I saw a few pieces of trash, but . . ." Iris shrugs.

Neil rolls his eyes. "Great, Iris. But I meant, anything *real*. Like an article of clothing that you know was Brooke's. Footprints that haven't been washed away. A sign of struggle. Something that might lead us to our next step." The power of being in charge is definitely getting to Neil's head. Good lord.

Iris flushes. "Sorry, *Neil*. I . . . just . . . How are we supposed to have any idea what to look for? Or, like, what does a struggle even look like in the woods? This is hard." Her excitement from before has dimmed.

Neil sets his jaw. "Well, now we'll do the same thing on the other side of the road, okay? Maybe she crossed over—it's a lot harder to walk on this side with the incline than it is by the cliffs. And at night, it's way easier to see over there, too."

This is getting frustrating, my pants are sopping wet, and the rain has starting lashing at us since we emerged from the tree canopy, but this was also my idea to begin with and I want to help Brooke, so I can't exactly back out. I guess I thought we'd stumble upon something huge, but it's starting to seem like that isn't going to happen. Iris said she saw a bunch of cops out here earlier today walking this area, so maybe there isn't much left to find.

We cross the highway once again and find ourselves at the Lookout, a wide clearing with scattered benches that tourists like to stop at as they're driving through town. From here, it's easy to look out and see the ocean. There's a fence that surrounds some of it, but it's broken in a bunch of places. The Castle Cove Council has really been slacking on keeping up maintenance around here.

I hang back. I've been to this spot about three trillion times in my life, but right now goose bumps are popping up all over my skin, and not just because I'm wet and cold. I wish I was at home, tucked in my bed, snarking at Iris about tutoring and about stupid Henry the VIII and his stupid wives.

Zora is the first to speak. "She could have slipped or something, you know. That's not an impossibility."

"I don't know," Neil says. "She grew up here—she knows not to get too close to the edge."

"But she was wasted," Spike murmurs. "Right? That's what I heard. She might have gotten dizzy or something. Passed out."

Iris shrugs. "She didn't seem *that* drunk when she was running. But I guess I was pretty far away."

Spike bends down on his hands and knees, close to the cliff's edge. My entire body quakes with a shiver.

"Hey!" I call. "Be careful. It's slippery. What are you looking for, anyway?"

"I don't know," Spike mumbles. "Hair caught in the cracks?" Iris turns to me. I think she's trying to gauge if I'm okay. I square my shoulders and give her a small nod.

"But if her boyfriend did it, I don't think she'd be here. He'd have, like, dumped her somewhere else," Zora says matter-of-factly. "Or maybe she's still alive, in a basement somewhere. Not implausible."

Jesus, that girl will not give it a *rest.* "Will you please stop speculating?" My voice is angrier than I intend, but honestly.

"Sorry," Zora shoots back. "But the perp is almost always someone the victim knew really well."

Iris steps forward in front of Zora. "We don't even know what—if anything—happened yet," she says. "Let's keep walking." I realize with a start that she's defending me to her friend. When's the last time someone defended me? Maybe never.

We start off again, but Neil hangs back, standing at the Lookout, watching the waves. He takes a picture of the water with his phone.

"Dude," Spike shouts. "You coming?"

"Yeah," Neil calls, sliding his phone back into his pocket. "Be right there."

We make it a few hundred feet down the path when a van screeches onto the shoulder of the road in front of us and slams to a stop. *KWB* is written on the side of it. The local news station. Great. Amazing. Fantastic. Just what we need right now. Reporters.

The van door slides open and a woman leans out holding a golf umbrella up over her head of red, curly hair. She waves. "Hey, kids!"

We all stop in our tracks. "Oh, hell no," Spike mutters under his breath.

"Kids!" the woman says again, fully out of the van now. A bedraggled-looking man climbs out behind her, balancing a giant camera in one hand with a little umbrella attached to its top. "What are you doing here? Are you aware you're close to the spot that Brooke Donovan, the missing girl, was last seen? Do you know her? Are you classmates of hers at CCHS?" Her eyes land on me, and her entire face changes. "Oh!" she exclaims. "Oh, I know who *you* are. Alice Ogilvie."

My heart sinks. I know who she is, too. Tessa Hopkins from the local news station. After my disappearance last summer, she would not stop calling, trying to get an interview with me. Brenda finally told her off and the calls stopped, but she does not take no for an answer easily.

"Alice, do you have a minute?" She motions to her cameraman, and he swings the equipment up onto his shoulder, dropping his umbrella on the ground. Better hope that thing is waterproof. "Can you tell me—did you and Brooke Donovan plan this? You disappear over the summer, and then she does hers a few months later? Keeping everyone on their toes?" She's in my face now, peppering me with all these stupid questions just like everyone else has been doing, like this is all my fault.

I don't even try to stop myself. I reach out and rip the microphone out of Tessa Hopkins's hand and throw it down Highway 1, then wave at her the stupid heavy flashlight that I've been lugging around.

"If you do not leave us alone right now, I will have my parents sue your ass off for harassment," I say. The cameraman lowers his camera and whistles.

"I don't think you can actually do that, Alice," Tessa Hopkins says, wiping a stray raindrop off her face. "Freedom of the press."

My nostrils flare. "*Watch* me," I say. I step toward Tessa Hopkins. Tessa takes a tiny step back.

"Just go, news-lady dude," Spike calls.

An irritated expression crosses Tessa's face. I'm sure she's not used to being bossed around by a bunch of teenagers, but *this* teenager has had about enough of this crap for one lifetime. After a beat, she reaches into her jacket pocket and holds out some cards.

"Fine. If any of you want to talk," she says, "you know how to find me."

Zora reaches around me and snatches the cards.

We watch as Tessa and the cameraman walk down Highway 1 to get her microphone.

Farther down the cliff's edge, the wind has grown even harsher, whipping rain into our faces as the sky dims. Neil keeps stopping behind us, scrolling on his phone, tapping away.

"Neil," Zora says, exasperated. "Pay *attention.*"

"I am," Neil says. "I'm paying a lot of attention, as a matter of fact. I'm checking the tide ma—" He cuts off as he peers over the cliffside.

"You guys?"

His voice is shaking.

We gather around him.

"Guys," he says again, pointing down to the sea.

Beside me, Zora makes a tiny, strangled sound.

I look down.

There, nestled against the craggy rocks, is a body.

A body facedown in a black leather jacket; long brown hair fanned out and floating in the water like seaweed; bare, bluish legs sticking out from a short, pleated cheerleader skirt. Being pelted by hard rain.

Time stops.

Brooke.

"See, even if she fell at the Lookout, her body would move around because of tidal activity and the currents," Neil whispers. "And she'd get batted around by displacement and boats and, like, things down there. She might have gotten stuck in a tide pool or something. If she shifted, you wouldn't find her there. You'd find her—"

"Here," Spike says. "Holy shit." He takes his phone out of his pocket. "We have to call the cops."

Two things happen then.

Zora vomits in the brush, and without even thinking, I reach for Iris's hand, my body beginning to shake with silent sobs.

The heavy silence is broken by a sound. "Holy hell," says a familiar, breathy voice. I turn and there she is, Tessa Hopkins, standing behind us, hand over her mouth.

· BREAKING NEWS ·

Anchor Ben Perez: Good evening. This is Ben Perez with the *KWB News at Six*. Tonight, we bring you an explosive update to the story that's been dominating headlines for the last two days in Central California—the story of Brooke Donovan, the missing seventeen-year-old high school student who is, of course, the daughter of Victoria Donovan of the Levy Cosmetics family, who were number 122 on the *Forbes* World's Billionaires list last year. We're told they are using their considerable political clout to put pressure on local authorities handling this case.

Anchor Valerie Metz: Thanks, Ben. Brooke Donovan vanished the night of Halloween—two days ago. She was reported missing by her grandmother, Lilian Levy of Levy Cosmetics, but it was initially assumed she had run away.

Ben Perez: That's right, Valerie. Our sources say that the PD has reason to believe that it's the body of Brooke Donovan. Our own Tessa Hopkins is on the scene. Tessa, are you there?

Reporter Tessa Hopkins: Thanks, Ben. Although the police had been searching in Castle Cove for Brooke Donovan over the past forty-eight hours, they had planned their biggest manhunt for tomorrow morning because of the rain. But, this evening, local teenagers discovered a body in the water, at the foot of the cliffs behind me. Is it Brooke Donovan? We don't know yet, pending identification by the family, but if it is indeed Ms. Donovan, many questions will need to be answered. How did she get into the water? Was it an accident? Or was it foul play? Stay tuned.

Ben Perez: Sorry to cut in, but I was just updated by our sources that the police already have a suspect in custody—we're trying to get more information on that now and will update you as more news comes in.

CHAPTER TWELVE

"I think people more often kill those they love, than those they hate. Possibly because only the people you love can really make life unendurable to you."
—AGATHA CHRISTIE, *CROOKED HOUSE*

MY HANDS HAVEN'T STOPPED shaking since we were at the cliffs earlier. I don't know when Iris and I separated, but one minute she was there, holding my hand, and the next she was gone. I got back home a while ago. Brenda drew a bath for me, and all through it, my hands kept shaking. After it. And now, still, they're shaking.

All because of stupid Brooke Donovan.

Who is *dead*.

A gasp and a sob breaks the silence of my bedroom, and I turn my head—actually physically *turn* my *head*—to see where the noise came from before realizing that, of course, it came from me. From my own mouth.

Brenda looks up from where she sits across the room, reading a book in the oversized bucket chair that I've had since middle school. "Are you okay, Alice?" she asks, voice soft.

I nod, blinking hard. That's the chair where Brooke used to sit when she'd come over back in the day, under the guise of doing homework together, but really to keep me company when I'd get lonely. We never talked about it, but I know it's true. I always preferred to go to her house; her mom was there, warm and inviting.

I wonder what it's like now in that house. Three became two and now two have become . . .

I cut the thought off before it can finish and roll over to my side, clutching my phone between my hands. Iris keeps texting me to check in, but I haven't responded. I don't know what to say.

Even mindlessly scrolling TikTok isn't helping; I keep running into video tributes to Brooke and all these comments about Steve. Apparently, someone saw him being brought into the police station earlier, and gossip is building. Between that and the fight on Halloween night, he's already becoming the prime suspect in the eyes of my classmates.

I think back to the other morning at school, how weird and disheveled he was, the scratches on his face. His missing shoe. I try to imagine it: Steve that night, angry, arguing with Brooke. Catching up with her after the party. Arguing some more. Getting closer and closer to the cliff's edge until—

A message dings on my phone from a number I don't recognize. Probably spam. When I open it, I see that it's only two sentences long, but it's definitely not spam.

They brought Steve in for questioning. Not looking good.

My pulse picks up.

Who is this? I type.

> **A friend**

>> A friend?? what friend? Kennedy is that
>> you? Do you think this is a good time to
>> prank me? I don't know if you've heard
>> but I've had a BAD NIGHT

> **This isn't kennedy**

I'm getting pissed. Like I said, I've had a pretty god-awful night, and I am not in the mood to play games right now.

>> WHO IS IT THEN?

> **Alice, I'm a friend okay? I promise.**

>> How do you know my name??
>> you know who I am?

> **Yes. Alice Ogilvie. I know you've been**
> **concerned about your best friend. Why no**
> **one was looking for her. I know you're smart**
> **and stubborn and you want to know what**
> **really happened to her**

>> Can you please be more specific about
>> who you are?
>> Do we know each other? What's your
>> name?

> **I can't tell you that. not yet. Just know I**
> **want to help. You can't tell anyone about me**
> **though**

Help?? How?

**I can get things. information. I know how the
cops in this town are.**

I start typing things and then deleting—I want to know
more . . . I want to know *everything,* but clearly whoever this is,
they are not going to share that with me right now.

Okay then what can you tell me

**Right now the thing you should know is
steve is at the police station and they're
looking at him hard**

I make a face at the phone screen. *I mean, that isn't new info
really. People were posting about it on social media.*

There's a pause in their response, and I think for a moment
they're gone. But then:

**Ok. Here's something. He's being formally
arrested.**

Wait what? arrested?

I sit up in bed, heart pounding.

"Alice?" Brenda says, concern threading through her voice.

"I'm fine," I say, keeping as much shakiness out of my voice
as I possibly can. I sink back down on my pillow, furiously typing.

HELLO??

Gtg I'm sorry. I'll be in touch soon.

I text the number a couple more times asking for more info, but there's no reply. How could they drop that bomb on me and just disappear? My heart is pounding a mile a minute in my chest. There has to be some mistake, right? There's no way that the cops have enough evidence on Steve to *arrest* him for this? A flash from earlier crosses my mind: the rain, the body floating, Brooke . . .

Brenda rises from her chair, and it's only then that I realize I'm whimpering. She comes over to me and puts a cool hand against my forehead. It's something she's done so many times before—when I'm sick, the night after I got my first period, the time when Steve and I got into a huge fight after Spring Formal sophomore year and he told me he was sick of being treated like a prop—but tonight it's different.

The touch of her skin against mine bursts something in my midsection, something that's been wrapped up tight for a long, long, long time, and all of a sudden, instead of telling her goodnight, I'm crying. Hard.

And because she's Brenda, all she does is nod and sink down onto the bed next to me and wrap me in her arms.

HP: I can't even process right now. In calc but they're letting us all go. Meet me at the Pit.

RK: This cannot be real. And I HATE that bathroom, but ok.

HP: I heard Steve is still at the station. Why's he still there?

RK: Maybe cause he did it

RK: Kinda wouldn't be surprised tbh. NEVER seen him like he was on Hween

RK: He was out of control

RK: Park?

HP: Do you think they drug tested him?

RK: Drug tested him?!

HP: Nm

RK: Uhh ok where are u I'm already in Pit

RK: Do you think he was doing DRUGS?

HP: What? no. you just said he was acting weird

RK: Well he was

RK: I bet they're going to bring us all down to the station again

RK: Talk to us or whatever about where we were

RK: I'm not showing them the video

HP: Haha

RK: *Haha*??? what's up with you

HP: Nothing . . . I'm kind of . . . hold on almost there

RK: What

HP: Brooke

HP: She's gone. She's GONE. This wasn't what was supposed to happen

HP: Fuck.

RK: I'm here. It's okay. I'm here.

HP: I can't deal

RK: I'm right here

HP: I'm freaking out

RK: It's okay, I'm here

HP: I don't know what to do

RK: No, I mean I am LITERALLY RIGHT HERE. IN THE BATHROOM. NEXT TO YOU. JFC, HELEN, PUT DOWN YOUR PHONE.

CHAPTER THIRTEEN

IRIS
NOVEMBER 3
5:32 P.M.

MAYBE IT'S HEARTLESS. MAYBE it's selfish, or cruel, to be doing this when a girl is dead.

But it's what we do when we don't know what else to do. We skate.

We went skating when Zora broke up with the girl from Carmel. We went skating when Neil's mom got her diagnosis. We skated through her chemo. We skated through her remission.

And now we're skating through this. Around and around Seaside Skate, pink and purple and orange lights blipping over the walls, some ancient disco hit vibrating from the sound system.

The announcement came over the intercom at school. That Brooke Donovan's body had been positively identified. That Ms. Westmacott was available for students who needed to talk. That school was over for the day.

And then, not on the intercom, but through texts and rumors and whispers, that Steve Anderson had been arrested for the murder of Brooke Donovan.

I texted Alice three times, that maybe we should cancel tutoring, since, you know, *Brooke*. Her *friend*. But she didn't answer. I told her I'd be at the rink, in case she wanted to talk.

I'm a little worried about Alice, to be honest. Not that I know her all that well, but kids were saying things in the halls. That since she hadn't shown up to school, maybe . . . she was in on it. I've watched enough crime shows to know that sure, the boyfriend usually *did* do it, but every once in a while, it turns out a girlfriend helped him. Not that I think Alice is *that* girlfriend, but just that . . . people have been talking about her for months, and rumors take a toll.

So here we are, gliding around the rink, an endless, soothing thing.

Spike zips up next to me, slows down, circles me. He's much better than I am, even though we've both been coming here since we were little.

"Steve Anderson," he says simply.

I give him a grim look. "Possibly."

He shrugs. "He seemed like a nice guy, but how well do we really know anyone, Iris?" He zips away from me.

I'm thinking I should check my phone in the locker, when I see her at the wall, waving frantically to me.

And what I see is *not* the Alice Ogilvie I know.

This is not the same Alice Ogilvie who's drifted around my orbit since kindergarten. That Alice was all sharp edges and *whatevers*, a vision of perfect hair and perfect clothes. Impenetrable.

The Alice standing before me as I slide to a stop is wearing sweatpants, a grungy cable-knit sweater, and her normally-blown-out-to-perfection hair is stuffed back into . . . a *scrunchie*.

"My god," she says, taking in the rink. "I haven't been here since Brooke dragged me here as cover when she was with Cole."

My eyes dart to Cole Fielding, usually so chipper and cute, dully handing out skates behind the counter. He was too shook to even try to flirt with me when I got my skates, which was very disappointing.

"Alice," I say. "I'm so sorry. About——"

"I'm in a *state*," she says softly. "That's the word that keeps running through my mind. Is that weird? A *state*."

"Alice. It's grief. You're feeling grief. Talk to me."

Her eyes briefly mist over.

"You heard, right? About Steve? Of course you did. Everybody has. Did you hear that other stuff? People are texting me now, you know. Like, *Hey Alice, did you do it? Did you help Steve?*"

"People are dicks, Alice." I pat her hand. For a moment, she lets me, then slides her hand away.

"Anyway, I've been up all night, ever since I heard Steve was arrest——"

She claps a hand over her mouth.

I stare at her. "Wait. How did you know last night he was arrested when it wasn't announced until *today*?"

Alice takes her hand away from her mouth. "Don't ask me. It's better you not know."

I stay quiet, keeping my face impassive so she can't tell what I'm thinking. Who would Alice know who *knows* things? And how would she even *know* someone who *knows* things?

I decide to just nod. I'll figure this out eventually.

Alice blinks. "So. Anyway, since I heard, I spent all night thinking about——"

Zora sweeps up and grabs my arm, pulling me back out. "Hey, Alice, come on out," she says. "Get some skates. It'll clear your mind."

"Iris!" Alice calls, frowning.

"Hey, we were *talking*," I tell Zora. "I know you don't like her, but she's trying to talk to *me*. Her friend *died*."

Zora sighs. "Fine. But whatever she says, don't get wrapped up in it, okay? I mean, you know what they're saying. She's quite possibly an accomplice."

She looks at me knowingly.

I slip my arm out of her grasp. "If she's an accomplice, then what am I? I'm possibly the last one who saw Brooke alive, right? Maybe it was *me*."

I stop back in front of Alice.

"That girl is so rude," she says, picking at her nail polish anxiously. She takes a deep breath. "Look. I think . . . all this might be my fault," she says. "You know? If I hadn't been so intent on going to that party? And if Steve and Brooke hadn't gotten into that fight? This might not have happened. Brooke might still be here."

My heart freezes. That's a crapload of guilt to take on, and I feel suddenly very sorry for Alice Ogilvie. "Alice, first of all, *no*. If it *was* Steve, it was *Steve*, and it's on him. I get pissed at plenty of people all the time and do I murd——"

"You said *if*."

"Yeah, so?"

"So you don't believe he did it."

"I didn't say that. I'm just a person who thinks that until all the evidence is in, nothing is a done deal. And I haven't heard *anything* about evidence, have you? And, like, didn't you watch that one show on Netflix? Where the cops basically coerced that kid into confessing he killed that girl? Who knows what went down at the police station. I watched that show with my old babysit—"

"I like murder, you know? I mean, not *murder*-murder, but reading about it. I spent a lot of time reading this summer. Agatha Christie. Mysteries. I like things that are puzzling."

"I'm aware." I don't know where she's going with this.

"And I've been trying to untangle stuff in my head. It just doesn't make sense to me. What could they possibly have on *Steve*?"

"Go on."

"I mean, did they even interview, say, Coach? Because I, for one, still find it hard to believe he wasn't calling every hotel and airline and searching every back alley for Brooke. Not trying to throw him under the bus, but from a purely investigative standpoint, it seems pretty suspicious to me that he didn't call the police about his daughter missing. Her grandmother did, and only after *I* told her."

Alice twists a strand of her hair between her fingers, deep in thought. "I just feel in my heart of hearts that something is wrong with this situation."

"I know you loved Steve," I say, trying to be kind, "but he very well may have done it. People aren't always what they seem."

"I really hate that line of thinking," Alice says. "I mean, I get it. But I hate it."

I shrug.

"Anyway," she says. "I just want to do some digging. Like what we did yesterday, with your notes, and the search. If it was Steve, I need evidence to show me that, and then I'll move on. But what if . . . it wasn't? Brooke deserves to have someone figure out what really happened to her."

Spike skates by me, tugging on the back of my shirt. I ignore him.

"And," Alice says, "if I'm going to find out what happened to Brooke Donovan, I'm going to need you to be my sidekick. You know people like Thompson don't think we can do it. Just like no one thought Agatha Christie could write an unsolvable mystery. People underestimate women all the time. And I'm sick of it."

She looks at me expectantly.

"Give me a second," I say.

I push off, skate away, arms pumping, head spinning. Prove it? Prove *what*? And *sidekick*?

Alice Ogilvie is a girl who was too stupid to run away and know to *stay* away, a girl who leaves ruin in her wake wherever she goes, and now her friend is dead and she wants me to . . . to . . . what? Turn all Veronica Mars and suddenly solve a crime that doesn't appear to need much solving? A girl's body was found; her boyfriend was arrested.

I'm an under-the-radar person. I like the rock I live under. It's quiet and safe here, and when it gets ripped away from me, like with the Thing, all hell breaks loose and it takes me a long time to stitch myself back together. I go to school, I study, and I skate. That's it. It's boring and bland, but it's what I have.

I pass by Zora and Neil, dipping in unison.

Still, something keeps chipping at me. I thought about Brooke a lot last night, too, the way her body looked in the water, her hair stuck in the crags of the rocks, her legs bare and bloated. That a girl had to die like that, cold and alone.

I hope Steve has a good lawyer, that's for sure. He's going to need it.

Something nudges at my brain as I pass Alice. She's watching me, waiting for my answer.

Alice said Coach went about his day after finding out Brooke never went home and wasn't at school. Granted, maybe he did something behind the scenes we don't know about, but it was Alice who contacted Brooke's grandmother, not Coach. There's something very off about that.

Not to mention . . . Kennedy. Kennedy was supposed to be Brooke's end-of-the-night stop and . . . what if it really was? The police did question the Mains, but what if that questioning wasn't thorough?

The possibilities are endless. Tantalizing. Not to mention the extra-interesting element of Alice's mystery contact.

I skate by Alice. She's holding Brooke's "Missing" flyer up as I pass by again, so that I can see what she wants me to see, what she knows is quite possibly the only way I'll say yes, because she has money, like she said, and I don't.

$50,000.

I know where I want to go. It's bookmarked on my laptop. Whispering Pines, way up north. Hidden. Away from Castle Cove and these people, like Alice Ogilvie, who walk around like they live in a golden bubble.

Like nothing bad can ever touch them.

But it has. Something bad has touched Alice Ogilvie.

I can see it in her face as I slowly stop in front of her. The way her eyes are desperate and pleading. The pain she has there for Brooke, which she'll probably never admit to, and that's fine, because you shouldn't force people to be vulnerable. Sometimes, you need them to be angry, and impetuous, and mean, and hardheaded.

Especially if you're going to, *maybe,* solve a crime.

"Okay," I say, taking the flyer from her hand. I fold it up and slide it into my pocket. "I'll do it."

"Excellent," Alice says. "The first thing we need to do is talk to Steve. I need to see him in the flesh and ask if he really did murder my best friend."

CHAPTER FOURTEEN

ALICE

NOVEMBER 5

9:42 A.M.

"Every murderer is probably
somebody's old friend."
—AGATHA CHRISTIE,
THE MYSTERIOUS AFFAIR AT STYLES

"I'M NOT SURE THIS is a good idea, Alice," says Brenda again as she turns her Lincoln Town Car into the parking lot of the Manzanita County Jail. We're southeast of Castle Cove proper, up into the hills near this tiny town named Blossom. The jail was originally downtown in Castle Cove near the police station, but back about ten years ago the Planning Commission decided it was an eyesore, so they moved it up here. It caused a lot of issues in the towns around the area. It was a messed-up summer; it was also the summer Remy Jackson was murdered.

"It's just Steve. You *know* Steve." We've been having this argument since Iris and I asked her to come along with us as our legal guardian. Thursday night, after we decided that our next and first step needed to be talking directly to Steve himself, we read on the jail website that apparently since we are minors, we can't just waltz in and visit him. We had to wait until he was arraigned and processed, and only *then* could we come.

Rules are so frustrating. I do not appreciate being treated like a child. But when I called the jail to protest, the man on the other end of the phone was decidedly unmoved by my arguments. "We'll be fine. Just come in with us, sign us in or whatever, and then you can play Candy Crush."

Brenda sighs her *Oh Alice* sigh, but pulls into a space a few rows back from the squat concrete jail. Honestly, you'd think they'd at least try to make it somewhat pleasant-looking for the people inside. How does anyone expect to rehabilitate people in a building this ugly?

The three of us get out of the car. Iris has been quiet most of the ride, I think because she's been listening to Brenda and me bicker in the front seat.

We walk inside the building, check in with the woman behind the bulletproof glass window, and take our seats to wait. A few minutes later, we're buzzed through the heavy doors into the visiting area with its round tables and chairs that are screwed to the floor. It's not until Steve appears, wearing an orange jumpsuit and a weary expression on his face, that it hits me.

Steve is in *jail.* Like, what the hell?

Clearly, I already knew this fact, but actually seeing him in front of me wearing an orange jumpsuit with a weary look in his eyes is like a kick in the stomach. He looks like . . . he looks like a *criminal.* My mouth goes dry. Everything I was planning to ask him flies out of my head as he takes a seat across the table from the three of us.

"Alice," he says. He looks like he hasn't slept in days. "Iris

Adams?" Then he notices Brenda. "*Brenda?* What the——" He shakes his head. "I don't know what all of you are doing here, but I can't handle this right now."

I swallow and pull myself together. Falling apart would do no one any good, not to mention would be extremely embarrassing. First things first.

"Steve," I say. "I'm here to ask you a question. Did you kill my friend?"

His mouth drops open. Next to me, Brenda stiffens. She glares at me like *Alice, what in the hell are you doing?* but I ignore her. This is what we came here to do.

Steve presses his hands against his eyes. He looks like he's close to coming apart at the seams.

"You can talk to us," Iris says softly. "You must be so scared. Just tell us what happened. Maybe we can help."

He runs a hand though his hair, squinting off into the distance, like he's trying to decide whether to stay or leave. He's quiet for so long, I can't take it anymore. I start to ramble.

"Steve, you showed up at school that morning and you were all messed up and I don't get it; you never used to drink during the season, did you? Why——"

"Alice," he interrupts. "Please stop. I've been in here for two days now and the guards are really not nice, and I . . ." He chokes on his words. "I don't know what's going to happen to me."

"Maybe if you talk it out with us, it will help," Iris says. "We want to hear your side of the story."

He gives her a wobbly smile. "Thanks, Iris." I bite my bottom lip to keep my excitement off my face. This good-cop-bad-cop thing Iris suggested we do is actually *working.*

Steve sniffs and then starts to speak. "Here's the thing. I don't *know* what happened."

"What do you——" I begin, but Iris kicks me under the table and I shut my mouth.

Steve continues, "So, I heard . . . about Brooke, and I swear the next *second* the cops were banging on the front door, saying they needed to talk to me down at the station. I didn't know what to do, so I went with them. They started asking me about that night, but I couldn't remember *anything* that happened after you left, Alice. I remember talking to you——at that point, I'd had like half a drink, total, I was pretty sober . . . but then we went back into the party, and after that it's like . . . blank. Completely blank. People told me that Brooke and I got into . . ." His voice breaks. "Into a fight? And she took off. But I don't remember any of that. The next thing I knew, I was waking up in the woods, feeling like I got hit by a truck. I realized I had a test, but I needed something in my stomach first, so I stopped by Dotty's Doughnuts." He shakes his head in frustration. "Everyone keeps asking me what happened——what I *did*——but I don't remember."

"Maybe you had more to drink than you think you did?" Iris says gently.

"No!" The word explodes out of Steve's mouth, and Iris visibly flinches back and Brenda puts her hand over hers. One of the guards lingering by the entrance to the room takes a step toward us.

"Steve," I say in a low voice.

He grits his teeth and drags in a breath before replying. "Sorry, Iris. Sorry. I just . . . it's so frustrating. All I've been doing is going over that night in my mind, trying to fill in the blank pieces, but it's like this black hole in my memory." He pushes his hands against his face.

"Do you have a lawyer, Steve?" Iris asks, concern laced through her words. She's really good at this.

"Yeah," he mumbles into his hands. "They assigned me some public defender. Ricky something. Randall? I don't know. She's nice, but . . ." He heaves a sigh, meeting our eyes. "Anyway, none of that matters. It's too late." He motions to the room around us. "Look where I am. I'm screwed."

I place my hand flat on the table between us. Honestly, like I told Iris, if he's guilty, he's guilty. If that's what we find, so be it. But, I was there that night, and I saw Steve. And he was *sober* when *I* saw him, but Iris said he seemed drunk when she watched the fight. It doesn't make sense, and I like things to make sense. "That's what we need to find out. Why you can't remember."

He puts his head in his hands. "Alice, just leave it. My lawyer is handling it, okay? There's nothing you can do."

I purse my lips. Just because I'm not some fancy *lawyer* doesn't mean I can't help. "Steve, I know we haven't been talking over the past few months, but I want you to know that I'm something of an expert on mysteries these days; I've spent a lot of time reading Agatha Christie novels and——"

He heaves a heavy sigh, interrupting me. "This is real life, Alice. *My* life. Not some stupid book." He turns away from us and motions to one of the guards stationed by the doors. The guard starts heading our way. "I have to go. I know you want to help, but please don't start doing your Alice thing with this."

—

As soon as we're back in the lobby, I grab Iris's arm. She has an excited expression on her face, her eyes sparkling.

"Alice, I——"

I cut her off. "We have to figure out why he doesn't remember anything, when he says he only had part of a drink."

"Alice——" Iris says, but I keep going.

"When I saw him that night, he seemed pretty much okay," I continue. "How did he go from sober to flat-out *wasted* in thirty minutes?"

Iris nods emphatically. "Yes, totally. But Alice—*listen* to me." A smile stretches across her face. "I know his lawyer. Ricky Randall. I *know* her. She used to be my babysitter."

My heart picks up. "Oh my god. That's amazing. You know Ricky? We need to talk to her! Do you know where she might be right now?"

Iris smiles. "Oh, that I do."

"Well then," I say, pushing through the jailhouse doors back into the sunlight. "Let's go find her."

CHAPTER FIFTEEN

IRIS
NOVEMBER 5
1 2:30 P.M.

ALICE OGILVIE STARES AT me across the booth at the back of the Moon Landing, fiddling with the red straw in her seltzer.

Brenda immediately decamped to the bar when we got here, under the belief that we were going to do some homework before I had to go to work in the back, washing dishes. Which is really what I do on Saturdays in the afternoon while my mom is tending bar. We've got notebooks and pencils, just to keep up appearances. Brenda's scrolling her phone and drinking tea.

"*That* one?" Alice asks. "*That's* her?"

She gazes at Ricky Randall nursing a drink at the far end of the bar, papers spread on the counter in front of her, briefcase spilling over with god knows what. She's furiously typing on a laptop, swiping strands of hair off her face.

"That's her," I answer. I'm used to people underestimating Ricky. In fact, I'm pretty sure she uses this to her advantage.

"The sweatpants and flannel shirt don't inspire much confidence," Alice says. "And . . . is she a little tipsy?"

Ricky Randall belches.

"Seriously," Alice says.

"All the best lawyers are somewhat disheveled and discontent, Alice. Plus, it's to our benefit to be in the know with Steve's lawyer. She can give us information on what's happening with his case and maybe . . . she can help us dig a little further into this *thing* we seem to be attempting to solve. It's good to have help."

"Oh, we can solve this," Alice says. "We're the perfect people, Iris. Don't you see? No one will be watching us. Who *would* think we were up to something? We're just dumb teenage girls, right?"

Something about that hurts, to be honest. I mean, we live with it every day. In class, on the street, everywhere. Teachers not calling on you but calling on boys. Cluck-clucking at our clothes and makeup. The eyes of men when I just want to buy a stupid cup of coffee at Dotty's Doughnuts. That cop at the police station, Thompson.

"Iris! Look at you, studying so hard on a Saturday afternoon."

Ricky Randall is standing at our booth, looking at Alice and me, her eyes a little fuzzy.

She extends a hand to Alice. "Ricky Randall, attorney-at-law. You and I have someone in common, don't we?"

Alice frowns before taking Ricky's hand in her own. "Alice Ogilvie," she says primly. "And yes, I suppose so."

"Mind if I sit?" Ricky says, not waiting for an answer. She slides in next to me, bumping me to the wall. She smells like a mixture of her preferred gin and ginger and the egg sandwich she must have just eaten at the bar.

I shrug at Alice, who is giving me a *Really?* look. My mother always says, "Ricky Randall dances to her own drummer, however drunk that drummer may be."

Ricky picks up one of my books. *In Cold Blood.* "Interesting choice."

"I have an essay due," I tell her. "And you know me, I like true crime."

She nods, twirling the red straw in her drink for a minute. "I feel like we need to get the elephant out of the room right away, don't you, girls?"

Alice and I look at each other.

"First, yes, I'm representing your ex-boyfriend for the murder of your ex–best friend, Alice Ogilvie. And I already know quite a bit about you from last summer. Believe me, the fact that my current client was also considered, *briefly,* a possible suspect in your disappearance isn't going to help him when we go to trial."

"Trial? Who said anything about a trial?" Alice asks.

"Alice," I say. "He's probably entering a not-guilty plea. Now the state will have to prove it. There will be a trial. And also . . ." I trail off, because the next part isn't so great, and I'm not sure Alice has really thought about it.

"You'll both be called to testify," Ricky finishes for me. "Iris because she witnessed the fight and saw Brooke running and can place her near the scene of the alleged crime. And you, Alice, because you are the ex-girlfriend and ex-friend who deliberately picked a fight with the deceased girl the night of the party, have a history of lying to the police, and, sorry to say, have no concrete alibi for the night of the murder."

Alice's face pinkens. "I didn't do it! How many times do I have to say this? I can't believe everyone is blaming *me*."

Ricky smiles. "Doesn't help that you just went to see your ex-boyfriend in jail. As a good attorney, I might try to spin that as you making sure he doesn't mention your part in the crime."

"Oh my god!" Alice shouts. "How do you even know we went to the jail?"

"I'm his lawyer, Alice. I know things."

"I am done," Alice says, dropping her phone into her purse. "Really, Iris? This? You want me to work with this?"

Ricky Randall laughs. "Calm down, kid. I wouldn't be doing my job if I didn't explore all the angles, right? I have a sneaking suspicion that two teenagers visiting a suspect in jail have more on their minds than making sure he has commissary money, so out with it. Why were you there? And what do you want from me? Because I know you want something."

Alice is still fuming. I turn to Ricky.

"Alice does care about Steve, but she cares about Brooke more. And we think, quite possibly, that there might be other people who could have . . . done it."

Ricky sets down my copy of *In Cold Blood.* "Oh, really?"

"Did the police interview *anyone* else?" Alice asks her.

I take out my notebook and pencil. Ricky glances at them. "Good girl," she murmurs. "Always take notes. Keep track of everything."

Ricky looks at Alice. "I can give you some information, but not all. The police did interview many people at the party, but with that kind of large crowd, it's impossible to know everyone who was there. They talked to Brooke's friends. They interviewed Brooke's father. Nothing seemed out of the ordinary, though."

Alice flicks her eyes to me. I nod, like *Go ahead.*

"I find it disturbing that Matt Donovan didn't call the police the instant he realized his daughter never came home, Ms. Randall. She was missing for ten hours before he waltzed into our school like nothing was wrong and then dismissed it as her probably running away——" Alice says.

"And Alice was the one who called the grandma," I say, interrupting Alice. "Lilian Levy. *Not* Coach Donovan."

"You don't say." Ricky leans back in the booth and crosses her arms. "That is a concern. But it could also be answered as, kids *do* run away. Sometimes more than once. Sometimes they have problems at home and stay at their friends' houses, like Brooke was doing with that obstreperous girl, what's her name——"

"Rebecca Kennedy," Alice and I say together.

"That's the one. I can't wait to interview her," Ricky says.

"Speaking of Kennedy," I say. "Brooke was supposed to spend the night at her house, but she never made it there, and Kennedy doesn't call Coach right away in the morning to tell him? I mean, I'm just theorizing here, but . . ."

"That's a bit of a stretch, Iris," Ricky says. "Not a bad one, but a long one."

"*Listen* to me," Alice interjects. "Brooke was my friend. I knew her my entire life, until she stole my boyfriend. Now she's dead and he's been arrested for it. Something just doesn't sit right with me. You can say that's stupid, but why *Steve*? What exactly do they have on Steve?"

Ricky sighs. "They found a red basketball sneaker in the

woods off Highway One, right across from the Lookout, which is where they think Brooke went over. Sneaker prints near the fencing on the cliffs. At *least* six hours of unaccounted-for time that night. Time *he* can't even recall and has no idea why he can't recall it——"

"He doesn't drink," Alice says. "So I don't get it. He said he had half a beer, but why would that make him not remember anything?"

Ricky shrugs. "Hard to say. The police didn't do tox screens for anyone they interviewed. Anderson was down there the day after Brooke disappeared; that would have been the time to tox-screen the boyfriend who fought with her just hours before she went missing, but it wasn't done. As you're personally aware, Alice, Castle Cove police aren't particularly adept at missing persons cases."

I look up from my notebook. "That's right. The fight. It's all on video. Plenty of people probably filmed you and Brooke, too, Alice, and also Steve and Brooke fighting."

Alice's face falls.

"So they've got that, too," Ricky says. "Video and statements from partygoers show evidence of a very large and strong young man behaving physically with a much smaller young woman. Not something you want in front of a jury, that's for sure. They've got traces of his hair in the woods, along with hers."

"But nothing . . ." I hesitate, searching for the right word. "Like, absolutely concrete? Like a . . . murder weapon or something?"

"Well, what they do have is buildable, that's for sure," Ricky says. "But no murder weapon at the moment. We also don't know exactly how she died. We know she went over the cliff.

The police obviously think it was Steve, but what precipitated her going over the cliff? Did he push her over? Did he strike her and she fell over? Did they struggle and she slipped? Did they fight in the woods and he dragged her across Highway One—"

"Stop," Alice says. "This is giving me a headache."

"I'm just laying it all out for you, Alice. This is serious stuff. We have to wait for a coroner's report to come back, Brooke's tox report, to know exactly how, or as close to it, she died, and in what manner, because that's what will determine formal charges against Steve at his preliminary hearing."

I write down *coroner's report, toxicology, hearing, manner of death,* in my casebook. "How long does that report take?" I ask.

"It depends," Ricky says. "Could be a few days, could be a few weeks. I suspect a preliminary report will be back in a few days."

Alice takes a deep breath. "Just tell me. If Steve goes to trial, if he's found guilty, what . . . what's he going to, you know, get?"

Ricky fixes Alice with a level stare. "Like I said, it depends on what else they have against him. Could be four years, if a prosecutor thinks it was involuntary manslaughter, which means an accident, but avoidable. If they can prove he did it, but never called for help, a prosecutor might press for second-degree, and that's maybe fifteen years. There's also . . ."

She hesitates.

"What?" I say. My hand is starting to cramp from writing so fast.

Ricky picks at the black polish on her nails. "If it's proved Steve took her to the cliffs for the express purpose of killing her, it changes to first-degree murder. It's a little hazy here, because you have to have evidence of that, which is hard. But if the coroner's report comes back and says she suffered additional injury *before* she went off the cliff? Was assaulted, injured in some way, something that's evidence of a struggle . . . we're talking twenty-five to life."

Alice's face is deadly pale.

"I'm sorry," Ricky says. "I'm just laying out all the avenues. It's my job to find enough evidence to prove that Anderson didn't do it. I have to create a road map of doubt for a jury. Poor kid, wrong side of the tracks, stumbles into a relationship with an heiress, can't handle the pressure, they fight, she runs away, he passes out in the woods and the next thing you know, he wakes up and she's dead and the cops say it's him."

"Well, that's exactly what he said happened," I say.

"Precisely. And that's the problem." She turns to Alice. "I'm sorry about your friend Brooke, but I have to tell you. This Anderson kid? Is like talking to a really good-looking piece of Play-Doh. He goes along with *everything*. He's like a bendable straw. Yes ma'am, this. Yes ma'am, that. I'm a bit surprised you dated him for so long. I pegged you for needing something a little spicier."

"He was very nice to me," Alice says sharply. "It's none of your business, anyway."

"It is my business, Ms. Ogilvie, because in order to prove my client not guilty, or get him a better deal, I need to cast shadows in the direction of who else might have done it. Which means you, maybe. I'm gonna play the angle that Steve is just a nice kid from the wrong side of the tracks who fell in with a rich girl, who's you, by the way, and made some bad choices."

"Fine," Alice says. "I don't care. I had nothing to do with it.

I only know that this seems like a rushed and careless investigation, like the police are grasping at straws just because Lilian Levy swanned into town and they're landing on Steve."

"His shoe was in the woods," I remind her.

"Well," Alice says to me, "that's our job to figure it out, then, isn't it? What we need to do is just what *you're* doing." She points at Ricky. "Create a reasonable doubt. Build a case that someone other than Steve did it, and how."

Ricky looks at Alice and then back at me. "Keep me in the loop, kids, but remember, I work for Steve, not you. And lawyers don't ask clients questions about guilt or innocence. We just try to get them the best deal possible. I just want you to do one thing for me."

She finishes her drink, stands up, and looks down at us. "Whatever you two are planning, try not to get killed. Because people who get nosy with the wrong people? Often end up dead. And I don't think Castle Cove needs any more dead girls, get it?"

She walks back to the bar, collects her briefcase, says goodbye to my mom, and ambles out of the Moon Landing.

"She's quite a piece of work," Alice says. "We're not going to *die.*"

"Alice," I say. "If you really want to do this, I want to make sure it's for the right reasons, okay? It isn't because you're still in love with Steve, right? Or because you think somehow this is a redemption arc for you?"

She narrows her eyes. "Redemption arc?"

"You know, bad girl makes good, solves her friend's murder, becomes a heroine in the town's eyes. That sort of thing." I'm watching her carefully. I have my own motives, which involve money, sure, but a girl did die, and it feels only right and correct that the proper person go down for it.

Alice shakes her head vigorously. "God no. I mean, did you *hear* her? She's representing Steve, but her job is also to make it look like *I* had something to do with Brooke's murder, and by gum, Iris, I am *not* going down for that. I was in the bathtub with a novel in my hand, not out somewhere cat-fighting with my former best friend and tossing her over a cliff by her hair."

She looks down. "Ugh, Brenda is texting me. She wants to know why we aren't studying and who that lady was."

I look back at her, sitting at the bar. "Tell her Ricky used to be my babysitter. And start studying because honestly, I do need to get paid for improving your grades even if we are about to . . . wait, what is it exactly we're going to do?"

Alice ponders this as she makes a show of opening her notebooks for Brenda's searching eyes. "Compile a list of possible suspects. Sleuth around, get this show on the road. And, you know, make a murder board. And frankly, with everything we're about to do, and my extensive Agatha Christie knowledge, this should count for freaking extra credit, am I right?"

I sigh. We are probably *this far* from donning trench coats, smoking Lucky Strikes, and slinking furtively around town, taking notes in a little black book.

Which doesn't actually sound all that bad, truth be told.

STEVEO33'S INSTAGRAM PAGE
COMMENTS UNDER LAST-POSTED PICTURE

{Photo of Steve and Brooke, their faces pressed together, big smiles on their faces. In the background is beach and sunshine. A perfect couple on a perfect day.}

TOP COMMENTS:

TheRealRKennedy Steve I can't believe you did this. Brooke was my BEST FRIEND!! I hope you burn in hell.

CCFan MURDERER

STeveAndersonFan Hey ur so hot DM me

Snub952 can't believe you in this picture with her. Were u thinking about killing her then to

JonasBros99 MURDERER

ItsmarkP23 Steve whyd you do it why ur 2 hot 2 kill sum1

Fishybanana MURDERER

AngelBlossom2 It's pretty obvious she didn't appreciate him. Steve DM me

> **TheRealRKennedy** YOU ARE A SICK HUMAN BEING
>
> **AngelBlossom2** Oh yeah want to come say that to my face????

Biebs4Pres MURDERER ROT IN HELL

Dono99 Brooke you were an angel a pure angel you were too good for this earth. Now you're in a better place with your mama ▲▁▲▁▲▁▲▁▲▁▲▁▲▁▲▁▲▁▲▁▲

Will_772263 Bro I can't believe they are saying all these things about you. It has to be BS right?

JeffersonKingCNN Are you a friend of the accused? If so, I'm interested in speaking with you. Please contact me at Jefferson.King@CNN.com

> **Will_772263** Ew get a life, vulture
>
> **Ahendo** I was friends with Steve! I'll email you shortly!
>
> **Will_772263** Henderson get a life

CHAPTER SIXTEEN

ALICE

NOVEMBER 5

8:02 P.M.

"From now on, it is our task to suspect each and
every one amongst us. Forewarned is forearmed.
Take no risks and be alert to danger. That is all."
—AGATHA CHRISTIE, *AND THEN THERE WERE NONE*

WHEN IRIS ARRIVES AT my house after working at the bar, I
lead her back to the room my mother refers to as the conservatory. It's a name I used to find stuffy and embarrassing but,
since getting into Christie, now find kinda awesome (don't tell
my parents). A lot of Agatha Christie's books take place in old
English country manors, and a bunch of her books and plays
have scenes set in conservatories.

I already have the room all set up. A stack of spiral notebooks sits on the marble coffee table along with a bag full of
string and notecards. To the side is the big corkboard on wheels
that we used for schoolwork during my house arrest.

It's now our murder board.

Iris walks over to the materials sitting on the table, poking
through them, and then looks up at me. "Nice work, Ogilvie."

"Thank you." I flush a little and turn to face the board so

she doesn't see. I'm not exactly used to hearing compliments from my family and friends. "I figured we can use this to map everything out. Poirot always talks about order and method in investigations, and this is a good way to get organized."

She blinks. "Poirot?"

"Hercule Poirot? Agatha Christie's main detective guy. He's, like, this world-famous detective who solves tons of nearly-impossible-to-solve mysteries. He always says that he relies on order, method, and 'those little gray cells' to figure out who did it."

"Gray cells?" Iris asks. "Like . . . you mean your brain?"

I nod. "Yes! So, like, he always used reason and logic and psychology to help solve his cases. One of the reasons we need to do this on our own, because clearly the cops aren't using *any* of those things in their investigation."

Iris picks up a stack of notecards and taps them on the table thoughtfully. "It's perfect. Also, I was thinking we need to make a casebook. Record everything. I already started making notes at the bar. Plus, anything that contact of yours happens to know—whoever it is." She shoots me a look. I give her a pretty smile and pantomime zipping my lips. I'm not about to admit I, too, have no idea who it is. "Also witness statements—those are *your* friends, by the way, Alice."

"*Ex*-friends," I mutter.

Iris rolls her eyes. "Ex-friends. Whatever." She grabs one of the notecards and scribbles some words on it before walking around the table and pinning it up in the center of the board.

BROOKE DONOVAN.

I raise an eyebrow at Iris.

"We can make a circle around her name, you know?" she

explains. "See how all the suspects are connected to her. What their motives could have been."

I nod. "Okay, yeah. That works."

"So. First up. People at the party." Iris grabs another card, this time writing *Steve Anderson*.

I open my mouth, but before I can speak, she says, "Alice, he's been arrested for *murder*. Of course he's a suspect."

I consider her words. "Alright. Proceed."

"Thanks."

On the same notecard under Steve's name, Iris writes, *Motive: it's always the boyfriend/jealousy/the fight/blackout. Evidence: sneaker that could be his was found in the woods near where Brooke disappeared, strands of his hair, 10 hours missing.*

She grabs a piece of string and heads over to the board with it and the card. She pins the Steve card up and then connects the string from Brooke's name to Steve's card, then walks back to me. Picking up the pen and another notecard, she writes *Helen Park.*

"Hmm." I consider the name. "Could be. Park and Kennedy have been best friends since birth, but when everything happened this past summer"—I ignore Iris's stare—"Kennedy and Donovan got way closer. Could be that Park got sick of the competition." I pause, considering. "She was always weirdly jealous of Brooke."

Iris writes, *Motive: jealousy. Evidence: ??* and the card goes up on the board next to Steve's.

"I guess next has to be Kennedy?" I ask, and then pause for a moment, thinking. Kennedy, with all her faults, was actually a pretty loyal friend to Brooke, not that I'd ever say that out loud. "She was drinking—Kennedy is *not* known for handling her liquor well," I say. "Brooke was supposed to sleep at her house that night, and she says somehow she didn't even notice she wasn't there until the next *morning*? How's that even possible? And she has a temper."

Iris furrows her brow. "That's a pretty weak motive, Alice." But she writes: *Motive: temper, where did Kennedy go after the party, why didn't she call the cops when she realized Brooke wasn't there? Evidence: ??*

"Alright. Who's up next?"

"Ashley Henderson?"

I shake my head. "Even though she's, like, going to be voted Most Likely to Murder Someone in the yearbook, she couldn't have done it. She was in LA."

"Are you sure? She could have lied. Maybe said she was going . . . hung around town in secret and then—"

I cut her off. "Nope, sorry, Adams. She was def in LA. She posted like four million stories on her Insta about it; all these pictures of her with Titi VanBaale, who's the star of the film, and so it couldn't have been her and . . ."

I trail off, realizing she's looking at me funny.

"What?"

She pauses and then shakes her head a little. "Did you just call me *Adams*?"

Did I? "I . . ." I'm not sure what to say. "Maybe."

Her expression is bemused. "Nothing. Just . . . nothing." She grabs another notecard. "Okay, so no Henderson. So we got the last of the Main Kids suspects?"

I shrug. "I think so?"

"Oh wait." She scribbles something down and tacks it up on the board without looking at me.

When I read it, my cheeks grow hot.

Alice Ogilvie.

"Is this because of what Ricky said in the bar?" I stand and move to grab the card so I can crumple it up and throw it in the trash where it belongs, but Iris blocks me. "I didn't *do* it, Iris."

"Alice, cut it out," she says. Her tone is sharp. I freeze in my tracks. "Sit down." She points to a chair and I sit. She crouches down in front of me. "Yes, this is because of what Ricky said. You heard her; you are going to be called to testify, if and when this goes to trial. You were there that night. And, we visited the main suspect in jail. If it gets to that point, Ricky might make it seem like you were in on it somehow and——"

"I wasn't!" God, will people in this town *ever* stop blaming everything on me?

"I know that," Iris says, voice soft. "You know that. But we have to make sure we keep all of that in mind. We don't want to get blindsided."

I flare my nostrils. "Fine. But in my opinion, there are about a billion people they should look at first. Like, any one of the people on our list. And we haven't even gotten past the Main Kids—Jesus Christ, *why* am I calling them that?—there are other people——"

"Alice," Iris interrupts. "I get it, but I think you understand. We have to. Okay? Up on the board you go." She walks back over to the board and writes below my name, *Motive: spurned girlfriend, aptitude for disappearing. Evidence: ??*

I clench my jaw. "Fine." I stand and pick up a card and a pen. "I'll do the next one. Five. Brooke's ex . . . hookup. Cole Fielding. Like I said, last spring . . . it was a thing. They were totally on the DL, but Cole kept pushing for more. Nobody knows about it, really, except me and Kennedy and Park, and Kennedy was

138

always jealous because she's been obsessed with him literally for years . . . wait! That could be a motive for Kennedy, couldn't it?"

Iris nods. "Yeah. Wait, hold on. What's *Cole's* motive? If he was so into Brooke and all . . ."

I shrug, scribbling words on the card below his name. "A broken heart."

"Ah. Fair. No stronger motive than that."

I hand Iris the card and she pins it to the board and then grabs another one, writing a name. "I think this might be the last . . ."

Coach Donovan.

"Finally," I say.

Iris nods. "You told me that all the trusts are in Brooke's name. Money can make people do crazy things," she says.

I nod. "No kidding. And like Kennedy said, Coach and Brooke haven't been getting along. She was staying out nights. He wasn't worried the day she disappeared. All of it. It's just . . . suspicious."

I grab the notecard from her hand and write *Motive: trouble at home. Money.* I walk over and pin it up on the board and then turn back to Iris.

She hesitates. "You might not like this one, Alice." She bites her lip and writes a word down on a card, holding it up to me.

Accident.

My jaw sets. "It wasn't. Brooke knew better." I can't wrap my head around the fact that all of this might have been simply . . . a mistake. My best friend, dying. It has to be more than that. It just has to be.

Iris considers me. "She was drunk. It was dark. People slip off the edge of that cliff. You know that. And if the coroner's report comes back saying her injuries are consistent with an accidental fall—"

"Wait." I hold up my hands. "How could they even determine that?"

"Physics?" Iris says. "If she was pushed, most likely wouldn't she be pushed outward? And not have, say, a lot of scrapes and injuries from tumbling down the actual cliffside? But if someone as strong as Steve pushed her, she might have fallen *away* and down, and her injuries would be from landing on the rocks and water below and then she got washed out?"

My head is swimming. "Maybe I should have paid more attention in physics."

"Perhaps." Iris tilts her head.

I grab the card from her hand and walk over to the board. I pin it up and attach a string to the center card, then turn back to Iris. "Okay. I think we're done."

She has an odd expression on her face. "I just remembered," she says. "The thing we forgot." She scribbles something down on a card and holds it up so I can see.

Unknown.

I wrinkle my forehead. "Unknown?"

She nods. "Yeah. I was just thinking . . . we're considering the obvious, what's right in front of us, because that's the way we want things to work. *The boyfriend did it. It was her dad. Jealous girlfriends.* But . . . like, what if it's something else? Something we can't see right now? Something—or *someone*—else. Think about Remy Jackson and the person who . . . did that. They're still out there." Her expression sends a chill down my spine. "Or"—she hesitates and then plunges forward—"what if it's an entirely new person? Someone we haven't even thought about? There were a lot of people at that party. There are a lot of people who might . . . not have the best intentions toward Brooke. Or her family." She gestures to the card. "Hence, *Unknown.*"

I shiver, even though I'm wearing a sweater over my pajamas and the heat is on full blast in the house.

Iris walks to the board and pins the last card up and then comes back over to me. We both fall silent, examining the board.

I can't stop looking at that last card.

Unknown.

For the first time, I'm a little afraid of what we might find, and what might happen to us when we do.

CHAPTER SEVENTEEN

WE ARE DOING WHAT detectives do—we're on a stakeout. First up, Brooke's house, to spy on Coach Donovan. Granted, it would be better if we were in a car a little less conspicuous than a silver Mercedes SUV, but there you have it.

Also, it is boring. And a little creepy, parked on the quiet street, looking up at Brooke's house, the windows like dark eyes.

We sit in the car, watching for . . . something. But the house, and everything inside, seems as still and silent as a stone. It's covered in vines and sits on the north side of the road. Unlike the houses that surround it, there's ample lawn space on both sides of the house and in front. It has a perfect view of the ocean from the hill.

"Brooke's mom built this house for her and Brooke when Brooke was just a baby," Alice says softly. "A few years later, Coach moved in with them. It seems like a perfect love story—

exiled from her wealthy family, a single mom moves back to her family's hometown, meets the love of her life who not only wants to marry her but adopt her child as his own."

She's not wrong. Most single moms would just be happy for some help. I start Googling *Matt Donovan, Matthew Donovan, Coach Donovan, Castle Cove High* on my phone.

"He's not here," Alice finally says. "No lights."

"That seems suspicious, doesn't it?" I say. "I mean, if my kid was . . . *you know* . . . I feel like I'd be at home, right? Planning a funeral? Making calls? Anything?"

"Absolutely," Alice says. She makes a note in our casebook. "How's the Googling coming?"

I put my phone down. "Nothing. Matt Donovan, blah blah blah, Coach this, stat that. One thing I don't get, though, is why did Brooke's mom marry Coach? I mean, he's nobody. The Levys practically bleed money. Why did Brooke's mom marry *him*?"

Alice shakes her head. "Victoria was different. I don't think she wanted to be a part of all that anymore. The family life. Their way of things. She wasn't into it. Yeah, she was fancy, but she was always about regular stuff. Baking cookies."

She pauses. "I mean, my parents hired a modeling coach for me at seven to take better family photos, and meanwhile, Brooke was out with the freaking *Girl Scouts* identifying mushrooms and making flower crowns."

"I remember that," I say softly. "She was in my troop."

Alice glances at me. "Victoria loved Coach. She lived in that giant house, but she had a small life. I know that sounds weird, but it's true. The one thing she agreed to was Brooke's debutante ball last year because Lilian insisted. Lilian lives in

Manhattan. Debutante balls are still a big thing with her crowd. Coach didn't go. Lilian is *not* a fan of Coach."

"Modeling classes?" I say teasingly.

She shrugs. "Don't knock it. I absolutely would have crushed making flower crowns, but my posture is *perfect.*"

She seems suddenly lost in thought.

Then she's all business, writing in the casebook and reading out loud. *"Surveillance of CD's home ends, nine-forty-five p.m. Suspect's house is dark, but where is suspect? Odd behavior for grieving person."* She snaps the casebook shut and starts the car. "Onward," she says in a firm voice.

Dotty's Doughnuts is tucked between the Taffy Queen and Shells Galore off Seaside Drive. We're on the western edge of downtown, by the boardwalk, where all the touristy shops are.

This is where Steve went after he woke up confused in the woods. To buy a doughnut and a latte before going to school. Alice parks and turns to me. "Proper detective protocol calls for coffee for our stakeout. It's what the best detectives would do. Two, Steve was here after he woke up in the woods. Which I think proves he didn't do it, because honestly, who commits murder and then gets a doughnut?"

"Well," I say, "I once saw a show about a guy who bludgeoned his mother to death in the kitchen and then cooked a full meal of pot roast and mashed potatoes, so anything is possible."

"Iris," Alice says wearily. "You seem like such a nice person and yet your brain is full of horrible things."

"The world is full of horrible things," I say, getting out of her car.

The second I open the door to the coffee shop, the scent of sugar and burnt coffee wafts over us. I head to the register and start to get out my wallet, but Alice waves me off. "My treat," she says.

Dotty is arranging powdered jellies in a bin in the front. She's a haggard-looking woman with slumped shoulders who frequents the Moon Landing. She glances up.

"Only to-go orders, girls, I'm closing up in ten," she says in a raspy voice. "Hope you don't want anything too complicated."

"Just a coffee," I say.

Alice presses a finger to her chin. "Mmm, what about an almond iced mocha with one of those bear claws? And excuse me, but aren't you . . ."

Dotty glances at her as she drops a bear claw into a bag. "I'm sorry?"

"I'm such a nosy nuisance, I know, but . . . you're her, right? The lady who saw Steve Anderson? *You know.* That *morning?*"

Dotty pauses, looking back and forth between me and Alice. "How did you know that?"

Alice leans in conspiratorially. "I know his sister. Sorry. She's a real blabbermouth."

"Dusty? Well, tell her she owes ten bucks for those beers I bought her over at the Moon Landing. And, yeah, he was here. You girls know him? Such a shame, really. That poor girl."

She hands me a coffee cup, and I turn to pump the urn.

"Was he, like, totally wrecked?" I ask carefully. I don't want to make her suspicious. "I heard he was super drunk that night. I mean, obviously, drunk enough to . . . *well* . . ."

Dotty scoops some ice into a plastic cup. "If you ask me—"

Alice cuts her off. "Oh no, half ice, please, don't fill it up all

145

the way, then I get less coffee. And just two fingers of almond, please."

Dotty frowns at her.

"If I ask you, what?" I urge in a gentle voice. I take a sip of my coffee. My mom says Dotty can talk for *hours.*

"He didn't seem that bad. I know drinkers, believe me, and he didn't smell all that awful, like you should after a bender, or whatever the news is saying. I tried to tell them that, but cops never listen. He was sleeping in his car when I got here, and then he came in and used the bathroom, sounded like he was hacking up a lung. Got a cinnamon crumb and a latte. Seemed mostly confused."

"Confused how?" Alice asks. She takes her almond mocha from Dotty and jiggles it delicately.

"Didn't know what time it was, jabbering about losing his phone. Couldn't remember my name and he comes in here all the time. It was more like he hit his head or something, not hungover."

At the jail, Steve said he was sure he'd only had half a beer. He *was* weaving when I saw him fighting with Brooke, but he was still lucid enough to yell at her and push her. How drunk could he have been that he remembers nothing after supposedly only having one drink, much less not remembering maybe, possibly, pushing his girlfriend off a cliff? Something doesn't add up, because when people pass out at the bar, they are *out,* according to my mom.

Dotty rings us up. Alice hands her a twenty.

"It's a shame, though," Dotty muses. "I know his family. They don't have much. This must be killing them. Wasn't he getting a scholarship to play college ball?"

"Yes," Alice says. "He worked very hard to get that. His mom worked two jobs just to save enough to send him to training camps and stuff."

Dotty shakes her head. "That's what I was thinking when I found his sneaker in the bathroom. Like, that kid probably needs this shoe. It looks expensive, you sure don't want to lose—"

"I'm sorry," I interrupt. "Did you say—"

"His sneaker. He went into the bathroom, like I said, and sounded like he was hacking up a lung. I went in to clean up after he left, because maybe he yakked or something, but there wasn't anything like that. Clean as a whistle, but there was this sneaker. Can't miss it. Big feet, those basketball players, am I right? I gave it to the cops when they came in later that day, you know, so maybe they'd return it to him, or whatever."

Alice says, "So, wait, when he came in, he was wearing both shoes?"

"What did I just say?" Dotty answers, exasperated. "Obviously, if I found his sneaker, and he was the first and only one here, it's *his* shoe. He walked in wearing two. Who could miss them? Bright red, like blood."

Alice and I stare at each other. The cops said they found Steve's sneaker in the woods.

But he was wearing both when he got here.

And then they . . . took it?

"Dotty," I say, trying to keep my voice calm. "Do you have, like, surveillance video?"

"Well, I don't know why you'd need *that,*" she says. She sets her mouth in a line. "What are you girls getting at, anyway?"

Alice's voice is smooth and sweet. "Nothing, nothing at all. My friend is just nosy. Maybe nosier than me."

Dotty frowns at Alice. "Doesn't matter anyway. The cops

147

took that, too, if that's what you're getting at. Said they needed it for evidence. And now the camera doesn't work!"

I grab Alice's change from Dotty and stuff it into the tip jar. "You've been very helpful. Thank you!"

In the car, I take out my phone and pull up Ricky Randall. Alice sees, and holds out her hand. "Here," she says, and tosses something into my lap. "Use this. I was thinking we might need to, you know, keep things on the down low."

"Is this a burner?" I ask her.

"Yes," she says, sipping her drink. "I picked some up when I was getting our investigation supplies this afternoon."

"I feel so official now," I say. "Like a real detective. I just need a drinking problem and a broken marriage and I'm all set."

I tap out Ricky's number, then type: *It's me*

Who's me?

"Use a code name," Alice says, looking over.

Me. My name is: In Cold Blood.
Oh for god's sake. Are you on a burner? You girls are going to get yourselves killed.
Dotty at Dotty's Doughnuts said when Steve came in, he was wearing both shoes, but he left one in the bathroom. She gave it to the cops. But you told us they claim THEY found it in the woods.
You don't say.

How did his shoe get in the woods if he was wearing both when he got here? I type.

> **This is odd. I'm not showing a formal**
> **interview with Dotty Schumacher in my**
> **files. Interesting.**
>> She says they took the surveillance
>> tape from that night
>> Which would show he was wearing both
>> shoes when he got here so. . . .
> **No mention of a surveillance tape in the**
> **police work**
> **I have to think on this.**
> **Be careful. Talk more later. Good job, In**
> **Cold Blood.**

I read Ricky's texts aloud to Alice.

Alice sets her coffee in the cup holder. "So, the cops took the shoe and what? Planted it?"

"Technically, I think the word we want to use is *frame.* Did the cops frame Steve Anderson? This is very perplexing."

I can hardly think straight. My heart is beating a mile a minute. My words come out in a rush.

Alice gives me a bemused look. "*Perplexing?* I think that coffee is really hitting you, Adams. We might have to do one more round of work tonight, because it looks like *you* won't be sleeping."

The thing about Castle Cove, for as much as it irks me, is that it's really beautiful. Especially at night, driving Highway 1, the sea to one side, placid and dark, the moon hovering like a pale gem. It seems magical, sailboats and yachts bobbing serenely in the club marina.

Except for the fact that a girl died in this water.

Alice parks the car. She points to a particularly garish house that's lit up like a Christmas tree and pulsing with music. "Gerber's. One of Steve's oafish friends," she says. "It's where everyone goes on Saturday nights."

My phone, the real one, not the burner one, buzzes. My mom.

You good?

Yes, I type back. *With Alice. Studying.*

Ok. Love you.

Alice watches me slide my phone into the pocket of my peacoat.

"Must be nice," she says softly. "Your mom looking out for you."

"Do your parents let you stay out late?" I ask gently. "Should you text them?"

She shrugs. "They don't care. They're hardly ever here. They work a lot, all over the place. My mom's in the film industry, and my dad . . . does something complicated with money that involves a lot of international travel. It's no big deal. I mean, I have Brenda, so. She put a tracker on my phone, after the thing in the summer. Can you imagine? I mean, I could disable it, but at least someone cares where I am, right?"

She looks out her window. I decide not to press it.

Alice clears her throat. "So all the Mains are here, probably. Kennedy, Park. I bet even *Cole*. Our list."

I take off my seat belt. "Okay, let's go ask some questions."

Alice widens her eyes. "Oh no, I'm not going in there. Do you remember what happened last time I showed up to a party uninvited? No, thank you."

"Well, we can't just sit in this car and wait for them to come out all night, Alice. What's the plan?"

She holds up her burner phone. "I'm going to make them come to me. Plus, I don't want them *knowing* what we're doing. Let's start with Park. She's the weak link."

She smiles at me, a glint in her eye, then starts texting on the burner. I look over her shoulder to read.

I know all about you

"Oh my god," I breathe. *"Really?"*

"I saw it in a movie," Alice says. "Plus, Poirot lies all the time in books to get people to reveal themselves."

The burner blinks.

Who the hell is this

I know what you did I know about
Brooke

Seriously this is not funny

Come outside right now, alone, or I'll call
the cops

No

Alice grunts.

I'll tell your dad

"She's scared shitless of him," Alice murmurs. "He runs everything with a tight fist."

We wait. And in a few minutes, Park appears from around the back of the house, in a red dress and gray coat, purse over her shoulder, peering around, phone in her hand. She looks freaked out.

Alice motions for me to slide down as far as we can in the seats, with just our eyes peeking over the dash. Park hesitates on the lawn. I hope she doesn't recognize Alice's car if she spots it.

I've been watching you. I saw what you did.

Park clamps a hand over her mouth, staring at her phone.

Is it eating you up inside?

"Oh my god," I whisper. "This is . . . a smidge mean."
"They were mean to me," Alice whispers back.

I didn't mean for it to happen. Please. You have to believe me. It was an accident.

Beside me, Alice's eyes widen. "Holy crap," she breathes.
Wait, did Park kill Brooke? That makes no sense. Plus, that would be too easy. The cops questioned her. Right now, stand-

ing on the lawn, she looks like a frightened little girl, whipping around, looking every which way, wondering who's watching her, talking to her.

What exactly did Park do?

She *was* the only Main crying that day in school when the cops came for them in the cafeteria, but . . . she would have broken in that interrogation room if this sort of *Scream* shenanigan is freaking her out. "Alice, I don't think——"

Alice holds up a hand.

> What a lovely dress you have on.
> Brooke had a dress like that. You were
> always so jealous, weren't you? Did you
> want to be Brooke?

Park whips around, takes a few steps, peering everywhere. She's starting to cry.

> **I just wanted her to pass out, that's all I
> didn't mean for him to drink it, please**

I gasp. Alice stares at me, an incredulous smile on her face.

> **She had everything all the time please
> whoever you are please just leave me alone
> I didn't mean for anyone to die**

Park drops to her knees on the lawn, her face down.

> **I love him**

"Wait," I say, stunned. "Did Park . . . drug Brooke's drink?"

"But *Steve* must have drunk it," Alice whispers. "*That's* why he was so weird. He *did* drink, but whatever Park gave Brooke . . . messed him up way more? No wonder he couldn't remember anything."

I grab the burner and type, *You drugged Brooke Donovan, Helen Park*

Please I'll do anything you want it was just
some Ambien

What a bad girl you are Helen Park we'll
be watching you

The front door of the house opens, and Kennedy steps out. "Park?" she calls. "Parkie, what's the frickin' deal? You puking?"

Park scrambles up, brushing off her knees, wiping her face. She shoves her phone into her purse and stumbles to Kennedy. They disappear into the house.

Carefully, still half down in her seat, Alice starts the car and slowly pulls away. Once we're far enough down the road, we both sit straight up, stunned, looking at each other.

"Helen Park tried to drug Brooke Donovan to get with Steve Anderson." Alice shakes her head.

"But then Brooke Donovan ran away and disappeared and later was found in the water," I answer.

"And Steve Anderson was arrested for her murder, but apparently he was deep in la-la land." Alice chuckles. "I did not have *Park* drugging Brooke on my bingo card."

Halfway to my apartment building, the burner Alice used for Park lights up.

Please don't tell my dad please please
please

I hold the phone up so Alice can read the message.

"That's what you get, Parkie," she says, her voice tough and pleased. "For messing with me."

Later that night, in my room, I text Ricky Randall. I do it from my regular phone and not the burner, because it's in my backpack and I'm too tired to get out of bed and get it.

> Helen Park drugged Steve Anderson's
> drink at the party. Ambien.

I don't know why you aren't asleep, Iris.
You've had a long day.

> She put it in Brooke's drink, but Steve
> drank it instead. He wasn't drunk.
> He was messed up on Ambien in
> combination with the alcohol.

Hmm. And you obtained this information
how?

> We pranked Helen and she admitted it
> on text.

I like your methods. Not sure they're
admissible in court, but I can call her in for
an interview. Wait.

> What

Did you say Helen Park?

> Yeah

155

Oh no. No way her dad's letting her in my office without some fancy lawyer in a suit. Did you know he assaulted Denny down at the Burger Hut with a Super Patty Meal? Said the burger wasn't cooked enough and threw it in Denny's face. I repped Denny. We won, but that guy's got a temper.

> That's what Alice said. Said Helen is very afraid of him. Also, your office is your car.

I stay mobile for my clientele.

. . .

Speaking of dads.

> Don't.

. . .

Iris.

. . .

> He hasn't been around since August and the incident.

Good.

> I gotta go to bed now

Forward me the Helen Park texts. I'll see what I can do. And Iris?

> Yeah

Be careful. Doing this. And with that Ogilvie girl.

> She seems cool. It's fine.

Good night, Iris.

> Good night, Ricky.

MURDER BOARD

Steve Anderson
Helen Park
Rebecca Kennedy
Alice Ogilvie
Cole Fielding
Coach Donovan
Accident
Unknown

BROOKE DONOVAN, AMERICAN HEIRESS:
FIVE FAST FACTS YOU NEED TO KNOW

News of Brooke Donovan's murder broke late evening November 2. Donovan, an heir to the Levy Cosmetics fortune, was discovered by classmates, who spotted her body at the bottom of the cliffs edging the town of Castle Cove. Here are five fast facts you should know about Donovan and the Levy Family.

1. Brooke Donovan lived in Castle Cove, California, since the age of five, when her mother, heiress Victoria Levy, married local basketball coach Matthew Donovan, much to the chagrin of Victoria's mother, Lilian Levy, founder of multinational makeup and skincare manufacturer Levy Cosmetics. Brooke was formally adopted by Matthew Donovan at the age of eight, at which time she took his last name. Lilian Levy grew up in Castle Cove in Levy Castle. But, when Levy was fifteen, her father, hotelier Charles W. Levy, went to prison for embezzlement and lost their family fortune. The Levy Castle is now

a Registered Historic Landmark and open for
tours and events. We're told Brooke was there,
attending a party, the night of her death.

2. After her father went to prison, Lilian Levy
moved to New York City with her mother to live
with family. Soon after, she started helping her
neighbor, a chemist, make creams and perfumes
for his small store. It was quickly clear she had a
nose for the business, and by the time she was
twenty-one, she was selling her preparations
to local pharmacies. Levy Cosmetics is now a
publicly traded corporation with a yearly revenue
of over $15 billion.

3. Victoria Donovan (née Levy) died two years ago
from a sudden heart attack while in remission
from breast cancer. After her death, Brooke
remained living with her father in Castle Cove,
even though her mother's family tried to strong-
arm him into sending her back to live with Lilian
in Manhattan.

4. Mirroring her mother's love life, Brooke Donovan
was dating a local basketball player named
Steve Anderson at the time of her death.

5. This isn't the first time the Levy family has been
embroiled in tragedy and scandal. First was
Lilian's father and the loss of their family fortune.
Then was Victoria's quick marriage, pregnancy,
and divorce from Brooke's paternal father,
Prince Juan Sebastian, third cousin to the king
of Spain, who left his wife and child shortly after

Brooke's birth to travel the world. A few years later, Victoria's youngest sister, Francine Levy, disappeared off a cruise ship while traveling in the Mediterranean, and her body was never recovered. The death of Brooke Donovan is only the latest in a long list of tragedies that the Levy family has endured, including the death of film star Mona Moody under mysterious circumstances at the Levy Castle in the 1940s. Some say they are cursed.

CHAPTER EIGHTEEN

IRIS
NOVEMBER 7
8:43 A.M.

IT'S A MADHOUSE AT school.

News vans everywhere, police trying to keep reporters behind a barricade. Teachers trying desperately to get kids inside and stop them from answering reporters' questions. I spot that KWB reporter, Tessa Hopkins, who's somehow managed to weasel her way around the barricade, intently listening to a very-well-made-up Kennedy. I swerve around some kids. I definitely don't want Tessa to spot me.

Alice is standing by her open locker, rooting around among crumpled papers and nail polish bottles.

"Are you ready?" I say sternly. She was resistant yesterday, but it needs to be done.

"Merde, Iris. *You* do it; you have a class with her. She's the *last* person I want to talk to."

"No, I'm doing the other thing. We agreed. You're handling

Kennedy. You did great with Park, but you can't do the burner thing again. It has to be face-to-face with Kennedy and we need to record it, just in case."

Alice smiles in a wicked way. "I texted Park again. I can't stop! It's hilarious."

"Alice."

"Okay, okay. But Kennedy hates me. You have no idea what it's like to have to talk to someone who literally hates you."

I consider this. Kennedy seems like the type of person who feeds off weakness. It would give her something to work with, to chew on. Alice could use this to her advantage.

"Cry," I tell Alice.

She narrows her eyes. "You want me to cry in front of that a-hole? I don't *cry*, Iris."

"Come *on*. Say you're sorry for the way you've acted. That you've been lonely without her and now that Brooke's gone and Steve's been arrested, you're . . . you're . . . a mess."

"You want me to be weak," she says flatly.

"It's the only way," I say gently. "Think of her as a hungry lion and you are but a tender piece of meat for her to devour. It's all for a good cause, right? For Brooke? And make sure Park isn't around when you do it. It might make her suspicious after the burner thing."

She blows a strand of hair off her face, but she looks unsure. Granted, I wouldn't want to talk to somebody who'd been cruel to me, either. In fact, it would make me sick to my stomach.

Suddenly, I remember what Westmacott said to me in her office. About Alice.

"Alice," I say quietly. "I believe in you. You can do this."

She blinks at me.

I say the only thing I can think of to convince her.

" 'She's had a long life of experience in noticing evil, fancying evil, suspecting evil, and going forth to do battle with evil.' That's you, Alice. Go do battle with evil."

A slow smile spreads across her face. "Iris, have you been reading Miss Marple? That's a line from *At Bertram's Hotel,* isn't it?"

"Good god, no. That's your thing. I just skimmed one of your books yesterday."

"Interesting," she says. "Okay. I'll do it. But I'm not going to like it."

Battle won.

I find Spike's dad, the head janitor at Castle Cove High, in the facilities office. He's always been a pretty cool guy. I have, on occasion, gone over to Spike's house on the rare weekend night I try to appease my mother about my lack of a social life, and while everyone is in the corner of Spike's living room staring down another round of D&D, I usually sit with Mr. Flick by the television as he regales me with the intricacies of betting on horses while we watch the races.

"Oh hey, Iris," he says. "Shouldn't you be in class?" He checks his watch, which has a tie-dyed band. Once, Spike told me his dad used to crisscross the country in an old school bus, selling homemade merch at concerts. Spike actually got his name from one of his dad's favorite albums.

"It's cool. I'm on pass," I tell him. It's a lie, but I know he doesn't know that. I'm an A+ kid with nary a scratch on my school record. Why would I lie?

Being an under-the-radar person is proving to have quite a few perks when investigating a crime.

"Can I help you with something?"

"Actually," I say, "you can. It's about Coach Donovan. He's, you know, going to be out for a while——"

Mr. Flick nods sadly. "Terrible stuff. I'm in shock about the Anderson boy, to be honest. Always seemed like such a good one, you know?"

"Me too." I wait the appropriate amount of time before I continue. "Anyway, some of the kids, we wanted to do a candle-light memorial for Brooke. Like, have her picture up and a place to put flowers and all that, but nobody wants to bother Coach at home and we thought maybe he had one in his office?"

"Can't you just take it off Instagram or whatever it is you kids are using these days?"

"Oh, haha. Well, you know, those types of photos aren't, like, well, probably appropriate, and we want something nice."

He nods. "Gotcha." He puts down his clipboard. "Follow me."

I trail him down the hall and up the L-wing staircase.

It suddenly occurs to me that, like, Mr. Flick is not just going to leave me there in Coach's office while I root around for god knows what. Perhaps Alice and I should have discussed more focused things to look for. Detecting is hard.

I need to get Flick away from here for at least a few minutes.

I pull out my phone.

Spike, I type. *Text your dad. Right now.*

The hell, Iris, I'm in band right now.

Just do it. Tell him you need him or
something and to meet you somewhere.
I need him away from Coach's office.

I can't just leave band!

JUST DO IT I'LL EXPLAIN LATER

**If you and Ogilvie are masterminding
something about Brooke I want in!**

Mr. Flick unlocks the door to Coach's office. "Here you go. Oh, there's one, a nice one, right there." He points to the wall. It's a photograph of Brooke, beautiful as always, in what looks like an extremely expensive and formal dress, standing in an ornate hall with dreamy-looking chandeliers.

"That was her thing . . . what's it called again?" Mr. Flick's voice sounds faraway almost. "Where the girls with money go? A big ball or something."

Brooke is wearing long white gloves, her gorgeous dress as white as snow.

"A debutante ball," I say slowly. "A kind of coming-out party."

Brooke's money required ritual and history, things like balls for beautiful girls. The annual regatta ball coming up at the Yacht Club. All that stuff.

"Ah shoot, hold on, Spike's texting me," Mr. Flick says. "Can you wait here? I gotta lock up after you leave. I'll be right back."

"No problem."

And of course he leaves. Because I'm Iris Adams. I'm not going to do anything *illegal.*

But that's exactly what I do as soon as I hear his footsteps fading down the hall.

I tuck the framed photo into my backpack, just to be on the up and up, and then I move around to Coach's desk. The drawers aren't locked. I mean, I don't even know exactly what I'm looking for, just that . . . I'm looking for something. I have to admit, I'm a little scared. My heart is beating like a mad thing in my chest. Also, it smells in here. I glance around. There's a box of sneakers in the corner. Shelves lined with team photos, plaques, trophies.

All I find in his drawers are pens, sticky notes, chewing gum, a pair of socks, and files on students. Which . . . interest me very much, but that's not what I came for.

I accidentally slam a desk drawer shut too hard, and the monitor on his desk blinks to life, the little box waiting for a password.

Hmmm.

From what I know of Coach, he's not the dullest bulb, but he might not be the brightest, either. If he's going to have a password, it's going to be something easy to remember.

I type in *CrystalCoveCougars.*

The password box shakes, *No.*

It can't be something about Brooke—that would be too easy, wouldn't it?

My phone buzzes.

DAD'S GONE

I TRIED

YOU BETTER TELL ME WHAT'S GOING ON

Damn it.

And then I see it, like the dumbass I am, just sticking right there at the base of the monitor, half hidden underneath an open can of Diet Pepsi.

A sticky note that says *CCHSHOOPS333*.

Castle Cove High School and *hoops* for basketball.

Bingo. I type in the password, and his email immediately pops on. He must not have closed the window from the last time he was here.

I hear whistling down the hall and the jangle of an enormous swatch of keys. Mr. Flick.

I scroll, but I have no idea what to look for. I take a quick picture of the window and stuff the password in my pocket.

I'm back around the front of the desk when Mr. Flick appears in the doorway. "All done?" he asks.

"Yeah," I say. "I took the debutante ball photo. I'll bring it back tomorrow, okay?"

"No later, alright?" He waves a hand in front of his face. "Jeez, it stinks in here."

"Probably the shoes," I say. "I didn't know one person could have so many sneakers."

He looks at the sneakers in the corner. "Nah, those aren't his. Those are leftovers from the team. Rich Colson over at Foot Locker gives the basketball team a deal on shoes, and you know how kids outgrow shoes so quick. Coach saves those and donates them to the Goodwill down on Bristol Street."

Mr. Flick is still talking. "I keep telling him to get them outta here because they stink up the place, but you know Coach. The only thing on his brain is winning and women."

He chuckles.

Sneakers. There are an awful lot of sneakers in that box. I peek into it. It's Nikes, mostly. Red ones. Steve was wearing red sneakers, according to Dotty. I'm trying to process this when something Mr. Flick said intrudes.

" 'Winning and women'?" I say.

His face reddens. "Oh, sheesh, I probably shouldn't have said anything. Not cool."

He makes a motion to shoo me out of the room.

"Actually, Mr. Flick, since it's just you and me, you can tell me. What do you mean exactly? I mean, I know Coach was dating Ms. Westmacott, but——"

"Oh, that ended way back when school started. I had to replace the tissue boxes in her office like four times a week."

I give him a sly grin.

The corner of Mr. Flick's mouth curls up. "Well, seeing as how it's *you,* Iris, between you and me? The guy is kind of a hound."

" 'A hound'?" I say innocently.

Brooke Donovan's devoted stepfather, beloved basketball coach, a lady-hound? Was he always this way? Or only after Brooke's mom died? There is obviously so much more to Coach Donovan than meets the eye.

"Is this womanizing a new thing for Coach, Mr. Flick? Or was he even this way before, you know, Brooke's mom died?"

My brain is spinning. I wish I had my casebook with me so I could take notes, because I'm thinking of what Alice said, about Brooke's money being tied up, and her fighting with Coach about something, and now that I think about it, why is a guy who married an extraordinarily rich woman still a high school basketball coach? Is anybody *that* good-hearted? What if . . .

"Iris," Mr. Flick says conspiratorially. "I could tell you *so* many stories about this guy."

"Oh, Mr. Flick, please do. Please, please *do.*"

CHAPTER NINETEEN

ALICE

NOVEMBER 7

11:43 A.M.

"Ah, I see you are an actress, Miss Marple,
as well as an avenger."

—AGATHA CHRISTIE, *NEMESIS*

I SPOT KENNEDY STUFFING books into her locker before lunch. She's alone, which is good, because I'm definitely not talking to her in front of people like Park or Henderson, but also bad, because it means I don't have any excuse *not* to talk to her. I can't believe Iris managed to convince me to do this. Referencing Miss Marple. She already knows my weak spots. It's rude.

Anyway, I have this under control. Hercule Poirot always drew out information from suspects by lying through his teeth and pretending not to know things, so they would trust him. And I just so happen to have a *lot* of experience with both.

I suck in a breath and march over to Kennedy. The hallway is mostly empty, outside of a couple of girls from my grade leaning against the wall across the way, chatting. They fall quiet as I head toward Kennedy. Out of the corner of my eye, I see one nudging the other. I ignore them. Miss Marple wouldn't let other people's opinions of her stop her from forging forward, and neither will I.

When I reach Kennedy, I stop, clearing my throat loudly. Her head is inside her locker, and she's intently looking at something on her phone with a little smile on her face. She jumps when she hears me.

"Ogilvie, what the hell?" She turns red and quickly locks her phone. "What are you *doing*?"

"Hello," I say, which admittedly isn't the most creative greeting. "Um . . ." I trail off. *Lie, Alice.*

She raises her eyebrows and then slams her locker door shut, swinging her Celine bag onto her shoulder. "Yes?"

"Hi, Kennedy. How are you? I've been worried about you. Because of Brooke and all, you know?" I bite my lip, looking down at the floor, forcing tears into my eyes. My bottom lip trembles. "It's just crazy. What they're saying about Steve. Everything that happened. I don't . . . I feel like maybe it's all *my* fault." My throat tightens. Dammit. I didn't even have to fake it. I blink, hard.

Kennedy's irritated expression slips when she hears the wobble in my voice. "Oh, Alice." She sighs heavily and pats my arm awkwardly. "Not everything is about you, you know. What happened is horrible, but it's not like *you* pushed Brooke off a cliff." She pauses, raising her eyebrows. "*Did* you?" She snorts. "Just kidding. We know Steve did it. Thank god they got him so fast. Could you imagine if he was still here, like, wandering around school, after *murdering* someone? Talk about creepy." She shudders.

I furrow my brow. "Do you really think Steve did it?"

She makes a face. "Alice, *hello*. He *obviously* did it. They have all that evidence and everything. Open-and-shut case. I ran into Coach yesterday, and he was saying how glad he is that it's done; how it's better this way because it's not going to turn into some three-ring media circus. Brooke deserved better, you know?"

I think about the news vans parked out front of the school. "Um, not sure that's true." It's odd to me that Coach would be *glad* that Steve is going down for this—even if he did it— because Steve always seemed like someone Coach was pretty fond of, through basketball.

She waves a hand. "Yeah, well, I don't know. He was sad and stuff. He might not even have known what he was saying. But, anyway, it's def better that Steve is behind bars. We were supposed to all go to the regatta ball together. I'm sorry, but I do *not* need some murderer messing up my photos. I would have had to, like, cut him out of them or something, which would ruin my entire aesthetic."

"Right." Good god. I forgot how Kennedy can be. I have to get her back on track. "So can I ask you something? It's been bothering me."

She considers me. "Mmmm . . . maybe."

I force my expression to stay frozen, fighting the reflex to roll my eyes. "That night—Halloween. After Brooke left the party? Do you think she could have run into someone else? Other than Steve?"

Kennedy looks annoyed. "Why are you asking me this, Alice? Why does everything have to be an *issue* with you? Just leave it alone, okay? We're all trying to move on. I already talked to the police and told them everything and Steve is in jail . . . it's done. And thank god for that."

I huff a breath. "Not everything is an issue, okay? *God.*" Ugh, she is so annoying. I need to get her alibi—if she has one—without *explicitly* getting her alibi, because then she might lie. Although, Hercule Poirot *does* say that sometimes lies lead you to the truth.

It comes to me suddenly. How Iris got me to talk to Kennedy in the first place. She knows my weak spots, and she used them to get me to do what she wanted. And boy do I know Kennedy's weak spot.

"Was Cole Fielding there that night?" I ask. Clearly I know he was, because I saw him.

She pauses midstep when she hears his name, a sly smile creeping onto her face. "Yes," she says. "Why yes, he was. Why do you ask?"

"I just heard that you guys were getting cozy." I nudge her. "You've been waiting for that to happen for *years*." I pretend like I'm excited for her, even though the whole thing is creepy.

"Right?" She leans toward me conspiratorially. "It was *awesome*."

Ew. Out loud I say, "Cool. By the way, how was Brooke handling the two of you getting together? She was always a little territorial about him. Did she care?"

"No. She said she didn't." She grabs her phone out of the side pocket of her bag and swipes a few times. "Look." She shoves it into my hands with an expression of triumph and then furtively glances up and down the hall. "Just make sure the volume is down."

I press Play and when I see what's—*who's*—on the screen, my mouth drops open. "Oh my god, *Kennedy*. Is that . . . you and Cole? Ew! Get that away from me!" I throw the phone at her and she catches it, laughing.

"He's hot! I'm not sorry! I deserve a nice piece of ass once in a while, too, you know. So if what you're getting at here is that you think that Cole had something to do with Brooke, he didn't, okay? See that time stamp?" She shoves the phone back in my face. "Says right there. We were together that night. He's over her. As you can see."

I could have lived my entire life without seeing a video like that and been happy. I make a face. "I'm going to have to put my head in a bucket of bleach now, thanks."

"Oh, don't be such a *prude,* Alice." A dreamy expression settles on her face. "You know even when Brooke was with Cole, I liked him. Most girls treat him like he's nothing more than a hot piece, but he is actually really—"

"Okay, thanks. I gotta go," I say, interrupting her monologue about Cole. I know from experience it can go on literally for *hours.*

Kennedy's mouth snaps shut and her expression shutters. "Fine, Alice. See you or whatever."

I pat her on the arm. "You know, Kennedy," I say, "when Steve's case goes to trial, they might ask everyone where they were that night, after the party. You'd get to show that video of you and Cole to the world."

Her eyes widen, and she looks down at the frozen image on her phone's screen and then back up at me in horror.

"Isn't that exciting?" I say with a sweet smile. "See you." And then I hurry away to find Iris as fast as my legs will take me.

MURDER BOARD

Steve Anderson
~~Helen Park~~
~~Rebecca Kennedy~~
Alice Ogilvie
~~Cole Fielding~~
Coach Donovan
Accident
Unknown

TEXT CONVERSATION BETWEEN
A. OGILVIE AND R. KENNEDY
NOVEMBER 7

3:03 P.M.

AO: Hey

RK: Why ru texting me, Ogilvie

AO: Calm down

AO: Can I ask you 1 more q

RK: OMG get a life

AO: I'll assume that means yes.

AO: Right after Brooke disappeared, you mentioned something had gone down bw her n Coach

AO: You said it was something w money

AO: Like what

RK: God you're nosy.

RK: I think she said something about him wanting her to make sure he still got his monthly stipend until she was out of college

RK: He wanted her to make him a trustee or something.

AO: A trustee?

RK: I don't KNOW alice. You know I don't talk about money.

AO: Um. since when?

RK: Whatev

RK: Is that all you needed?

AO: Yea

RK: GOOD. BYE.

CHAPTER TWENTY

IRIS
NOVEMBER 7
4:40 P.M.

Where are you???

IT'S LIKE THE EIGHTH text Alice has sent me.

My mother stares at me, her mouth trembling. "It's fine," she says. "He texted me, I blocked him. End of story. He knows not to come here because of the restraining order."

My stomach is in a tight knot. I want to tell her we should just go, leave now, use the money I've already saved. Run. But before I can get that plea out of my mouth, there's a knock on the door. My mother and I both freeze.

She holds up a hand to me and walks to the door. "Hello?" she calls.

From outside the door comes a familiar, breezy voice. "Am I in the right place? I'm looking for Iris?"

My mother's shoulders visibly loosen. I let out my breath.

It's just Alice. But then my heart sinks. Alice is here. I didn't want her to come here. I look around. We haven't cleaned in a few days—there's stuff lying everywhere, unlike Alice's spotless mansion.

My mother opens the door. Alice steps inside. "There you are! I have been looking all over for you. Hi, Ms. Adams."

"Alice," my mother says gently. "I'm guessing it's time for tutoring?" She glances at me. "I'll check in from work, okay?"

I nod. Alice looks back and forth between us, a thin line appearing between her brows.

I wonder what she thought of the trash overflowing from the dumpster in the parking lot. The desiccated pumpkin still outside 312's door. If she's annoyed by the lady in 316, blaring *Real Housewives* so loud we can hear it inside my apartment.

My mom lets Alice in and leaves, closing the door behind her. Alice smiles at me brightly. "You didn't answer any of my texts! I had to look up your address. I hope you don't mind."

"Sorry everything's so grungy," I say. "Kind of a step down for you, I guess."

Alice's face falls. "Iris——"

"I have to pee," I say. I walk into the bathroom, turn on the water full blast, and splash my face. He texted my mom. He's not supposed to. He's inching closer. I rub my face hard with a towel.

When I come out, Alice is staring at my laptop on the kitchen table, reading the page I have up. She glances up at me. "What's Whispering Pines? That's up north, right? You and your family going on a trip?"

I slam the laptop shut. I had a million tabs open. How to

change your identity. Stuff like that. I do not need Alice pestering me and figuring out my own plans for disappearing.

"It's just me and my mom and no."

"Oh. Does your dad travel a lot, like mine——"

"No. My dad's dead. And you don't have to say you're sorry or anything. It happened before I was born."

It's a lie, but one I can make with a straight face and one that I hope will shut Alice down.

"Oh," Alice says, her voice soft. "That must be really hard. I never really see my parents, but I can't imagine what it would be like to, you know, not have them."

"You can't miss what you never had," I answer. "Besides, my mom is stellar, so I'm good. No worries for me."

Alice is silent. I grab my laptop and put it on the counter, for something to do, and so I don't have to look at her face, because she looks . . . almost like she cares, and I don't want that right now.

"Your apartment's nice," she says, changing the subject, her voice bright and cheery. "I like the watercolors over there. Did you make them?" She gestures toward the kitchen wall.

I regard her carefully. Is she going to make fun of me? That seems like something a Main might do. "Yes, they're mine. I like it. Painting the ocean, I mean."

She peers closer at them. "I love them. They're so . . . pretty and calming. I wish I had some sort of talent. They make this room so cozy and warm——"

"You can stop, Alice. You don't have to pretend. I know it's gross here. You shouldn't have come. Next time just tell me where to meet you."

Alice frowns. "Actually, I do like it. And your paintings. It feels homey in here. Like people live here." She pauses. "I'm not some stuck-up princess, you know. Maybe you're the snob, Iris. Did you ever think of that?"

My face goes beet red. "Fine," I say finally. "Let's just get to it, okay?"

"Fine." Alice plops her purse on the kitchen table. "Kennedy . . . how can I put this? She was in flagrante delicto with Cole Fielding after Brooke ran away, and she has a very saucy time-stamped video to prove it. We can take them off the murder board, I think."

"Oh my god. They filmed it?" I laugh. Also, I kind of want to see that video, but I'm not about to tell Alice that.

Alice fans her face. "It's seared in my brain forever."

We look at each other and giggle at the same time, thoughts of Cole and Kennedy getting squirmy with each other stuck in our heads. Although, I do feel a tinge of jealousy thinking about Cole with Kennedy.

Okay, things are better now.

"Okay," I say, taking a deep breath. "Coach's office. I didn't get much, really. I only had a little time before Mr. Flick came back and—oh, he's Spike's dad. Did you know that? So I had to text Spike to somehow get his dad to leave Coach's office and leave me alone, but I did get this."

I show her my phone with the picture of Coach's email inbox. Some messages seem benign, like *Olive Garden wants you back!* But others are more interesting.

Alice takes my phone and ponders the photo. "A lot of emails from Lincoln Life and Beneficiary and something called Watson, Terwilliger, and Morton. Lawyers? Maybe that's the trust estate?

Kennedy said Brooke and Coach were arguing about making him a trustee so he could still get money after she went to college."

"Are they dated from before Brooke died?" I ask.

"Yup. So he was definitely trying to change things. And . . . oh wow."

She zooms in on my phone. "Coach has an awful lot of emails from teachers. Is that normal?"

"That's the other thing. Flick said Coach is quite the hound dog among the female staff at Castle Cove High. How many women was he juggling?"

Alice hands me back my phone. "Well, it looks like quite a few. Do you think Brooke knew about his extracurricular pursuits? Beyond Westmacott, I mean."

"How could she not? Right, so back to evidence. One, Coach doesn't seem all that devoted. Two, he's trying something funny with the estate? I don't know. And all the teachers? What if, just say, it was Coach, for whatever reason? What if he had help from someone? And the police have the wrong guy? And I'm thinking we might need help with all this. From the Zoners. This is a lot of stuff to research and gather, and other eyes might speed this along?"

Alice regards me carefully. "You might be right."

I breathe a sigh of relief. It's a lot of work, but that's not really the issue for me. The issue is something else. Getting that reward money and getting out, and the quicker we can maybe solve this, the quicker that happens.

Alice picks up her purse. "Get your things. That's the whole reason I'm here, anyway, is that we need to ramp up investigating Coach. We're going on a mission."

She's heading to the door before I can even grab my backpack. I hurry after her.

"So what's the plan?" I ask. We're sitting in Alice's car, down the street from Brooke's house. "We just waltz into Coach's and ask him, 'Dude, did you, by any chance, you know, off your own kid?' I don't think that's going to fly."

Alice glances at me. "Okay, don't get mad," she says. "I thought about that, and there's really only one way to search his house without him bothering us or making him suspicious. I have something. Look in my purse."

I pick up her purse from the console and rummage inside. I hold up a condom packet. "Really, Alice? I think this might be going a little *far*."

"Not *that*! Feel around the bottom. And, that's gross. He is practically an elderly man." She shudders.

I pull out a pill bottle, read the label. *Ariadne Ogilvie, Xanax, 3 milligrams.*

"Surprise!" Alice says.

"Alice . . . no," I say.

"Park did it to Steve!" she says. "And in 'The Third Floor Flat,' Hercule Poirot used ethyl chloride to knock out a suspect so he could have time to rummage through their pockets. I can't get ahold of that fast, but my mom's medicine cabinet is a virtual pharmaceutical wonderland, so here we go."

I jiggle the bottle in my hand. "This is wrong. Very wrong."

Alice sighs. "Do you think he's going to say anything incriminating to me? Like, *Oh yes, Alice, thank you for asking, why yes I did push Brooke off a cliff.* No. And we need uninterrupted time to look through his office. Find some stuff about the trust Kennedy keeps talking about."

"We?"

"I go in, make small talk. Funeral stuff. Offer to get him a drink. Plop in the pills. I looked it up. He'll be out in no time. I text you, turn off the security system, let you in the back way, we go upstairs, yada yada yada."

There are a million ways this could go wrong and a million more reasons why this is horribly unethical. *Drugging* someone. But murdering someone is *also* horrible, and if it *was* Coach . . .

I sigh. There are an awful lot of morally gray areas to being a detective.

"The only way I can justify this is by saying that teachers are always asking us to apply fictional stories to our real lives, so in a way we're just doing applicable research," I tell Alice.

"And committing a few felonies, of course," Alice murmurs.

I take a huge breath and let it out slowly, slowly, slowly.

"Alice Ogilvie, what have you done to my life," I say softly.

Alice slows halfway up Brooke's street.

We pull up at the looming, three-story Spanish-style we staked out before.

"Maybe it was all just an act. On Coach's part," I answer.

"I guess that's what we're going to find out," Alice says.

"Don't forget," I say. "Turn your phone on. Record everything he says before you, you know."

She presses a button and my door pops open. "Happy lurking," she trills.

The *hell*.

I'm crouched behind a thicket of bushes at the end of Brooke's driveway, watching as Alice marches up to the lavish double doors and presses the doorbell. A few seconds later, Coach Donovan appears and waves her in.

The doors close.

Sweat begins to prickle on my forehead. Regret floods through me.

What the hell are we doing? In what world did we possibly decide that sending Alice into the house of someone we think might be a *murderer* was a good idea? Because, you know, what if he *is*? I creep up the side of the yard, sticking close to the house, and ease around the back.

The backyard is like some tropical oasis.

A glistening, narrow, probably heated pool with a Jacuzzi to boot. A freestanding bar and a pool house. Fancy-looking lounge chairs and tables and palm trees. And then, right smack in the middle of a well-tended, lush green lawn, a huge trampoline.

These *people*. As soon as I think it, I'm ashamed. Maybe Alice was right. Maybe I *am* the snob.

My heart is like a drum in my ears. I can feel sweat pooling under my arms, even though the day is overcast and cool. I check my phone. How long has it been? What if he's strangling her? What if he's got her on the couch, a beautiful and pricey pillow pressed to her mouth?

The sliding glass door opens, startling me. Alice peeks her head out, waves me in.

"Security system?" I say.

She points to a square box on the wall. "Done. Brooke and I used to sneak out at night. They never changed the code. Let's go." She starts to go up some stairs.

"Hold on," I say. "I kind of want to . . . I mean . . . he's out, right?"

She raises an eyebrow. "Go see for yourself. I'll be upstairs."

She hustles up the stairs, and I walk slowly to the front room. There he is, slumped on the white couch, his mouth open, hands splayed next to him. Should I poke him? Listen to his breathing? What if she gave him too much?

He gives a little snort. Good. Alive, at least.

I look at the beer bottle on the table. He's out. But we need to make sure, maybe, that he doesn't suspect anything when he wakes up?

I run into the kitchen, grab some more beer bottles from the fridge, and start pouring them out in the sink drain. I leave two on the counter and take the other two back out to the front room, nestle one next to him on the couch, and put the other on the table in front of him.

Then I run up the back stairs to join Alice.

I find her in a room in the middle of the hallway.

From what I saw in Coach's office at school, he's no more organized at home, because this place is a *mess*. Alice is sitting in his desk chair, scrolling through his email.

She shakes her head and holds up a Post-it note scrawled with *JORDAN6!* "Will people never learn about passwords?" she says. "Like, literally stuck to the keyboard."

A printer in the corner springs to life. She's printing stuff out.

Papers all over his desk, sneakers everywhere, dirty T-shirts, trophies on shelves, some crusty-looking takeout boxes. The rest of the house, or the little I've seen of it so far, seems so pristine and untouchable. Maybe this room is the only place Coach feels like himself. I kind of feel a little sorry for him.

And then I don't, because peeking out from a box in the corner is a boob. A photograph of a boob. A boob, I find as I slowly pull it from the box, that belongs to the lunch lady, Mrs. Yang.

Mrs. Yang. I drop it from my fingers like it's hot.

"Hurry up," Alice whispers. "I don't know how long exactly he's going to be out. I crushed up like three of those things."

"Three?"

"Well, they looked *tiny.*"

Next to Alice, I rifle through the papers on his desk. It's mostly school stuff: exams he's grading for his history class (looks like Park failed one), basketball stats and rosters, schedules. The things in his desk drawer are very interesting: nicotine gum (Coach smoked?), a condom packet (what the hell, but I guess, good for practicing safe sex, Coach Donovan; and oh my god, *everyone* seems to have condoms handy; it's like Condomalandia in Castle Cove!), dental floss. I open the bottom file drawer.

Oh.

So Coach *can* keep things in order. Because these folders are all labeled in neat handwriting: *Victoria, Brooke, Family Medical, Insurance, House Repair, Taxes, Pet Health* (oh dear god if there is a dog in this house and it comes after me), and . . .

. . . *Last Will and Testament of Victoria Levy Donovan.*

"Will!" I shout.

"Take it!" Alice shouts back.

I grab a copy of the will and jam it into my backpack. Taxes seems complicated, so I skip it. Insurance seems good, so I shove that one into my backpack, too. There are a couple of credit card bills on his desk, so I snag those.

Alice grabs my arm. "Did you hear that?"

I freeze.

From downstairs comes a loud, annoyed, and brittle voice.

"Foolish oaf. Look at you. Just look at you!"

"Oh my god," Alice says. "It's Lilian. Brooke's grandmother. Oh. My. God."

There's a sound, like someone hitting something.

"What is she doing?" I whisper. "She's going to wake him up."

"Grab everything," Alice says. She heads out the door, and I scrape all the papers from the printer into my backpack. And then I pause.

Coach's phone is right there.

From the hallway, Alice whispers, *"Iris."*

There's probably so much on this phone. Too much to just look at and screenshot right now and—

I drop it into my backpack, heart thumping, and join Alice at the top of the stairs.

An odd clump-clump sound, like a cane, echoes from downstairs, growing louder.

Lilian is walking in the kitchen, getting perilously close to the back stairs.

"Stay here," Alice says in a low voice.

I stand at the top of the stairs, out of sight, pressed against the wall. Alice clatters down the stairs.

"Hello, Lilian."

"Well." Lilian's voice isn't so annoyed now. "Alice Ogilvie. My word, what a beauty you've become."

It sounds almost . . . sad.

Oh. Brooke. Alice . . . of course, would remind her of Brooke.

"I trust you've viewed my son-in-law, drunk on the couch. I'm not particularly thrilled with *that*. To what do I owe your presence in this house, may I ask?"

"He was fine when I got here," Alice says smoothly. "And I just wanted to pay my respects. And then he kind of . . . dropped off. I was upstairs, looking in the bathroom. I was worried maybe he'd, you know, taken something?"

"I should only be so lucky. This is a terrible business, what's happened, but at least he'll be out of my hair for good this time. He's been a thorn in my heart for a decade."

Thorn in her heart? My pulse jumps. *Interesting.*

"Is that so?" Alice says mildly.

"Don't get me started. Now, help me up the stairs. My sister Caroline's at the funeral home. I need some documents in the office and a dress. You'll help me. You know what Brooke liked. She should be buried in something she liked."

Her voice has softened again.

"Yes, of course," Alice says. "But do you want to sit awhile? Talk? It's been so long and I . . . I'm just so sorry, Lilian. I'm especially sorry I had to be the one to text you about Brooke."

"Thank god you *did,* my dear. I wonder just how long Matthew would have waited to ask for help. I'm positively mortified by his behavior, though I can't say I'm surprised. He's certainly . . ." She trails off. "Never mind."

There's a pause, and then Alice says carefully, "He's what?"

"Don't mind me. Just the muddled emotions of an old woman getting the best of me. My family has long been a tangled mess. Misfortune is an unnatural air I'm forced to breathe.

After a while, you don't know any different. Just help me up the stairs so I can get these things done. I don't want to sit. I've had a hip replacement. The doctor had cleavers for hands and it feels as though he replaced my mottled bone with wood."

Oh god. They're coming up the stairs. I whirl around, open the first door at the top of the stairs, and close it softly behind me.

Clomp. Shuffle. Clomp. Shuffle.

"You'll help me pick out something lovely, won't you, Alice?"

"Of course, Lilian. Brooke has tons of beautiful dresses. Oops, watch your step." Alice's voice is unnaturally loud.

"You don't have to shout, dear girl. It's my hip that's gone bad, not my ears."

They need a dress.

Slowly, I turn around, my heart sinking clear down to my feet. My body runs cold.

Polaroids clipped to string along the walls, a vision board, fairy lights, a plush-looking canopy bed, pom-poms delicately tucked atop the vanity mirror, the crimson and gold Castle Cove High colors gleaming in the shafts of late-afternoon sunlight streaming from her balcony doors.

I'm in Brooke Donovan's room. Frantically, I look around. There's one other door, but it's probably the closet, so I can't hide in *there,* because *that* is where they'll look for a dress.

The balcony is the only choice. There is no other way out of this. There is absolutely no way.

I open the double doors, step out, and look down.

I can climb over the balcony railing and try to drop down, possibly breaking my legs in the process. Or maybe I can grow wings and fly through the air to the pool and drown, which seems more and more palatable by the minute.

Or I can do what I am doing without even thinking about it, because I can barely feel my body anymore, at all, because sheer adrenaline has made me a tight, electric thing. So far today I have stolen documents, seen the lunch lady's boobs, and drugged a high school basketball coach.

I've done all that; I can do *this*.

I hoist myself on top of the balcony railing and half jump, half fall, onto the trampoline below.

CHAPTER TWENTY-ONE

"Take no risks and be alert to danger. That is all."

—AGATHA CHRISTIE,

AND THEN THERE WERE NONE

MY HEART IS PRACTICALLY exploding through my chest as we reach Brooke's door. I have no idea where Iris went, but I have to assume it was into one of the rooms close to the top of the stairwell.

Lilian pushes open the door and I brace myself, expecting to see Iris frozen in front of us, or her feet sticking out from under Brooke's bed.

Instead, the room is empty. I breathe a sigh of relief, then notice the balcony doors; they're open, a breeze lifting into the air the long silk drapes that Brooke and her mom picked out for Brooke's thirteenth birthday. Oh good lord; did Iris jump out the window?

"That's odd." Lilian walks around me to the doors, pulling them closed and turning the lock. "Matthew really is losing the thread." Her mouth puckers. "Not that I expected any different." She turns back to me. "You'll learn, Alice dear, that as you get older, people surprise you less and less. Now, if you'll be so kind, can you show me where Brooke keeps—I'm sorry, *kept*—her dresses?"

Ten minutes later, dresses in hand, we make our way back downstairs. Coach is still knocked out on the couch.

"How much did that man drink?" Lilian considers him with obvious distaste. "I will never understand what my daughter saw in him." She shakes her head. "She could have had anyone she wanted, but after Brooke's father did what he did . . ." She shakes her head. "No matter. The past is the past. Best to leave it there." She approaches Coach's motionless body and pokes it with her cane. He grunts and rolls to his back, drool snaking down his chin. Gross.

It appears Lilian has the same thought, because she wrinkles her nose and pokes him again, this time much, much harder.

"Ow." He comes to with a groan, flailing his arm out in the direction of the cane. His eyes are glassy and bloodshot, and his hair is mussed, sticking up everywhere off his head. When he sees Lilian and me standing there, he blinks a few times. "Wha—" He rubs his eyes. "What happened? Lilian? Alice? I don't . . ." He struggles up to a seated position, knocking over the beer bottle next to him. He looks at it in confusion. "Did I drink . . ." He sees the bottles strewn on the table, and his face grows red. "Did I . . . oh god." I almost feel sorry for him; he looks so out of it and lost. But then I remember he might have killed my best friend, and that sympathy goes right out the window.

"Lilian, I didn't realize you were coming over," he says, his words slurry.

"I needed a dress. For Brooke. Don't worry, Alice helped me. Since you were . . . incapacitated."

"I don't know how that happened . . . ," he starts.

Lilian cuts him off. "I'm sure you don't. That said, Matthew, I think we need to have a conversation. About where we go from here. I think we both know we're entering our final chapter together."

Well, *this* sounds like a conversation I should hear. I start to take a seat on the couch and then realize Lilian is looking at me pointedly.

"Yes?" I say sweetly, giving her my best innocent smile. But I should have known better than to try and play the master.

She raises a brow. "Thank you for all your help, Alice, but you may go now."

"I—" I think fast, trying to make up a reason I should stay, but she's quick for an old woman who just had hip surgery. Before I can say another word, she has me by my elbow and is leading me toward the front door and shutting it behind me.

Outside, I realize that I better get a move on and figure out where the hell Iris went. I send her a text as I'm hurrying to my car but am stopped short by a rusty Honda swinging into the U-shaped drive. It parks next to a black Bentley that must be Lilian's. Her driver sits in the car, playing on his phone.

I squint into the falling dusk, trying to make out the new-comer, but the car door swings open before I can place them.

"Hi, Alice," says Ms. Westmacott, surprise tingeing her voice, as she steps out of the car. She leans back in and pulls a big cardboard box off the passenger seat. "What are you doing here?"

I think the question is really what the hell is *she* doing here? Are she and Coach dating again? Brooke would be so pissed; she was so happy when Coach finally dumped that lady. Brooke always said Westmacott was super intense and annoying, but I think she was mostly jealous that her dad was spending so much time with someone other than her.

I hold up a hand in greeting. "Oh hey," I say, and continue on my way to my car. "I was just helping Coach out. Funeral stuff. Gotta run."

Westmacott, of course, starts talking like we're having a conversation in her office, and I freeze in my tracks, turning back to her slowly.

"This is all so sad, isn't it, Alice?" She balances the box she's holding on one arm to gesture to the house behind us. As she does, the box slips. She attempts to grab it, but it clatters to the ground, contents spilling out onto the driveway. "Shoot." Her face goes red, and she bends and starts to throw things back into it.

I sigh. I need to go get Iris, but I have a bad feeling it would not look great if I ignored my guidance counselor when she was in need. "Can I help?" I walk over to her.

"No. No," she says without looking at me. I grab a ratty T-shirt off the ground, but she yanks it out of my hands. "I said, *no.*" Her tone freezes me in place as she throws the shirt into the box, where it lands, draped over the rest of the contents.

She turns to me, forcing a smile. "Sorry. It's just been a day. This is Matt's stuff. From when we were dating. It's . . . well, sometimes, no matter how painful it is, you have to let things go. I'm sure you understand that, Alice."

Good god, why is she bringing that stuff over here *now*? Like, talk about bad timing, lady. Whatever. The last thing I want is to get drawn into weird teacher drama. I put on my prettiest smile. "That's nice of you. So sorry, but I really do have to go."

And with that, I turn and head straight to my car.

I find Iris a half mile down the road, tromping down the side of a grassy hill, dirt streaked across her shirt. I flick on my blinker, slow, pull onto the narrow shoulder, and stop. I climb out of the car, waving at her like mad.

"Down here!" I call when she sees me. I'm about to say more, when a truck zooms past us on the road. We should probably get out of here.

She runs the rest of the way down the hill, straight past me, and to the car, pulling open the passenger-side door. "Let's go!" she says as she drops her bag onto the floor of the car.

I drive like a madwoman back to my house, squeal to a stop in the driveway.

"Where did you learn to drive like that?" Iris says. Her face is a little green.

"Last summer, I spent some time in Tuscany and had a moped. Honestly, Castle Cove's hills are nothing compared to——" I cut off, realizing she's looking at me in amusement. "I'm a good driver," I mutter. "Whatever. Can we get to the important part now, please? Gimme that bag!" I grab the bag at Iris's feet and haul it up into my lap. "We need to look at all of this," I say, digging through it. "Wait—his phone?" I pull it out of the bag, holding it up like a trophy. "You got his phone? OMG this is *amazing*, Iris!"

"I know. Who knows what he's been up to? This might give us some clues. But wait." Iris holds up a hand. "I want to see what's on there, too, but we need more space. We need to spread all this stuff out and really see it. Also, we should get help from my friends. Spike and Neil and Zora? Are you still okay with that? There's a lot of stuff to go through here—we have to do it fast." She pauses, eyes searching my face.

They *were* helpful the other night. I nod. "Okay. Just make sure Neil knows who's in charge."

In the house, we yell a quick hello to Brenda in the kitchen and hurry upstairs, where I grab my laptop from my bedroom. Then we head straight back down to our investigation room. It's time to get serious.

Once in the room, Iris starts pulling stuff out of her bag. She carefully sets down onto the coffee table a phone, the credit card statements, the email printouts, the file folders, and the will, and we gaze at it in awe.

I grab the phone off the table first. "I can't believe we have his *phone.* This is gold." I tap the screen, and a photo of Brooke, Victoria, and Coach appears, sending a little shock through me. I clench my jaw, ignoring the photo, and I type in the most obvious passcode, Brooke's birthday. It vibrates. Wrong. I try *123456* next, because Coach is many things, but a brainiac is not one of them. It vibrates again.

"Try *070573,*" Iris says. Her laptop is now set up on the table in front of us, and she's bent down in front of the screen, reading something off it.

"What's that?"

"His birthday." She meets my eyes and smiles. "I just Googled it."

"Smart." I type in the numbers.

And the phone opens.

"Whoa," I breathe.

"Oh my god." Iris straightens from her computer, meeting my eyes. "Okay, okay, first, look at his texts! Or, like, his email? I don't know—how do old people communicate?"

"Texts, I think?" I say, and then something dawns on me. "Oh crap. We need to do it quick, though. I just realized that once he notices it's missing, he'll probably ping it to figure out where it is."

"Oh, you're right," Iris says. "Let's work quick because I do not want to get arrested."

"We won't. We can do this," I say. I sound more reassuring than I feel, but what choice do we have?

I swipe over to his messages, scrolling down the list of names. I stop when I see it: *Brooke.*

Jesus. The last few messages between them were all from her—

Dad are you around? Need a ride.

Heading to the lookout. Pick me up there?

Hello?

Brooke texted Coach that night? Why would he claim that he hadn't heard from her the next morning when I saw him in the hallway? My stomach knots. "This is weird. . . ."

"What is?" asks Iris. I hold the phone out so she can read the screen. "The texts from Brooke?"

"Yeah . . . I mean, no, the texts by themselves aren't, but . . ." I tell her how Coach acted like he hadn't heard from Brooke the morning of November 1. "But, look, she *did* text him. After the party, in that gap of time between her leaving and . . ." I trail off. I can't bring myself to say the words, still.

Iris reads the texts again, brow furrowing. "That's . . . that's *really* sketchy of Coach. Why would he lie to you? Unless . . ."

"Unless he had a *reason* to lie," I say. "We should definitely take photos of these or something before we ditch the phone. To make sure we have copies."

Iris nods. "Good call." She snaps a picture with her phone.

I click on one name that's just listed as *Kevin.*

Where are you? You better show up this time. It was also received on Halloween—at 11:56 p.m. Coach had not responded.

I nudge Iris. "Look at this one!"

"Why was someone asking Coach where he was at midnight on a school day?" Iris says. She grabs the phone from me and scrolls up the conversation. "There's only one more text between them . . . Wait—it was sent earlier that day. *Meet me at midnight tonight.*" She wrinkles her nose. "Normal people don't plan meetings in the middle of the night."

"No kidding," I reply, taking the phone back from her, staring at the messages. "There's something super shady about that."

"I think we need to find out who Kevin is." Iris scribbles *KEVIN* down in her notebook in big block letters along with the phone number.

"Let's see what else is in here." I click over to some of Coach's other messages. There's one to a contact listed as *RA* that says, *My security system is malfunctioning.*

"Do you know what this means?" I show it to Iris, who shakes her head.

"Google the number to see who it is?" she suggests. "That just sounds mother-sucking cryptic."

"Good call." I type the number into my search bar and press Enter. "No results," I tell Iris.

"Hmmm," she says, thinking. "I guess he *could* have been having issues with his alarm system."

"Yeah," I say. I swipe back to his main list of messages. There are a lot of names I recognize as teachers at our school—*female* teachers, including Westmacott.

"Ew, I just saw Westmacott at Coach's," I say with a shudder. "I do *not* need to see what *they're* texting about, thank you very much. Although"—I skim their last few messages—"these aren't so much sexts as *Sorry I'm breaking up with you because my daughter doesn't like you* ones. Jeez, Coach. Way to throw Brooke under the bus there."

"Wait, back up. Westmacott was at Coach's?" asks Iris. "Why?"

"I know, random, right? She said she was dropping some of his stuff off."

Iris makes a face. "That's some odd timing. I mean, his daughter just died."

"Right? That's what I thought, too." I shrug. "Then again, she's a strange lady."

I turn back to the phone, clicking on a few more text conversations. "Good lord. This is nuts. In a *ton* of these messages to teachers he must have been dating, Coach uses Brooke as an excuse as to why he can't see them anymore. I mean, I know that she didn't like Westmacott much when they were dating, but I don't think she ever *knew* about most of these people. She would have been totally skeeved out." I start reading a few of them out loud to Iris. "*I can't see you anymore. Brooke is too fragile. Will miss your*— Eww, oh my god, definitely not reading the rest of that out loud. Okay, thank you, I have seen quite enough." I hold the phone away from me, pinching it in two fingers. Between those messages and Kennedy's video, it's quite possible I have been permanently scarred.

"Check his pics next," says Iris excitedly.

I glance at the time on the phone. At least thirty minutes have gone by since leaving his house. What if he pings the phone and comes to find us? What if he pings it and sees it's at *my house*?

"Okay, but we have to ditch the phone soon," I say. "I'm surprised he hasn't already activated Find My iPhone. Lilian must be giving him an earful. Where are we going to put this thing? Should we throw it back onto his front lawn?"

She shakes her head vehemently. "We can*not* return to the scene of our crime, Ogilvie."

Fair enough. "Okay. Let me think." I open his photos app and glance down at the first picture as I say this. It's a very, very, *very* disturbing shot of Ms. Weaver, the drama teacher, wearing nothing but a bra.

"Ew! Ew! Ew!" I throw the phone at Iris, who looks at the screen in horror. "Okay. I'm done with this. Seen enough. Let's ditch it, please."

We're interrupted by a commotion at the door of the room.

A male voice that sounds a lot like Neil says, "Hey, what's up!" I look up to see Spike, Neil, and Zora standing there holding several boxes of pizza, a flustered Brenda behind them.

"Do you know these people, Alice?" she asks. Shoot, I forgot to tell her they were coming. I haven't exactly had a lot of visitors in the past few months, so she must be wondering what is happening.

"We told you, we were *invited*," says Zora.

"Yes, sorry, Brenda. I meant to tell you. They're here for a . . . class project." I cross my fingers that none of them disagree.

"Yup," says Spike. "A class *project*."

Neil winks at me.

I close my eyes. I better not regret this.

CHAPTER TWENTY-TWO

ZORA AND NEIL PUT down pizza boxes on the coffee table, and Spike looks around at Alice's investigation-room handiwork, settling on the murder board. "From a purely practical standpoint, I agree with putting Coach here. Stepdad, inheritance, probably insurance money, meeting whoever this person *Kevin* is. It's all very seedy Lifetime movie, but Cole Fielding," he murmurs, looking at the murder board and then back to us. "Really?"

"He's not a suspect anymore; that's why we crossed his name out," Alice says. "He was, but he was, um, doing some very lascivious things with Kennedy that night. On video. So. He has an alibi."

Spike blushes. "Alrighty, then."

Zora folds a piece of pizza in half and pulls off some dripping cheese. "He was hooking up with Brooke last spring, Spike. How could you not know that?"

She studies the board. "Did you guys make a timeline yet?"

"Timeline?" I ask. I'm still trying to take pictures of Coach's texts, but it's getting tedious.

"Yeah, you know. Where everyone was the night of the party, especially after. Alibis need to cohere to timelines. What's Brooke's estimated time of death? I haven't seen any info on the news about an autopsy report. So, like if Coach has an alibi during the time they think she died, perhaps he didn't do it, you know? Does he have proof of where he was?"

Alice and I look at each other.

"We were *getting* to that," she says. "Let me see what I can do."

She pulls out her burner phone. Her contact. Of course.

"Iris," Neil asks, sitting next to me. "What exactly are you up to?"

He slips Coach's phone from me. A giant smile spreads across his face. "Iris Adams, *why* do you have Coach's phone?"

Alice grabs it from him. "It was an accident, obviously. We were there gathering information, and we *need* to return it before he notices."

"Wait," Spike says. "You were where getting what? And how exactly is having that phone an accident?"

Alice sighs. "We went to Coach's, we looked in his office, we got a bunch of stuff"—she points to the will, the credit card bills, and the folders on the table by the pizza boxes—"and we also got his phone. We've been taking pics of his texts."

Zora whistles. "That's like fifteen kinds of robbery at once, people, but also, please explain to me how you were able to get this. At Coach's house. Without him knowing."

Neil takes the phone back from Alice. "Don't take photos. Too long. We need to duplicate it and then I'll take care of it."

He grabs my phone, his laptop, and Coach's phone and goes and sits in the corner, typing fast.

"Uh. Does he know what he's doing?" I ask.

Spike nods. "Yes. Don't question it. The less you know about Neil's capabilities, the better. Also, this board sincerely lacks spice. We should have photos of our victim and our suspects. The string is a nice touch, but I like strong visuals. Mind?"

He fiddles with a printer on a desk in front of the fireplace and opens up his laptop. In a few seconds, a photo of Brooke slides out. He tacks it to the murder board above her card. There she is, beautiful and laughing, on the beach, her shoulders slightly sunburned.

"I remember that day," Alice says softly. "That's before I was with Steve, when it was just the two of us."

We're all quiet, looking at the girl on the board.

Spike puts his head down, goes back to printing out photos.

"He's gonna want that phone back, you two," Zora warns.

Alice clears her throat. "We incapacitated Coach, you don't need to know how, just that he's currently very, very foggy. We have some time, I think, but not a lot."

She checks her phone and nudges me. "It's going to take my person some time. Can you check with yours?"

> It's me. We need you. Can you come?
> Have some info for you and do you have
> autopsy report?

Hello, ICB. Tell me where you are and I need
food.

I text Ricky the address and turn to the room. "Someone's coming who can help. In the meantime, here's what we know and what we think we know."

"Wait, who's coming?" Spike says, looking up from the photos he's printing out. "How many people are involved in this now?"

"I'll get to that," I say. "First, we saw Steve in jail. Bottom line is, he said he remembers nothing after the fight at the party. Says he woke up in the woods, confused—"

Alice interrupts. "But that can be explained, because later, we found out Helen Park drugged Brooke's drink, to knock her out so Helen could hook up with Steve—"

"But Steve drank it instead," I finish. "That's why he can't remember anything except waking up in the woods and then going to Dotty's Doughnuts."

Zora tilts her head. "Helen Park is drugging people now?"

"Yup," Alice says. "Everyone assumes Steve was drunk, but he wasn't. It was alcohol and Ambien."

"And I thought Helen was such a nice girl," Spike says. "She's always borrowing my pencils in calc and *returning* them. No one *ever* returns them."

"You have a low bar for kindness, Spike," Zora says.

"But," I say, trying to get them back on track. "The police say they found one of Steve's sneakers in the woods and prints by the Lookout, where Brooke went over. But Dotty says Steve was wearing *both* of his shoes when he came in to get coffee and left one in the bathroom when he was washing up. She gave it to the cops to give back to him and suddenly—"

"They say they found the sneaker in the woods," Alice says.

"Plus, the surveillance tape at Dotty's that would prove Steve was wearing both when he came in? The police took that, too, and there's no record of it in the files."

Zora gets up and starts pacing, munching a piece of pizza. "Hmm. That seems . . . like a frame-up? Did the police put the shoe in the woods? Why Steve?"

"That's what we're trying to figure out," I say. "We don't think the police ever considered any other people as suspects."

Neil stands up. "That's crazy, if it's true. The Castle Cove PD framing softhearted basketball players? Didn't see that coming."

He hands my phone to me and tucks Coach's phone in his pocket. He slides one of the pizza boxes off the table. "I'm out. I can handle Coach's phone. I deliver pizza to his house like three times a week. If he's messed up from whatever you gave him, he won't remember making the call. He likes me. I tutor half his players."

He turns to leave right as Ricky arrives in the doorway.

"Who are you and why are you taking the food?" she asks. "I'm starving."

Ricky's eyes travel the room, taking in each of us and all the evidence we have spread out. "Let's lay down some ground rules. First of all, I'm Steve's lawyer. Second, I don't know any of you. Except for Iris. And Moneybags here. I never saw you, you never saw me. Agreed?"

"Moneybags?" Alice says. "That's a tad rude. Is that really necessary?"

"If the shoe fits, Moneybags," Ricky says.

"I'm liking all this secrecy," Zora says. "Very mysterious."

"Great," Ricky says, sitting down. "What do you have and what do you need to know?"

Alice stands up and goes to the murder board, now filled with printed photos of Brooke, Coach, Cole, Kennedy, and Alice herself. She unpins hers and turns it around so it's just a white page.

"For the sake of brevity, everyone," she says, "I did not kill my former best friend. Moving on, in order to eliminate suspects, we need to know what time Brooke died. Approximately."

"Autopsy time," Spike says, cracking a seltzer water.

Ricky dips into a folder on her lap. "Detective Thompson will be giving a press conference tomorrow, formally charging Steve Anderson with the murder of Brooke Donovan. I'm hoping it's involuntary manslaughter, which means it was unintentional. He'd get four to six years, maybe. Second-degree means a possible fifteen years. But it all depends on what the coroner's report, the final version, that is, says. Everything right now will be based on the initial findings. What we don't want, especially if a jury trial is involved, is the option for first-degree murder, because—"

"That's twenty-five to life," I tell Zora and Spike. Zora whistles.

Alice grimaces, then quickly rearranges her face so it's a blank slate. I think she doesn't want the other kids to know how much twenty-five to life scares her.

"I've got initial details from the coroner's report. It's a little hairy, so are you ready, people?"

We all nod.

Ricky reads from a document in her lap. "Brooke Donovan went into the water between approximately eleven p.m. and two a.m. Since her body wasn't found until two days later, there was significant decomposition owing to salt water, strong currents, and sea life. What's interesting here is the cause of death."

Ricky looks up from her documents. "This is real life, guys. Not a book or a movie, you get it?"

"Just say it," Zora urges. "We're not children."

"Actually, you are," Ricky answers. "Her skull was fractured, most likely from the fall to the rocks, before she was swept out. Scratches on her hands, knees, legs, possibly from hitting the cliffside on the way down. Decomposition due to time in water. Time of death between midnight and two a.m."

Alice's fingers are wound tightly together. "That's not . . . I mean, awful? I mean it is, of course, because she's dead . . . but, it seems like she was just pushed?"

Ricky nods. "Or fell in the middle of a lovers' quarrel, and the alleged assailant never contacted authorities. It's possible a final report will say, had someone been called, she might have lived. We don't know how long she might have been alive. At the bottom.

"The good news, if you can call it that, is that Steve is a pretty good citizen. Mentors kids, never in trouble. Handsome, clean-cut. A jury will *want* to think he's not a killer. He could be *their* son. Not a drinker, though he apparently passed out in the woods. It's entirely possible he *did.* How the sneaker got there after Dotty's is another matter. And I wish to hell he could remember *something.*"

"But he was drugged," Alice interjects. "Of course he remembers nothing!"

Ricky gives her a sympathetic look. "I know that, Alice. But the police didn't tox screen him. That won't hold up in court. There's no proof, even if your friend comes forward, though I love the *Riverdale* vibes of what she did. It might raise some concerns with a jury, but also . . . it might raise other issues. People on Ambien? Have been known to get violent and exhibit odd behavior. Which also leads me to the videos of your friend, a big guy, manhandling his much smaller girlfriend. Like I said in the bar, if a jury sees *that*? Not good."

"Damn," Spike says.

"But what if the police planted the shoe?" Zora asks. "What about that angle?"

Ricky closes the folder on her lap and reaches for a slice of pizza. "Does anyone have any beer? I'm dying for a beer."

"We are *children,*" Alice reminds her.

"Right," Ricky says, winking. "You just drink at parties in the woods." She looks at Zora. "If you want to make a case for the police scapegoating Steve, that's fine, but I'd need some evidence of that, because that's a . . ." She makes an explosion gesture with her hand.

"Ricky," Alice says, exasperation in her voice. "You've told us everything that's going to bring Steve down. What exactly is your defense of him? I mean, that's your *job.*"

Ricky lets out a slow sigh. "My defense is . . . my client had an altercation with his girlfriend, *possibly* exacerbated by being drugged, and then he passed out in the woods, so he couldn't have done it. I mean, that's it. If they charge him with involuntary manslaughter, he'll serve some time. It'll go down as an accident. I'd love to know why a sneaker belonging to him suddenly appeared in the woods after the fact, and I'll bring this up, but Dotty isn't the most coherent witness. Mainly . . ." She pauses. "Mainly, like you, I have to lead the jury in the direction of someone else who could have done it. Plant a reasonable doubt."

She looks at Alice pointedly.

"Just *stop*," Alice says.

"She's right, though," I say. "Not that you did it, Alice, but she has to make it look like someone *other* than Steve could have done it, to distract a jury. You're kind of a natural fit."

"Sorry, Moneybags," Ricky says. "I might lean in the direction of another person, too. I don't know yet. I have reams of interviews to read through; I have to talk to Anderson again. There could be someone else out there, not on your board. Who knows?"

"Wait," Zora says. "Interviews? Because . . . did they interview Coach Donovan? I'm asking because this . . ."

She holds up some papers.

". . . is the last will and testament of Victoria Levy Donovan, which says that once Brooke turns eighteen, Victoria's money transfers to her, and Coach is no longer a trustee, whatever that means, and oh my god . . ."

Alice grabs the will from Zora. "Oh, holy moly," she breathes.

"What?" I ask, jumping up and peering over her shoulder. She points to a specific section and reads out loud as I follow on the page.

```
If at any time before the age of
eighteen, the beneficiary, BROOKE LEVY
DONOVAN, becomes deceased or suffers
irreparable bodily injury requiring
long-term care, her legal guardian,
MATTHEW PAUL DONOVAN, will receive
a lump sum of five million dollars,
```

```
payable upon relinquishment of all care
activities, legal guardianship, legal
matters, and claims to any and all of
BROOKE LEVY DONOVAN'S assets now and in
perpetuity.
```

"Guys," Spike says, waggling the credit card bills at us. "Looks like Coach was in the hole for about three hundred grand."

"So, Coach!" Zora says. "There's a whole lot of iffy stuff here right now. Owes money, meeting mysterious guy the night his daughter is pushed off a cliff—"

"Doesn't answer his daughter's texts that night, asking for a ride," Alice continues.

"Wait." Ricky throws her half-eaten slice of pizza on the coffee table. "Brooke texted him? He specifically said in his initial interview that he hadn't heard from her."

Alice looks at me and I look at Alice.

Alice hands Ricky my phone, which is now, sort of (and for how long?), also Coach's phone.

Ricky skims the phone and hands it back to Alice. "I don't even want to know," she says. "How you got this, who duplicated it, etc."

Ricky opens her folder back up and reads from her notes. "Matt Donovan's alibi, Lucy Hollister, confirmed he was at her house from two a.m. to around three a.m., but he can't account for where he was before that. Says he was grading papers. After that, he says he went home and went to bed and assumed Brooke was at her friend's house. Besides the phone, what else do you have? I need *everything* you can think of."

And then all of us start talking at once, telling her about the text from Kevin, Brooke's fights with Coach, and his canoodling with teachers.

In the middle of this, when no one is looking at me, I text Alice.

> That person you know who knows things. Can you press them about the sneaker and the police? Because why would they move the sneaker and try to frame Steve? Maybe your friend can find something out. Dirty cops?

In the back of my mind, though, even if we have *some* evidence that seemingly implicates Coach, anybody on that board could have still done it. Especially *Unknown*.

MURDER BOARD

Steve Anderson

~~Helen Park~~

~~Rebecca Kennedy~~

~~Alice Ogilvie~~

~~Cole Fielding~~

Coach Donovan

~~Accident~~

Unknown

TIMELINE

OCTOBER 31

ALICE

9:00 p.m. Alice arrives at party, altercation with Brooke and Steve

9:30 p.m. Alice leaves party

IRIS

9:35 p.m. Iris sees Alice driving away from Levy Castle on Highway 1

9:45 p.m. Iris encounters Brooke running on Highway 1

Last known sighting of Brooke

COACH

9:00 p.m. to 10:30 p.m. Grading?

10:30 p.m. to 2:00 a.m. *UNKNOWN*

10:30 p.m. First text from Brooke (unanswered)

10:38 p.m. Second text from Brooke (unanswered)

10:40 p.m. Third text from Brooke (unanswered)

2:00 a.m. to 3:00 a.m. At Lucy Hollister's house

3:00 a.m. Home (allegedly)

7:55 a.m. Alice sees him at school

KENNEDY
8:00 p.m. to 11:00 p.m. Castle party
11:30 p.m. to ?? Time-stamped video with Cole Fielding
?? Kennedy goes home. Brooke never shows (doesn't realize this until the next morning)
7:52 a.m. Alice sees her at school

COLE
Same as Rebecca Kennedy

STEVE
8:00 p.m. Party
9:15 p.m. Altercation with Brooke
10:30 p.m. Leaves party
2:00 a.m. to approximately 7:15 a.m. Claims he fell asleep in woods; no proof
7:25 a.m. Confirmed at Dotty's Doughnuts
8:00 a.m. Confirmed sighting at school

BROOKE
8:00 p.m. At party
9:15 p.m. Altercation with Steve
9:45 p.m. Leaves party; seen by Iris Adams on Highway 1
10:30 p.m. First text to Coach (unanswered)
10:38 p.m. Second text to Coach (unanswered)
10:40 p.m. Third text to Coach (unanswered)
Estimated time of death: 12:00 p.m. to 2:00 a.m.

CHAPTER TWENTY-THREE

ALICE
NOVEMBER 8
11:22 A.M.

"It's like all those quiet people, when they do lose
their tempers, they lose them with a vengeance."
—AGATHA CHRISTIE, *THE ABC MURDERS*

AFTER HISTORY, I'M WALKING to my next class, scrolling
through my phone, when I slam into a brick wall.

"Ow!" I jump back and my phone clatters to the ground.
Rubbing my shoulder that collided with the hard thing, I bend
to grab my phone.

"Hello, Alice," says a low voice above me. A familiar voice.
I look up from my crouch, realizing that what I ran into was in
fact not a brick wall but a person. A very, very tall person, with
a very, very angry expression on his face.

Coach. Standing in front of me with his arms crossed, face
red and eyes blazing. I've never seen him this mad, not in person, but immediately a memory hits me. Last year, Steve showed
up at my house after one of their away games, shaken, rambling about how Coach lost his temper during the second half

and got kicked off the court. I haven't thought about it until now—it had seemed like an exaggeration. But now I get it. The look on his face is pure fury.

Oh. Oh *no*. My stomach drops. This is bad. I rise slowly, phone in hand. I start to text Iris—*SOS* or something to inform her that I'm pretty sure I'm about to get murdered—but before I can, Coach grabs my phone.

"I don't think you need that right now."

I swallow, plastering on a smile to keep my mouth from shaking. I remind myself we're in a very public place. The hallway is buzzing with my classmates. Safety in numbers.

"Hi Coach. I'm *so* glad to see you're feeling better!" I say, somehow managing to keep my voice steady, even though there's a good chance I might puke at any moment. God, I really should be an actress.

"Don't try to pull that with me. We need to talk, Alice," he says in a quiet voice. He looks around, seeming to register for the first time the many, many eyes watching us. "Let's go to my office, please."

He must think I'm much stupider than I actually am, if he thinks that's going to happen.

I shake my head. "I'm sorry, Coach, but I'll be late for next period if I don't leave right now." I try to dart past him, but he's already in front of me. Damn, for a giant man he moves quick.

"Alice, this is not a joke." He drops his voice even more, leaning toward me. "You were at my house yesterday . . . ," he starts, "and my office was a *mess*. And then some kid showed up with a pizza that I didn't order and asked to use my bathroom. After he left, I found my phone stuffed in my bathroom medicine cabinet, and I'm sure I didn't put it there." The expression in his eyes sends a chill down my spine. "You need to tell me *right now*—what happened?"

I tilt my head, blinking at him innocently. "I'm not sure what you mean? I came to your house and we chatted. You were . . . drinking," I whisper. "I know everything with Brooke has been hard. When Lilian showed up, I tried to cover for you, but you know how bossy she is . . ." I trail off. "Anyway, I really have to go——"

He cuts me off. "Alice Ogilvie, I know you did something to me yesterday. I know I didn't make that mess in my office—at home *or* at school. My picture of Brooke at her debutante ball is missing. I didn't think much of it until yesterday, but now . . ." His eyes narrow. "*And* I'm pretty sure . . . I'm *pretty* sure I only had one beer. I'm going to find out what you did, you better believe it." He's moved uncomfortably close to me. I take a step back and he steps forward. A wild expression has transformed his face. His voice rises. "I always knew you were trouble. Coming into my house and encouraging Brooke to do all sorts of things. And after what you pulled last summer." He sneers. "I hope you realize that no one will believe you even if——"

"Is everything okay here?" a voice from behind interrupts him. "Coach Donovan, what are you doing at school?"

I turn and find Ms. Westmacott, arms crossed, wearing an odd expression. "Is everything okay here, Alice?"

Coach steps back. It appears to be dawning on him that coming into school to confront a seventeen-year-old girl was not his smartest move. A large crowd has gathered, and several people have their phones out, recording us.

He clears his throat. "Yes. We're fine. I was just talking to

Alice about . . . details. You know, with the funeral." He hands my phone back to me.

Westmacott looks between us, her gaze locking on me in a way that makes my skin prickle, and I nod. I just want to get the hell out of here and tell Iris what happened, and if going along with Coach's stupid lie is the way to do it, I don't care.

"I thought I heard . . ." Westmacott pauses and then shakes her head. "Never mind. Matthew, I'm sure Alice has to get to her next class. I'll walk you out."

Coach hesitates, then nods. As Westmacott turns to lead him away, he leans down close to me one last time and growls, "I hope you know this isn't over, Alice Ogilvie."

I give him my toothiest smile and flutter my fingers *goodbye* at him. But as soon as he rounds the corner and the crowd around us disperses, I slump back against a locker and type out a text to Iris with shaking hands.

Tessa Hopkins: I'm live at the Castle Cove Police Department. Any minute now, Detective Thompson, the lead investigator in the Brooke Donovan case, will formally announce charges against eighteen-year-old Steve Anderson. Anderson is expected to be charged with involuntary manslaughter.

Detective Thompson: Good evening. I'll be giving prepared remarks and taking questions after. As you know, Brooke Donovan went missing on Halloween night after a large party at the Levy Castle. We initially suspected she had run away, based on the fact that another adolescent in Castle Cove disappeared in a similar manner last summer. That particular teenager returned of her own volition. Unfortunately, that was not the case with Ms. Donovan.

We believe Ms. Donovan fought with her boyfriend, Mr. Anderson, on Halloween night, and the last known sighting of her was on Highway One shortly after their argument. After interviewing her friends and family, particularly Mr. Anderson, it became evident to us that his actions the evening of her disappearance were highly suspect. There were a number of troubling inconsistencies during interviews with Mr. Anderson. In addition, items belonging to the suspect were found in the approximate area where Ms. Donovan was last seen alive. Ms. Donovan's body was found two days after her disappearance. The initial coroner's report states that she likely died due to injuries sustained in her fall from the cliff. Whether she was pushed or fell after a struggle, we do not know yet. At this time, we offer thoughts and prayers to the victim's family and ask that they are given privacy and time to mourn. This was a thorough and intelligently run investigation, with many thanks to the special help from Mary Malone, who came in from out of town to assist in leading this investigation. At this time, Steven Anderson is being charged with involuntary manslaughter. Upon receipt of the final autopsy report, this charge could change significantly.

Tessa Hopkins: Detective Thompson, can you tell us more about the evidence linking Steve Anderson to Brooke Donovan's death? Was his DNA found on her body or near the crime scene?

Detective Thompson: Now, she was in the water for two days, and as you know, there can be significant decomposition and other effects from salt, debris, and sea life. DNA testing is being conducted from evidence found at the cliff site, the body of the deceased, and the wooded area.

Reporter: What other evidence do you have linking the suspect to the victim's murder?

Reporter: Can you tell us if Brooke was still alive for a time after she fell?

Reporter: Had she been sexually assaulted?

Reporter: Do you have DNA linking Anderson to Donovan?

Reporter: Where is Brooke Donovan's phone?

Detective Thompson: We are in the process of compiling DNA evidence. We do not believe she was sexually assaulted. Several partygoers recorded a physical confrontation between Ms. Donovan and Mr. Anderson that evening, which leads us to believe Mr. Anderson left the party later that night, seeking Ms. Donovan out, and that he located her in the woods, where a struggle occurred.

Reporter: Were there ever any other persons of interest in this case?

Reporter: Can you tell us the link between Brooke disappearing and the earlier disappearance of a girl

222

last summer? Weren't they both involved with Steve
Anderson and have you questioned the other girl?

CNN: Detective Thompson, can you explain why
you waited two days to begin the search for Brooke
Donovan? She was a seventeen-year-old missing girl,
and yet your department issued no Amber Alert. You
didn't interview witnesses for two days, and there are
rumors her stepfather did not contact police for several
hours after discovering she was missing.

Detective Thompson: As I've said, we believed the victim
may have been copycatting an earlier disappearance.
Don't get me wrong here, buddy, we did everything we
could, based on what we had at that time. We didn't
issue an Amber Alert because we did not feel this was a
kidnapping case. Her stepfather stated his daughter had
been having trouble—

Mary Malone, lead investigator: If I could just step in
here one moment, thank you. The Castle Cove Police
Department is to be commended for an impeccable
investigation concerning a difficult, and somewhat
troubled, girl. Mr. Anderson is a star athlete under
a great amount of pressure. His background is quite
different from Ms. Donovan's, and we are operating
under the assumption that academic and personal
pressure may have caused him to snap. He's had issues
with violence in the past. He was inebriated the evening
of the mur—

Tessa Hopkins: Can you tell us what issues of violence in his past? If he was inebriated, was there a toxicology screen done on Mr. Anderson?

Mary Malone: There was no tox screen at the initial interview; it was still thought Ms. Donovan had—

CNN: It seems problematic about the lag time between her disappearance and a search. Can you—

(Voice from the crowd): I gave you his basketball sneaker! What happened to his sneaker? Is that what you say you found at the Lookout because—

Mary Malone: Thank you for your time.

CHAPTER TWENTY-FOUR

"DID YOU SEE IT?" Cole Fielding says in disbelief. "The press conference, I mean."

He passes a pair of skates over the counter to me. "I saw it."

I did see the press conference. Spike texted me the link, and I definitely recognized that scratchy voice in the crowd outside the police station: Dotty Schumacher. After she asked where the sneaker was and they shut down the conference, a chill went down my spine. Something is *definitely* up. Something *very* bizarre, and I hope that Alice's contact has something concrete for us soon, because if we're going to posit some sort of police cover-up, we need to know now.

"I'd like to kill *him,* to tell you the truth," Cole says. "That asshole. Brooke never did anything to anybody, you know? I mean, he was out of control by the end of the party, for sure, but

I didn't think he could do *this*. I guess you can if you're drunk, maybe? But Steve's not known for partying hard."

I pause, then decide just to say it. "We think maybe he wasn't so much drunk as . . . like, there was something in his drink, you know? It was a huge party with tons of people. Maybe somebody dosed someone's drink and Steve was the one who actually drank it." I'm not going to mention Park's name.

Cole frowns. "That's extremely creepy, but yeah . . . maybe that would explain him being so extra. I still can't believe it, though. I mean, Brooke is *dead*. I've never had anyone I know die before."

He scrapes some hair from his eyes, which are shining with sadness.

Is it wrong that Cole seems so bereft about Brooke and I still can't stop fixating on his pillowy lips and perfect skin? Yes, it's probably wrong in a thousand different ways.

I take my skates, walk away from Cole, and sit down and put them on. Spike, Neil, and Zora wave from the rink. I need time to think. Skating will help. It always does.

"Iris." It's Alice, out of breath. She's trying to rub off the admit stamp for the rink. "This is gross," she murmurs, wetting a finger and rubbing furiously on the back of her hand.

"Alice, please tell me your contact has something we can use."

"He's working on it," she says. "I think . . ." She pauses. "I think we have to stay on the Coach angle. I've racked my brain, and I can't finagle a way we'd be able to pin this on anyone else. Not even Kennedy, as much as I'd like that."

I look at my skates, thinking. "Well, what's the next step?

We gave Ricky all we have right now on Coach. Do you want to stake him out again?"

Alice purses her lips. "I'm thinking."

I finish tying my laces. "Go get some skates."

"Um, *no*."

"Um, *yes*. Skating will help you think."

Alice pouts, but gets up and goes over to Cole to get skates.

"I don't really recall how to do this," she says when she gets back, holding her skates primly. "And who else uses these? I don't want anything *fungal*."

"Just put them on, Alice." I'm rolling in a small circle around the bench. Coach coming to school and cornering Alice has me nervous and itching to move. Can he figure out that we duplicated his phone? And that it was duplicated to *mine*? I already have the Thing; I don't need another violent man after me.

Alice falters a little standing up. I catch her elbow. "I'll help you. Just relax. You remember how to stop, right?" I show her how to angle the skate to use the toe stop.

"I have successfully avoided PE for three years," she says, exasperated. "I do not need *this*."

We glide onto the rink floor. Spike and Zora zip up. Neil is out by himself on the other side of the rink. "We need to help Alice," I tell them. "And we need to ponder."

Spike links his arm with mine, I link to Alice, and Zora links up on Alice's left side.

"I feel like I'm in the middle of a sandwich," Alice sighs.

"Okay," I say. I feel instantly better, clearer, now that we are on the floor and moving. "Here's what we have: Coach was in debt. He's set to get five million now that Brooke's dead—"

"He was hooking up with several teachers and, from his credit card statements, it looks like he was buying them all quite pricey baubles—though that doesn't make him a murderer," Zora adds.

"He broke up with Westmacott because, according to Kennedy and various texts from Brooke on his phone, Brooke was pissed he might marry her—"

"Also," Alice puffs. Her face is pink from exertion. "He was pressuring Brooke to make him a trustee and extend his monthly stipend until she was out of college. And who's the Kevin dude who so desperately needed to meet Coach on Halloween night? I feel like Kevin—"

"The Kevin thing is bugging me, too," Zora says. "If Coach didn't answer Brooke, was he with this Kevin person and why? And, if we think he *did* kill Brooke, did this Kevin help him? Then after it's over, Coach heads to Ms. Hollister's house for sexy love?"

Spike breaks off from our group and flips around to face us, skating backward. "Coach has big credit card debt; his story about that night has holes. It's obvious they didn't really investigate him. Like, at all. I mean, *I* would. Boyfriend, dad. Anybody she was having problems with."

"Let's not forget the text he sent with that cryptic message, too," Alice says. "I can't figure that one out. *Was* it just about the alarm?"

"Part of me wonders if Lilian is somehow involved in this," I say. "I mean, anything is possible. Maybe to squash bad publicity, get it over with, get someone in jail, move on. Maybe she paid a cop to plant the shoe. Who knows. People with money do weird things. Once I saw this show where a grandmother paid her least favorite grandson to take the murder rap for her favorite grandson."

"That's cold," Spike says, shaking his head and glancing at Alice. "Rich people, out here framing poor people for murder just because it's an inconvenience."

"We're not all like that," Alice shoots back. "I don't lump you guys together. Anyway, nice try, Iris, but I highly doubt Lilian would do anything like that."

"Park's rich and she tried to drug Brooke!" Zora shouts. "Kennedy's making sex tapes! Believe me, that's going to show up on TMZ."

"You guys smoke weed," Alice points out.

"Yes, but we don't force it into someone's drink, so to speak," Spike says. "And there are no sex tapes here. This is a virgin crowd. Except for Zora."

I break out from the group and turn to face them, skating backward next to Spike. Alice wobbles, but Zora holds her up.

"Okay," I say. "Steve's second court appearance is tomorrow. Coach seems scared. He confronted Alice at *school*. Practically *threatened* her. That means he's got a lot to hide, in my opinion. We have to do something and do it fast. Brooke's funeral is Friday. We all need to be there, watching Coach. I'm leaning toward Coach. And yeah, maybe he had help."

"Right," Zora says. "We need to find the mysterious Kevin. Find out what's what with him. This is a superb angle. Maybe a kidnapping-ransom attempt gone wrong. Coach owes money, needs money, is pressuring his kid to make sure he gets more, she won't do it, maybe he partners up with this Kevin person to kidnap Brooke for ransom, but it all goes horribly wrong."

"He's not going to *tell* us anything," I say, frustrated.

"He might," Alice says. "If he thought it was Coach contacting him. We have his number. We'll just text him from one of the burners, have Coach say he got a new phone to explain the different number, say it's urgent. That we need to meet up——"

"This is getting good," Spike says. "But we can't just show up, five kids——"

"Alice's car breaks down," Zora says. "Spike, you can fiddle with it. Auto shop is about to come in handy. We'll get there early. He'll happen upon us and——"

"Oh," I say, something dawning on me. "And we are afraid and alone, we don't know this town, we're foreign exchange students at a school that matriculates murderers, please help us . . ."

I lock eyes with Alice. She knows what I mean.

Neil catches up with us, panting. "Wait, what did I miss? What's happening?"

"Three years of French is about to pay off, that's what's happening, Neil," Alice says gleefully. "Ah putain ça va être chaud!"

MURDER BOARD

Steve Anderson

~~Helen Park~~

~~Rebecca Kennedy~~

~~Alice Ogilvie~~

~~Cole Fielding~~

Coach Donovan

~~Accident~~

Unknown

Kevin???

CHAPTER TWENTY-FIVE

ALICE
NOVEMBER 8
5:32 P.M.

"Use your eyes. Use your ears. Use your brains—if
you've got any. And, if necessary—act."
—AGATHA CHRISTIE, *DEATH ON THE NILE*

"SO, HERE'S THE DEAL," I say to my companions as we whip
around the tight curve on the way out of downtown back to
Highway 1. "Hercule Poirot—"

"Who?" mutters Zora from the back.

I'm tempted to turn around to glare, but, as I learned from
my time in Tuscany, that can be very dangerous. Instead, I snap
"A world-famous detective" at her, push my sunglasses back up
onto my nose, and steer the car into the turn ahead. The hardest part of this particular section of road is how at sunset, the
sun will very literally blind you when you come around this
curve. And it's sunset right now.

"Jesus, Alice," yells Spike from the back seat. "Can we please
not die? At least not until we have a chance to figure out who
the killer is?"

"Sorry," I say without really meaning it. At least I have their attention. "So, as I was saying, Poirot. He was this great detective in Agatha Christie's novels and—"

"She knows he was fictional, right?" I hear Zora mutter. The girl is really working my last nerve.

"And," I repeat, "okay, so keep in mind this was like one hundred years ago. But one of Poirot's favorite investigative techniques was to use the fact that the British thought foreigners were not as smart as they were against them. He'd play up his French-ness—even though, of course, he was Belgian—and trick them into disclosing way more info to him than they would have otherwise. Like, using their biases against them or whatever. I think that's what we should do here to figure out who this Kevin person is, and what he wanted with Coach."

The car's silent for a moment, and then Spike says, "Alice, that's brilliant."

"Yeah, I think that's a great plan," says Iris from the passenger seat.

"Let's do it," adds Neil.

There's a beat, and then another, before finally, begrudgingly, another voice from the back seat chimes in. "Okay, that works," Zora says.

I pull onto the shoulder on the forest side of Highway 1 a half mile down from the spot where "Coach" agreed to meet with Kevin.

"Are you guys ready to get your French on?" I turn to face the four of them, smiling wide. This is going to be fun.

I pop the hood and we all hop out of the car. Spike walks around to the front and opens the hood, pulling it up and propping it on the little metal stick. He leans over and starts to tinker with whatever is under there. An engine, I presume? Neil walks around to join him and starts giving instructions.

"Par-le-vous French?" Iris looks at me with raised brows and a big smile. "How does that sound?"

"Perfect. As long as the guy doesn't actually speak French, I think we're good."

"Got it!" Spike exclaims, holding up a small black thing with a triumphant expression. "The car is officially broken. At least, for the moment." He grins and slips the part into his pocket. He and Neil start hopping around pumping their fists, which is actually quite endearing.

I glance at Iris, but her face is impassive. I'm really starting to ship those two hard, but I get the feeling Iris is not on board. "When he gets here, Spike and Neil, go back and pretend like you're fixing the car, okay? Zora and Iris can hover around you guys, acting worried. Iris, maybe rub some dirt on your face or something. Look really pathetic. And I'll do most of the talking. Sound good?"

Everyone murmurs in agreement.

"Do you think that's him?" Zora is looking down the road at a car that's approaching. It has one of those really loud engines that rattle everything within a mile radius of it.

Neil glances at his wristwatch. "I bet it is. Right on time."

I grab my burner out of my back pocket to see if he's messaged "Coach" about his arrival, but there's nothing new after our correspondence earlier, when I texted him pretending to be Coach and said to meet here at 5:30 p.m. Kevin replied, *OK you better have it this time,* but that was it. I have no idea what to expect from this meeting, but I have to say I'm glad Iris and I have backup right now.

As the car draws nearer, we scatter. Neil and Spike duck back under the hood, and Iris and Zora pace behind them wearing distraught expressions.

I hurry over to the side of the road and start waving like mad, trying to get the driver's attention. My fingers are crossed that this is, in fact, Kevin, because if it's not, this is going to be super awkward. The car slows and its blinker turns on, indicating it's going to pull over.

Darting back toward my car, I put on my most helpless *What is going on here?* face, heart pounding in my ears.

"What're you kids doin' out here?" The man in the driver's seat has a thick black mustache and a gravelly voice. "Car break down?"

"Oui," I say. "Ehh . . . le automobile. It, um, it is not start and we cannot have it work again. Nom d'un nom d'un nom!" I'm not sure what I just said made any sense, but I remember Poirot saying it in *Death on the Nile.*

The man gives me a long look. "You French?"

Oh god, he knows that was French? What if he—

"Don't speak it myself," he continues, and I let out a breath. "But my daughter took it at Castle Cove High."

"Oui!" I say again. "Castle Cove High. We . . . how do you say? We attend! Foreign exchange." I gesture between the five of us, and Spike and Iris nod emphatically.

"Exchange students, eh? Been a sad few days for the students there. Donovan's kid, dying and all." He shakes his head, muttering to himself. "Donovan tends to get himself into trouble.

Gotta say, part of me was surprised it wasn't him who ended up at the bottom of that cliff."

I pretend like I have no idea what he's saying. "Oui. Dead girl." I frown. "Cette pauvre petite."

"Gotta be a little scary for you all," he continues, mostly to himself. "Coming all this way to the great United States of America, only to be confronted with this whole mess." He heaves a sigh. "You know what, let me see if I can assist you kids. I got a meeting in a few, but Donovan can wait. He's kept *me* waiting enough as it is."

"Merci, mon ami, merci." I bounce up and down, clapping a little, as he gets out of his truck. This is perfect. Not only is he already spilling info, but this has to be Kevin.

He walks over to Spike. "What seems to be the issue?"

"Err . . . break-a-down?" Spike says, motioning to the inside of the hood. "I . . . oui oui oui!" He gestures to the car and backs away from the man, face bright red.

"Sorry, sorry." I hurry over to them. "His English? Very bad." I shoot a look at Spike to convey that he better keep it together or *else* and turn back to the man. "Help is from you . . . er . . . we appreciate."

He laughs a little laugh. "You're trying so hard, sweetheart." I bristle. What a tool. At least he firmly believes that we speak little to no English.

"Mais oui," I say demurely, batting my lashes at him. "You say . . . there is a meeting? You have?"

He looks up from the engine. "Ah, nothing to worry yourself about. I'll be okay. Just meeting a man who owes me some money."

"Mon-ey?" I make a face and shrug. "Qu'est-ce qu'il y a?"

Coach owed him money? Who is this guy?

He shakes his head. "No idea what you're saying, but it sure sounds pretty. I'll tinker here for a bit—but first I have to make a quick call." He holds up a finger. "Be right back." He walks a couple of feet away from me toward the tree line, phone pressed to his ear.

"Hey, Ernie," he says to the person on the other end without bothering to lower his voice. "Yeah. Almost there. Got a little sidetracked, but Donovan's made me wait long enough for this money as it is; he can stand to be on the receiving end for once." He pauses, listening. "Yeah. Yeah. No, I get it. I *get* it." His tone has changed from easygoing to angry. "Yes, he knows he needs to get it to me or he's gonna start losing limbs—" He cuts off. "Yeah, I know a hundred grand is a hell of a lot of—" He cuts off again, listening, his face growing redder as the seconds tick by. "I told him we're not placing any more bets for him until— Ernie, I'll *get* it. Trust me, okay? It's under control." He hangs up with a heavy sigh, pushing a hand through his hair.

"Sorry 'bout that." He comes back over to the car. "Had to check in with the boss. Donovan sure loves his horses. Too bad he can't pay up when they lose." Sticking his head back under the hood, he starts poking around again. "You know, you kids are lucky. I remember being your age. No worries. No bills to pay. Was easier then. Now I have to deal with these jerks all the time, people who don't know how to pay their debts, people who think they're entitled to be cut a break. I'm getting a little tired of it, to be honest." He straightens up and wipes his forehead with the back of his arm, streaking it with oil. "Had to send my kid through college somehow, though. This world ain't cheap." We meet eyes, and I shrug like I have no idea what he's saying.

"Kinda nice, talking to you kids. Refreshing, not to be judged."

"Ah, vraiment!" I reply, just to say something.

He smiles a little. "That's right. Well, nothing looks awry in there to me. Maybe the engine just needed a break. Why don't you try it now?" He motions to the car and makes a steering motion. I catch Spike's eye and gesture that he should replace whatever part he took out while Kevin's distracted.

Kevin walks me around to the driver's seat and I scoot inside, babbling random French phrases to stall. "Le roi est mort—vive le roi! Quelle page? J'ai oublié mes devoirs!" I used that last one a lot sophomore year, which explains my B–. I have an ear for language but am opposed to the assignment of work that I'm supposed to do at home. Clearly, considering Iris and I have pivoted our tutoring sessions to an out-of-the-box learning experience that will benefit both of us way more than rote memorization.

"Try it out." Kevin motions with his hand for me to push the ignition button. I pray that Spike's had enough time to rejigger that part into the engine. I turn it, and the car roars to life.

Kevin bangs on the roof of the car with excitement and pride. "Hot damn. Still got it."

"Merci, merci," I cry, joined by Iris, who walks toward us, babbling "merci" over and over again. This ruse would have been much easier if I weren't the only French speaker in the crowd.

"No problem at all." Kevin pulls his phone out of his pants pocket and checks the time. "Good thing, too, because I have to split. Gotta see a guy about a horse." He chuckles, waving to us as he heads over to his car and pulls back onto the road.

We watch him drive away silently. His taillights disappear

around the bend, and Iris folds over, hands on her knees, giggling. "He totally fell for it. That was amazing!"

Spike snorts. "Good thing we didn't really need that guy to fix the car. He had no clue what he was doing."

"'Course he didn't," says Zora, rolling her eyes.

"Guys," Neil says, interrupting our glee, a serious expression on his face. "Guys. Do you know what this means? Kevin must be a bookie. And Coach owed Kevin *money*. Lots of money, from the sound of it. Money that he wasn't paying up. He had a week? From Halloween? *Or else?* And on Halloween Brooke is murdered, and Coach inherits a *ton* of money that he desperately needed." He pauses, pinning each of us with his eyes one by one. "I really *do* think Coach Donovan killed his daughter."

A chill runs down my spine. Somewhere along the way, I sort of forgot that this entire thing was about Brooke being . . . dead. A lump builds in my throat, and I let out a little gasp of air. As I blink back the tears that have started gathering in the corners of my eyes, a cool hand slips into mine and I turn to find Iris, standing next to me with a sad expression on her face.

After dropping off all the various Zoners at their respective homes, Iris and I are alone in the car. We're quiet now, coming off the high of our luck with the ruse and the subsequent reminder that we're doing all of this because my former best friend was murdered.

I turn into the parking lot of Iris's apartment building, pulling to a stop in a space close to the building. She's silent next to me.

"I'll text you later?" I ask, turning toward her. She doesn't answer. She's staring out her window at something. I can't really see her face.

"What are you looking at?" I lean over to look, and realize she's making a little gasping noise under her breath. "Are you okay?"

"I—" She clears her throat, chest rising and falling fast. She looks away from the window, back at me, her face pale. She looks terrified.

"What's going on?" I lean forward again, unsnapping my seat belt, and this time I'm able to get a glimpse of an older man, leaning against a run-down car, his arms crossed over his chest. "Who is that guy?"

"It's"—Iris licks her lips—"probably just somebody for the lady in 115. She gets a lot of visitors." Her hands are trembling in her lap.

"Do you want me to walk you in or something? Should we call someone?" I reach into the center console and pick up my phone. "That guy looks like bad news, Iris."

"No. No. Please don't. It's fine. I'm going to get out and run up to my apartment—I'm quick, you've seen me. And I'll lock the door and stuff, I promise. Okay? I'll be fine." She gives me a shaky grin that I think is supposed to reassure me. My stomach turns. Something is not right here. She's not telling me something, but I can't force it out of her, so I nod.

"Okay. I'll wait until you're inside."

"You don't have to—" she starts, but I cut her off.

"I will wait until you are inside, Iris," I say firmly, and she nods.

She opens her car door and runs for it. The man straightens, moving in her direction, and I do the only thing I can think of—lock the car doors and start honking the horn, over and over again. The sound reverberates in the night, and several lights snap on inside apartments on the first floor. The man freezes about twenty feet away and turns back toward me, an awful glare on his face.

Holding up my phone, I lean forward toward the windshield and snap a couple of pictures of him. Evidence, should I need it. He must see me do it, because he yells, "Hey," and starts toward my car. Merde.

I have to get out of here. I put the car into reverse with a trembling hand and back out of the space.

My phone buzzes with a text from Iris. *Inside.*

Thank god she's safe.

At the man's car, I slow, managing to take several shots of its body and license plate through my window. I hurriedly send all the photos to my source, who seems to know everything, with the message *Can you try to run this license plate for me??*

There's a tap on the back of my car, and through the rear-view mirror, I see the man. He caught up to me. Oh my god.

I press my foot down on the gas hard, screeching out of the lot as fast as my car will go.

TEXT CONVERSATION BETWEEN
A. OGILVIE AND I. ADAMS
NOVEMBER 8

7:44 P.M.

AO: Just checking on you

7:49 P.M.

AO: Iris? You there?

7:52 P.M.

AO: I'm a little worried

IA: Hey

AO: HEY! Are you ok

IA: Yeah fine why

AO: Oh. ok

IA: Just watching *Criminal Investigations*

AO: As long as you're ok

IA: Yup. I'll see you tomorrow.

AO: OK

CHAPTER TWENTY-SIX

IRIS
NOVEMBER 9
10:45 A.M.

I'M TRYING TO CONCENTRATE on Ms. Hollister, who I have now seen way too much of, in way too many compromising ways, because I can't stop thinking about the Thing. The way he was just . . . there. Waiting for me in the parking lot. The way I don't even remember running up the stairs to my apartment and opening the door. I just remember a fog of fear descending over me. I pushed the couch in front of the door. I called my mom. I called the police. I said he was breaking the order, but by the time they got there, he was, of course, gone. He's so good at disappearing when he needs to. If I didn't hate him so much, I'd ask for lessons.

And now I'm tired from being up too late. I'm behind in my schoolwork because of this whole investigation thing, and I can't afford to not do well. He ruins everything. He's always ruined everything. Why did he come back in the first place? If you disappear, just stay *gone.*

My skin is prickling. I can't think about this here, right now, in school, my safe place. I need to get him out of my head, concentrate on the one thing that can help me disappear. I pull out our casebook and start scribbling.

Coach owed a lot of money. Credit cards. Betting. About to lose a limb. Bullying daughter to change terms of trust. Where is Brooke's phone? Why didn't the police ask to look at his phone so they could see the texts from her? Would he throw her phone in the ocean? I would definitely throw it in the ocean, right? Get rid of it immediately. But wait—can't you ping the last location of someone's phone? Did the police do that? Would it show her texts to him? Maybe Alice can ask her contact if the police ever tried to locate the phone. And why, why didn't we try to press the bookie harder on the other angle? How do we know he didn't help Coach? We just let him go because he seemed nice, but—

A familiar sound blares from my backpack as I'm working in the Coach casebook.

Oh. No. I scramble to unzip my backpack and get to the phone to turn it off.

Ms. Hollister whips around from the whiteboard. "How many times do I have to remind everyone that phones are to be *off* during class time!"

Beside me, Ashley Henderson whispers, "Busted, nerd girl," just as I shut off the phone.

"Ms. Adams," Ms. Hollister says. "Is your personal life more important than polynomials?"

"No ma'am. I'm sorry," I answer, staring straight ahead.

"Get with the program, Ms. Adams. Turn it off. Keep it off. Or off you go to Principal Brown's office."

I make a motion like I'm putting the burner back in my backpack, but I tuck it under the hem of my flannel.

Ms. Hollister is in a *foul* mood. Which I can understand, since she's apparently the only alibi for a *murderer.*

As soon as she turns back to the whiteboard, I glance down.

Hey

In Cold Blood

We have a wrinkle

Turns out my client now wants to plead

guilty to involuntary manslaughter to avoid

a trial. I can't convince him to stick it out.

You and Moneybags need to call me stat

My heart starts sparrowing in my chest. What the hell? Steve is now . . . flipping his plea?

"Nerd girl," Henderson says quite loudly. "Is that your phone, *again*?"

Ms. Hollister turns back, pissed.

"Out," she says. "Right now."

I grab my backpack, and I'm in the hallway in under thirty seconds. I'm not going to the principal. I duck down the science corridor to avoid the hall monitor.

This is all . . . awful. Who changes their mind and pleads guilty?

I text Alice. *Steve now says he's guilty. No trial. Meet me in the Pit. Need to call Ricky.*

The fuck, Alice writes back.

Then I book it to the Pit.

—

Alice bursts into the Pit five minutes later.

She puts her hand on my arm. "You want to talk about last night?"

Her voice is tender, but it cuts me just the same. I cannot tell her about the Thing. I just cannot. He's a sore that lives in me, and to let him out . . . I can't. I just can't. Not even to Alice, whose hand on my arm is too warm, too kind. We're sidekicks, not friends. You don't make friends when you're planning to vanish.

"It was nothing," I say quickly. "It was like I thought. He was there for the lady in 115."

Alice takes her hand away. "If you say so."

I can tell she doesn't believe me, but we've got more important things to think about right now. I already have Ricky's name pulled up on my regular phone. I press Dial and put it on speaker. She picks up right away.

"Yeah, so." It sounds like she's eating something crunchy.

"What the hell, Ricky," Alice says. "What's going on?"

"Steve is changing his plea, kids. I'm gobsmacked. His best chance for less time was a trial. I would have done my damnedest to sway a jury toward reasonable doubt. I can't get through to that kid. Just said he changed his mind and that's that. If you kids have anything on that police-frame-up angle, or something extremely damning toward Matt Donovan, now is the time."

"It was Coach," Alice says desperately. "We have proof."

"We've got *stuff*," I say into the phone, my words echoing in the bathroom. "We met with that guy last night, the one who Coach was supposed to meet on Halloween but never did. He's a bookie. Coach owed him a hundred grand. Which means, if Coach was getting five million if Brooke died——"

"You met with a bookie?" Ricky sounds impressed. "Huh. Didn't think you had that in you. This is getting very tangled at the moment. I can't just waltz over to the DA's office and say, *Hey, Parker, I think you have the wrong man.* He'll laugh me out of his office."

She's quiet. Too quiet. Alice looks at me, frowning.

"Anderson's flip is driving me batty," Ricky finally says. "I have to do what he says, because I'm his lawyer, but I think it's time to play dirty."

"Dirty how?" I ask.

"Step one, go down to the police department, tell them what you have. They'll look at you like you're stupid teenage girls, but you're used to that. It will be *on record* that you visited and raised concerns about the case and offered them evidence that points *against* Steve Anderson being guilty and points *to* Coach. They'll ignore you. But they'll have to take notes about your visit, what was discussed, and log it into the investigation file."

"Got it," Alice says.

"I just wish I knew what made this kid change his mind," Ricky muses. "I fear some sort of . . . manipulation."

Alice and I look at each other.

"What are you saying exactly?" Alice asks. "Are you saying someone bribed Steve to change his plea?"

"Rich people like to make things go away," Ricky says.

"I told you!" I crow. "I told you, Alice!"

Alice scrunches up her face. "It's *not* Lilian."

"Girls!" Ricky shouts. "Focus. I'm just tossing things out. I can't get all the files from the police at the moment. I'm getting stonewalled. I need to *prove* no one but Steve was seriously considered a suspect. I need to raise doubt. So I need you to get down there and raise a stink."

I look at Alice. She shrugs.

"Like, should we do that right now?" I ask. "I mean, I'm technically supposed to still be in calc."

There's a pause on the other end of the line. Then Ricky sighs.

"Girls," she says. "Please believe me that you will never, ever, ever in your entire life use calculus after high school. Not once. But if you don't go down to PD right now, you will definitely be using visitor passes to see your friend in prison for a crime he possibly did not commit."

CHAPTER TWENTY-SEVEN

"It is the courage, the insistence,
the ruthless force of youth."
—AGATHA CHRISTIE, *FIVE LITTLE PIGS*

WE BOOKED IT TO the police station as fast as humanly possible and signed in at the front desk, only to wait. In fact, we've been waiting a solid *hour* for someone to come talk to us, and I've had just about enough.

"Excuse me?" I call to the sergeant sitting behind the front desk. She ignores me. "Um, excuse me?" I stand and walk over to her. "We have been waiting for*ever* to talk with someone. Did you tell Detective Thompson we're here?"

She heaves an irritated sigh. "As I told you, Detective Thompson is busy with important police business. There are se—"

"There he is!" I yell, spotting him behind her at the far end of the hallway. I don't wait for her to respond. I hightail it past her desk, shouting, "Detective! Detective! Wait up!"

"Miss!" the woman shouts behind me, but I ignore her.

Thompson glances down the hall, catches sight of my

approaching figure, and puts his head down like he thinks if he can't see me, I can't see him or something.

"*Excuse* me." I pick up my pace and manage to reach Thompson just before he ducks through a door. "Detective *Thompson*, I need to speak with you," I call out.

He turns back to me, holding a steaming cup of coffee. Clearly, he's been just *slammed*. "We need to chat about the Brooke Donovan case. I have some information that might interest you," I say.

The woman from the front desk has caught up with me. "Sir, I am so sorry," she pants. "She ran right by me and——"

"It's okay, Bertie. I know how slippery Alice Ogilvie can be."

Ew. Talk about rude.

I ignore the comment. I'm not going to let him rile me up. "I *said* I need to talk to you," I repeat.

He waves Bertie off, taking a tiny sip of his coffee before responding. "Oh? Is that right?"

"Yes." I put a hand on my hip. "I have information. Information that will blow the case wide open," I say. And suddenly I feel less Agatha Christie, more *CSI*.

"Well, Alice. Too late for that. The case is closed. We have our man. You know that, right? Steve Anderson is pleading guilty. It should be a pretty open-and-shut case, if you ask me." He starts to walk away, but I reach out and grab the sleeve of his suit before I think about what I'm doing. He stops and looks at his sleeve, then looks at me, a warning in his gaze.

"Sorry." I snatch my hand back. "But this is *important*. I mean, you're a *detective*. Aren't you supposed to try to detect things? Like, the fact that Steve wasn't drunk that night? He was *drugged*?"

Thompson assesses me. "Drugged?"

"Yes! Someone spiked his drink!"

"And you know this how, exactly?"

I pause. "I have my sources."

He rubs the bridge of his nose. "I'm sure you do, Alice."

I know how he feels about me and what I did last summer, but this is real. Steve is *not* guilty, and there's a murderer walking around. "You know I'm not going to leave until you listen to me," I say, "so you might as well not waste any more of our time."

He sighs. "Alice, I'm too tired for this; I was up half the night with a screaming newborn. You have two minutes. Go."

"Okay, so first of all, the basketball sneakers," I begin. "You talked to Dotty of Dotty's Doughnuts, so you know that Steve went in there that morning. Dotty saw him at seven-twenty-five a.m.—with *both* sneakers on—and she says he left one of them in the bathroom and she gave it to the cops later that day, along with the video footage from her security camera. So how could that sneaker in the woods be his? Unless one of your guys planted it there." I give him a meaningful look, which he ignores. "I don't understand how you're overlooking that. Not to mention, where did the record of your conversation with Dotty go? Where is the surveillance video from the coffee shop? Dotty says some of *your* guys took it, but now it's just . . . vanished into thin air? That's awfully odd, don't you think, *detective*?"

"Alice—" starts Thompson, but I barrel over him.

"Also, like I said, I have information from a *very* reliable source that Steve really *hadn't* been drinking that much Halloween night—he was drugged. But you have no evidence proving he was either drunk *or* drugged because, did you even give him a toxicology test after you brought him in? No! And there's

Brooke's dad—Coach Donovan. Did you guys even look at him? Or at *anyone* other than Steve? Did you know Coach owes hundreds of thousands of dollars in outstanding debt? And that he benefits monetarily from Brooke's death? Like, *really* benefits. And he and Brooke hadn't been getting along before she died. They were arguing—about *money,* from what I hear. And the morning after she disappeared, he acted really shady at school. Like, he wasn't even going to call you at all until—" I cut myself off. No need to tell him about how I called Lilian. "In conclusion, if I were you, I'd take a look around my own department. Because your guys are clearly mishandling this case *pretty freaking badly* if you ask me."

I finish and stare at Thompson. He's silent for a beat, and then his eyes narrow and his mouth pulls up at the corner into a sneer, his expression morphing from tired to mean.

"First of all, Alice," he grinds out in a low growl. "Not that I owe *you,* a teenager, an explanation of how we have conducted our investigation, but yes, we spoke to Dotty Schumacher about the sneaker. That said, Dotty Schumacher is not a reliable eyewitness. I can't tell you how often she calls here with some cockamamie story or another. The sneaker was found in the woods by two of my men, logged, and tested. It had Anderson's prints on it. There's no record of Dotty giving them the sneaker, because it never happened. Unfortunately, Dotty's memory has gotten quite spotty over the last year. As evidenced by the quality of her bear claws," he mutters. "Second, Matthew Donovan is a respected and admired member of the Castle Cove community who has brought our basketball team to victory three years running. When I spoke with him after his daughter disappeared, he *cried*. Why would he do that, if he'd been the one to kill her?"

"He——" I start, but Thompson holds up a finger.

"And third, and most important, Steve has now confessed to the crime."

"But now he's——"

"Here's the thing." Thompson's voice hardens. "This isn't one of your high school melodramas. This is real life. This is a *murder* case, one where we got our guy, where he admitted to doing it. So I recommend that you take your theories and go write some *Veronica Mars* fanfiction. And please, leave police business to the *police*."

My jaw sets. I knew that this was going to be the reaction when we came here. Ricky said we had to, but these cops—they don't want to listen.

"It's time for you to go now, Miss Ogilvie." He motions to someone behind me, and Bertie reappears at my elbow. "Thank you for your concern, but we are handling this. I would *strongly* suggest that you stay out of it, if you know what's good for you."

Bertie motions for me to follow her out, but I stay firmly planted where I stand.

"It's time for you to go, Alice," repeats Thompson, eyeing me.

I narrow my eyes at him. This . . . this *jerk* thinks he's so high and mighty because he's a police officer? Well, clearly that's pretty meaningless work, considering how much they're bungling this case. "You know, Officer Thompson," I say in my sweetest, deadliest voice. "You might think I am just some dumb teenage girl, but you're going to be in for a rude awakening when we blow this case wide open and prove that something shady is going on in this town. And you better believe it's all going to come down on your shoulders when that happens. You can kiss your pension goodbye."

"Okay, that's about enough. Sorry about this, Officer Thompson," Bertie says. She grabs me by the elbow and pulls me down the hallway. She's much, much stronger than I would have given her credit for, because no matter how hard I struggle against her grip, I'm stuck.

When we get to the front desk, she marches me past Iris and through the door out into the cool Crystal Cove air. "There will be no more of that, you hear me, Ms. Ogilvie? Or else," she says, mouth set in a hard, thin line. She marches back into the building just as Iris walks out.

"Wow, Alice, you just got kicked out of a police station. That's badass," she says.

I rub my arm. "Ow. These cops are crazy. They wouldn't even listen to me. And that one—Bertie—I swear to god she just threatened me a second ago." I sink down to the curb and put my head in my hands. "What are we supposed to do now, then? Let an innocent person go down for this—"

"Calm down." Iris's voice is soft but firm. "Take a breath, Alice. And relax. I have a plan."

CHAPTER TWENTY-EIGHT

IRIS
NOVEMBER 9
9:30 P.M.

I KNEW ALICE WOULD love my plan, because Alice Ogilvie is all about gossip, manipulation, and lies. I'm not judging her for it. For Alice, they're simply her lifeblood. And in this instance, the trickery in her veins is going to come in handy.

While Alice was doing her slippery best to get Detective Thompson to listen to her without, you know, exposing *our* crimes, I was texting with Ricky Randall, who was giving me step three, which is swaying the court of public opinion.

You need to make a ruckus, she'd texted. *It's your only shot at this point. Tell people the cops are hiding something. That the investigation is being mishandled.*

I had an idea.

—

As Alice listened to me in the parking lot of the Castle Cove Police Department, her grin spread as wide and beautiful as the ocean on a clear day.

"We have to use what works best for stirring people up," I tell her. "Where do people enjoy giving opinions they know nothing about? Where do they enjoy taking part in a big old conspiracy-driven pile-on?"

Alice laughs. "On the internet, of course!"

I nod. "Exactly," I say. "We have to hit adults and our esteemed peers where they hang out most often. Adults equals Facebook; our peers are dancing it out and weeping over on TikTok and Instagram."

It only takes us ten minutes to get to Dotty's Doughnuts. Alice pulls into the parking lot and stops in a spot directly outside where we can see Dotty Schumacher move around behind the counter, wiping the Formica, arranging doughnuts on a half-off tray by the register.

"Operation Castle Cove Corrupt starts now," I say, opening the car door.

If we can't get the police to investigate Coach, we'll have to put the pressure on. Police do not like bad publicity.

The little bell above the door jangles as we walk in.

Dotty glances up and grimaces. "Oh. You two again."

"Yes! We're back! Just can't get enough of these sweet treats!" Alice announces. "Two small coffees, please. And that jelly doughnut, thank you." She smiles pleasantly and then turns to me.

"I just can't believe it. I mean, I'm *heartbroken.*" Alice's voice trembles convincingly.

"It's totally disgusting," I answer smoothly. "I mean, but cops are cops, right?"

Dotty pauses as she slips Alice's jelly into a paper sleeve.

"I mean, they *know* who did it, and still, they're going to let that poor guy go to prison. I just can't imagine. They have *evidence* it was someone else," Alice says, letting out a heavy sigh.

"Well, you know this town. It's always the poor people who get shafted, never the rich. Guess Coach Donovan has some good friends at the station," I say matter-of-factly.

Dotty glances up, shifting her gaze from me to Alice.

"You two talking about that basketball player? You know something about the coach?"

"Well . . . ," I say slowly.

Alice adds some creamer to her coffee. "There are a *lot* of things about the coach, to be honest. I mean, who *is* he? He wasn't born here, like you and me, you know? And, full disclosure, I was *friends* with his daughter. Brooke. The *victim*. The things I could tell you about that house . . ."

Dotty's mouth is hanging open. "Like what? Can't say I ever trusted him. He seemed okay, but like you said, he's not from here."

Alice takes a sip of her coffee. "Between you and me, the coach? Like, after Brooke's mom died, he was always pressuring Brooke about money, because her family set it up so he only got a little every month to take care of Brooke. Until, you know, Brooke turned eighteen. And it would all be hers. Nothing for him. But——"

I cut off Alice. We can't say *too* much, or we're going to veer into some ugly territory. "Suffice to say, Dotty? He owes a lot of money to a lot of people and the only way out? I think? Was maybe——"

Dotty's eyes widen. "Oh lord. Yes. It's always like that, in the shows. Insurance money? And probably that big old house they got up there. My friend used to be the maid there, but he let her go. After the lady died. Said he was kind of a touchy-feely one, too."

She makes a face.

"He was canoodling with half the teachers at school!" Alice says. "Can you imagine?"

Dotty shakes her head. "It hurts my heart to think of it, to be honest, someone doing that to their own kid? But I've been around. I've watched enough things and read enough on the webs to know that money—"

"Makes people do bad, bad things," I finish for her. "Anyway, it looks like the police? *Maybe?* Have been . . . compromised? And Anderson? My personal opinion? He's just . . . giving up. Who knows? Maybe he got paid off, too, like the cops who planted that sneaker you found."

Dotty refills the coffee urn. She appears to be thinking very, very hard. "I tried to tell them at the press conference. About the sneaker. I shouted it! But then they hustled me out and told me to keep my mouth shut."

"I saw that and I am so sorry. You were just trying to be *heard,*" Alice murmurs, shaking her head.

Dotty looks around, like someone might overhear her, even though the shop is empty.

"And then, all of a sudden, my brother's parking tickets, poof, disappear."

"Really?" I say breathlessly.

She nods and lowers her voice. "And they told my brother, like, don't ask about it, don't say anything, just be grateful. And said to, get this, 'rein your sister in.' "

Alice raises her eyebrows at me.

"*That* sounds ominous," I say to Dotty.

"Right? Creeped me out," says Dotty.

"You know what *I* heard?" Alice says conspiratorially, leaning close to Dotty. "I heard *the family* doesn't want a scandal. Lord knows, *that* family has had enough scandals for a lifetime, but can you imagine?"

"It's a tale as old as time," Dotty agrees. "Rich people get away with it. It's the rest of us that pay."

She shakes her head angrily as she rings us up. Alice hands her twenty dollars.

"I just wish there was some way we could help that kid," Alice says. "But you know the police. And what can you do now that he says he's guilty? All he has is some court-appointed lawyer. They're never any good."

I choose to ignore that.

"Oh, I *know,* honey. I just wish there was something I could do," Dotty says.

Alice shrugs prettily. "Me too. Don't you, Iris?"

"Yeah, I sure do." I pull out my phone casually.

Dotty's brow is furrowed.

She's thinking. She just needs a little push. I keep scrolling on my phone, watching her furtively.

She holds out Alice's change.

"Oh no, no, you keep it. Please," Alice insists. "I'm just so sorry that no one is listening to you about the sneaker. You are like the one person who knows the truth and . . . no one cares. If only people would pay attention, you could be the one who finds justice for Brooke."

Dotty frowns thoughtfully.

Bingo.

"Oh, you know what?" I make sure to say this to Alice, instead of to Dotty directly. "Look, I forgot, I've been so busy studying, but these people, this group"—I squint at my phone— "they started a protest group. For Steve. Look. The hashtag #CastleCoveCorrupt."

I angle the phone to Alice and she peers over. "Wow, that's a ton of hits. Have you seen this, Dotty?" She tips the phone in Dotty's direction. Dotty leans into my phone, inspecting all the posts using #CastleCoveCorrupt on Facebook.

"Oh, I see," she says. "Oh, that's good. I might read those later. Maybe I have something to add, right?"

"Yes, absolutely," Alice says. "You should speak out, Dotty. Like we said."

Dotty keeps reading, but I slide my phone away gently.

"You have a good night, now," I say. "We've gotta go study for an English test. Sorry to keep you."

I nudge Alice away from the counter, and we slip out the front door.

As soon as we're back in the car, we settle in, pretending to be sipping our now-lukewarm coffees while sneaking looks at Dotty.

She wipes the counter. Throws out some old doughnuts, comes and locks the door, turns the sign around to "Closed." Walks back behind the counter, switches off the doughnut display lights. Then she stands there, very still, just thinking.

And she slips her phone from her pocket.

"Let's go," I tell Alice. "Park on a side street."

"I think this is really going to work," Alice says breathily, pulling out of the lot.

By the time she parks the car a few streets down, I'm already looking up Dotty Schumacher on Facebook, because that's where old people do all their talking and complaining.

Her page is unassuming. It's filled with doughnuts, grand-kids, a vacation to Disneyland, Dotty in black Mickey Mouse ears and eating an inappropriately long corn dog.

Alice is leaning over my shoulder. A chortle of laughter erupts from her, and I have to guess she's gotten to the post.

10 P.M.

Feeling pretty awful. Thinking about the way our town just chews up all of us trying to get by. Thinking about that basketball player from the high school. I heard the police didn't even look at anybody else, just set their sights on him. Here's the thing—he was wearing both shoes when he came in! He left one in the bathroom, and I gave it to the cops, but then they said they found it in the woods??? Give me a break!! They even took my surveillance tape, that shows he was wearing 2 shoes!! Something stinks down there at the police department!!! I mean, what about the dad, right??? Rich jerk. Seemed okay at first, but he's not from here, you know? He's not a Castle Cove–r. Probably going to inherit a bunch of money now. Sick of it, to tell you the truth. Wish there was something to help that poor kid. Musta just given up and decided to plead out.

Randy Boolen: Did they even investigate the dad?

Sarah Carter: Do they even have evidence against the kid?? Didn't he say he was all wasted in the woods and

stuff? Maybe the cops pressured him. Cops lie all the
time to get you to say things.

Denise Donrik: What the hell is that about the
sneaker????

Lila Canarsie: Castle Cove Police, man. Of course
they'll blame the poor kid. That's the way this stupid
town works. Let me tell you about my brother . . .

"Okay, Alice," I tell her. "Do it now."

Alice pulls up the fake profile I created while I waited for
her at the police station. I found some pictures of a nice-looking
middle-aged woman on the internet, and we named her Annie
Devlin. Dotty accepted her friend request approximately ten
minutes before we walked into her doughnut shop. Because of
course she did. Everyone wants friends, lots of them, and what
owner of a doughnut shop wouldn't want to befriend Annie
Devlin, "Doughnut Enthusiast"?

Alice, as Annie Devlin, begins replying to Dotty's post.

If you ask me, this whole thing is really suspicious. I
fancy myself something of an amateur detective, ha ha,
not to toot my own horn, but in stuff like this, where
money is involved, it's almost ALWAYS THE FAMILY.
OR THE COPS. There's a lot of chatter about it. Just
look up #CastleCoveCorrupt

"Is your heart beating really fast?" I ask Alice.
"Duh," she says. "But I am here for it."

My phone buzzes. Spike.

DONE, he texts.

After I get home, I start scrolling after Spike's text and I can't stop. He and Zora have been busy.

It's like an endless machine. #CastleCoveCorrupt. Everywhere. Instagram. Twitter. Facebook. TikTok. Spike and Zora and Neil must have made a dozen accounts, cribbed hundreds of photos, crafted pristine but short profiles, and created a monster. People have latched on to it like crazy.

> **Bongwater420:** I thought everyone was entitled to justice, but not in Castle Cove, I guess

> **Instagraham:** Did that kid even have a lawyer when they first brought him in? No lawyer would have let him go from not guilty to guilty. You gotta fight!

> **MillieHenson:** Was there EVEN an investigation?

> **Jeffboyardee:** Mad shit going down hearing stuff about that Coach

> **SarahMart:** Did she have ANY OTHER BOYFRIENDS they could have looked at

> **StitchBitch22:** Seems really sketch that kid flipped his plea like that.

> **In.Cog.Nito:** Rich family probably bought off the cops/ kid to avoid a scandal

FrancesFarley: I heard that coach was selling painkillers on the side

GerbersDilemma: WAS HE SUPPOSED TO INHERIT MONEY IF SHE DIED

LouFletcher: One time that coach totally lost it in class and flipped a desk, lol, I was there, thought he was gonna go apeshit on us

BettyBonkerBooks: Have those cops even said what evidence they have against the kid?

AntonioBolano: Yeah a sneaker in the woods but that doughnut lady says the kid left it at her shop and she gave it to police and whammo, suddenly they "found" it in the woods

FrankPalazzolo: If they found clothes fibers or his hairs in the woods, of course it looks like he was there, he slept there. Did they scrape his nails for her DNA?

AlanIver: Don't forget Remy Jackson they totes shoved that under the rug 2 and they never found that guy

SolerSystem: I saw 3 cases up north, teenage girls disappeared maybe a serial killer

AshleySmashley: You don't even know half of what happens at CC High, I could tell you shit

SqueakyPete: He was hooking up with half the teachers at school, everyone knew

CharmedLifeSteve: once saved my ass in middle school, he's a decent dude

PoorTony: Dumb as a rock, but not a killer. Why did he say he was guilty

KBMarino: Def needs a better lawyer but if you have no money, you get no love

Justice4Steve: Cops always pin it on poor people

HankKilgore: Someone shd go 2 jail but not Steve

And on and on, each one tagged with #CastleCoveCorrupt. I feel a little queasy.

Queasy because . . . this is what we set out to do, yes, and we have some convincing things that need to be looked at, like the will, those texts on Coach's phone asking him to pay up, the texts he ignored from Brooke. Harassing Alice in the hallway.

But does all that equal murder? Part of me thinks yes. Part of me is on the fence.

But all of me thinks Steve Anderson did not kill Brooke Donovan.

The sound of my mother's key in the lock jars me, and I sit up on the couch, rubbing my eyes.

"Oh, you're up," she says. She looks tired. "I thought you'd be in bed by now. Don't you have a test tomorrow?"

She slips off her bar apron and sets it on the coffee table in front of me, the coins inside clinking. She sits down next to me on the couch and leans back.

"I was studying," I say. I pull out the bills from the apron, smoothing them into neat piles of ones, fives, tens. I used to love to do this when I was little. Make the piles. And I learned early on how quickly it would all go away. Into the Thing's pocket.

"Dotty came in late tonight," my mom murmurs. "She was full of talk about Steve Anderson and bad cops. She seems to think something's up."

Carefully, I say, "Oh yeah?"

"Oh god, yes. She was rambling about that girl's father? Stepfather? Didn't you have him for a class?"

"Freshman history," I say. "A lot of sports metaphors."

But she's not listening because she's fallen asleep, her head lolling against the back of the couch, mouth open. I cover her with a blanket. Take the bills and the apron into the kitchen, put the bills into the kitty jar, methodically separate the coins into their own jars.

Everything we have, we scrape for.

I look at my phone again.

> **BurberryGirl:** Didn't that coach even offer a reward, haha funny if it turns out to be him, lol
>
> **LoverOfClouds:** Payin up to put yoself in prison, noice
>
> **ShaysAnatomy** Grandma put up the reward cash

I look at my mom on the couch.

Coach, whatever happens, he'll lawyer up. Probably some fancy lawyer will offer to take him on, what with the media that comes with being the widower of an heiress, headlines. The whole deal. I've seen it on *Forensic Files*. Good-looking guy that smells of money charged with murder; another good-looking guy in an expensive suit with a gleaming car and perfect sound-bite will arrive to save him.

Coach will be fine. But Steve and me? No one's really looking out for us, are they?

I want that reward money.

The burner phone buzzes.

Ricky Randall.

Good job. Step 4 soon.

The Castle Cove Gazette
NOVEMBER 10

PUBLIC OUTCRY OVER STEVE ANDERSON CASE

Unless you've been living under a rock, you're aware that Levy Cosmetics heir Brooke Donovan was murdered on Halloween night and her body was discovered off the coast of Castle Cove. Several days later, her boyfriend, high school basketball star Steve Anderson, was arrested for her murder and was going to plead guilty to involuntary manslaughter. Castle Cove's elite breathed a sigh of relief. An open-and-shut case . . . right?

Yet, overnight, a movement has started online under the hashtag #CastleCoveCorrupt that alleges that the cops in Castle Cove have seriously bungled their investigation. In a Facebook post, Dotty Schumacher, of Dotty's Doughnuts, accused the department of hiding information and even planting evidence.

Some of the more salacious posts we've seen around the internet go even further, positing the reason behind Anderson's switch to a guilty plea might be even more sinister—that he's being paid to be the fall guy.

Rumors about local teacher Matt Donovan, adopted father to Brooke, have also started, questioning just how much he might stand to inherit from Brooke's death.

At the moment, we're still looking into where that hashtag originated, but since Wednesday evening, it's exploded on all the social networks and reached far beyond our fair town. Yesterday it was trending on Twitter.

CHAPTER TWENTY-NINE

ALICE
NOVEMBER 10
1 2:34 P.M.

> "When the sun shines you
> cannot see the moon," he said.
> "But when the sun is gone—
> ah, when the sun is gone."
> —AGATHA CHRISTIE, *DEATH ON THE NILE*

BRENDA HAD SOME APPOINTMENTS down in LA today, and with her gone I decided that instead of attending school, I should probably spend the morning on our investigation, trying to figure out how we can prove Coach is guilty. Priorities and all. Public opinion is well and good, but if the cops are in on all of this somehow, we're going to need more than that to put the right person behind bars. I thought briefly about texting Lilian—her pockets are deep and I'm sure she knows people who have seen situations like this before—but Iris's words niggle in the back of my head. I really don't think Lilian is in on it—whatever *it* is—but . . . what if I'm wrong? I can't risk it.

I'm scrolling through all the new comments left on Facebook about Coach and Steve, getting more frustrated by the second, when my phone vibrates with a text. It's from that number—the one who keeps sending me stuff about the case. I sit up straighter and read.

All it says is: *Go to Joe's Diner. 1:15 p.m.*

> Can we meet finally?
>
> **No. I'm leaving files for you. Booth 3b in the back of the place. It'll be taped under the north-facing bench.**
> **And alice don't come early. If I see you there, the info is leaving with me**

Dammit. How did they know what I was thinking? .

> Fine. I don't know why you wont just tell me who you are tho

There's a pause, and I start to worry that I scared them off. I'm typing out another text when the reply finally dings on my phone.

> **All in due time, Ogilvie**

Forty minutes later, I'm parked in the empty lot behind Joe's Diner, slumped in the driver's seat. I'm only one minute early, but I don't want to risk spooking them.

The diner has been around forever—since like the 1980s— and, as far as I can tell, it hasn't been updated much since. On the roof of the building is a huge neon sign that spells out *Joe's* in cursive. I swear to god, people who live downtown complain that it keeps them awake at night. You can see the thing clear from the highway. The inside of the restaurant is all pinks and yellows and bright blues. And the waitstaff wears, no joke, *Spandex uniforms*. Like, I'm sorry, but talk about tacky. According to Kennedy, her dad used to work here when he was younger, before he went away to college and came back with a business degree and his first million. She's shown me the pictures of him in a neon-orange Spandex onesie, even though I most definitely did *not* ask to see them.

At precisely 1:15 p.m., I hop out of my car and head into the diner via the back entrance.

It's quiet inside. There's only one customer sitting in a booth by the front door—an older man slurping soup. That can't be my anonymous source . . . can it? I assess him for a long moment until he raises his head, giving me a puzzled glance. I shake myself out of it. Stay on course, Ogilvie.

Keeping my head down, I hurry toward the back of the restaurant and slip into the booth I'm pretty sure is the one anonymous described, doing my best to be quiet so as not to draw attention.

"Hello," I whisper, just in case someone is listening. The only response is the hum of the heating system switching on overhead.

I lean down, patting along the bottom of the wooden booth, and my fingers touch something papery. *There it is.* I try to pull it off, but the angle is awkward.

Crap. I think I have to . . . I start to slide downward, pulling myself between the tabletop and the booth, until I'm crouching on the ground. There it is—a large envelope duct-taped under my seat. No wonder I couldn't get the thing off from above;

there has to be at least a half roll of tape on here. I get to work peeling it off.

The envelope is almost free when I hear a nasally voice from above.

"Um, can I help you?"

I peek out from the gap above my head and see the waiter.

"What are . . ." He trails off, probably because he recognizes me from around town. I am sort of infamous these days. "Alice Ogilvie?" Yup, there it is.

I put a finger to my lips, yank the envelope the rest of the way off the bench bottom, and slip out from under the table, settling back down in the booth.

I blink at him prettily. "Oh hi."

"What were you . . ." He looks like he can't decide whether to finish that question.

I hop out of the booth, envelope in hand. "Pretend you never saw me, okay?" I'm about to head out, when I realize he might know some important information. "Actually—you might be able to help me."

"Me?" He points to himself, confusion in his eyes.

"Yes, you. Have you been here all afternoon? Did you see someone come in here, sit in this booth?" I gesture over to it.

He shakes his head. "No. I got here maybe five minutes ago. The shift just changed."

"Is the other person still here?" I look toward the back of the restaurant, like I might catch a glimpse of them.

"Nope. June took off. I think she was headed to Santa Barbara for the weekend to see family." He pauses. "Do you want anything? A coffee? Something—"

I shake my head. "No," I say brusquely. "Thank you, I need

to be going now." I brush past him, heading down the hallway and out the back door again, the envelope grasped tight in my hand.

Back in my car, I rip open the top of it, emptying its contents onto my lap. Inside are two unmarked folders.

In the first one, there's a photo—the one I sent off the day I saw that old car at Iris's building. The one she was so scared to see. The one she wouldn't tell me anything about afterward. Under that are a few pages—incident reports on a guy whose last name is, curiously, Adams. The same as Iris's. He's older, about the right age to be her dad . . . except Iris told me her dad was dead. I skim the papers quickly. He's been arrested a bunch. Domestic violence, mainly, from the looks of it. And, it appears that there's a restraining order against him. Taken out by none other than Iris's mom. What the *hell*?

What was this guy doing at Iris's house? Did she *lie* to me about her dad being dead? She wouldn't have . . . would she? Does this have something to do with why she was looking up that Whispering Pines place? I consider texting her to ask but remember her face the morning after when I asked her about it, how it slammed shut. There haven't been many times in my life where I've treaded lightly, but I have a feeling this needs to be one of them.

So instead, I set that folder aside for future reference, and open the second one.

Which is a *gold mine.*

"Whoa," I breathe, looking at the single paper inside. The visitor log from the jail. *Steve's* visitor log.

A list of names. It's short. It appears Steve hasn't had many visitors.

Marcus Anderson

Maryann Anderson

Steve's parents. It looks like they've come to visit him a bunch since he's been in jail, because their names appear several times on the list.

Ricky Randall

Alice Ogilvie

Iris Adams

Dusty Anderson

I'm surprised to see his sister's name. They were never that close, but I guess desperate times.

And then, a name I don't recognize.

Ruthann Bollinger

Ruthann Bollinger?

I type the name into Google. A ton of results pop up. I start clicking on them at random.

> **Ruthann Bollinger of the Bradford Media Corporation**
> **spoke to reporters yesterday about the upcoming**
> **global merger of LMC and . . .**

Okay, yawn. This is the sort of thing my dad always talks about—global mergers and acquisitions stuff—and whenever he does, my brain totally zones out. I stop reading and scan down the article to find a photo of a group of old men and women, all wearing stiff smiles and business suits. God, grownups must be so bored with their lives.

Under the photo is the caption *Pictures: Bradford Media Corporation's Ruthann Bollinger, Greta Bradford, and Sandy Ackerman with India Media Group's Leslie Leifer, Daniel Ahuja, and Deepash Patel.*

I furrow my brow. I'm not making the connection to Steve. The name Bradford is familiar for some reason, though. I Google it and realize why: Greta Bradford is the richest woman in the United States. Duh, I've heard my parents talking about her because every year she's on the *Forbes* list of billionaires.

I don't get it. I know Iris mentioned Steve could have been bribed in jail and flipped his plea because of that, but what's the connection? Why would some random person who works for a billionaire's media company care about Steve and Brooke and Castle Cove? Did she know Brooke? Or the Levy family?

I don't know what I'm looking at—not yet—but I have a strong suspicion that if we figure that out, we'll figure out exactly why it's not Coach Donovan behind bars.

• BREAKING NEWS •

Ben Perez: I'm sorry to interrupt your morning
programming, but in a startling turn of events in the
Brooke Donovan murder case, new details have emerged
about the manner of her death. Reporter Tessa Hopkins
is on the scene at the Castle Cove Police Department,
where a press conference is about to begin.

Tessa Hopkins: Thanks, Ben. I'm live at the police station
right now, where any moment, Detective Thompson is
expected to announce the results of the coroner's report
and new charges against Brooke Donovan's alleged
murderer, her boyfriend Steve Anderson. Anderson was
expected to plead guilty to involuntary manslaughter
and to receive—oh, wait, we're starting.

Detective Thompson: Thank you, ladies and gentlemen,
for your patience with our investigation. At this time, we
are charging Steven Anderson with first-degree murder
in the death of Brooke Donovan. I'll let Dr. Tavi Henry
speak now. Dr. Henry will deliver the results of the
autopsy examination.

Dr. Henry: Thank you. Preliminary testing indicated Ms. Donovan died of her injuries from the fall. Subsequent testing has revealed that her skull was fractured prior to the fall, most likely from a blunt object. In addition, abrasions sustained to her legs and the palms of her hands indicate that Ms. Donovan likely slipped, or was pushed, from the ledge of the cliff, but held on for a period of time. Impressions found on the backs of her hands are consistent with the sole of a shoe, or sneaker. This leads us to believe that Ms. Donovan released her hold on the cliffside from a force—

Reporter: "From a force"? What does that mean?

Dr. Henry: Forensic examination would indicate that her alleged killer stomped on her hands in order to cause her fall. After falling, she did sustain additional skull injuries. However, it is our belief that—

Tessa Hopkins: Are you saying Steve Anderson struck her before she fell? Approximately how many times and with what?

Reporter: Would she have lived if she hadn't fallen from the cliff?

Dr. Henry: It is possible she would have lived had she not fallen from the cliff. It is possible that her skull fracture would not have been the primary cause of her—

Reporter: Do the prints on her hands match Anderson's sneakers? What about the DNA test—

Reporter: What was the blunt object? Has it been found?

Detective Thompson: Excuse me, Dr. Henry. We have not located the object used to strike Ms. Donovan's skull. At this time, we believe the impressions on her hands will match the sneakers belonging to Steve Anderson. There were metallic flakes embedded in her skull, which we think may have come from a trophy of some sort. Mr. Anderson had accepted a Youth Basketball Mentor Award from the YMCA earlier that day. We believe he took the object from his car and used it on Ms. Donovan as they fought in the woods or cliffside.

Tessa Hopkins: Do you have anything to say about the public concern over the handling of this case, Detective Thompson? Many Castle Cove citizens think the police are responsible for planting Mr. Anderson's shoe—

Detective Thompson: Those rumors are entirely unfounded and a stain on the great men and women of this police force. Mr. Anderson had agreed to plead guilty to involuntary manslaughter, ma'am. You don't do that if you're innocent. At this time, the charges against Mr. Anderson have been altered to reflect new evidence. He'll be charged with first-degree murder, which carries a maximum of life without parole. Thank you.

Reporter: Where is Brooke Donovan's phone?

Tessa Hopkins: Who were the police who said they located the shoe in the woods?

Reporter: Where are you looking for the object?

Voices in crowd: Castle Cove Corrupt, Castle Cove Corrupt

CHAPTER THIRTY

This is bad. Deep breaths. See you soon.

I SHUT MY EYES. I don't even want to look at Ricky's text. As soon as that press conference ended, the school erupted. Nobody could listen in class. Everyone went crazy.

Steve. Life in prison. Blunt object.

Spike looks at me. He's been glued to his phone. "A trophy, Iris? Bashing somebody's head with a trophy and kicking them off a cliff? That's . . . hateful. That's *personal*. I feel sick."

So do I. I've been texting Alice every five minutes since I heard, and she hasn't texted back. I'm starting to get worried.

And my mom has been giving me looks from behind the bar ever since we got here. Those looks that mean, *Oh, how sweet, my daughter is* with *someone.* I'm ignoring her. Spike is Spike, and

I am not detonating my plans for a boy. And plus, hello? Steve Anderson is getting life in prison.

I'm rapping my knuckles on the booth table. This is so, so bad.

"Can you believe it? These posts, they're spreading like wildfire," Spike says. "Castle Cove Corrupt is still going strong, even with . . . this new stuff."

"Yeah," I say, distracted. "Have you seen Alice around today? She's supposed to meet us here and she's late."

"Maybe she ditched to go get her hair done or something."

"She has a little more depth than you give her credit for, Spike. I don't think she'd go to the salon when her ex-boyfriend is probably going to get life in prison."

"Jury's still out on that. So what's our next step?"

"Ricky. She's coming here with an update."

I keep tapping my fingers on the sticky table as I think. It's not like Alice to just, well, disappear. I mean, at least not any*more.*

"Hey, Iris?" Spike puts down his phone. "I was thinking, maybe, after all this? That maybe you might want to go to a movie or something?"

"Yeah, that sounds great," I say, craning my neck to see if Ricky's here yet. "Let's get everyone together. We should ask Alice, too—I bet she'd like to go."

"No, I meant, like, just you . . . and me."

Spike, nice and cute Spike, tangled hair flopping at his shoulders, pushes his glasses up his nose nervously. My heart starts thumping fast, but then just as quickly . . . deflates. There's a whole world in his eyes right now, I can see it happening: movies and hand-holding and sharing popcorn and all of that.

But that isn't me. Not right now. Because I'm only half here. The other half is going to vanish. I should have asked Alice about this. How to let someone down easy. Would she know? She must know. Alice seems like the kind of person who would know those things. Dammit. Am I *friends* with her?

"Spike," I say quietly. "Listen."

But before I can say more, Ricky appears at the edge of our booth, dressed more professionally than I've ever seen her: decent black suit, white shirt, gold necklace, and my god, her hair actually looks *blow-dried.*

My mother already has her drink ready at the bar, and Ricky grabs it and walks back to our booth. She slides in next to me.

"Where's Moneybags?" she murmurs, sipping her drink.

"I don't know where Moneybags is, at the moment. I think all of us are dying, to be honest. What the *hell* is going on?"

"The first rule in detective work is never to lose your partner, Iris," Ricky says. "Just like your suspect, you need to be aware of where they are and what they're doing at all times."

"Like they could be double-agenting?" Spike asks, cramming fries into his mouth.

I watch him swallow. Even if I were to ever, like, be with someone, I would prefer they not put thirty-six French fries into their mouth at once. Four, tops.

"Double-crossing," Ricky says with a grin. "Or compromised. Someday we'll have a little tutorial on investigative work, but now is not that day."

She opens her briefcase and pulls out some papers.

"Well. What a day, huh? I'm due back at the police station in a little bit. Short answer, they have no blunt object, so they don't have the murder weapon to compare to Steve's prints.

They still have the sneaker, but the fine print on the autopsy report about the impressions on the backs of Brooke's hands also notes that the impressions are slight and might have been compromised by her being in the water. Yes, she was probably kicked down, it's true. But can they match Steve's sneakers to those faint prints? Who knows. Made for good television, though."

"Did you talk to Steve?" I say. "I mean, what is he thinking . . . *now*?"

"Thanks for bringing that up, Iris. My client is currently sedated. La-la land. When I broke the news, he promptly became hysterical at the thought of life behind bars and had some sort of small seizure, I think. Kept saying it wasn't supposed to go down like this. I'll check in on him later. My guess is once he's lucid, he's going to have a lot to say. Nobody wants life, I'll tell you that. Which is good. We want a trial. That's the best possible scenario for us."

"But what about the other stuff?" Spike asks. "You know, like you thought somebody might have paid him off?"

Ricky takes a big gulp of her drink. "That's what I'm hoping he'll spill when he wakes up. I need him to tell me that, offer me some bona fides, because I've got no proof of that. Do you? Or you, Iris?"

Spike and I shake our heads.

"It's time for step four, Iris," Ricky says.

I take out my casebook and dig around in my backpack for a pen. "I'm ready."

Ricky Randall taps my casebook.

"I've got plenty on Donovan, that's for sure. At least enough for an investigation. Do I have the exact thing I need? A blunt object that might possibly be a trophy? I do not. Do I have something else, more concrete? I do not."

"So . . . what now?" I ask.

"I need to keep pushing focus away from Steve and more to the police and Matt Donovan. I can't use what you have about Donovan with the DA because you obtained it illegally. So I need you to make what you have available to the *one* person I know who cares only about the story and not about fussy little legal details like illegal information leaks to the press. Someone who will blow this up big-time, and quick. Make a huge gap and let the police fall through it."

She downs the rest of her drink in one swallow, stands up, collects her briefcase, and places a card on the table between me and Spike.

Tessa Hopkins.

When we look up, Ricky Randall is gone.

"Shit," Spike says. "The crazy TV lady."

"Right." I text Alice again. Wait. Nothing. I listen to the echoey sound of Spike's straw at the bottom of his glass, sucking at emptiness. It's annoying and I want it to stop.

"Give me that," I mutter. He pushes it to me and I take it, walking over to the bar, wedging myself between an old woman doodling in black ink on a cocktail napkin and a guy playing Angry Birds on his phone. My mom is down the bar, gently talking to a weeping woman. I sigh.

"You seem a bit young for an establishment like this."

I glance to the left.

My heart practically drops to my feet, out of my shoes, and proceeds to roll halfway across the sticky bar floor.

Lilian Levy is perched on the barstool next to me, the tips of her exquisitely painted nails moving the red straw in her drink in circles around the inside of the glass. The red straw matches the red frames on her glasses.

My cheeks are hot. How I wish Alice was here right now. She'd know exactly how to handle this. "I . . . my mom works here. She's right down there. Kids can be here before seven, but not after."

"Mmm," she murmurs. "My father used to bring me here when I was little. Ordered me Shirley Temples, though of course I'm having something quite stronger than that now. I can't say this place has changed much. He did like it here, though. Said it felt real. I guess I just wanted to remember that right now. What's real."

She goes quiet, her eyes getting a faraway look. I would like to believe she's a mean old rich woman, but I can't. Right now, she's just a grandmother who lost her granddaughter.

"I . . . I knew her," I finally say. "Your granddaughter. Brooke. We went to school together. I'm so sorry."

Her eyes flicker to mine. "That's very kind of you. I've lost everyone now. My daughters. My granddaughter. I had a husband once and I lost him, too, but this feels different. This emptiness."

The enormous sapphire ring she's wearing catches in the light above the bar. She laughs softly when she sees me looking at it. "This means nothing. It's beautiful, but it doesn't take away a broken heart. They say money makes you happy. It doesn't. It just makes you more comfortable in your grief."

My mother comes over and exchanges a look with Lilian

Levy. Lilian nods ever so slightly, and my mother refills her empty glass. "You have a lovely daughter," Lilian says. "Very smart. Agile."

"Why, thank you," my mother answers. She gives me a strange look, because of course she does. I'm talking to a rich old woman in a bar. But wait . . .

"I'm sorry, what did you say?" My blood gets cooler. Smart? *Agile?* She knows nothing about me.

Lilian Levy chuckles. "Iris Adams. The last person, well, second-to-last, to see my Brooke alive. Don't look so surprised. Do you think I haven't combed over the police interviews? I know who every player is in this tragedy."

She swivels on the stool so she's facing me. Her face is smooth, powdered, black mascara clinging elegantly to her eyelashes. "Were you frightened when you jumped from my granddaughter's balcony? Don't think I didn't know you were there. I could hear you and Alice scuttling around upstairs like mice when I came into the house. But I played along with Alice. To see how far she'd take it. I was . . . impressed when I went to close the doors to Brooke's balcony. Impressed to see a tiny, sprite-like figure darting up the hill in the exact lumberjack-style shirt you're wearing right this very minute."

"I . . ." I'm stuck. She *saw* me? What else does she know? Also, I'm wearing flannel. Lumberjacks wear *wool.*

"Come now, Iris Adams. You and Alice, bless her flighty brain, have something up your sleeve. You don't think the boy did it."

Her eyes are pinning mine. I can't look away. There's something in them. Sadness, grief, but also . . . a spark of interest.

If I don't say something soon, I'll lose this. And I can't lose it.

"No, we don't," I say finally. "In fact, we think someone paid him to say he did. And so . . . was it *you*? You might as well tell me. There's no way I could prove it, anyway. I just want to know."

She laughs so hard, tears pool in the corners of her eyes, and she reaches for a cocktail napkin, dabbing at them.

"Oh my," she says, crumpling the napkin and setting it on the bar next to her doodled napkins. Stars, hearts, suns. Something a little girl would draw.

"That's very rich. Dear girl, if I thought that boy killed my granddaughter, I would take care of it."

A chill runs through me. *Take care of it.*

Her eyes are no longer laughing.

"I didn't pay that twit. If he wanted to plead guilty, so be it. If he gets life now after all this new mess and he's innocent, so be it. Don't you understand? It doesn't matter to me who did it. I will still have lost everything. I will *never* have peace. I just want to bury my granddaughter and go home. Castle Cove is no longer my home."

"But someone," I say. If not Lilian, who? "Someone did pay him, right? That's what we think, anyway, and also, we think . . ."

Do I dare say Coach Donovan? Alice says Lilian hates Coach. Maybe she thinks it's him, too, but like she said, it doesn't matter to her anymore.

She's picked up her pen again. Her shoulders are slumped, like the air has gone out of her.

Star, heart, sun on the napkin.

"It must be hard on you, your mother working here. But I imagine you two get by somehow. I remember that, having nothing, having to work my way back into the world. But I did it. I went from a castle with eighteen bedrooms and a private zoo with llamas to a sixth-floor walkup in the East Village to a grand brownstone off Central Park and a seventeenth-century home in Scotland. My name is on the lipstick half the women in the world wear. Sixty percent of women slap the jeans I designed on their asses every day. *I* did that. I earned it. I earned my place in the world."

She slides a slim leather wallet from her purse, slips out two twenties, and folds the doodled napkin around it.

"I suspect your interest in my granddaughter's death has much to do with the reward. Am I right, Iris Adams?"

I'm silent, ashamed.

"Don't be cowed, dear girl. But you have to work for what you want. That's the way of the world when you have nothing. They make you struggle for it. I did. You can, too. But it never hurts to have a little leg up, does it?" Her phone vibrates and she stands slowly.

She puts her wrinkled, bejeweled hand on my shoulder and leans into my ear. "I love a good mystery as much as the next person. I can't wait to see how this plays out."

Lilian Levy winks at me. "My car is here. Good luck to you, Iris Adams."

I watch her walk out of the bar, leaning on her cane.

My mother comes over, scoops up the empty glass and the crumpled napkins. "What was *that* all about?" she says.

I shake my head. "I don't know."

Across the room, Spike is giving me the *What's going on?* hands-up-in-the-air gesture.

"Oh, Mom," I say as she's walking away. "Your tip."

I pick up the folded napkin, the stars and hearts and suns

bleeding through the soft tissue. I unfold the napkin and hand my mom the twenties.

Inside the napkin, among the hearts and stars, is written *Penny Jefferson* in spindly script. I walk back to Spike. Penny Jefferson? What was that nutty old lady thinking? Maybe she had one too many drinks, thinking about her old life in Castle Cove.

I slide into the booth across from Spike, lay down the napkin between us.

"That was Lilian Levy," I say, grateful to have something to focus on besides Spike's apparent interest in me.

Spike's eyes pop. "I'm sorry, *what?*"

"Ha, don't worry, I asked if she paid Steve off and she intimated that if she thought he did it, she wouldn't bribe him, she'd kill him. Which, *scary*. Then she said I have to earn it, whatever that means."

Spike looks at the napkin. "So you saved her ramblings for a souvenir?"

I shrug. Earn it. Thanks, rich lady. So helpful, like I didn't know that already.

"Iris."

I mean, I live my stupid life *earning* it. And who the hell is this lady, getting a thrill by watching me run up a hill? *Impressed* by that?

"Iris." Spike pounds his fist on the table.

"What?" I yell back.

"Penny Jefferson," he says, a little bit of spit flying from his mouth, his cheeks flushed. He holds up his phone.

I squint at it. Some picture of a smiling, brown-haired young woman, the arm of a handsome young fellow looped around her shoulders. Something about his eyes seems familiar, the way they bore into the camera. Tousled blond hair, just another good-looking guy.

```
Penny Jefferson, the wife of billionaire
Paul Bradford, reported missing
```

"Thanks, Spike, for another missing girl story. I don't have enough of those," I say.

"Look closer, dummy. Look closer at Paul Bradford." He shoves the phone at me.

The article is over twenty years old. I scroll down, find other photos in color. And then I see it. A flare of recognition in those steel-blue eyes staring at me, the same way they did when I answered a question about Napoleon incorrectly in freshman history class.

"Holy shit," I say. "Is that——"

"I think it is!"

Steel-blue eyes, setting the hearts of many teachers at Castle Cove High on fire. The nose is a little different now, the jawline less prominent, softer somehow.

"This is Coach. Matt Donovan is Paul Bradford——"

"And *that* girl went missing too——" Spike says.

I drop his phone on the table and pick up my own.

Alice, I text. *Alice ALICE.*

I send her the link to the Penny Jefferson article.

COACH DONOVAN IS PAUL BRADFORD
PENNY JEFFERSON, Alice

Google Penny Jefferson + Paul Bradford
I will be at your house in fifteen minutes

𝕾𝖆𝖓𝖙𝖆 𝕮𝖗𝖚𝖟 𝕿𝖎𝖒𝖊𝖘

APRIL 23, 1997

Disappearance of Local Woman
Puzzles Santa Cruz PD

Last Sunday afternoon, while on a camping trip with her husband, Paul Bradford, in the Santa Cruz Mountains, Penny Jefferson, 23, went missing. Bradford said Jefferson told him she was going on a solo hike to see a nearby waterfall while he set up camp. After almost an hour had passed with no word from her, he grew concerned and went to try to find her. There was no sign of her on the trail to the waterfall or at the falls themselves, so Bradford alerted authorities. Bradford related that Jefferson had, in recent months, been struggling with a substance abuse problem as well as serious depression. The Santa Cruz PD was dispatched, and shortly after, search efforts began.

Three days later there is still no sign of Jefferson, despite the best efforts of local authorities. Bradford is the son of media mogul Peter Ford Bradford III.

Under the article are more headlines and photos. I scroll down.

MAY 17, 1997

Still No Leads in Jefferson's Disappearance
Husband Paul Bradford Comes Under Fire

AUGUST 5, 1997

Remains Discovered in Santa Cruz Mountains Could
Be Missing Local Woman

AUGUST 8, 1997

Santa Cruz Community Rallies Around Jefferson
Family
Discovered Remains Not Those of Daughter
Penny Jefferson

AUGUST 23, 1997

Media Empire Heir Addresses Gossip Regarding
Involvement in Disappearance of Wife

OCTOBER 23, 1997

Six Months After Penny Jefferson Disappearance,
Here's What We Know

Penny Jefferson Declared Legally Dead by Family a Year After Disappearance
Husband Paul Bradford Leaves Town Amid Public Scrutiny

"This is huge," Spike says.

My breath is caught in my throat. Threads are desperately trying to attach to one another in my brain. Matthew Donovan used to be Paul Bradford. Matt Donovan used to be mega, mega rich when he was Paul Bradford. Paul Bradford's wife went missing and was never found.

Rich people can do anything. They can erase lives. They can make new ones.

This is exactly what Ricky Randall wanted.

When we Googled Matt Donovan, nothing came up but basketball and community fundraisers and Castle Cove High and Victoria Levy and millions of other Matt Donovans out there living their Matt Donovan lives.

Because . . . Matt Donovan is not Matt Donovan at all.

CHAPTER THIRTY-ONE

"Very few of us are what we seem."

—AGATHA CHRISTIE,

THE MAN IN THE MIST

I'M PACING THE WIDTH of the conservatory, sipping a cup of tea and thinking about the latest twist in the case. Steve might be charged with first-degree murder and face life in prison? Coach Donovan might be Paul Bradford. Paul Bradford might be Coach Donovan. Coach Donovan might be a *billionaire*? The guy who once wore the same pair of ratty sweatpants to school for a week straight, until Brooke finally intervened?

Not to mention, someone from the Bradford Corporation just so *happened* to have visited Steve in jail?

Through the windows of the room, I can hear the faint crash of the ocean against the bottom of the cliffs. It's windy out tonight—the blustery fall wind tapping branches of redwoods against the roof. It's appropriately spooky.

The door to the room swings open, and Iris and Spike appear.

"Iris, you *genius.* I am freaking out. This is *so crazy*," I say by way of greeting, stopping in my tracks for a moment. "This is becoming more and more like an Agatha Christie novel by the minute! Like, so many of her books have people who use hidden identities to get away with murder." I start counting on my fingers. "Let's see, there's *A Murder Is Announced, Murder on the Orient Express, Murder in Mesopotamia* . . . "

"I cannot believe Coach Donovan might be, like, *a whole different person,*" Spike says, taking a seat on the couch and folding one long leg under his body.

Iris perches on the arm of the big blue chair, all casual, like she didn't just manage to blow this thing *wide open.*

"Where did you find this info?" I say to her. "This is *awesome.*"

Iris blushes. "Thank you. I actually . . . well, I ran into Lilian Levy. At the bar."

"At the Moon Landing?" I ask incredulously.

"Yes," says Iris. "And she gave me this big speech about working for what you want, which I thought was really annoying at first, because, hello, you're a billionaire, lady, but then she left this napkin behind. . . ."

"With the words *Penny Jefferson* on it!" exclaims Spike, who looks like he's about to burst.

"I cannot believe you and Lilian Levy were hanging out." I shake my head, smiling at the thought of it. "Okay, so I have to tell you something from my end, too. I got another text from that anonymous source, that told me to go to Joe's Diner. Where I found—get this—Steve's visitor log from the *jail.*"

"Excuse me," says Spike. "Who is this *contact?*"

"We are unsure about that at the moment," I say primly. "Anyway, that's not the point. The point is that there was a name on it I didn't know, so I Googled it. And, it turns out that the person works for the *Bradford Corporation*."

Iris's eyes pop open wide. "You mean . . ."

"Yes!" I exclaim. "And, I felt like it was something big, but of course I didn't figure it out until you sent me that text. Paul Bradford is the *son* of—"

"Billionaire Greta Bradford," finishes Iris, jumping up to stand. "And this woman whose name you saw—"

"Ruthann Bollinger," I interject.

"Wait, did you say *Ruthann*?" She hurries back to our casebook and starts flipping through pages. "I thought so. Look at this, right here! *RA—Ruthann.* Do you think that's who Coach texted the morning after Brooke disappeared?"

My mouth drops open. "Holy—"

Iris is thinking hard. "That weird message. Where Coach said his security system was faulty or something. It must have been some kind of—"

"Code," I interrupt. "For help. I bet his family made him communicate with them by code if he needed something."

"He must have known he'd be looked at for all of this, and if he was . . . he knew it would be *bad* for him," says Iris. "All of this stuff . . . it would have come out."

I nod, heart pounding. "*Yes.* And they must have come right away. To help. I found a bunch of pics that had both Ruthann and Greta in them, together. Articles that talked about the two of them working together closely. Ruthann is for sure not just some rando who works there. She's, like, Greta's right-hand woman."

Iris heaves a breath. "My head is spinning. Coach's first wife disappeared. Was *murdered,* maybe? Did Coach do that? Did he leave town and change his name? And like, have *plastic sur-*

gery? Are we living in the plot of one of those soap operas my grandma used to watch?"

"I mean, his first wife fell off a cliff," says Spike. "Under uber-suspicious circumstances. Not the worst idea to skip town and get a new identity. I bet you his parents were more than happy to make the situation go away."

Iris shakes her head. "What I don't get is, why did Lilian let her daughter marry that man? Do you think she knew from the beginning that Coach was Paul Bradford? And, moreover, did *Brooke's mom* know?"

I stop in my tracks, thinking about what Iris just said. *Did* Victoria know? She was married to him for ten years. He formally adopted her only kid.

"God. I hadn't even thought about that part of it. Victoria and Coach had this whirlwind romance—Brooke once told me that her grandma didn't know until after it had happened that the two of them had gotten married. So, maybe Lilian figured it out after that, but it was too late." I shiver. "It's all so creepy, thinking that Coach has been around all these years and maybe no one ever really knew him at all."

Spike sits back against the couch cushions, rubbing a hand against his cheek. "But Coach has all that debt. Credit card, gambling, all of it. Why not just ask his family for money? If they're so rich and all?"

I shake my head. "My best guess would be that they told him not to contact them unless it was an emergency. Like, a real one. Like this."

"Hmm," Spike says. "Makes sense. They wouldn't want a trail back to them, if they could help it. So do we think . . . do we think that once Coach's—*Paul's*—mom got wind of this mess, she got someone to pay off Steve? To confess to the murder that Coach-slash-Paul committed?"

I shake my head again. "I don't know for sure, but otherwise the fact that this Ruthann person visited Steve in jail is a *very* strange coincidence, don't you think? And that outgoing call from Coach's phone to RA the morning Brooke went missing . . . That would be an awfully big coincidence, if you ask me."

"Agreed." Iris rummages in the front pocket of her backpack and holds out a business card between her fingers. "Ricky gave me this card"—Spike clears his throat and she rolls her eyes—"gave *us* this card earlier this afternoon. Look at it."

I walk over and pluck it from her fingers. On it is a name:

TESSA HOPKINS
ANCHOR / REPORTER
KWB

"Ricky wants us to leak the info we have," Iris continues. "To that reporter. The one who was there the night we found Brooke's bo—" She catches herself. "Brooke was found. You yelled at her, remember? Anyway, Ricky says that she'll help us."

"Yeah. I know Tessa," I say to Iris. "Not only was she a huge B that night on the cliff, she *also* harassed me after I got in trouble last summer. She wouldn't leave me alone. I don't know. . . ."

"She would be perfect, then," Iris says. "You have to admit, she's determined. Who better to help take Coach down?"

I sigh. Involving Tessa seems like a gamble, but then again, what choice do we really have? This is our one shot to *really* sway public opinion and prove the cops totally messed this case up. And Iris is right, Tessa is nothing if not persistent, which was incredibly annoying when she was focused on me but could be just what we need to crack this case wide open.

I walk over to the murder board and point to the new additions. "I printed out the visitor log that I obtained from my source, and a bunch of the articles that trace Penny Jefferson from the time she disappeared up until the time she was declared dead." I point to the top-right section of the board. "And photos of Paul Bradford and the person now known as Coach Matthew Donovan."

Spike gets up and walks over to the board, scrutinizing the two pictures. "Man, seeing Paul and Coach next to each other . . . it's giving me the creeps."

"No kidding." Iris walks over and stands next to him. The two of them look back and forth between the images. "Like, the blue eyes are the exact same. The chin is a little bit slimmer and his nose is different. . . . Those are easy things to change, though—right, Alice?" Iris looks at me.

"Excuse me, how would *I* know?" I say. My nose is very much my own, thank you kindly.

Iris walks back to the couch and grabs a file off the coffee table. It's labeled *Coach* and has all the articles we've printed out and collected on him, along with the will and other materials that we found in his office.

She settles back down onto a cushion. "Okay, here's what we need to do before we call Tessa. Ricky said we should make sure all our stuff is in one place so we can give it to her—copies of Coach's texts, the will, all of it. A file of the evidence, including this new stuff. *Especially* this new stuff, really." She points to the board. "I bet you Tessa will have a way of looking back into the Bradfords and digging up even more info on Paul."

"I didn't find anything more when I was Googling, but maybe." I pause and think for a second. "I guess Greta probably has the resources to make sure certain stories are no longer written about her dear son Paul."

Iris holds out the file. "Spike, take this." She sounds so bossy. I smile. "Make copies of everything inside."

He salutes her and takes it from her hand, heading over to the machine I moved in from my dad's office.

"In the meantime . . ." Iris pulls our casebook out of her backpack, opening it to a blank page. "We have to make our file for Tessa." She starts scribbling away. I walk over and take a seat beside her, reading over her shoulder.

Suspect: Matthew Donovan

Real name: Paul Bradford of the Bradford family. One of the richest families in the world. Suspected to have murdered his first wife, after which time he disappeared and resurfaced more than ten years later with a new face in Castle Cove, CA. A few years after that, he married Victoria Levy, of the Levy Cosmetics family.

October 31

1. Cannot account for time between 10:30 p.m. and 2:00 a.m.
2. Texts on phone reveal message from Kevin (bookie) to meet at midnight on 10/31; meeting never happened

3. *Owes bookie a LOT of money (100k)*
4. *Credit card statements reveal 300k in personal debt*
5. *Trust states limited monthly stipend for BD's upkeep*
6. *Trust states stipend ends upon BD's 18th birthday*
7. *Will states 5 mil upon BD's untimely death before age of 18*
8. *Texts reveal fractured relationship with BD due to money issues*
9. *Verbally harassed AO in CCHS hallway, witnessed by guidance counselor*
10. *Ignored Brooke's texts the night she disappeared and then lied to Alice about them*

She finishes and we both fall quiet, reading the list over.

"Wow," I say. "This does not look good for Coach."

Iris's mouth quirks. "No, it doesn't."

She turns to me. "I mean, people can hide so *many* things."

I know she's talking about me and my disappearance, but I can't help but think about the man outside of her house. The guy who might be her dad; the same person she claimed was dead. I open my mouth to say something, but Spike ambles back over, clutching a sheaf of papers.

"Is it time? Can I do it? Please?" he says excitedly, setting down the papers on the table in front of us.

In unison, Iris and I say, *"No."*

I look at Iris; she looks at me. She holds the card up so I can read the number.

I tap the number into the burner phone, hit Speaker, and hold it out so we can all listen.

It rings. And rings.

"What do we say when she answers? How do you even *do* this?" Iris says, bouncing up and down on the couch next to me.

"I told you to let me!" Spike says. He changes his voice so it's deeper. "I have some information you might find impor—"

I hold up my hand.

"This is Tessa Hopkins, KWB News. To leave a message related to a broadcast, press one. For confidential information, press two."

Iris and Spike are both staring at me.

I press two with a shaking finger.

We could ruin someone's life with what we're about to do. I think about Coach making us waffles in the mornings, laughing with Victoria and spinning her around the kitchen. How he'd come to all of our dance rehearsals back in middle school. But then I remember how Agatha Christie once said, "People who can be very good can be very bad, too." And good lord, who changes their name? Who has *plastic surgery* on their face so they can change their identity?

Only someone who has done very bad things.

"Tessa Hopkins, you don't know me, but I'll be looking for you at Brooke Donovan's funeral tomorrow. Don't brush me off. I know what happened to Brooke, and I have proof." I press End and look up.

"Noooiicce." Spike nods approvingly and holds up his hand to high-five.

Grudgingly, I return his five.

CHAPTER THIRTY-TWO

ALICE

NOVEMBER 11

11:22 A.M.

"Why harrow oneself by looking
on the worst side?"
"Because it is sometimes necessary."
—AGATHA CHRISTIE, *SAD CYPRESS*

IRIS IS WAITING FOR me in the parking lot of the cemetery the next morning.

"Are you ready for this?" She has on black retro-y sunglasses with sparkles on the corners, a surprisingly good look for her. I can't tell if she's talking about the funeral, Tessa, or something else entirely, but I nod. I'm ready for it all.

Around us, funeral-goers wearing black trickle out of their cars, walking toward the gravesite in small groups. I recognize some of them from school—a bunch of teachers, including a pale-faced Ms. Westmacott, are walking up ahead of us—but there are a lot of people our age who I can't place.

I shove my hands deep into my coat pockets. "Who *are* all these people?" I ask Iris. "I'm not that bad at recognizing the people from school, am I?"

She makes a face. "Not to be rude, Alice, but you might be.

We've gone to school together for ten years, and you didn't even know my name. Although, to be fair, I don't think that these kids go to our school." She nods over to a clump of people to our right, all wearing black shirts with white lettering that says #CastleCoveCorrupt.

One of the guys in the group catches my eye. "Corrupt cops!" he yells, throwing a fist pump into the air.

My mouth falls open. "Oh my god," Iris mutters under her breath.

My heart is thumping about a million times a minute in my chest. I knew the hashtag had picked up steam. Last night, Alec Downey, that TikTok creator who's always getting word out about social justice issues, posted about it on their page. The post already has over five hundred thousand views and one hundred and fifty thousand shares.

The comments section was full of people agreeing, talking about the toxic divide between the rich and the poor in Castle Cove, and even bringing up other examples of the cops doing shady stuff in the past here. There were also some people who mentioned the possibility of protesting, but I didn't think they'd actually show up, especially not to the funeral.

It's working.

Along the far edge of the parking lot, news vans are set up and reporters are milling around trying to flag people down for interviews. It's a madhouse.

Iris nudges me. "There's Tessa." She nods to the KWB van, where Tessa stands, barking orders at that same tired-looking cameraman from the night at the Lookout. "We need to keep an eye on her—make sure she doesn't leave before we get a chance to talk."

I snort. "I doubt that'll be a problem. Knowing Tessa, she's probably dying to know who left her that message last night. I'm betting she'll wait around after to see if they find her."

We've almost made it to the lawn when I hear someone calling my name. I turn and see Rafael Ramirez hurrying toward us, waving. My heart skips a beat. The last time I saw Raf was . . . a while ago . . . during what was one of both the best and worst experiences of my life.

"Who is that?" Iris whispers, nudging me. "Do you know him?"

"Umm . . . yes," I tell her. "That's Raf. Ramirez? He went to CCHS and graduated a few years ago? Played basketball with Steve?"

She shakes her head.

"I guess I'm not the only one who doesn't know every person who goes to our school," I tease. She rolls her eyes.

"Hey, Alice," Raf says breathlessly when he catches up to us. "How are you? This is all—" He cuts off, noticing Iris. "Oh, I'm sorry. I'm Raf." He extends his hand, like he's a grown-up person. Typical Raf. Iris takes it and shakes.

"Iris," she replies.

"Hi, Iris." Raf holds up a hand to shield his eyes from the bright midday sun, squinting in the direction of the crowd of people. "Alice, how are you holding up?"

"I'm fine," I say merrily. "Just fine, thank you."

He gives me a long look. "Fine?"

"Fine!" I reply. "You can stop asking me that now."

"Alice, I'd like to help just like—"

I blink at him. The last thing I want is for him to finish that sentence. "You being here is very kind."

"I just——" he starts, but I cut him off again.

"It was great seeing you, but we have to go." I hook my arm through Iris's and start dragging her away.

"What was that?" she hisses.

"Nothing, like I said, he went to our school. Was friends with Steve. He sort of knew Brooke, but not that well, so it's nice of him to come today. Now back to the actual important stuff—like watching Coach." I point ahead.

In front of us are several rows of white folding chairs, where the family sits, waiting. An elegantly dressed Lilian Levy is holding hands with her sister, Caroline, who's bawling. Coach Donovan is in the first chair, nearest to the head of the grave. His mouth is set in a fierce line, and he's wearing sunglasses and a rumpled black suit. None of the other family members are speaking to him.

My nostrils flare. He doesn't deserve that seat.

We're approaching the grave site. There's a hole dug into the earth and a pile of dirt to one side. My stupid hands start shaking, so I stick them back into my pockets as we approach. I take a breath. I can do this. We're here on a business matter, and I will not, as Agatha Christie put it, mix up sentiment and reason.

Iris and I find Spike, Zora, and Neil standing toward the back of the crowd and join them. It looks like almost every faculty member from school has come. I spot Park and Kennedy and some of the other Mains across the way, the guys jostling each other and laughing like they think this is some sort of party.

As we wait for the ceremony to begin, I start to register the whispers around us.

I heard he pushed her off the cliff because when she turned eighteen, his source of money was going to dry up.

He def looks like a murderer.

Creep. Poor Brooke living in that house alone with him for all those years.

I swallow. I know it's what we wanted, but listening to strangers speculate about Coach and Brooke and her murder . . . it hurts in a way I didn't expect.

The far side of the crowd parts, and the guests quiet as the minister emerges. He walks up and stands next to the headstone, and the sight cracks something inside of me.

"I can't do this," I whisper, starting to back away, out through the people gathered around me.

"Let me through, please," I say as I push past them, keeping my voice down because the last thing I want is to cause a scene, but if these people don't let me out of here, I am going to literally freak out.

I don't exhale until I reach the edge of the crowd. I head to the nearest palm tree and sink down to a crouch under it, the tightness in my chest slowly releasing.

"Alice?" Iris is panting slightly from following me. "Are you okay?"

I rub my eyes and realize they're wet.

I'm crying.

"Yeah," I answer, though I am clearly lying. I take a big, ugly sniff. I am not an attractive crier. My mom always used to say that to me when I was younger—*Alice, you are much prettier when you smile*—which is about the time I stopped allowing myself to cry. "I'm fine."

"You know . . ." Iris takes off her sunglasses and squints into the California sunlight. "It's okay. If you're not, you know—if you're not okay. She was your friend."

The lump in my throat aches, but maybe a little bit less. She sits down next to me and takes my hand, twining her fingers through mine, and we sit and watch the funeral from afar.

An hour later, most people have departed. The reporters have started packing up their equipment. From our spot under the tree where we've been camped, Iris nudges me. "She's still here."

She nods in the direction of Tessa Hopkins, busily scrolling on her phone while her cameraman loads up the van.

I nod. "Let's do this."

Iris takes the folder of information out of her bag, and we head over to the van. I clear my throat. "Excuse me?"

She ignores me.

I put a hand on my hip and clear my throat again, louder this time. "Um, *excuse me?*"

Tessa finally looks up. She raises a perfectly sculpted brow and says, "Alice Ogilvie? Can I *help* you? If you've finally come looking for your five minutes of fame, I hate to say it, but your story is so last season." She gestures around us. "This is what the people are interested in now. Blew your disappearance right out of the water."

I glare at her and open my mouth to snap a response, but Iris elbows me, shaking her head. *Stay on message,* she mouths. She turns back to Tessa. "We have some information we think you'd be interested in. Information about *this.*" She gestures back toward the site of the grave, holding out the folder of information toward Tessa, who looks at it with disinterest.

"A folder?"

Iris shakes it. "No, you don't get it. It's *us.*"

Tessa's eyes narrow. "Who is *us?*"

God this lady is annoying. I point to Iris and then back to myself. "We are. We are us."

Tessa looks at me for a moment and then rubs the bridge of her nose. "You kids today, you all speak in riddles, I swear to god." She snaps her fingers to the cameraman. "I don't have time for this. I've got to be on air in an hour." She hikes her purse up her shoulder and turns to go.

"No, no wait," Iris calls out. "Alice is trying to say that we're the ones who called you. Last night. On the tip line. Ricky Randall sent us."

Tessa stops in her tracks and turns back to us. "Oh, is that right? Interesting. You two?" She arches an eyebrow. "Let me give you a tip, girls. First rule of being a source? Leave your name and number so I can call back. It's all confidential out here in news-land."

"Listen," Iris says, frustrated. "Just *take it* already and stop lecturing." She holds the folder out again. This time Tessa takes it between her exquisitely manicured fingers and opens it. As she starts to read what we put together, her expression begins to shift from condescending to curious to . . . shocked.

She looks up from the folder at us with wide eyes and a pale face. "This says you think Matt Donovan might be . . . Paul Bradford? The son of the Bradfords, who no one has seen for the better part of two *decades*? Jesus Christ. Do you know . . . do you two know what you might have stumbled onto here? If that's true? This could be the cover-up of the century. How did you happen upon this?"

"We can't reveal our sources," I say. "But we're almost positive it's true."

A wicked grin plays on the edges of Tessa's mouth. "You said

Ricky Randall sent you, huh? And how did you two get mixed up with a character like Ricky?"

"She used to be my babysitter," Iris says.

Tessa Hopkins barks out a laugh and slams the folder shut.

"Get in the van. We're going for a ride."

CHAPTER THIRTY-THREE

IRIS

NOVEMBER 12

5:04 P.M.

ALICE IS BOUNCING ON the comfy blue chair in her conservatory. We're fixated on the giant flat screen above the fireplace, waiting impatiently.

"When?" Alice keeps saying. *"When?"*

"Hush," I tell her. "Didn't your parents ever teach you to be patient?"

Alice looks at me blankly. "No. Is that a thing?"

On the screen, the anchor is promising breaking news in the Steve Anderson case. Tessa had told us in the van, as she flipped through our investigation folder, that it would take time, because she'd have to verify everything. "I'm not an idiot," she'd said. "I don't want to get fired or sued, to be clear, but I'm also not above, you know, playing a little fast and loose. And I need to tell the detectives on the case what I have and give them time to respond, or not."

"To *what?*" Crushed between camera equipment, coolers, cords, and cables in the back of the van, Alice was indignant.

"If even half of this is true," Tessa told her, "it means the police didn't look at Matt Donovan closely, for one. And two, if the connection between his phone call to Bradford Corp., and the Bollinger person contacting Steve, pans out to prove money changed hands in exchange for a guilty plea . . . that's, like, well, career-making for me, and I don't want to mess it up. Three . . . if we find out cops were on the payroll, oh wow, that's . . ." She shakes her head, stunned by it all.

"Castle Cove Cover-Up," called the cameraman from the front seat in a singsong voice.

"Shut it," Tessa said. "You have two jobs: making me look good and driving."

"Eh," he calls back. "You know the police in this town bleed green, not blue."

"So what, then," I said. "We wait? How long?"

Tessa paged through the documents in our folder. "A few hours? Tomorrow? Just keep your eyes peeled."

"You won't . . ." I hesitated. "You promise you won't name us?" That's the last thing I need. To be front and center on the news when I'm trying to make myself as invisible as possible.

"No, anonymous sources are protected. I can't be compelled to reveal your identities even in court. Shit, if journalists had to reveal their sources, we'd have no news to deliver."

The cameraman snorted.

Tessa looked from Alice to me, a smile spreading across her face, her brightly painted lips revealing sparkling, white, expensive teeth.

"I'm going to take a guess and say a lot of this wasn't obtained, oh, on the up and up. Would I be right?"

"I'm sorry, we can't reveal that information at this time," Alice said gleefully.

"Evasiveness. I like it," Tessa responded. "You two are quite the detectives, aren't you? I'm impressed."

My focus is pulled back to the television as the commercial ends and Ben Perez, the news anchor, who had previously been reporting on a local woman's seashell Etsy shop, fixes his face into a serious expression.

"And now, breaking news in the Brooke Donovan investigation. We're going live to the Castle Cove Police Department for a special report by Tessa Hopkins."

"Holy moly," Alice breathes.

My stomach is squeezing tightly. Spike texts me. *IT'S HAPPENING.*

"Thank you, Ben." Tessa Hopkins flips her hair and stares directly into the camera.

"This is her moment," Alice says excitedly. "Can you see it? She's *thrilled.*"

I can see it, how her body is positively electrified, and it makes me a little uneasy. I can also hear a lot of noise around her. Is that . . . chanting?

"Castle Cove Corrupt! Castle Cove Corrupt!"

"I'm here at the Castle Cove Police Department, where just a few days ago, Steve Anderson was preparing to plead guilty to the murder of heiress Brooke Donovan. But what was initially an involuntary manslaughter charge was changed to first-degree murder, after a coroner's report stated that Brooke Donovan was bludgeoned before her fall from the cliff."

Tessa Hopkins pivots slightly, taking a few steps, putting herself in front of the chanting crowd. "In a shocking turn of events, Anderson has now recanted his admission of guilt. And while police have so far remained firm that evidence puts Anderson at the crime scene that evening, KWB has recently learned some explosive new details that put the entire investigation of Brooke Donovan's death into question."

She takes a deep breath. Her moment has arrived.

"Anonymous sources have revealed that Matthew Donovan, stepfather to Brooke Donovan, was *also* a suspect in the disappearance of his first wife, Penny Jefferson, in 1997, when he was using the name Paul Bradford. If that name sounds familiar to you, it should. The Bradford family runs the largest media company in the world. To be blunt, they are literally the richest family in America. Penny Jefferson's body was never found. Her family declared her legally dead a year later. Shortly after that? Paul Bradford mysteriously vanished from public view."

On-screen, two photos appear. One is Paul Bradford, handsome and happy, chiseled jaw, piercing blue eyes. The other is Matt Donovan, handsome, older, dark hair shot through with gray, the nose slightly more angular, the jawline softer.

But the piercing blue eyes are the same.

"Oh wow," I breathe. "It's amazing, seeing those photos so big. Together."

"Damn," Alice whispers.

Tessa's face returns to the screen. "Based on what we've been able to verify, Paul Bradford ceased to exist a year after Penny Jefferson's disappearance. Matt Donovan appears in Castle Cove some years later, accepting the position of history teacher and basketball coach at Castle Cove High. Now, your brain is probably spinning at this point. Why would Steve Anderson confess to a murder and then so suddenly pivot? Where was Matt Donovan the night of the murder? Sources reveal that while Donovan had an alibi for part of the evening, he doesn't have an explanation for his whereabouts between midnight and two a.m., the time the coroner says Brooke Donovan was likely killed. He's also heavily in debt, and documents obtained by KWB show that in the event of Brooke's death, the person Castle Cove knows as Matt Donovan was set to inherit five million dollars."

She pauses. "Our question now is, what did the Castle Cove Police Department know about Matt Donovan at the time of Brooke's disappearance? Was Paul Bradford's family . . . involved in Steve Anderson's initial plea? There are many questions to be asked in the coming weeks and, as you can see, plenty of people want answers."

The camera pans to the left.

"Oh my god," Alice says.

There are tons of people, all in black #CastleCoveCorrupt T-shirts, just like at Brooke's funeral, chanting it over and over. They have signs now, too. *Corrupt Castle Cove PD. CastleCove-Corrupt. Truth Now. Detain Donovan.*

Good, part of me thinks. Serves that horrible Detective Thompson right.

Tessa Hopkins swings now to the right, and suddenly, there's Ricky Randall, unsmiling, dressed in the same black suit we saw her in at the bar. She looks so young here, outside in the sun. She usually looks so grizzled in the darkened atmosphere of the Moon Landing bar.

"With me now is Steve Anderson's attorney, Ricky Randall.

Ms. Randall, what can you tell me about the bombshell new information for this case?"

Ricky takes a deep breath before speaking. I wonder if she's nervous. This is certainly no assault-by-beef-patty case. This is big-time.

"It's my belief that a number of potential suspects were not fully investigated at the start of this case, including Mr. Donovan. While I can't divulge specific information concerning evidence against Mr. Donovan, I can say that I firmly believe my client, Steve Anderson, is innocent. I believe his initial plea is the direct result of complicit financial manipulation. I believe the Castle Cove Police Department has much to answer for, and I will find justice for Brooke Donovan and Steve Anderson."

Tessa Hopkins looks back into the camera. "Ben, as you can see, this is only the beginning. When I asked Detective Thompson, the lead investigator on the case, if Matt Donovan or any other suspects were fully looked into before Steve Anderson issued what we now believe might have been a coerced confession, his response was *No comment.* When we visited Mr. Donovan at his home today, he did not answer the door. The Bradford family spokesperson has also refused to comment. We're unsure at this time if Donovan has retained an attorney. We'll keep you up-to-date as this story continues to break."

Alice mutes the television and lets out a shriek.

"This is amazeballs!" she shouts gleefully, doing a little dance in front of me on her plush rug.

My phone vibrates. I pull it out. I don't recognize the number.

Miss you and your mom

My heart freezes.

"Iris?" Alice's voice is like a knife in my ear, sharp. "Iris, what's up?"

But my phone buzzes again. Hands shaking, I check it. *Please don't be him, please don't be him again.*

It's not. It's Spike. I exhale.

HOLY HELL ARE U WATCHING?? CHANNEL 10, NOW

I look up. Alice is now glued to the television screen as KWB shows live footage of a black SUV hurtling down the highway, several cop cars in pursuit.

Alleged suspect in murder case in high-speed chase, reads the chyron. *High school coach wanted for questioning in the death of his daughter . . . news of first wife's disappearance . . . possibly changed identity . . .*

"Oh my god," Alice says. "Oh. My. God. Is that?"

"Coach," I say, trying to keep my voice calm. I shove my phone into my backpack, stick my hands under my thighs so she can't see them shaking.

HE'S ON THE RUN!!! Spike texts.

"Well," Alice says matter-of-factly. "This is certainly escalating, isn't it?"

"Yes," I say weakly. "It certainly is."

I block the Thing's number.

TRANSCRIPT, MATTHEW DONOVAN,
CASE #2987A

Recorded Interview, November 12
Location: Castle Cove Police Department
Conducted by Officer M. Thompson & Officer J. Metz
9:47 p.m.

Thompson: Well.

Thompson: Here we are. I can't say we saw this coming.

Thompson: Why don't you start by telling me whether I should call you Matt Donovan or Paul Bradford.

[pause]

Thompson: I'm going to need you to answer.

Matthew Donovan: My legal name is Matthew Donovan.

Metz: And did you assume that name after the disappearance of your first wife, Penny Jefferson?

Donovan: Yes.

Thompson: Your lawyer, Aaron Mathison, is present, correct?

Aaron Mathison: That's correct.

Thompson: Why did you run, Matt?

[inaudible whispering]

Thompson: Please speak up for the microphone.

Donovan: Wouldn't you?

Metz: Answer the question, please.

Donovan: You think I did it. You think I killed my kid, but I didn't. I didn't kill my first wife, either. But after that . . . why wouldn't I run? I had to change my *life* because of that. You've got nothing on me.

Mathison: Matt, please.

Thompson: Where were you between ten-thirty p.m. and two a.m. on the night of October 31?

Donovan: I graded papers. I told you. Then I went to my friend's house. A lady friend.

Metz: Your daughter texted you three times, Matt. You never answered. Why?

Donovan: I was grading papers. I was busy. We'd been fighting. We needed a little time.

Thompson: Fighting about money?

Mathison: I'm advising my client not to answer.

Thompson: Noted. Matt, I gotta tell you. This is a real hole you're in. Let me be plain here. Rich guy suspected in disappearance of first wife. Her body's never found. He disappears off the face of the earth, a year later. Then he crops up, with a new name, new life, new wife, money again. But not . . . too much money, am I right? Victoria kept you on a tight leash?

Donovan: I loved her. I didn't care about her money. Whatever her mother wanted to do in regards to financial stuff, I went along with it.

Thompson: You said you were fighting with
Brooke. Were you angry enough to kill her?
Needed that money from the will?
Mathison: I'm advising my client not to answer.
Donovan: You guys are pieces of work, you know
that?
Mathison: I'm advising my client to remain
silent.
Donovan: You've got nothing. This is a—
Thompson: Matt, you're a great coach, aren't
you? I love the games! Never miss one.
Donovan: I enjoy my job.
Thompson: Lots of awards, plaques, perks from
local businesses. Free sneakers from Foot
Locker! Go, Cougars!
Metz: Go, Cougars!
Thompson: Matt, back in the summer, you
accepted a Youth Basketball Coach Award from
down at the Y, is that right? On or about
August 30?
Donovan: Correct.
Thompson: Must have been a big night. What did
you do?
Donovan: I don't remember. Ceremony. Dinner
with my girlfriend, back to her house—
Metz: Which girlfriend?
Donovan: Carol Westmacott.
Thompson: Hard to keep track, I guess.
[silence]
Thompson: Matt, can you tell me why when we

searched your house earlier today, we found a YMCA Youth Basketball Coach Award trophy coated in dried blood? We've also found a sneaker in your home that appears to match prints taken from the woods and the Lookout.

Donovan: What? No. No. No, that—

Mathison: I'm going to advise my client not to answer any further questions.

Donovan: This is *not* happening! You are *not* doing this to me. I'm not doing this again. You don't know who you're dealing—

Mathison: Mr. Donovan, please.

Metz: Your family would do anything for you, wouldn't they, Mr. Donovan? A mother's love is a mighty thing.

Donovan: You guys are downright despicable. You know that? You think I don't know about what you've got going on? If I go down, the rest of you are sure as hell going down with—

Thompson: At this time, Mr. Donovan, I'm placing you under arrest for the murder of Brooke Levy Donovan.

CHAPTER THIRTY-FOUR

ALICE

NOVEMBER 18

12:15 P.M.

"Truth is seldom romantic."

—AGATHA CHRISTIE,

MURDER IS EASY

STEVE IS FAMOUS. HE'S out of jail, and everyone is talking about him on the internet like he's the freaking Jean Valjean of Castle Cove. Willing to go down for something he didn't do to provide for his family. For his sister's future. He's literally gained one hundred thousand followers on TikTok since last week, which is especially amazing considering he's never posted anything on his channel. Last I heard, he was being flown out to Chicago on a private jet for an interview with CNN's Jefferson King. Sure, he might be in big trouble eventually, because after all, he *might* have taken a bribe, but right now no one seems focused on that. It's all about him being a hero.

Another alert about the case beeps into my phone, this one about the state's internal investigation of the Castle Cove Police Department. They've already put several people on administrative leave—including Bertie, the cop who tossed me out of the station a few weeks ago so rudely—and the media seems to think there are more to come. I would have guessed Thompson would be first to go, but according to Ricky, he's been cleared—apparently, he's not a dirty cop. He's just a jerk. And, Greta Bradford is now under investigation for witness tampering and bribery, which has made all of this not just national news—it's reached the international media. Ricky was interviewed on the BBC yesterday.

At first, I loved all these updates, but it's starting to get annoying. All this talk about Ricky and Tessa and freaking *Thompson,* but no mention of us at all. All because Iris insisted that we be anonymous sources. I was okay with it at the beginning because I didn't want the Bradfords—or Thompson—coming after me, but now it's like . . . *hello.* We solved this freaking thing and literally got an innocent man out of *jail,* and no one even knows.

I slam my locker shut and stalk down the hall with a sour feeling in my stomach. When Hercule Poirot solved cases, he was *celebrated.* Everyone said he was the world's greatest detective! People were in *awe* of him. It's not that I need all that—not really—but at the same time, it would be nice to be recognized. I'm happy justice is on its way to being served, now that Coach has been arrested and is awaiting trial, but also—I did something. Something *big.* For the first time in my life, I did something really *good.* And no one knows.

I'm heading to the library to meet Iris, which is not a place I have ever been. Honestly, I didn't even realize our school *had* a library until Iris mentioned it earlier and told me to meet her there.

I push through the big double doors and find her sitting at

one of the long tables in the center of the room, her laptop in front of her. She's the only one in here, outside of a librarian who's standing behind the front desk fiddling with a stack of books, and I appreciate the quiet. It's nice. Calm. I make a mental note to come back here more often. Maybe I could . . . study.

Iris waves as she sees me approach. "Hey."

"Hey," I say, sliding into the chair next to her. "Did you hear the latest about Steve? Going on CNN? Like, wtf. What about the people who actually *solved* the case? I love that Tessa is just taking all the credit. Like, all she did was open a file folder with a bunch of stuff *we* put together in it. She didn't even . . ." I trail off as I realize Iris is staring at me. "What?" I snap.

"Alice." She seems annoyed. She sighs, looking down at her computer keyboard. "Nothing. Never mind."

"Never mind, *what*?" I know I'm in a bad mood, but I would have thought she of all people would get it.

"I just . . . We didn't do this for the fame, did we, Alice? We did it for Brooke." She tilts her head, appraising me.

I clench my jaw. "No. But . . . this is the one thing I've done in my life that worked out *well*. Like, after everything last summer, it could have changed how everyone saw me in this stupid town. Maybe my parents would actually be proud of me. Stay in the same room as me for more than five seconds. I just want a little recognition—is that too much to ask?" I hit the table with my fist, hard, and Iris freezes, her eyes pinned on it.

"Sorry," I mumble. "I'm just . . . never mind. It's fine." I swallow. God, I'm really losing it. Since when do I give *emotional speeches*? I flip my hair back off my face and sit up straighter. "Never mind. I am over it, as of now. Moving on." I wave a hand.

Iris searches my face with her eyes, then nods. "Okay. If you say so. I mean, Alice, you know I'm here . . . if you want to talk or whatever. About last summer. Or your parents. Or . . . whatever. Right? That's what having friends is all about."

I swallow. That was certainly not what having the Mains as friends was about—at least not since Brooke and I started drifting last year. That was all sarcastic remarks and backhanded compliments. Maybe I can trust Iris with real stuff, though. It would be nice to have a friend, someone to talk to, like I used to talk to Brooke back in the day.

"I gotta use the bathroom," Iris says, standing. "I'll be right back, okay?" She pauses, looking down at me. "You'll be okay here, right? While I'm gone?"

I smile. "Of course." I waggle my fingers at her departing figure. My phone beeps again. Somehow in the last week, I ended up on this group text with Park and Kennedy, which is mostly the two of them talking about boys—Kennedy keeps bringing up her night with Cole on Halloween, which is all sorts of *ew,* but because of it, I realized Iris and I—well, *I*—messed up a little in our investigation. It doesn't matter now, obviously, but apparently Cole left Kennedy that night around 12:30 in the morning. He wasn't with her all night like I'd thought. Basically, I know *way* too many details about their night together.

Right now, Kennedy and Park are talking excitedly about how a producer from the Lifetime Channel contacted Kennedy's dad about potentially doing a film version about all of this. Kennedy is, of course, convinced that someone *amazing* is going to play her.

I read their back-and-forth dispassionately for a while, before realizing that Iris is taking forever in the bathroom and I am *bored.* Her computer is sitting open next to me, so I figure while

I'm sitting here, I might as well do some online shopping. I am about to pull up Google when I register what's on the screen.

Whispering Pines Lodge.

Why is Iris looking up this Whispering Pines place again? I read down the website, but it just looks like a kind of run-down motel up north. I don't get Iris's obsession with it.

And then, an email appears in the upper right-hand corner of the laptop. An email from Whispering Pines Lodge. Without even thinking, I click it.

> Dear Iris,
>
> Thank you for your inquiry. Yes, we do offer discounted monthly rates. You indicated you likely want to stay with us starting at the end of this month for an extended period of time? We do book up around the holidays, so I'd suggest you make your reservation as soon as your plans are certain.
>
> Best,
> Rosalind White, Manager & Owner

I skim the email over again, and then again, my heart beating faster with each read. Why is Iris booking a monthly rate at a place up north? Is she leaving town? I get that her dad is maybe not a nice guy, but how could she do this after everything that just happened? After what we did together? After that little *speech* she just gave me?

I was just starting to feel like I could trust her, that I had a real friend who I could count on for the first time since Brooke, but clearly, she's been keeping incredibly important things from me. My hands start to shake. I have to get out of here.

Without bothering to close the email, I pick up my bag from the floor, about to haul ass away from this lying liar, when there's a voice behind me.

"Alice, where are you going?"

I turn, eyes blazing, and find Iris standing behind me with a puzzled expression on her face.

She looks down at her computer, the email still open on her desktop, and back at me. "Were you looking at my stuff? You don't have any business looking at my stuff, Alice."

"What's in Whispering Pines?" I ask her. Maybe there's some logical explanation for this. Maybe there's some reason that every single time I've asked this girl a question about herself or her dad or that *place,* she's pushed me away.

She's silent, staring at me, hand gripping the back of the chair where I was sitting just moments before.

"What is in Whispering Pines?" I repeat.

For a brief moment, her mouth trembles, and I think she's going to tell me. She looks down at the floor, blinking hard, but when she meets my gaze, her eyes are fire. "Who do you think you are, looking through my things? You don't own the world, Alice Ogilvie."

"Were you planning to . . . what, Iris? Move to some motel in the middle of nowhere? Were you even going to *tell* me before you left? I thought we were friends." My voice shakes.

Her eyes narrow. "You think we're *friends*?" She laughs a mean little laugh. "That's funny. You don't know the first thing about me. I know you're used to your friendships being surface-level, but news flash, *Alice,* that's not a real relationship." Iris's mouth presses into a line. "What's on my computer is none of your business. This is your problem, you know that? You think everything revolves around you. You think *Brooke's murder* occurred in order for you to redeem yourself. This isn't about *you.*"

My mouth falls open. All the frustration and sadness clogging up my system vanishes in an instant, replaced by hard, cool, deadly calm. Iris thinks she knows me? She thinks she's seen the real Alice Ogilvie? She doesn't know me at all.

"Who are you?" I say, everything crystal clear all of a sudden.

"What?" Iris frowns. "What are you talking about?"

"Who *are* you, even?" I repeat, my voice rising. "Some loser who was assigned to tutor me? You think any of this has anything to do with *you*? All you wanted was the money. The fee for tutoring me and the reward for finding Brooke's killer."

At the word *money,* her face falls and I know I hit the mark.

"Why *do* you need the money, anyway? I mean, other than the obvious." I wave a hand. "It's funny, we talk about me all the time. What's *your* story, Iris? The one time I was in your apartment, you freaked out. What's up with that man who was in the parking lot that night, huh? I know that was your dad——" Iris sucks in a breath, mouth falling into a frown, and I falter as something tells me I might have gone too far.

An oppressive silence presses into the room, against my skull, against my lungs. A part of me wants to backtrack——apologize, tell Iris to forget everything I said——but her words run through my head. *You think everything revolves around you. This isn't about you.* She thinks the only reason I did any of this was for *myself*? Sure, I've been a little mad that I'm not getting the thanks that we deserve, but I did this for *Brooke*. Because, no matter what anyone thinks, I cared about her. And I miss her. My throat tightens.

Iris opens her mouth like she's about to speak, but before she can, we're interrupted by a voice. The librarian who'd been in the corner is now beside us.

"Excuse me, girls," she says, looking back and forth between us. "I'm not sure if you realize this, but this is a quiet space. I'm sorry you're in a tiff, but I'm going to have to ask you to take this elsewhere."

I lick my lips and give her my best smile. "So sorry. We're fine. I was just leaving anyway." She nods and walks back to her desk.

I start to leave, but before I do, I lean over close to Iris's face and hiss, "Spoiler alert, Iris: if anyone is going to get the reward money, it's me. I'm the one who called her about Coach. Brooke was *my* best friend. I'm practically her family. You're nobody. You're not going to be seeing a penny of it. And you know what else? You're fired. As my tutor. We're done. Finished. But, you'll be happy to hear that your pay is waiting for you in Westmacott's office. Since that's all you ever cared about, anyway. I'll see you around, *loser.*" And then I hike my bag up onto my shoulder and walk away.

CHAPTER THIRTY-FIVE

IRIS
NOVEMBER 18
12:45 P.M.

I CAN'T BELIEVE I was so stupid.

She called me a *loser.*

I'm walking fast through the halls, on my way to Westmacott's office, knocking my shoulders into practically every person I pass. I hate Alice Ogilvie with a white-hot fervor right now. With every fiber of my being. How did she know that about my dad? What was she pulling behind my back? If she wanted to know, she should have just *asked* directly, not pretended like I'm just another mystery for her to solve, like Brooke. Not that I would have told her everything—I might have told her *something,* at least—but she could have at least asked, if she wanted to know so bad.

Though, if I'm being honest, what would I have told her, anyway? What words do you possibly use to tell your kind-of friend that your dad hits you and your mom? Not even the police cared.

Mother-*sucker*. Jesus Christ, I'm crying in the hallway of my high school, which is something you never live down. Those stupid Main girls, Kennedy and Park, pass by me and whisper. Screw Kennedy. Tomorrow I'm asking to switch biology lab partners. She can get someone else to carry her. These kids and all their privilege. It makes me sick. Floating through life on a cloud of money.

How could I have been so stupid? Alice is right. I was never going to get that money. Lilian was just playing me, wasn't she? To do her dirty work for her by telling me about Penny Jefferson. Or maybe gaming me, like it's fun for her to see how far the poor girl will go for money, what the poor girl is willing to do. And I call myself a *detective*? I knew I never should have gotten involved with Alice Ogilvie. My grades suffered. I skipped school. I jumped out a *window*.

Lilian Levy was wrong in the Moon Landing. I'm not *smart*. I'm not *agile*. It was right there, the whole time, in front of me, and I couldn't see it. That I'd never get the money if it was Coach.

Just like I couldn't see Alice for what she really was. Just a manipulative, awful person. Thinking she'd get *famous* from this? That people would *like* her again?

I got lulled into it, thinking she was different. I let little bits of me open up and look what happened, because that's what happens when you do that. You get hurt. People pull out the knives.

Freak, someone murmurs. *Go cry in the bathroom, nerd.*

I pause outside Westmacott's door and wipe my face angrily.

And I hate myself. For being stupid about not thinking the money thing through clearly. And for being . . . like Alice.

Alice wanted recognition. I wanted money.

Both of us lost. Both of us are liars.

I *hate* Castle Cove.

I go to knock on the door, but suddenly Westmacott's voice rises behind it.

"No, I just want to leave him a message. That's allowed, isn't it? Why is this so hard to understand? Doesn't he get to make phone calls?"

I take my hand away from the door.

"Yes, I know he could call me if he chose to, but I need to get a message to him. Can you just write it down?"

Her voice is high-pitched and, to be honest, a little scary. I hear the sound of a phone receiver being slammed down and then Westmacott's voice, forlorn.

"I'm just trying to *help* him."

I'm about to walk away, because obviously, Westmacott is having some sort of *moment,* when Cole Fielding saunters by, hair in his face as usual, glowing and perfect.

He grins at me. I'm ashamed of myself for grinning back, but he's so goddamn good-looking, I can't help it. I have a crush. I'm not an *idiot.* And I know there's Spike, but . . .

If only Cole Fielding weren't so hell-bent on being some sort of leather-jacket-wearing generic high school motorcycle bad boy, he might be halfway decent. Only he's not wearing his leather jacket today. He's wearing some run-of-the-mill thrift-store sport coat, complete with elbow patches.

Sadly, this makes him even more attractive.

"Don't be shy, Adams, everybody needs their time in the beanbag."

He reaches out and bangs on Westmacott's door and laughs.

"Coming!" she shouts from inside. "Just a minute."

"Thanks a lot, Fielding."

"Heh. I love pranking you, Iris. Makes your face get all cute and glowy."

Even though my heart is cracking in half and I would like to set this whole place on fire, I blush.

"Yup, see? There it is. Ha. Gotta jam. Have a shift at Seaside. Maybe I'll see you there." He grins at me.

"Maybe," I say.

"Cool. Check you later, Adams." He walks away down the hall.

The door opens. "Iris, yes, I'm so sorry. I've been . . . not myself. Come in, please."

Westmacott looks flustered as she goes to stand by her window, gazing outside.

"Sorry," I say. "I can come back?"

"No, no. It's alright. I've been so discombobulated lately—have I forgotten an appointment with you?"

"No, I just . . ." I hate myself for stammering. Get it together, Iris.

"Alice Ogilvie just fired me."

Ms. Westmacott frowns. "She did what?"

"She fired me," I say again. "I don't really want to go into it. It doesn't matter. But she said my money was waiting for me. Is it here? Can I have it?"

Westmacott rummages in her desk. "Yes, it is. Her mother is often out of town, so she made the check out in advance. Alice is at a B-minus at the end of the quarter, so you've obviously done your job, but I'm very concerned at the moment. Did you two fight? I thought you'd become friends?"

She's holding the envelope in her hands, away from me.

Her nails aren't as nice-looking as they usually are. The polish looks peeled.

"You thought wrong," I say.

Ms. Westmacott starts to hand me the envelope and then pauses, bringing her hands close to her midriff.

Three thousand dollars. That's something, along with what I already have saved. A total of five thousand four hundred twenty-two dollars. Maybe that will convince my mother. Maybe it will be enough. To get somewhere.

"Are you alright, Iris? I know things are *very* confusing right now. They certainly have taken a turn, haven't they?"

"I just want my money. It's mine. I *earned* it." Take that, Lilian Levy.

Ms. Westmacott nods. "Alright, Iris." She holds out the envelope, and I practically snatch it from her. "If there's nothing else, the next time I see you, I'd like to start talking about colleges and scholarships."

"Right."

I'd like nothing more than to tell her there won't be any talk about colleges and scholarships because I'm taking this money home, and counting what I've saved, and come hell or high water, I'm getting my mother into a car and we are driving away from here, right now, forever, because there's nothing left for me here. Not one thing.

But I don't. I just tuck the envelope into the pocket of my peacoat and turn to go.

"It's all good, Ms. Westmacott. See you around."

CHAPTER THIRTY-SIX

IRIS

NOVEMBER 21

5:45 P.M.

SPIKE AND ZORA AND Neil are splayed out in Spike's living room. I'm on the recliner, feet up, my stomach in knots. I didn't want to come. I just wanted to hide in my room, frankly, but Spike made me. "You don't want to miss this! It just gets better and better, you know? And think about it: you, and we, had a hand in all this. It's kind of cool, in a way."

Zora looks up from her phone. "Your friend coming?"

I frown. "No."

"You two were joined at the hip. What's up?"

"We had a fight."

Spike raises his eyebrows. "You two? I thought you were all lovey-dovey. That's not cool. You okay?"

Neil murmurs, "Girlfight, girlfight."

"Shut up, dude." Zora leans toward me. "What happened?"

I don't really know how to tell her about the fight I had

335

with Alice. How would I explain that we fought because Alice thought all this would end up with people praising her? That we fought because she found something out about me, something I try to keep very, very hidden?

I mean, I get it. She didn't like to talk about her life, either, and I never managed to get out her whole story, but that girl's life . . . might be lonelier than mine. Where are her *parents*? Her friends are shallow snobs who, well, drug each other to steal one another's boyfriends, for starters. Her best friend was *murdered*. And she hated that friend (rightfully) for stealing her boyfriend and then she . . . died. The thought makes me shudder. The last feeling you had for a friend before they died was loathing. That . . . has to be a lot.

And I never really pressed her on that. Maybe I should have.

And it makes me sad. Because even though I'm mad at her, I know, deep down, that all Alice ever really wanted? Was to be goddamn loved. Her parents are incommunicado, she's being raised in a ginormous, echoey, admittedly freaking gorgeous house by a nice woman, but . . . who loves Alice? Where are they? Yeah, she treated Steve like an object, most likely, and he broke up with her, and he fell in love with someone else. And then Alice, being Alice, flips out and decides to disappear, so people will *miss* her.

I mean, how sad is that?

And then she thinks she can fix all that, and have her whole life back, like nothing ever happened.

Just like pretending her disappearance never happened. Something dark is in that girl, to have just . . . up and left like that.

That's something I understand.

And how do I explain to Zora that I fought with Alice partly because I was mad about not getting reward money? That's definitely not a good look.

"Um, dude, you look like you're having very many interesting thoughts over there," Zora says. "You want to share?"

I have tears in my eyes. Can Zora see? I quickly look down at my phone, where I'd like to see a text from Alice but won't.

Goddammit. I miss Alice Ogilvie.

It's true. I hated seeing her in school last week. I thought maybe she'd go back to the Main kids, but she didn't. She just sat by herself in the cafeteria, scrolling her phone.

Neil laughs. "You sound like Westmacott, Zora. 'Let's share. Here, feel the beanbag. Be the beanbag,'" he imitates.

Zora humphs. "Did you see they're starting a probe? Into malfeasance by the Castle Cove PD?"

Neil snickers. *"Probe."*

"Oh my god, shut up, you are seventeen, not seven," Zora shouts.

"Shush," Spike says. "It's starting."

We all look up. Tessa Hopkins is sitting in a beautifully lit room, facing four uncomfortable-looking women.

Westmacott, Sharon Yang the lunch lady, who will never really be anyone but Lunch Lady to us, Ms. Hollister, the calc teacher, and Patty Hansen, the history teacher.

"Boo!" Neil shouts. "Boo to you, Patty, for that C-plus on my Henry the VIII paper!"

"I'm here today with four of the women at the center of the Matthew Donovan murder allegation. It was revealed last week that Donovan was formerly Paul Bradford, heir to the Bradford family fortune. As Paul Bradford, he was a suspect in the disappearance of his first wife, Penny Jefferson, more than twenty years ago. Bradford changed his name and underwent plastic surgery to avoid the notoriety associated with that case and has been living a lie in Castle Cove for many years. His mother, Greta Bradford, is currently under investigation for witness tampering related to the Brooke Donovan case. A trial date has been set, and Donovan is presently in jail. Tonight, these four brave women speak out about the Matt Donovan they knew."

The camera pans out, so we can see all five of them in the room. Westmacott is on the left, Lunch Lady Yang in the middle, then Ms. Hollister, and Ms. Hansen on the end.

"I hope she asks Lunch Lady why Taco Tuesday was canceled," Spike says. "That's some breaking news I could definitely get behind."

Tessa Hopkins does her patented mini hair flip.

"What can you tell us about the man you knew as Matt Donovan?"

There's an uncomfortable silence, until finally Ms. Hansen speaks. "He could be very charming, you know? He had—has—these eyes. They just seem to really see you. Like he understands you."

"Or maybe," Spike says in a deep voice, "he's just trying to figure out the right way to push you off a cliff. Seems to be his modus operandi."

"Oh yeah," Lunch Lady says. "Treated you really nice."

"I mean, the gifts," Ms. Hansen says, fingering her bare neck, where an expensive pearl necklace was seen in her Facebook photos, and which has now, according to Ricky Randall, been taken into evidence.

"Right, the jewelry," Tessa Hopkins says. "The weekend trips to Santa Barbara. But didn't you wonder how he could afford all that? On a teacher and coach salary?"

Lunch Lady and Hansen look at each other.

"Well, you know, he *had* money. I just figured, he had something, right? I don't know. I mean, now that I've had time to think about it, I guess he was probably . . . you know, like they say. Using Brooke's upkeep money." Ms. Hansen looks teary.

"He lied a lot," Westmacott says suddenly. "We know that now. But you believed him, because nice guys can be hard to find. You get so many awful ones before you get one decent one. I was just so grateful."

She looks down at her lap, her lip quivering.

"Aw, Westmacott," Spike says. "That's kind of breaking my heart, girl."

Ms. Hollister nods. "You just don't see certain stuff, because you're in love."

Westmacott's eyes drift to Hollister. Her lip isn't quivering anymore, and her eyes look . . . really hurt.

"This is awful," Zora murmurs. "They all have to sit together and listen to each other talk about a guy they were *all* in love with, probably, like, overlapping. Is this even allowed, by the way, before Coach has gone to trial?"

"Paul," Neil says. "His name is Paul Bradford."

"He was still our coach," Zora says.

"I'm not sure Tessa Hopkins's ethics are concerned about that," I say to Zora. "But I'm sure they can't talk specific evidence or anything."

"No one seems to care much about ethics at this point," Neil says, stretching out on his back on the floor. "I mean, Anderson's going on *Oprah*. I thought you weren't supposed to benefit from a crime."

"He didn't commit the crime," I say. "So he can cry to whoever he wants and make money off it."

"That reminds me," Zora said. "Iris, your weird lawyer lady. Has she said anything about Steve being, like, charged for something? I mean, first he said he was guilty, then he took it back, so doesn't that count as perjury or something? I mean, he accepted a bribe and *lied*."

My fingers are hovering over my phone. "What? No, I don't know. I mean, she hasn't said anything to me about it."

Just text her, my brain says. Text Alice. She should be here. We can be her friends. Well, not *me,* not for much longer, but Spike and Zora and Neil will take her in. They'll take care of her.

"Dude got *around,*" Neil says. "How did these ladies not know about each other?"

"Let's talk about . . . the other things," Tessa says gently. "He started out as a gentleman, roses and candles and bubble baths, but what happened then?"

"I wanted to get married," Ms. Hansen says firmly. "And he flipped out. Said it would never happen, he still wasn't over his wife. Didn't want to upset . . . Brooke."

Westmacott's hands are practically white, they're wrapped so tight together in her lap.

"The second wife," Lunch Lady says. "We didn't know about the first one then. At least, I didn't."

"I didn't, either," Ms. Hansen says.

Westmacott says softly, "It was certainly a surprise to me."

Her face flushes.

"I think," Lunch Lady says, "he was just interested in rich women, really. Like, he wasn't gonna marry us unless we had money. And he was real shady about all that stuff. Always complaining—"

Ms. Hollister nods. "That the monthly trust for Brooke wasn't enough and that when she turned eighteen—"

"He'd lose access. She'd get her money. That he'd be left in the cold."

Ms. Hansen snorts. "Right. Well, now we know about the five mil."

"And it was odd, him coming over *that* late at night? On the night it happened, I mean." Ms. Hollister twists a strand of her hair between her fingers. "I mean, normally, he'd come over earlier, and then leave. But I was already asleep when he got there and he seemed . . . nervous."

"He could go for hours, too, if you know what I mean," laughs Ms. Hansen.

"Um, this has taken a gross turn," Zora says. "I need to bleach my brain."

"They seem kind of . . . cavalier," Spike murmurs. "A girl is dead and they were dating a murderer."

"Not Westmacott," I point out. "Look at her. She can barely keep it together."

Westmacott is breathing heavily, her neck flushed and prickly. I feel sorry for her. I mean, they'd just broken up, this happens, and now she has to listen to these other women talk about Coach . . . in bed. That's got to sting. And the one person I want to talk to most of all about it is Alice Ogilvie, who would say catty things about Westmacott and the other women, and probably drop a jillion Agatha Christie quotes that only she understands, and just generally be . . . Alice. Complicated and charming and mysterious and annoying.

I will miss that.

CHAPTER THIRTY-SEVEN

"Sensationalism dies quickly,
fear is long-lived."
—AGATHA CHRISTIE,
DEATH IN THE CLOUDS

MY MOM FLEW HOME for Thanksgiving. My dad couldn't—
claimed the deal he was doing in China was about to close.
Thanksgiving is an American holiday, Alice, he told me when we
talked a few days ago for the first time in weeks. *In the rest of the
world, life goes on as normal.*

At first, I thought my mom finally realized that maybe I
could use the company or something, what with everything
that's been going on. But as soon as she got up to the house
yesterday, she announced that she had booked an impossible-
to-get hair appointment down in LA on Friday morning, first
thing, which she just *had* to take. *It's Alfredo Dominguez, Alice,* she
said. *He does Reese Witherspoon. You understand.*

I nodded like I did, thinking, *Well, at least one of my parents
will be here and we can have Thanksgiving together,* except in the next
breath she told me that she'd have to leave early afternoon on

Thanksgiving to get down there and check into her hotel. God knows she wouldn't want to keep *Alfredo* waiting.

So, the house is empty, again. I'm wandering from room to room like I expect to find another human being somewhere, but I know I won't. Brenda had made plans to go see her daughter and her family down in San Diego when we heard my mom was coming home. She left last night, after making sure that I was going to be okay and leaving me enough food for the next few days. She told me she could stay, if I wanted. That she'd cancel her plans. But I told her to go. I'd be fine.

And I *am* fine. I've been alone before, more times than I can count, although in the past there was always someone I could convince to come keep me company. Steve, Brooke, Kennedy, Park . . . someone whose presence softened the sharp edges of emptiness in this house.

Anyway, when my mom left a few hours ago, I went to grab my phone, but realized there's no one left to call.

Clouds have started to gather in the sky outside the window. When I wander into our formal dining room, the shadows from the weird coat of armor my dad picked up a few years ago in Italy dance across the far wall of the room, and my skin prickles. I can't stay here.

I hurry to the front hall, grabbing my coat and bag, and head out the door as fast as my feet will take me.

Ten minutes later, I'm sitting in my car in front of an apartment building. I'm not sure what I'm doing here. Iris and I haven't spoken since the incident in the library. Even though I've thought about texting her a hundred times, I don't know what to say.

I've never gotten into a fight with someone before that hurt so much and come back from it with our friendship intact.

Clutching a pie under one arm, I trudge up the stairs toward Iris's apartment, palms sweating more with each step I take. The whole drive here, I was going over what I might say—*I'm sorry. You don't have to tell me anything about your Whispering Pines or your dad if you don't want. Can we please hang out again?*—but as I approach her floor, it all seems stupid. God, how do people *do* this sort of thing? Apologizing sucks.

As I reach the third floor, there's a loud shout from one of the apartments up ahead. The holidays really bring out the best in people.

Outside 317, I wipe my palms on the front of my shirt, take a deep breath, and knock. As I do, I hear another shout. *Wait.* Is that—it sounds like it's coming from inside of Iris's apartment.

I knock again, louder this time.

There's a scuffling sound from inside, and then the lock scrapes back and the door cracks open a few inches. Iris's face appears in the crack, hesitant.

"I have pie," I say, holding it out to her as a peace offering. "I'm so—"

"Alice, you can't be here." There's a noise behind her, and she flinches. "You have to go."

"Wait—" But before I can say anything more, she slams the door in my face.

CHAPTER THIRTY-EIGHT

OF COURSE WE SHOULD have left. As soon as I brought home that tutoring money, we should have left. Right then and there. But real life gets in the way. It always does. Nothing ever goes according to plan. I should have learned that by now.

Real life is spending two tearful days convincing your mother that you can go, that you have this money, and *Please, Mom, please, let's just take this chance.* But Castle Cove is her home, it's all she's ever known. The sea, the Moon Landing, the cemetery where her parents are buried.

Leaving what you know is scary. Starting over is scary.

But I did eventually. I convinced her. I showed her the money. I showed her the confirmation for the little room at the motel in Whispering Pines. We can stay there until we find something else. People need bartenders everywhere. It's a mobile trade. Her boss at the Moon Landing says she knows someone who knows someone who needs someone at a bar there. We packed only what we needed. We stuffed a cooler full of food. I could feel it. Could taste it in my mouth. Freedom. The crisp cool air through the open car window as we drove down the highway at night. What it would be like, away from him. Away from all the worry of him.

But we didn't make it in time. I was stupid. I thought maybe he'd be with his other family for Thanksgiving, because that's where he usually is.

I thought it might be Spike, or even Alice, as strange as that sounds, when the knock came at the door.

But when I open the door, there he is. The Thing.

"Hey, girl," he says. He chucks a finger under my chin, the way he always does. He looks thinner than the last time.

My whole body turns cold.

Behind me, my mother says, in a tiny voice, "Jeff."

And my father says, "Patsy, did I catch you on your way out? You got your coat on."

He squeezes by me. Reaches behind me and closes the door. Grazes the standing lamp next to the door. Gently positions it back.

"Cold out there. Don't want that cold getting in here."

It's hard to explain what your body feels like when it's afraid, really afraid, of being hurt. All the memories of the before hurts come back, hurtle through you, kind of shut you down. Things hurt less when your body goes numb.

My wrist last summer, that wasn't the first time. It was just the first time it was visible to anyone else.

My dad is looking at the small living room, at my mother in her coat, her eyes down, at our hastily packed two suitcases, the cooler, and three grocery bags stuffed full of what we thought we'd need.

"What's going on?" he says.

My father has a voice like a knife. Brutal and to the point.

My mother swallows.

"Patsy?"

I can see it, whatever bravery she has, draining away, her body wilting by the second.

"Iris? You tell me what's happening right now."

"You aren't supposed to be here," my mother says woodenly. "We have the order."

"Leaving," I say. "We're leaving. Away from here. *You.*"

I don't know where it comes from. I couldn't tell you. The words are just out. I have one hand in the pocket of my peacoat, holding on to the envelope full of money.

And then he starts walking toward my mother, the words coming from his mouth loud.

That's when there's another knock on the door.

I open the door just a crack.

Alice. Holding up a pie in a tin.

"I have pie," she says hesitantly. "I'm so——"

"Alice, you can't be here," I say. Keep my voice even. Measured. "You have to go."

She looks confused. "Wait——"

I slam the door in her face.

My loose hand creeps around the stem of the standing lamp.

I watch from above, as everything begins to move very slowly, like in a dream.

CHAPTER THIRTY-NINE

ALICE

NOVEMBER 24

2:35 P.M.

I LEAVE THE PIE on the ground outside the apartment door. If I bring it back home, tomorrow Brenda will ask me what happened, and I don't know how to explain this. Something is wrong, I know it, but—

The thought is cut short by another shout from inside Iris's apartment. I freeze.

Should I knock again? Iris made it very clear that she wanted me to leave, but I don't think this is normal. I need to do something. I pull my phone out of my back pocket and there's a message waiting from my source.

**Update: the lab found unidentifiable DNA on
Brooke's clothing**

I type out a reply with shaking fingers.

                    i need help

You okay?

                    no

Where are you?

                    Im at my friend's place

                    im scared

                    there are noises—I think something is
                    wrong.

                    i think she might be in trouble

Where

                    Seaside apartments

Call 911. I will be there in 10

Heart pounding, I dial 911 and tell them what's happening. I'm finishing the call when there's an even louder shout from inside Iris's apartment, and a moment later the door swings open. I jump with surprise and hurry toward the stairs as fast as I can. Behind me, I hear footsteps coming fast.

When I hit the top of the stairwell, I look back and see a skinny, rough-looking man running toward me. The same man from the rap sheet my source left in the folder that day.

Iris's dad.

Fear boils in my belly, and I'm tempted to run before he can catch up to me. It's what I would have done a month ago. Run away from this issue that isn't mine, go back to my big, empty house and lock the door behind me, pretend like I was never here. It's what I always did with Brooke and those other girls, and maybe if I hadn't—maybe if we'd all just cared about each other a little bit more—Brooke would still be here with us in-stead of . . . dead.

The fear hardens and then flames into something different. Anger. I am Alice *fucking* Ogilvie, and I didn't just solve a murder to run away from some jerk who clearly has been making my friend's life a living hell.

He's at the top of the stairs, a few feet away from me now, taking the steps down two at a time. A waft of beer hits me, and I notice a trickle of blood running down the side of his face.

Nice work, Iris.

As he passes, I stick out my foot and catch his ankle.

He grunts, arms flailing as he loses balance, and then falls onto his left side, hitting the cement stair below and rolling down, down, down until he thumps against the wall at the bottom, hard.

"Ow!" He curls into a ball of pain, arms clasped around his legs, and then his head turns, slow, so slow—I swear to god, time slows down—and he looks back up toward me with blazing eyes. My entire body is shaking. I have to get out of here before he stands up again.

I run. As I pass him, he reaches out a hand, grabbing at my ankles, but I pivot away, jumping down the next flight of stairs and the next until I'm at the bottom.

I don't know what to do. If—*when*—he gets up, he's going to come after me, and he is much, much bigger than I am. I need evidence. A record of his existence.

In the parking lot, I frantically scan the cars in the lot for his. I spot it in the far corner and run over to it, peering inside the windows. There's a crowbar half hidden under the passenger seat. Good lord; he has a weapon? I don't know what I'm doing, but I know that I am not going to let this guy get away with doing this to Iris or her mom ever again.

350

I start taking pictures. License plate. The crowbar. Anything else I can think of that could be used to identify him. That could be used to put him behind bars.

Behind me, I hear movement. Heart in throat, I turn, and see nothing, but then a loud groan cuts through the air. A moment later, another. Is he getting up? What if he's going back to her apartment? I won't let him do that.

I pop open my trunk and grab the first thing I see—a rope that somehow relates to the stupid horse my parents gave me. I have no idea what I plan to do with it, but holding it makes me feel at least minimally safer as I hurry back toward the stairs. From where I'm standing, I can see the spot where he landed.

It's empty.

Dread quakes in my stomach. Where did he go?

And then I hear them—shuffling noises. Coming down toward me. A voice inside my head is screaming, *Get in your car, Alice! Get out of here!* But I can't leave. I can't leave Iris here with that man, alone. I grip the rope between my fists, tight, and stand my ground.

A moment later, he enters my sightline, hitting the bottom of the stairs. He's almost to me. What am I doing? This man has at least a hundred pounds on me; I can't take him. This has to be one of my worst plans ever.

Then two things happen simultaneously: Iris's dad appears out of the bottom of the stairwell, stumbling toward me with the meanest expression I've ever seen, and I hear the wail of a siren in the distance, heading this way. The noise distracts Iris's dad for a moment; he's only about ten feet from me now, and I tighten my grip on the rope, thinking maybe this is my opportunity to do something. To stop him somehow. But then he turns back to me and we lock eyes, and a trickle of absolute dread rolls down my back.

Merde.

A wicked smile crosses the man's face, and I realize exactly why Iris was so desperate to leave town.

"Stay back," I scream at him, but he just laughs and my stomach turns, and he starts moving toward me again, reaching out, when another car swings into the parking lot, a civilian car, but with a driver who I would recognize anywhere.

Rafael Ramirez.

Of course. He's interning at the station during his freshman year at Castle Cove Community College. He mentioned it last summer, when I ran away from home and he found me with a crashed car and a headache on the side of the road and spent five days with me, helping me, but I had forgotten. It makes sense he'd do this.

His cousin was Remy Jackson.

CHAPTER FORTY

IRIS

NOVEMBER 24

2:52 P.M.

MY MOM IS HOLDING me. My head feels fuzzy from where he hit me. We're sitting on the floor. Her jacket is torn, the buttons scattered on the carpet around us. We don't say anything, because what is there to say? We have been here a million times before.

"Iris?"

It's Alice, her voice trembling.

"Iris, I called the police. They're here and they——"

I don't want her to see me this way. I don't want her to see *this.* I just want to disappear.

"Please, just go away," I say.

"Iris, that guy, I——"

"I said, *go away.*"

"Iris," my mom says quietly. "She's your friend."

"Go back," I say, harder. "Go back to your big house, and all your money, and all your rich friends. I don't want you here, don't you *get it*? Some people can't be saved."

I watch her face crumple. She hesitates, then turns and runs to the door, bashing into some guy coming in. He grabs her arm, but she shakes him off, disappears outside to the landing.

"Let me see," he says, bending down to me. "I need to see if you need medical attention. I'm guessing the guy in cuffs in the parking lot, this is his doing?"

He seems familiar somehow, but I can't place him. I can barely think. Why is he so young? Cops can't be this young. And he's not wearing blue.

He's feeling my face, his fingers gently probing. "Gonna have a shiner there," he murmurs. "He doesn't look so great, either. Which one of you clocked him?"

"Me," I say.

"The police will be up soon. What happened?" he says, looking at my mother. "I'm going to encourage you to file a restraining order."

"I did. Before. Last August," my mom says. "We were leaving. *Leaving*-leaving, you know? And he showed up. It's my fault. Wait, who *are* you? You're not a cop."

"I . . . I'm an intern. Criminal justice project. It's complicated. You can trust me. Tell me."

"Mom—"

"He was hurting me and she was just protecting me." My mom cuts me off. "She hit him, with that lamp. And then he was on her and the money—"

"Money?" He's looking around at our messed-up apartment, the suitcases, the grocery bags torn, contents all over the floor, my casebook. I wanted to take it with me.

Something is pricking at my brain as I look at his youthful face. I wish my head would clear.

"She was tutoring a school friend. It was her payment and it came out of her pocket and—"

"That's how we got him to go. I told him to take it, take it all, and just leave," I say.

The guy reaches out and takes my casebook. Opens it.

He looks at me, a puzzled expression on his face.

A series of clicks goes off in my brain. He grabbed Alice's arm at the door. He's young. He's . . . handsome in an easy way. He's not wearing sunglasses today, like he was at the funeral.

Rafael Ramirez.

And then . . .

"You," I say. "It's you. You're Alice's contact, aren't you?"

"I am," he says back. "And you're Alice's partner in crime."

CHAPTER FORTY-ONE

ALICE

NOVEMBER 24

3:33 P.M.

"Love can be a very frightening thing."
"That is why most great love stories are tragedies."
—AGATHA CHRISTIE, *DEATH ON THE NILE*

I'M BACK HOME, AGAIN. Back to this stupid big empty house, all alone. I'm sitting outside in my car, in the driveway, because I can't bring myself to go inside. Adrenaline and fear are coursing through my body, flashes of the rage in Iris's dad's eyes running through my head. If Raf hadn't shown up when he did . . . I shake my head. I can't go there.

I lean back in my seat, close my eyes against it all, everything that's happened in the past month—its weight slamming against me like one of those stupid waves on the cliffs below. Raf was my anonymous source. Brooke is dead. Her dad *killed* her. It's too much, too heavy in the silence of my car, and I turn the ignition back on so I can at least hear some music. I miss Brenda.

Hi, I text her.

She writes back immediately.

I miss you.

My mouth wobbles.

I miss you, too.
Are you okay?
Yeah. Just . . . it's quiet here.

There's a pause and then bubbles start. *I'm sorry. I will be home soon.*

I know, I text. The last thing I want is for her to feel guilty for going to see her daughter. *I'm fine.*

**I know most people are busy today . . . so
here is a suggestion. Why don't you go
visit your horse? Snowflake? You know you
haven't been out there in a few months.**

I roll my eyes. My stupid horse? But then, an image pops into my mind, unbidden, of that stupid horse in its stupid stable all alone. Just like me.

Maybe.
Love you.
Love you.

I drop my phone into the cup holder in the center console. I guess I'm going to see my stupid horse.

—

Green Gables Stables is way up in the hills that overlook Castle Cove. I've only been a few times since Snowflake was gifted to me and there's no service up here, so it takes me a few wrong turns before I finally find the place.

I pull into the parking lot in a cloud of dust. It's empty; there's only one other car parked across the way, but I guess I shouldn't be surprised. Who comes here on Thanksgiving?

An uninvited answer pops into my head: *losers.* That's who, Alice. Losers. My throat tightens. Shut up, brain. I slam the car door and tromp across the dirt into the empty stables. Halfway down the row, I find it—my horse, Snowflake, standing in its stall chewing on hay. I stand there for a minute, watching it eat. What do people *do* with horses? Like, pet them? I don't even know.

I walk into the stall, and Snowflake whinnies. We lock eyes for a minute, and I swear to god, it's like—I don't know, something passes through me. This calm. Brenda always tells me that riding horses is like therapy, but I never really believed her. Maybe I *should* try it.

I heave the saddle off the ground where it's sitting and manage to figure out how to hook it around her body, and then put on her bridle.

I'm about to lead her out of the stall, when I hear someone enter the barn and the clip-clop of another horse. My back stiffens. I really do not want to run into a horse lover right now and get into a long, extended conversation about riding. I have to get out of here.

I whisper sorry to Snowflake and start to unbuckle her halter as quietly as possible, when I hear the voice again.

"At least I'll always have you, Oliver."

What kind of horse name is Oliver? A stupid but oddly familiar name . . .

It's on the edge of my brain. Why do I know that name? I give Snowflake one last pat, sneaking out of her stall into the corridor that bisects the rows of stalls and walking quietly toward the voice. I want to solve this mystery.

As I creep closer, the person speaks again in a singsong voice, "You know I never meant for any of this to happen. It was all a mistake. Matthew was never supposed to end up in jail. But sometimes things have a way of working out, I guess."

I register the words as I'm peeking around the edge into the stall. What are they talking about? Coach Donovan and jail and . . . my skin prickles as I suddenly remember the text that Raf sent me earlier. The one about the extra DNA.

My heart starts pounding. I need to get out of here. I need to call Raf. I grab my phone from my back pocket, spinning around to leave, but my foot catches on the uneven ground, and I tumble forward. My phone clatters a few feet away from where I land.

"Alice?" says the voice. "What are you doing here?"

And, there she is. Standing above me, wearing her ugly tunic with the cutout squares and stars pasted along its neckline. Except, one of the stars is missing.

Oh my god. A denim star. I reach into my jacket pocket and touch it with my fingertips. The star I picked up in the woods the night we went to look for Brooke.

It's her.

Ms. Westmacott.

CHAPTER FORTY-TWO

IRIS

NOVEMBER 24

3:35 P.M.

MY MOTHER IS GIVING a statement in the front room while I'm in the bedroom, talking to another cop. A different one is taking pictures of my swelling eye.

"Your father was threatening your mother, physically, and that's when you hit him, with the lamp?" The woman has kind eyes. She's speaking gently.

"Yes," I say. Rafael Ramirez is sitting in a wicker chair in the corner, looking through my casebook.

"And you state that after the altercation, you gave him money to leave?"

"No," Raf says, lifting his head. "He took the money from you? Isn't that right? I think that's what you told me. He stole it."

"I—" No, no, that's not what happened. Is it? I close my eyes, trying to remember.

"I know this is hard, honey, but think back, and open your eyes, again, please, for the photos."

"She told me he stole it," Raf says. "That's another charge. In addition to assault and battery. If I remember my homework correctly."

He and the cop share a private look.

Oh.

The cop taking my statement speaks quietly. "Sometimes it's hard to make domestic cases stick, so whatever you can remember, helps."

Click. Flash.

They mean I could put him away, at least for a little bit. Maybe.

I swallow.

"It's confusing. He was hitting me. And my coat . . ." I reach down, finger my torn pocket. "He got ahold of it and said he was taking the money so we'd never be able to get away."

I hold my breath.

The cop writes it all down.

My mother makes tea. "It's what I do, I guess," she says sadly. "Make people drinks in stressful times. I don't understand any of this, least of *that*."

She motions to my casebook. Raf has it open on the kitchen table. The police have gone. We'll have to go down to the station in a few hours for more questioning.

"I wish you'd told me," my mother says. "That's all so . . . dangerous. But strangely, I'm proud of you, too. Trying to do something. For Brooke."

She sets down cups of tea in front of us. Looks at the mess in the front room.

"I suppose I'll straighten up a bit."

Raf watches her start to pick up papers and food that spilled from the cooler.

"Has Alice talked to you about what I told her?" His voice is low.

"In case you didn't notice, Alice and I are not generally speaking right now," I answer. My head throbs. "And you know what? I have some questions for *you*. Like, how did you and Alice actually meet? Do you have something to do with where she went this summer? I know she wasn't alone. I just *know* it. And if you two are like a thing? She is *seventeen,* dude, and I think that's bull——"

"Iris." Raf's voice is firm. "I'm nineteen. I went to CC High. I know Steve. I even remember you. You were a Mathlete freshman year, right?"

I nod.

He sighs. "I want to tell you about Alice, but I can't. Because that's Alice's story to tell, not mine. And it's not what you're thinking. Not at all. All I can say is that the Alice Ogilvie you think you know is not the real Alice Ogilvie."

I drink some of my tea too quickly, burn my mouth. I am fuming and my head hurts and my eye hurts and I feel like I'm electrified with pain inside me. Tears sting my eyes. What I want to say is, *I know that better than you think, Raf,* but I don't.

"You and Alice have done a fantastic job with all this, Iris. I know I wasn't too much help. I'm amazed by what you two did, but I have to say, I have doubts. That's what I'm trying to tell you, and what I was trying to tell Alice last night when I texted her, but she wasn't listening."

"Alice really enjoys not lis—"

"*Iris.* They recovered minute traces of DNA on the leather jacket Brooke was wearing when she was found. Very faint, because of the seawater. Two sets. No matches in the system."

I set my teacup down. My head is spinning now. "Wait, what?"

"Two sets. It's at least something that should be followed up on, especially now, but some of the detectives down at the—"

"Stop." I hold up my hand. Something is forming in my brain, but I can't get a handle on it. "Wait. She was found in a leather jacket?" I only glanced over the edge of the cliffs that night we found her body. Just enough to see her legs and skirt. Her hair in the cracks of watery rocks. Everything was kind of a blur, because there she was, *dead.* I don't remember seeing the leather jacket.

"Yes. I messaged Alice about this last night, but she never answered."

He grabs my laptop and pulls up a site. "I want you to take a look at these photos. I'm very sorry. It's going to be hard, I know. It's Brooke. After she was pulled from the water."

I swallow hard.

Her bloated face. The seaweed in her hair. The deathly, dull color of her skin.

There's a flashing in my brain. Something not right with the way Brooke looks.

"Iris, in your interview with Thompson, he asked what she was wearing and you never said she was in a leather jacket when she ran by you."

"She wasn't. She was just in her Halloween costume. The cheerleader thing. That means—"

I pick up my phone, hands shaking, and blaze through her IG feed, photo after photo after photo. No Brooke in a leather jacket, not one photo. And it's not even the kind of jacket she'd wear. It's old and worn, and she'd have had a pricier one. Girls like Brooke, they don't have leather jackets like this.

Raf blows out his breath, looking at her IG. "Did you ever see Coach in a leather jacket, Iris? Think back."

"No," I say, shaking my head. "Never. Not his style. Not Steve, either."

It's a kind and caring thing to do when a girl is in the woods, crying, cold. To give her your leather jacket to keep her warm.

My blood stills, looking at Brooke's lifeless body in the leather jacket.

You love someone, to take care of them like that. Or the idea of them.

Unknown. The word from our murder board flashes in my brain.

"It's not Coach," I shout. "It's not Coach!"

CHAPTER FORTY-THREE

"The human face is, after all, nothing
more nor less than a mask."
—AGATHA CHRISTIE, *SAD CYPRESS*

"OH HI," I SAY to Ms. Westmacott from the ground, plastering on one of my patented fake smiles even though my ankle is throbbing. She looks like she can't decide how to act right now, like she's not sure what I heard, if anything.

Good. I'd like to keep it that way.

I continue, "So funny, seeing you here!" I force out a carefree laugh as I struggle to stand. I need to get my phone.

Once I'm on my feet, words start spilling out of my mouth. "Remember a while ago, I told you I have a horse here? And you said that you do, too! Which is such a coincidence, isn't it? Who would have thought we'd both end up here today of all days—Thanksgiving. How funny." I'm inching my way closer and closer to the haystack that my phone disappeared into, but every time I put any weight on my ankle, my breath catches in pain.

"Anyway, my mom just texted and said dinner is ready—they're expecting me, you know—and so I have to take off in a minute, but I'll see you at school next week, right? Right. Okay, great!"

"Wait a second, Alice." Her voice is calm, so calm, but there's something bubbling beneath its surface that sends a shiver down my spine.

"Oh," I say. I make it to the stack of hay and reach into it, ignoring the sharp prickles on my arm. I feel something hard and wrap my hand around it. "I wish I could, but I really do have to get going, I'm sure you get——"

All of a sudden, she's coming toward me, fast. "I said, *wait* a second, Alice, please." This time, the words are not so pleasant as they leave her mouth. This time, they exit in a low growl, and I know that she knows. She knows that I heard her.

I need to get out of here. I shove my phone into my back pocket and spin around, but a hand lands on my arm hard and yanks me back. I twist away, but her fingers press into my arm deep, nails digging into my skin.

"Ow, get *off* me!" I pull away, but she doesn't let go. I topple back onto my butt, the air knocking out of my chest and my ankle screaming in pain. She falls forward onto her knees, grip loosening for a second as she tries to regain her balance.

I scramble up, grabbing at the nearest thing to me, which turns out to be a mop. Great.

"Don't come any closer!" I hold the handle of the mop toward her like a sword.

"Alice." She gives a little laugh. "You're being silly." She takes a step toward me.

"I'm not!" I poke the air between us with the mop's end and she jumps back. "Stay there." I have no idea what I'm doing. I want to turn and run again, but I worry she'll catch up with me as easily as she did the first time. I'm not exactly an Olympic athlete, and I'm worried my ankle might be sprained. "I heard you, back there. I *heard* you, talking to your stupid horse. About Brooke! About Coach. Why did you do it? Huh? Brooke never did anything to you!"

I realize tears are sliding down my cheeks. *"Why?"* I say again, the word cracking in half as it hits the air.

Her eyes narrow. "I *knew* you heard me, Alice Ogilvie. You're always sticking your nose into places where it doesn't belong. You and poor Iris—god do I wish I'd never paired the two of you up, you've been nothing but a bad influence on her since day one—stomping around town like you think you're Nancy Drew, solving crimes. You say Brooke never did anything to me? She did the same thing to me that she did to *you*. She came between me and the man I loved. That night when I saw her on the side of the road, all I wanted to do was talk. I wanted to understand. But she was so upset, so drunk. . . ."

She takes a step forward, and I stab the air between us with the end of the mop again. "Stay there!"

"Fine, fine." She holds up her hands and stills. "What you don't understand, Alice, what *no one* understands, is that Matthew was going to marry me. We *loved* each other. And then he broke it off, because of Brooke. Apparently, she didn't think I was good enough for him." Her mouth sets into a deep, angry scowl. "I was there that night with that box of Matthew's things—I was going to throw it over the cliff, because I was *done* with him. But then I heard Brooke across the highway, sitting all alone crying in the woods, and I knew I needed to help. And then maybe she would tell her dad he should marry me. Maybe then she would think I was good enough." She shakes her head.

"I put on a pair of Matthew's old sneakers because it was so muddy, and I was wearing heels . . . and then I walked across the road to see if she was okay. I should have known that would never work. Poor little rich girl. Not as angelic as everyone thinks, if you ask me. Brooke was awful when she saw me; she told me he'd *never* marry me. That he never loved me. She was acting like everything was *my* fault, like I wasn't being kind by trying to help when clearly none of her friends had cared enough to make sure she was okay. She started screaming, so I reached out to stop her, and I guess I slapped her? I don't know. All I know is, the next second, she was running across the street toward the cliffs."

A faraway look appears in her eyes and she shrugs. "I caught up with her there—I ran track in college, did you know that?—but she tripped over something. Fell to the ground. I needed her to stop, to listen to me, so I did what *anyone* would do. I grabbed one of Matthew's basketball trophies out of the box of his things, and I hit her. I needed her to *listen* to me. That's all. And then she got up and . . . slipped. I don't know how it happened. I tried to reach for her, but she was too far away. By the time I got close, she was hanging there, the poor girl, over the edge, head bleeding, her fingers turning white. *Carol,* she said to me, *Carol, please help.*"

She cocks her head, remembering, as dread blooms in my midsection.

"I thought about it. You know? I did; I thought about it. But, then, at the end, I realized that, well, without her there, it would mean Matthew would be free. We could be together, you know?" She smiles at me, like we're the same. "You of all people should understand that, Alice. How love sometimes makes you do bad things. But Brooke was a nuisance. And, now she's gone. It's better for both of us, really." She steps forward, extending her hand. "Now, if you'll hand me that mop, please."

"Brooke was my *friend*, you bitch." I smack her hand with the end of the mop, and she flinches back, rubbing it with a hurt expression. "We are not the same. I tried to *help* Steve when he was in trouble. I didn't murder his fucking girlfriend."

I've never cursed in front of a teacher before, but I have a feeling that Westmacott and I won't be at the same school much longer. One of us is not getting out of here to return, and it's not going to be me. This time, I don't hesitate—I throw the mop at her with all my strength and turn and take off running as fast as I can.

Which, it turns out, is not fast enough.

I'm barely halfway to the exit when I hear footsteps and a second later I'm tackled from behind. I topple with an *oomph*, landing flat against the floor of the barn, dirt caking the inside of my throat and mouth. I scramble forward, pulling myself away, but she grabs my bad ankle, her grip like a vise, and yanks. Something cracks, but I ignore it. I have to get out of here. I kick my other leg wildly, breaking free, and pull myself up to stand, but my leg buckles as I put weight on it. I sprawl back onto the ground.

Westmacott crawls toward me, dirt streaked on her face and through her hair, fury etched into every one of her features.

"Why couldn't you leave it alone, Alice?" she spits at me. "I never wanted anyone else to get hurt. I just wanted to be *loved*." I see her pick up something out of the corner of my eye, but before I can register what it is, it's coming toward me, hard and fast, and the world goes black.

CHAPTER FORTY-FOUR

"IRIS," RAF SAYS. HE'S driving faster than he should, but who cares, I guess? He's a cop. Or a cop in training, at least? What does a Criminal Justice intern even do? "Are you sure?"

"Listen," I tell him. "Look."

I hold my phone. Cole Fielding's TikToks. His IG. Lounging around in his leather jacket, looking dashing in a tousled, somewhat filthy way, hair in his eyes. How could I not know? How could I be blinded by him?

"Cole Fielding, Raf. He dated Brooke. I mean, not dated-dated, but you know, hooking up. Then he moved on, I guess, and she went with Steve. I don't really know, I don't follow that stuff all that much at school—"

"Get to the point, Iris."

"Anyway, this is his leather jacket. This is the jacket Brooke is wearing. And when I saw him the other day outside

Westmacott's office, he wasn't wearing it. He's been wearing that jacket since freshman year, Raf. It's his *thing*. And I know Kennedy—"

Raf shakes his head. "You're not making sense."

"Kennedy. A Main Girl. It doesn't matter. But she said they hooked up after the Halloween party, but it was earlier, and that means Cole did have time to find Brooke after and—"

I break off.

"Do something. Maybe they fought. I don't know. Was he jealous of Steve? And I'm killing myself here because he was on our board, Raf. And we wrote Cole off because of the Kennedy video, but . . ."

"But what about the trophy?" Raf says. "The one in Coach's house?"

"I don't know! Maybe he stole it when they were together? He's kind of sketchy, but so handsome you forget that? Maybe he stole it to sell later? I don't know. But that's *his* jacket."

"Okay," he says finally. "Here's what's going to happen. We're gonna go to the rink, and be real nice, and I'm going to do the talking, okay? All we want is a DNA test and some questioning. Let me handle it."

I'm punching my phone.

> Alice. It's Cole Fielding.
>
> Alice
>
> Where the hell are you

He pulls into the parking lot of Seaside Skate. "Hell of a lot of people here for a hol—"

"People have crappy lives, Raf," I say, practically shouting. "Not everybody wants to eat turkey with people they dislike. They want to watch movies, or skate, or be anywhere but home."

Raf nods. "Point taken. Hey, hold up——"

But I'm already out of the car and running for the entrance.

He catches up with me inside. I'm digging in my pockets for the entrance fee.

"Can't let you in without paying," Lizzy Mancini, the girl behind the counter, says. She goes to Castle Cove High, too. "Twenty bucks for two people."

I give Raf a pointed look. "Kinda had all my money stolen earlier, Raf."

He shoves twenty dollars at her, and she stamps both our hands.

Inside, the rink is hot and sweaty and disco music is blaring. Multicolored lights swivel across the room, turning the skaters pink, purple, red, blue. Cole Fielding is behind the skate rental desk.

Even though Raf said to let him do the talking, I can't. I'm done. I want this *over.*

"Oh hey, *Eyeeerriiis.* Fancy seeing you here."

I have to kind of shake my head to clear my thoughts because good god, he is *cute,* but also, quite possibly a murderer and that makes me extremely disappointed.

I hold up my phone, showing him the photo of Brooke, cold and dead on the ground.

"Is this your mother-sucking jacket, Cole? Where were you the night Brooke died, after you hooked up with Kennedy?"

Beside me, Raf groans. "Cole, we just want to——"

Cole's face drains of color. His mouth trembles. "Oh god. Put that away, Iris. What the hell? That's *disgusting.* I would nev——I loved her. I *did.* But you know, wrong-side-of-the-tracks thing. She went for Steve-O."

His face is crumpling in a way that makes me feel both sympathetic *and* angry.

"*Look* at it, Cole. And tell me the truth. You went there. You were mad. Something happened. That's *your* jacket."

"That's . . . oh god. It wasn't *me,* Iris. I'll take whatever test you want. Take my frickin' blood, but I wasn't there. I mean, yeah, that's my jacket, but I don't know how she got it. I don't . . ."

Neil and Spike zip up to us in their skates, Zora stumbling along behind them.

"Oh hey, Iris, you want to skate?" Spike says hopefully.

I ignore him, concentrating on Cole. The three of them, Zora, Neil, and Spike, hover around me and Raf.

"Where's your jacket, Cole? You weren't wearing it when I saw you outside Westmacott's office. You haven't been wearing lately. *Where* is it?"

I don't know what's wrong with me. I'm shouting. I can't even hear what Raf is trying to say beside me.

"Westmacott? I don't know. I mean, I don't really remember. She gave me a ride home after detention on Halloween, and that's the last I saw of my jacket. I was kinda high, to tell you the truth, and she had me take some boxes of shoes and trophies and stuff to her car in exchange for a lift. I got hot, I took my jacket off. . . ."

Trophies?

My brain turns. Turns again. Does a spin. I can't breathe.

The bloody trophy in his house. The box of his things in the corner of Westmacott's office.

In unison, Spike, Zora, Neil, and I say, "Holy shit."

Alice, text me back
Alice where are you
ALICE IT'S WESTMACOTT

CHAPTER FORTY-FIVE

ALICE
NOVEMBER 24
4:50 P.M.

"We never know the whole man, though
sometimes, in quick flashes, we know the
true man."

—AGATHA CHRISTIE, *AN AUTOBIOGRAPHY*

I COME TO ON hard ground, something sharp stabbing into
my back. I reach around and grab the offending object. Straw.
What the . . .

And then it all comes rushing back into my throbbing brain.
Why I'm here. What just happened. *Shit.* How long was I out?

I push myself up from the ground, the world swimming. I
touch my forehead, and my hand comes back wet and red. Blood.
I have to stop her. Westmacott. She murdered my friend.

Up on my feet, my ankle screaming in pain, my head
screaming in pain, I force myself to walk. Out, out of the barn,
into the falling dusk —there's Westmacott, sprinting to her car.
I must not have been unconscious for very long. I can catch her.

I head to my car, dragging my leg behind me, but when I get
to it, I see why Westmacott is still here. Why she took so long to
leave. My tires are all flat. That bitch slashed my *tires.*

Behind me, a car door slams, and I turn. Westmacott is in her car, engine on, and she's heading straight toward me. Holy—

I don't even think. Instinct takes over, and my body flies to the right, landing hard on the patchy grass and hard dirt next to the driver's side of my car. She hits the trunk of my car with hers, hard, spinning out and then coming to a stop across the lot, her engine steaming.

My entire body hurts. I groan, pushing myself up to sit. Squinting through the falling night, I can barely make out Westmacott's form, still in the driver's seat. I wonder if she hurt herself in that collision.

I have to get out of here. I have to go get help. My phone. I grab it from my back pocket. Its screen is shattered, but the phone still works. Thank god.

Except, there's no signal. My heart sinks. Why didn't I think of that? We're way up in the hills, and service is notoriously spotty here.

I look around the parking lot, but it's empty other than my useless car. How can I leave? I *need* to leave.

And then it hits me.

My horse.

I need to ride her. I need to ride her, fast, and go get help.

I hobble back into the barn, pushing myself to move faster than my ankle wants to. Good thing I saddled her before I was so rudely interrupted. I think back to my lessons when I was little, trying to remember the details about riding.

When I reach the stall, I grab her reins and she follows me out of the stables, which is very nice of her because I'm not sure what I would do if she didn't. I certainly have no idea what I'm doing.

Back in the parking lot, I realize I'm too late. Westmacott

is awake. I see her through her car window, rubbing her head, looking all around in a daze, and when she catches sight of me and Snowflake, she frowns.

A moment later, her engine roars to life.

We lock eyes and a shiver runs down my spine. I have to get on Snowflake before she can hit me again. She clearly has no regard for human life, but I'm pretty sure she'd never hurt a horse.

Snowflake whinnies beside me, like she can sense my anxiety.

"It's okay, girl," I say. I pat her side, put my foot in the stir-rup, and then pull myself up onto her back, ignoring my ankle, ignoring the trembling of my hands, ignoring the picture of the mangled girl from horse camp threatening to emerge from the depths of my brain.

Westmacott's car is speeding toward the exit of the lot, and she pulls out onto the backcountry road, going way too fast.

I have to catch her. She's not going to get away with this. Murdering my friend. My *best friend.*

I kick Snowflake's side, and we take off at a gallop, breath catching in my chest, hands tightening around the reins. At the end of the parking lot, we turn right, the direction Westma-cott's car went. It's starting to rain.

Can a horse even run as fast as a car? I have no idea. But I have to try.

The road is windy up here in the hills, narrow with brush on either side, no streetlights, and with the darkening sky and the rain blurring my vision, it's getting harder and harder to see.

At a V intersection, Snowflake slows, awaiting my instruc-tion, and I listen hard for the sound of an engine, and finally hear it up to the left.

I kick the horse's side again, and we move. Snowflake is hauling ass, breathing hard, and then there she is—Westmacott—in front of us. We're catching up. I steer Snowflake into the middle of the road, heart pounding, praying to the universe that no cars appear in front of us, because if they do, I am *screwed*.

We're close. So close. If I leaned over, I could probably touch the tail end of her car.

"GO!" I yell to Snowflake, who apparently understands me, because she picks up her speed and now we're beside the car. I move the reins, and Snowflake veers to the right, and so does Westmacott. I *knew* she'd never harm a horse.

One more time, a swerve to the right, and Westmacott's car follows, but she must have turned the wheel too sharply, because she starts spinning out of control. I pull on Snowflake's reins, and we slow, watching as the car in front of us veers off the road, its tires squealing.

A *crash* echoes against the hills as it smacks into an enormous redwood tree, its hood crumpling. Snowflake rears up at the noise and I hold on with all my strength, then find myself petting her head, whispering, "It's okay, girl."

She calms. An eerie silence descends over the mountain road, the only sounds the hissing of the broken car engine and the pitter-patter of the rain on the road. Smoke starts to billow out of the hood a second later, and I realize that I probably need to get Westmacott out of there in case it blows up or something.

I slip off Snowflake's back and unhook the reins from her bridle. "Good girl," I whisper. "You stay."

The car lets out a loud hiss. Shoot. I need to hurry.

I run over to the driver's-side door and find Westmacott slumped against the wheel, head bleeding. I can't tell if she's alive or dead. Yanking the door open, I grab her arm, and she startles.

"Get off me," she whines. "Just leave me here. My life is ruined already, can't you see that?" I think she's crying.

"You should have thought about that before you murdered my friend," I reply, grabbing her under her arms and pulling with all my might. She pops out and we collapse onto the ground, her on top of me.

A second later, she's up on her hands and knees, crawling away.

I reach out and catch her ankle, holding on with all my might even as she kicks, and tug her back, hard.

"Ow," she cries as something inside her leg pops. *Ew.* We both collapse onto our backs, breathing heavily. I need to make sure she doesn't get away again. I army-crawl back over to her and drape myself across her chest.

She starts to rant. "Get off me! Alice Ogilvie, I will have you know that this is going to go on your permanent record! Assaulting a teacher—why I've never—"

"Please, do shut up," I say, reaching around and pulling the scrunchie out of my hair and stuffing it hard into her mouth. I have heard just about enough from her.

I wrap the reins around and around her arms, pinning them to her body, and then secure the whole mess with one of those sailor's knots I learned how to make at horse camp. Who knew they'd come in handy someday?

Snowflake is standing on the paved road beside me, watching it all. When I finish, she snorts in approval, and I remember what Agatha Christie said about horses. *Wonderful things, horses. Never know what they will do, or won't do.*

She was sure right about that.

CHAPTER FORTY-SIX

IRIS
NOVEMBER 24
4:55 P.M.

"SHOULDN'T YOU PUT OUT an APB or something, dude? On the counselor?"

From the back seat, Spike's voice sounds a little scared. We're in Raf's car, still in the parking lot of Seaside Skate.

Raf grits his teeth. "Not a cop and I did not want all of you in this car, and yes, calling in about it now." He gets out of the car and pulls out his phone.

"Why is there pie in this car?" Zora asks.

"Alice brought it. To my apartment. It's apology pie. My mom gave it to Raf."

"Is it homemade?" Spike asks. I ignore him. I'm thinking about two things at once.

Alice and the trophy.

If Westmacott was taking his things back to Coach's house that day, that's why the trophy is there. If Westmacott somehow ran into Brooke, on the road that night, of course Brooke would talk to her. She's the guidance counselor; she's her father's ex-girlfriend, she—

"Brooke would have trusted her," Zora finishes for me as I've been thinking out loud. "She needed a ride. The box was in Westmacott's car. Cole's jacket. Brooke was cold. Westmacott gave her the jacket to make her trust her."

Spike nods.

"But," I say, looking at them both in the rearview mirror. "Because you hate that girl and you want her gone."

"If that girl was standing between you and the man you loved, yes," Spike says.

"Holy shit," Neil says slowly. "We put the wrong dude in jail."

I'm getting really worried about Alice. I shouldn't have treated her that way when she came to the apartment. Why isn't she, I don't know, texting me back and telling me to go to hell? I wish she'd do that right now, because I have a funny, tight knot in my stomach that something isn't . . . right.

"Iris?" Spike says.

"What?" I turn around. "Sorry, that came out too harsh. I'm a little distracted right now."

"I get it," he says softly. "But what happened to your eye?"

I look back down at my phone. "Nothing. Fell, is all."

Wait. Alice told me once that Brenda put a tracker on her phone. I text Brenda.

> Have you heard from Alice? I'm sorry, I
> can't get ahold of her.

"No, you didn't," Zora says flatly. They're all squeezed in back there, Neil and Zora and Spike, still with roller skates on. We left so fast, they didn't bother to take off their skates.

I freeze.

"Everybody knows," Spike says quietly. "About what he does. He came back, didn't he?"

"Shut up," I whisper.

"We're not stupid," Zora says. "Your wrist last summer? And eighth grade, remember? Graduation. I saw him, pushing you. Like that weird way, with his hand on the back of your neck."

"Stop, please." I can feel it, all over again, the way his fingers pressed into my skin that day, dug into my flesh.

"Iris," Spike says. "He's an asshole. And if you want to talk, I mean, we're here. He should not be hurting you."

"I just want to find Alice right now, okay?" I say. I hate the way my voice is small. I hate the way I tried to hide everything, and *everyone knew.* "And Westmacott."

My phone buzzes. Brenda.

> **Hello, Iris. I suggested that Alice go to the stables, but it looks like she isn't there right now. She's on Ridgeview Road and County 6. Does she know someone there? Here's the location. Is everything alright?**

What the hell is she doing there? What's on Ridgeview Road? I lean over and rap on the driver's-seat window, motion to Raf.

Never lose track of your partner, Ricky said. *If you do, it means they're in trouble.*

Raf gets back into the car. "Okay, there's a unit headed over to Westmacott's apartment. Who am I dropping off first?"

"Nobody," I say. "We have to find Alice first. I'm worried about her."

"Well," Raf says, "that's great, if we knew where Alice *was.*"

"I do, sort of." I show him the pin on my phone. "Somewhere here."

He starts the car, sighing. "Okay, off we go. It's like I'm at Castle Cove High again, driving around in a car with a bunch of kids. I hope to god nobody's high and makes me stop for food."

In the rearview mirror, Neil sheepishly raises his hand. "I mean, I am. High. And kind of hungry, so can we stop and get some——"

"Eat the pie!" Raf shouts.

Spike's eyes meet mine in the rearview mirror. The kindness in them makes me want to cry, so I avert my eyes and look out at the road.

"Drive faster," I say.

"Going as fast as I can, but if you'll notice, it's now raining, and I'd rather not kill us all," Raf says.

"So, Westmacott, huh?" Zora muses. "I don't think I saw that one coming. Why didn't we ever think of Coach's, uh, lovers?"

"I don't . . . I don't really know," I say. "Maybe we just aren't any good at this."

"I'd say we did pretty good," Neil says, his mouth full of pie.

"Wait," I say. It's hard to see. The rain is smearing the windshield as fast as Raf's wipers can brush it away. "What is that? Is that a car accident?"

Up ahead, there's a car off the road, its hood smashed against a tree, the driver's-side door hanging open. There are bodies in the road and—

"Is that a horse?" says Neil. "Or am I *that* stoned?"

"Call 911," Raf says, slowing the car down. "Tell them there's been an accident on Ridgeview and County 6. Stay inside the car."

He pulls the car to the side of the road, jumps out.

Neil calls 911, but no one listens to Raf and we all jump out, too, the others skidding as their skates hit the ground. Thunder is cracking the sky, and we're drenched the instant we're outside the car.

One body is lying on the ground, the other is sitting up, hunched over, wet, bright blond hair plastered against her jacket. The horse, standing in the brush, whinnies.

Alice.

I drop to my knees. She's rocking back and forth. Beside her, Westmacott is squirming. She's tied up, a scrunchie shoved in her mouth.

"It was her," Alice says in a small voice. "It was her. I have it. I have it all. On my phone. Take it."

She holds it out to Raf, her hand trembling. He takes it.

"She told me everything. At the stables, and then . . . I thought she was going to kill me. She literally tried to kill me."

Rivulets of blood are running through her pretty hair, the rain turning them pink, staining her hoodie.

"But I did it, Iris. I didn't give up. I wanted to do something right, for once, you know?"

"I know." I pet her hair gently. "And you did."

"I lied. I'm a liar, Iris."

"No," I tell her.

"I am. You know, in the summer? I meant to go. I didn't just run away. I smashed that stupid vase. I left my phone on purpose, all my things. You make fun of me, for the Christie stuff, but that was the one thing that got me through all summer. Through everything. Did you know she planned her own disappearance? To get back at her husband. He was cheating on her, so she took off and crashed her car and checked into a hotel under his mistress's name. I did the same thing. And you know what? It felt good."

Her voice rises.

"You should know that about me. I mean, you guessed, right from the start, that I did it on purpose. Out of spite. But you should know, it felt *good* to make everyone worry."

She struggles up. I hold her elbow, helping her. Rain drips from her hair.

"I mean, *finally,* people missed me. And I thought things would change," she said. "My mom would stay home more. My dad would call more. Steve might come back to me. But nothing changed. Nobody really cared where I was after all. Or why. Except him."

She smiles at Raf.

"Don't go being gross," she tells Zora and Neil, who are exchanging looks. "It's not like that. I crashed my car. I didn't have my phone——"

"I was on my way to my parents' cabin," Raf interjects. "She was on the side of the road. What should I have done, ignored her?"

"I convinced him to just leave the car there. He took me to his cabin. We played Clue for five days and ate Cheetos and watched VHS tapes of *Murder, She Wrote,*" Alice says. "He told me to forget about Steve. Forget my parents. All of it. Move on. That something, someday, would happen to me, something that would give me purpose. It was the best time of my life. Until now. Until this."

She looks at me.

"I did this," Alice says quietly. "*We* did this."

She punches me lightly in the arm.

"Sirens," Spike says. "Help is coming."

In the distance, an ambulance and police cars are appearing in the slicks of rain.

Alice sighs. "I'm really tired."

She looks up at Neil, Zora, and Spike, blinking.

"Are you . . . ," she says wearily. "Are you guys wearing *roller skates?*"

EPILOGUE

IRIS

DETECTIVE THOMPSON LOOKS UNCOMFORTABLE, but you can see he's trying not to show it. There are tons of microphones in front of him and cameras flashing.

"Tonight, I'm here to announce that we have arrested the person responsible for the murder of Brooke Donovan. This has been a complicated investigation from the very start. This afternoon Carol Westmacott, a counselor at Castle Cove High School, was taken into custody. Ms. Westmacott confessed. While I cannot share all the details with you right now, they will be forthcoming. Matthew Donovan has been released and is no longer an active suspect in this case. I'd ask for your patience as we work hard to resolve the rest of this investigation, but I can tell you that we are confident in our case against Ms. Westmacott. The charges that have been filed in relation to the murder of Brooke Donovan are entrapment and manslaughter. Additional charges against Ms. Westmacott that will be forthcoming and related to a different aspect of this case include attempted murder, assault and battery, stalking . . ."

The camera cuts away from Thompson to Tessa Hopkins, in the KWB studio.

"You've just heard from Detective Thompson concerning breaking news in the Brooke Donovan case, which has taken, I must say, several twists and turns since Steve Anderson was originally charged and then changed his confession from not guilty to guilty, which is now thought to be the result of an alleged bribe from the Bradford family. I'll be updating our viewers as this case continues to unfold, but I'd like to take a moment here to say that leads in the case against Carol Westmacott were not the sole action of the Castle Cove Police Department. Some of them came to me via our tip line from concerned members of the Castle Cove community. While I can't reveal my sources at this time, I do want to say thank you to them."

Alice clicks off the television.

Spike gathers up blankets and a cooler, and Neil grabs the pizzas, and we follow them outside and down the path to the beach, where Raf is stoking a bonfire. It's cold out, and the heat from the fire feels nice. In the distance, sailboats are wobbling along the water. The Yacht Club regatta ball is tomorrow. Workers are putting up lights. They look like little moons in the sky.

Alice flicks out a blanket and settles down, wiggling with happiness. "I'm so glad that someone mentioned us, even sort of anonymously."

"Me too," I say, sitting on my own blanket. "Look, you finally got some recognition for all your hard work."

Ricky Randall groans as she sits in the sand and opens the cooler. She cracks a beer. "Eat that pizza, you guys. I didn't buy it to waste it."

She raises her bottle to me. "Little Iris. Look at you. And Moneybags. Solving crimes."

"Please," Zora says, pulling her knit cap down over her ears. "They needed so much help. There are tons of things we could have done to get this solved quicker. I mean, come on. They put a guy in jail who didn't do it, and what were you doing to Cole Fielding? He's a fuckboy, not a killer."

"Innocent people go to prison," Ricky says. "More often than you might think."

"I still don't get it," Neil says from across the fire. He's wrapped in a wool blanket. "I'm so confused about how Westmacott did it, and like, why."

Alice sighs. "Let's see if you can follow along, Neil. Brooke fought with Steve and ran away. Iris ran after her, but didn't find her, because Brooke was in the woods. Iris went home. But—"

Zora cuts in. "Westmacott drove by a little while later and saw Brooke and pulled over. It was cold, so she took Cole Fielding's leather jacket—"

Raf interjects, leaning back in the sand, the flames making his face glow. "Which he'd left in her car after she gave him a ride home from detention. He also helped her take a box of sneakers, DVDs, trophies, and other stuff of Coach's from her office. She was going to return them to Coach, but then she decided to throw them off the Lookout spot. Which is when she saw Brooke across the road. She was wearing good shoes, so she put on a pair of Coach's sneakers, red Nike Zooms, just like Steve's. She had Brooke put on the jacket to stay warm—"

"Being nice, I guess," Alice says. "But then she and Brooke fought, because Brooke was drunk, and hated Westmacott, and Brooke said that Westmacott would never be her mother, ever, and that Coach would never marry her—"

I cut in. "And Brooke ran across Highway One to where Westmacott's car was on the cliff side, and Westmacott followed her. They had another fight. Westmacott grabbed a trophy from the box on the ground and hit her. Brooke slipped over the edge and was hanging there."

"My turn," Ricky says. "Instead of helping her up, Westmacott stepped on Brooke's hands until she went over."

"Because she's crazy," Spike says. "I don't think she had a plan-plan, but she went with it, after the fact."

Raf slips a piece of pizza from a box. "The sneakers Westmacott used to step on Brooke's hands have been found in Coach's office, where she must have planted them, just like she decided to take the box to his house after Brooke's murder, to make sure the trophy would be found *there*."

"But what about Steve?" Neil asks.

"Steve did go to the woods looking for Brooke," I say. "But then he passed out. The shoe Dotty found at the doughnut shop? The cops took it, and stuck it in the woods, because—"

"Allegedly," Ricky says, "when Coach's family, the Bradfords, heard what happened, they started grinding some considerable gears to point everything in a direction *not* at Coach, who had that little problem with his first wife before. But this

is all *alleged,* at the moment, because this probe is still being conducted."

"Probe," Neil murmurs. Zora groans.

"It all worked out in the end," I say. Though I do feel queasy, about Coach. But I mean, what are the chances that *two* of the women in his family suffered strange fates? Is that *my* fault? Something is definitely up with that guy.

Raf laughs. "I don't even know what to say. I'm kind of flabbergasted, to tell you the truth. I mean, Alice Ogilvie riding a horse to catch a killer and then hogtieing her in the middle of the road. It's a little unbelievable."

Alice tilts her head and says in a singsong voice, "I *am* awesome."

Spike gets up and sits down next to me on the blanket.

"You didn't get any money, though," he murmurs. "The reward. What would you have done with all that money, anyway?"

"Technically, she did solve the case," Zora says. "But do you really think that Levy lady is going to give Iris the money? I mean, her son-in-law was almost sent to prison."

I can feel Alice looking at me. I know she's sorry about what she said to me during our fight, that Lilian wouldn't give me the reward money. She said it to hurt me. And Zora doesn't know what Alice and I know about Lilian and how she feels about Coach Donovan.

But I have a secret, and it's inside a beautiful, creamy, expensive card in the pocket of my peacoat.

> *Dear Iris,*
>
> *What a time you have had. I knew you had it in you. I've learned quite a bit about you in the past several days. Your*

circumstances. Your life. There's a burning in you for something, I can feel it. Alice, too, though don't tell her I said that. She's much too full of herself as it is. You did your work admirably. As I said the night we met, there can be no justice when a life has been taken. Solace is an elusive thing. I am, however, confident that the right person has now been apprehended. And thus, I owe you a debt of infinite gratitude. Please accept my eternal thank-you. I look forward to meeting again. I have a feeling we are not quite done with one another.

> *Best,*
> *Lilian Levy*

I'm going to tell them. I swear I am. It's only fair. After all, I'm not the only one who worked on this case. There are five of us, and everyone should get their fair share.

But for now, I'm just going to let myself enjoy the feeling of a fifty-thousand-dollar check between my fingers. Because who knows when anything that amazing will ever happen to me again?

"Your stitches are healing well, Alice," Raf says. "Probably not too much of a scar."

Alice touches her forehead gingerly. "My mom will make me see a plastic surgeon, probably."

"Keep it," Zora says. "Adds character."

"Definitely." Ricky Randall burps. "You're gonna need to look tough for that next case you two take on."

"*What* case?" I say. "No, thank you. Never again. And I have too much going on. PSATs, applications."

"My schedule is full," Alice says firmly. "I mean, manicures, winter formal, since I'm missing the regatta ball, *studying,* which is new for me. And I would prefer not to have someone attempt to murder me, ever again."

"I did like jumping on the trampoline," I say quietly. "I mean . . . in retrospect, that was cool."

Alice smiles at me.

"There's Remy Jackson," Zora muses. "They never solved that. And Mona Moody, the dead Levy Castle starlet, if we're looking for glamour."

"We?" Alice says.

"I feel like our talents weren't properly utilized this time around, Alice. I'm willing to work more with you, it's true," Zora says.

"Let's just eat our pizza, okay, everyone?" Raf reaches out and takes another slice.

"Hmm," Alice says. "Remy Jackson. And a starlet plunging to her death off a veranda."

She pulls out her phone and starts Googling, the screen reflecting on her face.

"Alice," Raf says.

"Raf," she says.

I can't help it. I lean over and look at Alice's phone. *Fourteen-year-old girl found dead in seaside town, investigators have no leads . . . mysterious, magical Mona Moody . . .*

Then I don't. I look back out at the sea. *Breathe in, breathe out.*

"Come on, Iris," she says. "What do you say?"

Ricky grins at me. Like she said in the bar, never let your partner out of your sight.

My phone buzzes. I look down.

**I'll forgive you for thinking I was a killer if
you skate with me sometime, Adams.**

Oh god. My stomach flips. Cole Fielding. What is happening
to my life? Why can't things just be *normal*?

Maybe that thing Detective Thompson said about me is
right. Maybe trouble does follow me around. It sure follows
Alice Ogilvie.

We might as well make some trouble together.

WHERE TO GET HELP

Though *The Agathas* is, at heart, a fun book about two teen detectives, there are some very serious issues within this book.

Iris Adams is a child victim of domestic abuse. Her story might be your story, or it might be the story of someone you know. If you or someone you know is living with domestic abuse, or you suspect they might be, here are some resources to help:

CHILDLINE
childline.org.uk

REFUGE
refuge.org.uk

During the party, Steve and Brooke have a physical altercation. Though this is explained as caused by both of them being under the influence (and that is not an excuse), teen dating violence is real. If you feel unsafe in your relationship, here is a resource to help:

RESPECT NOT FEAR

respectnotfear.co.uk

If you need to talk to someone, anytime, anywhere, about anything, confidentially:

SAMARITANS

samaritans.org

ACKNOWLEDGMENTS

LIZ: Oh hi, Kathleen. How are you today?

KATHLEEN: Hello, Liz. I can't believe this book is a thing! I feel like we have a ton of people to thank for making *The Agathas* happen.

LIZ: Absolutely! First and foremost, our illustrious editor, Krista Marino. When we approached Krista with this idea, her enthusiasm for it made it all the more exciting. Krista, your eye for plot holes and character motivation elevated this book into something it wouldn't have become otherwise. We love that you love Iris and Alice as much as we do!

KATHLEEN: Krista is a gem and saved us many times. The entire team at Delacorte was outstanding and worked tirelessly to make this story of two unlikely teen detectives come to life. We'd like to heartily thank Lydia Gregovic, Beverly Horowitz, Barbara Marcus, Alison Impey, Tamar Schwartz, Colleen Fellingham, Kathy Dunn, Kelly McGauley, and Jenn Inzetta. And we cannot forget our agents, Andrea Morrison and Julie Stevenson! We drafted an outline and a spreadsheet, and started writing in secret (oopsie!), only telling them what we were doing when we felt we had something exciting and cool in the hopper, and their support (and surprise! And encouragement!) was invaluable. I still remember not wanting to tell Julie until we had, uh, actually finished an entire draft and you were all, "Kathleen, chill out." You were always telling me to chill! Kind of like how Alice is with Iris . . .

LIZ: Uh . . . Kathleen, I have a confession. I told Andrea about this book before we even started writing it. BECAUSE I HAVE NO CHILL EITHER. But yes, our agents are incredible and have been so supportive through this entire process. Thank you also to our film agents, Hilary Zaitz Michael and Olivia Burgher at WME, for your enthusiasm for this project; it's so wonderful to work with the two of you!

KATHLEEN: Your lack of chill and utter belief that the impossible can be done is why you are Alice and I am Iris. So I will thank YOU for messaging me every day during a pandemic summer in which I was very much isolated and depressed to talk about writing, which spun into talking about our mutual love of mysteries and true crime, which somehow turned into "Ha, ha, if I wrote a mystery, I'd do THIS," and me saying, "Well, I'd do THIS," which turned into "Well, wouldn't we then do THIS, and wouldn't that plot point go HERE," and then . . . suddenly we had a spreadsheet, and an outline, and two girls from the opposite sides of Castle Cove came together and—

KATHLEEN: Please let me give a brief shout-out here to my son, who was extremely excited about this book idea from the get-go and alerted us very early on that the name we had cho-sen for our town was the exact same town where the Scooby-Doo kids live.

LIZ: YES. That was an invaluable piece of information to receive for sure, and I thank him from the bottom of my heart. I'd also like to thank YOU, Kathleen, for . . . (we're going to get sappy for a second here, folks; you've been warned) writing this book with me. *Girl in Pieces* was one of the books I read when I was first starting to write YA, and it really touched me so deeply in so many ways; I remember when I first found out I had the same editor as KATHLEEN GLASGOW and I about died. And now we've written a book together!!! It's still incredible to me. So thank you. And to any readers out there who are also aspir-ing authors, please know that wildest dreams might actually come true someday, if you just keep moving forward. (Okay, sappy moment over.)

KATHLEEN: Wait, did you just pause in your acknowledg-ments to go post on Twitter?? Liz! Your endless enthusiasm for every aspect of writing this book (drafting, editing, fine-tuning, marketing) astounds me! THANK YOU. I said very early on when we first met, after I read and loved *The Lucky Ones,* that you and I were similar in so many ways, and that turned out to be a gift when writing this book.

KATHLEEN: Let's talk about cowriting from two different time zones. Thank you for texting me every morning to get out of bed and write my chapters!

LIZ: Look, Kathleen, I have a social media addiction. It's a thing. Anyway, you are very welcome. So many people have asked me how it was to cowrite remotely, to which I've replied it worked beautifully. As you found out, I'm not much of a night owl, so the time-zone thing ended up being a positive, I think.

KATHLEEN: Lest people think everything was cheery, Liz, let's not forget that time we had a brief creative tiff and suddenly your character was throwing a phone at my character's head.

LIZ: All in service of the PLOT, of course. And, while we're speaking of plot, we should thank a few experts who helped us make sure we were correctly describing the inner workings of the legal system. Amy Salley, particularly, was an invaluable resource (as well as being one of my favorite people!) and patiently bore with us as we threw a slew of questions at her about the court system and how it works in the Real World. K. J. Brower was also enormously helpful and always willing to answer even my most outlandish questions.

KATHLEEN: I'd like to thank *Forensic Files* and weird tabloid-y crime stories that inspired me to send you all those "Liz, I had a thought . . ." texts, like, four days before a draft was due to our editors. I mean, wow, you really put up with a lot from me. Also, I need to thank Dr. Justin Cetas for answering my questions about the decomposition of bodies in seawater.

LIZ: Since we're thanking people, I would also be remiss if I didn't thank Anna Elisa Mackowiak, whose help with the French language enabled me to properly write the chapter where Alice and her friends trick a bookie (kids, don't try that at home). I'd also like to thank my friends: Jeff Bishop (you are just the best; wow, Jeff, thank you for everything; I hope you know that I will continue to send you at least 20 TikTok videos daily until I take my final breath), Suzanne Park, Alex Richards, Rocky Callen, Kyrie McCauley, Nora Carpenter, Mike Lasagna, Eva V. Gibson, Jenny Howe, Jessica Goodman, Hannah Sawyer, and all the other wonderful people I've met since selling my debut. Thank you all for bearing with my writing-inspired dramatics at one time or another. Particular thanks to Dante Medema. You're the sort of nemesis every girl dreams of finding someday.

LIZ: I also need to thank my friends back in LA, who I miss dearly. And, a special thanks to Brenda del Cid for inspiring the name of Brenda, the character. We miss you every day!

KATHLEEN: I hope Jeff Bishop appreciates his shout-out within this book! Writing is often a solitary enterprise (though not entirely, this time, since I like to say that I only had to do fifty percent of the work; get yourself a cowriter, people!) and when you come up for air, there are people that bring you back to reality in the best ways. Major high fives to Janet McNally, Karen McManus, Lygia Day Peñaflor, Shannon Parker, Beth Wankel, Jeff Giles, Holly Vanderhaar, Elizabeth Noll, Julie Schumacher, and my mailman, who never fails to ask me, "You working on something exciting today?" That daily encouragement kept me from napping and got me back to the writing desk because finally, one day, I was able to say, "YES."

LIZ: Family thank-you time! To my parents, who have always been so encouraging of my writing; thank you for prodding me forward, even when I wanted nothing more than to quit. To Tori and Nick, who I now live about ten feet away from—it's lovely living near you and your kids, and I am so glad we finally made it happen (the one good thing to come out of the Pandemi Moore). To Joel and Kate & family: thank you for buying approximately fifteen copies of *The Lucky Ones* and being so, so supportive through the years. And, to my in-laws, thank you, also, for supporting my debut, talking it up to everyone you know, and for being such a wonderful group of people to marry into—I am a lucky woman.

KATHLEEN: Ima need Joel and Kate to up their game and buy at least fifty copies of *The Agathas,* Liz. Work your magic.

KATHLEEN: Liz, did you go back to making TikTok videos? We should probably wrap this up.

LIZ: Joel and Kate are on it. And TikTok is my life, Kathleen, I can't help it. In conclusion, and (as they say) last but very much not least, I need to thank my husband and my child, the Kowit Boys, who are my heart. I love you both times a billion trillion.

KATHLEEN: Thank you to my kids, who have upped "Are you done yet?" to "Way to go, Mom!" You two are my heart.

LIZ & KATHLEEN: And a giant thank-you to every reader out there who makes a writer's dream come true. Never stop reading. Never give up on your dreams.

KATHLEEN: We should stop. I might cry, and I have to go pick up my kid from horse camp. Last words, Liz?

LIZ: As the great Agatha Christie would say: "If the little grey cells are not exercised, they grow the rust." Remember to use your little grey cells, friends! And we hope you love Alice and Iris as much as we do.

ABOUT THE AUTHORS

Kathleen Glasgow is the author of the internationally best-selling novel *Girl in Pieces, How to Make Friends with the Dark,* and *You'd Be Home Now.* She lives and writes in Tucson, Arizona.

kathleenglasgowbooks.com

Liz Lawson is the author of *The Lucky Ones.* She lives in the Washington, DC, area with her family. You can find her on all social media platforms at @LzLwsn.

lizlawsonauthor.com